THE DESERT IN THE GLASS

C.C. LUCKEY

First paperback edition October 2019

Front cover art by Patricio "Pokérus" Thielemann

ISBN 978-1-734-12810-9 (paperback)
ISBN 978-1-734-12811-6 (ebook)

Published by Patient Corgi

CONTENTS

Part 1

TERATA

Settle, Arizona was a one-bar town on the fringes of a parched, ugly country dotted with grimy homesteads arranged in wagon circles around a supersized grocery store. Main Street—an unnecessary title, as it was the only well-paved route in town—provided driveway access to Royal Empire Liquor and City Bank on the west side and Helter Oasis, the local pub, on the east.

Main Street connected to Route 64 with an onramp that served as the town's only lifeline to the outside world. After Main passed through town the asphalt endured for a couple miles but sputtered and quit when it met the county line. The gravel road beyond was dubbed "Sunshine Highway" by leery locals who sat in broken plastic chairs on their crumbling porches and eyed each passing car with burning suspicion.

As you drove through town, you'd be quick to notice two garish pedestal signs which flanked the entry to Royal Empire Liquor's crumbling parking lot. The one on the far side simply read "Lottery-Liquor-Beer." On the near sign, "Royal Empire" was scrawled in gold script over a chipped and faded painting of a king's crown studded with sparkling jewels. The nameplate was studded with ancient gum globs and fliers for swap meets, garage sales, and an amateur wrestling show.

The establishment blatantly did not live up to its namesake.

As Joanna pulled her rental car into the liquor store driveway, the bottom scraped on the uneven gutter, loudly announcing her arrival. She had already felt self-conscious in the sexy, cherry-red convertible; now she felt positively on display. Every sunbaked head in town turned and stared while she parked the car and cut the ignition. The *locals* knew about the dip in the liquor store driveway. The *locals* didn't drive around in shiny new cars with the tops down. The *locals* knew she didn't belong here.

She sat still for a minute, pretending to root around in her purse while waiting for the watchers to become bored and move on. Signs plastering the liquor store windows advertised a "Big Sale": $8.99 jumbo beer packs, cheap tequila, and bags of ice in various sizes. A lanky teenager leaned against the wall at the corner, smoking a cigarette.

Now that she had parked, the heat of the sun was no longer being swept away by the highway wind. Her skin was starting to burn and her lipstick was melting. Joanna zipped her purse shut. She stepped out of the car and tried to close the door without slamming it. As she walked through Royal Empire Liquor's open doorway, a tired bell ding-donged and a raspy voice called from the back, "*Hangonasec, I'm in the john.*"

She meandered down the center aisle and picked up a local newspaper, a red licorice rope wrapped in a crinkling cellophane wrapper, and an iced tea from a cooler with a squeaky lid. The newspaper was titled "Settler Times" and had yesterday's date on it. Good enough. She wasn't really interested in the local news anyway, just the real estate prices for comps. The back page featured rows of gritty black and white pictures of barren chunks of desert. "Great Investment!" said one. And another: "Legacy Estates! Cheap Land!"

Joanna set her items on the counter and waited for the clerk to finish his business in the back. A postcard from Illinois was affixed to a wall safe with a magnet which stated, "I Love My Job, It's The Work I Hate." Men's magazines and a grimy wireless phone sat on the counter behind the cash register. Atop an empty Pepsi can a cigarette smoldered, sending up little smoke signals in the hot breeze coming through the front door. She inhaled deeply, enjoying the aroma. What she wouldn't do for a smoke…

Joanna heard a grunt and a flush from the back room. Within a minute—not enough time to have washed his hands, surely not—a man with a lopsided smile stepped to the counter. He wore a sun-bleached flannel work shirt which bore a name tag that read "Granger."

"Evenin', darlin'. Sorry 'bout the wait. My old plumbing is starting to give out, I think—and I don't mean the toilet! Old age is a *bitch*. Don't you never get old!" Granger said. He chuckled at his wit.

How was Joanna supposed to respond to that? "I'll keep it in mind," she managed with a weak smile. "Do you have today's paper, by any chance? It's not super important, but I noticed this one has yesterday's date on it."

Granger took up his station behind the counter, inhaling sharply as he settled himself on a warped metal barstool with a wince followed by a low groan. "Well now, that is today's paper, actually. See, that's a weekly publication. We don't have enough news around here for a daily effort—not us little folk out here in the land that the Lord forgot." Granger offered a wide grin, showing off an eccentric row of yellow teeth and a few gaping holes. Muddy tobacco and coffee stains streaked the enamel, and an alarming dark spot peeked out from his gums.

"Okay, no problem." Joanna wrested her gaze from his teeth, and her attention landed on a tray of click pens printed with "I ♥ Las Vegas."

"I'll take a pen, too. But…Las Vegas?" Joanna said.

"I know, we're a long way from Sin City. But tourists will buy anything."

"You get tourists out here?"

Granger grinned and wiped his nose with his finger, then punched keys on his cash register with an artistic flourish, pausing to point at each item as he tallied the price. "Let's see here. Paper, drink, candy, souvenir pen. The damage is, ah…three twenty-nine oughta do it."

Joanna handed him crumpled bills and three dimes.

"Could I also get directions? I'm looking for a road called Sunshine Highway, and my GPS reception cut out about ten miles ago. I think I'm a little turned around."

"Ah, directions. Well now, that…*that* will cost ya," Granger rumbled in a deep voice altogether different from his cheery customer-service tone. His thumb lingered too long as he pressed a sticky penny into the palm of her hand. He flashed her another tarnished grin and Joanna's heart thumped against her breastbone. The friendly stranger had vanished, and was replaced by an escaped convict with madness in his eyes and a powerful lust for disoriented young women. Joanna took a step backward, ready to run.

But Granger's face softened before she turned to bolt. "Aww, just foolin' with ya, city girl! Sunshine's a ways north yet, just keep along Main Street and you'll see it in another two and a half miles er so. Keep an eye out for the big old abandoned motorhome on the right, can't miss it." Granger's gruff grandpa demeanor returned as he held out her receipt with a wink.

"Thanks." Joanna took the receipt, but kept her distance. She didn't want to be here any more. Granger was all smiles now, but she sensed he was dangerous; not the type of person you wanted to upset, especially if you weren't a local.

"Real quick, hon, before you go—if you don't mind me asking, what business do you have out on the highway?"

"Oh, I'm a realtor. I'm on my way to check out some property."

"Oh yeah? Whose property would that be?"

"Um, I prefer to keep my client information confidential-"

"The Guerreros? The Cunninghams? Wouldn't be…couldn't be the old Hench Ranch, would it?"

"I really can't say. I'm sorry, but I have to get going! Thanks again for the directions."

Granger grunted, annoyed. "You can tell me, honey. I'm just curious, I won't tell anyone…pinky promise." He held out his hand with his little finger extended.

"Thanks again! You've been very helpful!" Joanna swept her items from the counter and waved back with a giddy smile. "But I have to get going. See you!"

Outside, she tossed her purchases into the passenger seat and fumbled for the convertible's door handle. Was she a coward? Paranoid? Honestly, she couldn't tell. The desert was making her feel nervous—crazy, even. Hundreds of miles of granite sand in every direction, burning winds, and the quiet, incessant heat. The land felt alien and indifferent, not a habitat meant for humans. In the city you could find help if you needed it, usually. But out here, the reality of death by exposure or predators ran right up to your door. The place was untamed, and the people here lived closer to nature than Joanna was used to.

There was movement behind Royal Empire Liquor's glass door. Between a sign listing the store's hours and an ad for Kool cigarettes, Granger's sagging face appeared. He stepped up to the glass door and arched his back, stretching as he watched Joanna fumble her keys from her purse. She released the parking brake and turned the key in the ignition—and the car didn't start. The engine turned over once, then shuddered to a halt.

Joanna waved again at Granger, while forcing a nervous *I'm-sure-everything's-all-right* smile. But he was not smiling back; he watched her, intense and steady, with that bedlam look dancing in his eyes.

Her imagination raced. How dangerous was he?

Would he lunge through the liquor store door to pull her from her car, lock her in the back room and chain her to his bed—no, it would be a *cot*, just a metal frame with a thin, stained mattress—over a tattered carpet littered with men's magazines and empty beer bottles? She imagined herself lying in a fetal position, naked and hurt, watching his boots shuffle close as he smacked a tire iron into the palm of his hand. Or perhaps his tastes ran simpler—he would simply leave her on the linoleum floor of the liquor store, bleeding out for all to see, right next to the cooler with the discount beer with an "I ♥ Las Vegas" ballpoint pen lodged in her neck. He would loom above her stiffening body, admiring his work. *Seeya, city girl,* he would say, as his cigarette dangled and bounced at the corner of his tarry mouth.

Joanna swallowed hard and tried the ignition again, turning the key with enough strength to hurt her fingers. When the car jumped to life, Granger moved away from the glass like a ghost fading from a mirror in a haunted house.

2

Main Street gave up and disintegrated into rubble at the top of a low, treeless hilltop as barren as a mayor's scalp. A heat-warped metal sign, speckled with rusted pits from shotgun blasts, was barely legible; "Sunshine Highway." Someone had scrawled a message across the bottom: *Welcome to the end of the world.*

Joanna found the abandoned motorhome at the

edge of town, just where Granger had said it would be. As she drove up the hill, it loomed into view like a face peeking over a sanitarium wall. The front windows had been smashed, leaving huge, dark eye sockets, but the black-tinted side windows were intact. Local youths had spray-painted the storage panels with strings of nonsense letters and shapes.

As all slowly decaying things do, it had a rich history and a long memory. The 1981 Coachmen Deluxe was crashed into a freeway median by its first owner within a month of purchase. The man died, but the RV lived on, refurbished and sold as a salvage title. For years it served as a cozy home for a woman and her daughter in northern New Mexico, until the daughter died under mysterious circumstances; her body was found in pieces, strewn about the living room area. In the late '90s, the RV had served as a tour bus for a rockabilly band, until the drummer died of a heroin overdose its tiny bathroom after a show at a dive bar in Arkansas. The bank repossessed the motorhome, then sold it to a silver-haired widower who dreamed of exploring the west coast just like Huell Howser. He had only crossed two states before suffering a coronary, hunched over on the little fold-down coffee table while parked outside a diner in Amarillo. The sheriff found him face-down in his final carry-out meal of chicken-fried steak and eggs. The motorhome was driven to its final resting place after being stolen from a used car lot by a desperate family of undocumented immigrants. They made 800 miles in just ten hours, until they were pulled over by a drunk state trooper who forced them to kneel in the shadow of the vehicle before blowing holes in their heads—an act of self-defense, he later told the court. The judge nodded, the investigation was dropped, and the motorhome was abandoned where it was stopped on the little hill where Main met Sunshine.

From then on, no one desired ownership of the motorhome except the vermin of the Mojave desert. As the years passed it became a familiar landmark in Settle; the locals referred to it as The Winn, despite it not being a Winnebago. Outsiders who visited the town found the abandoned motorhome ugly and forgettable. To the locals who knew it well, it exuded an undeniable malevolence. Its empty front windows gazed out at the desert, lost in thought. Animals sheltered there, stumbling through the chunks of broken glass to make nests in the dashboard, but nothing could live there for long. Occasionally, it emitted a strange, ripe smell—like melting plastic and spicy sweat. The locals never set foot inside it or attempted to move it further out into the desert; the miasma of bad luck surrounding the thing was palpable. You could almost taste it.

As Joanna drove past, she caught the stink of it for just a moment. The side paneling was splattered with crusted eggs and bird shit. Bullet holes riddled the storage compartments. What she could see of the interior was spook-house gloomy, waiting for a new owner, or at least a visitor. The Winn watched the little red car pass by, staring at Joanna with the same expression Granger had given her on her way out the door of Royal Empire Liquor. She quickly looked away.

The motorhome was two and a half miles north of downtown Settle, marking the entrance to the unincorporated chunk of desert known as Sunshine. The end of the asphalt was abrupt, resulting in a three inch drop-off to the gravel road which made the convertible's shocks complain. Dust rose up from the sides of the car no matter how softly she pumped the gas. Renting a convertible had been such a mistake.

Joanna's cell phone rang and startled her. It had been hours since she'd had any satellite reception. She fumbled it out of the empty ashtray and it rang again, vibrating in her hand until it slipped from her fingers. She grabbed for it, trying to fish it out from under her feet while simultaneously pulling over to the side of the road. In a desperate lunge for the phone she stepped on the brake too hard. The car came to an abrupt stop, whacking her forehead on the steering wheel just as she finally grasped the phone between her first finger and thumb. She yelled "Damn it!" before she could stop herself. Her voice echoed softly back to her by the distant hills: *damn it… damn it…*

"Hello?" she said, breathing hard. "This is Joanna speaking."

A burst of static accompanied her co-worker's voice. "Joanna! It's Mitch! I just wanted to check in and see if you made it to Settle County yet! You doing okay out there?"

"Yeah, I'm on Sunshine right now. I'm on my way out to the property."

"Well, that's great! I think everything's going to work out real well for you with this client! Real big client, too! You have fun, okay? Knock 'em dead!"

Mitch always talked like that. It was exhausting, but a little bit charming, too. You don't meet many total optimists, and Joanna found Mitch—while not exactly the smartest guy on the planet—kind of refreshing. Of course, it was all part of being a real estate agent. It was the persona he had developed to excel at his job, so that was who he was now, regardless of what he had been like before becoming an agent. It was the price of success.

"Okay, Mitch, I'll try. Thanks again for the lead. I really appreciate it."

"You bet! You totally got this in the bag!"

The connection ended before Joanna could say goodbye.

3

Sunshine Highway, while unpaved, was well-worn. It snaked up into exposed desert hills which were blistering during the day and frosty at night. There was more brush flanking the road here than there had been on Main Street, and it was twisted and sharp—the kind of vile thorns that hook into your clothing and refuse to let go.

The residences flanking the highway were mostly vans and campers inhabited by aging outcasts who never really found their footing in normal society. Some were drug addicts, a few were paranoid, but most were not totally crazy. Local law enforcement did not bother them unless they left their tiny homesteads, and they rarely ventured from their carefully marked territories except to trade the welfare checks they cashed at City Bank for food and water at Royal Empire Liquor—or, if they had the means to get there, the big-box grocery store.

As Joanna drove past, residents peeked out of windows framed with time-stained curtains. The desert dwellers stared at her rental car as it gleamed on the gravel road like a Christmas ornament left on a dead tree. Joanna felt their eyes upon her but she stared straight ahead, acting unaffected. She checked to make sure her doors were locked before remembering she was driving a convertible, and stopped just long enough to put the top up.

Five miles down Sunshine Highway, the road ended for good. Joanna's car lurched and bobbed into the raw open desert, rocking through potholes and grottoes worn deep by heavy winter storms. She could see faint tracks where car tires had driven through recently, but the way forward was overgrown with desert shrubs that caught in the car's undercarriage as she passed over them. Joanna spotted a tilting wooden sign carved in the shape of an arrow, which read "Hench Territory, 1/8 mile." Squinting her eyes in the late afternoon light, she saw the dark silhouette of a house on the horizon with a smaller building next to it. The sun was directly behind the structures, making it impossible to pick out any details. The windshield visor was no help at all. She hoped she'd found the right place: it was the end of the road.

A figure stepped in front of the car. Joanna slammed on the brakes, sending her cell phone once again clattering to the floor and tipping her purse. Its contents down the side of the passenger seat: makeup, tampons, loose change. The convertible came to an abrupt halt, skidding a few inches along the desert hardpan.

"Hello?" she called out. "Is someone there? Did I… did I hit you?"

Like a country magician, a gawky young man stepped out from the billowing clouds of dust. "Saw ya comin' a mile out, thought I'd meet ya out here! I'm Gus Hench. Sorry if I spooked ya. Welcome to Hench Ranch."

4

The interior of Hench House resembled a rustic estate from a spaghetti western. Curtains spotted with blush-colored roses muted the early evening sunlight. To the right of the front door, a low wall supported a row of coat hooks fashioned from old horseshoes. Joanna's steps were loud on the hardwood floor, dark with decades of polish, dusty in the corners. Thick grey cords of fluffy spiderweb swooped from an upper corner of the entryway and slowly danced in the air. The entry opened onto a quaint parlor, ready to greet guests of quality; a reception neatly appointed with cushioned rococo chairs and a glass-topped table supporting a huge silver cigarette lighter. In an amusing display of awkward grandiosity, Gus bowed and gestured toward the parlor with open arms and a crooked smile.

Joanna entered the room and stepped back in time. An opulent but faded rug of brown and burgundy crushed under her heels as she crossed the floor. While Gus fetched his father, she sat on the edge of a gilded chair and admired the room's artifacts. Cloudy oil paintings of Hench ancestry adorned the wood-paneled walls, which met the ceiling with elaborate crown molding carved with tiny roses. A wide desk and red leather chair was situated in dusty rays of slanted light under a four-paned window. Over an ornate fireplace hung the portrait of a stern-faced aristocrat of the old west, tanned and hardened, wearing his best Sunday finery with lace at his chin. On his left arm hung a young wife, sallow and thin with straw hair and sad eyes.

"You must be Miss Joanna Durand! Welcome to Hench territory!"

Filling the parlor doorway was an incredible mountain of a man. His neck creased under his chin, then protruded before meeting the top of his chest, which was flat for a few inches before embarking on the massive curvature of his folded and swaying belly. Arms the size of Easter hams chafed against his sides. The wooden floor creaked as he rocked his girth back and forth, ambulating across the room towards Joanna.

She jumped up and held out her hand. "Mr. Hench, I presume! How nice to meet you!"

The skin of his fingers was soft and warm. He pressed her hand briefly, then dropped it and turned toward the writing desk. "Just Charles, please. Don't get up on my account! Go ahead and have a seat, darlin.'" He settled into the red leather chair with a deep sigh.

"Ceegar?" Charles offered.

"Oh, no, thank you. I quit smoking years ago, doctor's orders," Joanna said.

"Well, whiskey then, at least. I insist."

"Oh, no, thank…"

"I never drink alone, darlin'. Drinking in private is the truest sign of an alcoholic, my father always said. Please, do me the honor of joining me, so that I may indulge. Pretty please?" Charles pleaded with a coy smile.

Joanna relented. "Gus!" Charles hollered. "Bring the rye!"

Gus disappeared from the doorway, leaving Joanna and Charles in uneasy silence.

"An ancestor?" asked Joanna, looking up at the oil painting over the fireplace.

"Yes ma'am. Us Henches have been around a real long time, and we plan on being around a lot longer. Just not around *here,* if you take my meaning."

"Yes, of course. It can be so refreshing to move," Joanna said. "My colleague mentioned that you-"

"Just a moment. Gus will be back shortly, I've no doubt. Pleasure before business, I always say. We'll have a drink before we start."

They lapsed into silence; a nightmare for Joanna. She was not adept at small-talk—at least, not without advance warning that she might need to invoke it—and she had not prepared any specific topics. In the silence, her ears focused on a shrill ticking clock that perched on the hearth: it was the loudest sound in the world. Charles was untroubled by the lull in conversation. His attention shifted from the painting over the fireplace to a bird outside the window, and finally to a piece of paper on his desk. He shuffled his feet and scratched his chest.

Charles was the host, but Joanna had called the meeting, so she was responsible for it. She should be talking about something, but what? Perhaps she could talk about the weather, or the town. She opened her mouth to speak even as she was unsure of how she would begin.

But she heard Gus returning, finally. The young man's thudding boots clomped down the hall until he appeared in the doorway, gripping a crystal highball glass in each hand with a bottle of high quality rye tucked under his arm. After handing Charles his glass, Gus set the bottle on the desk and placed Joanna's glass on a coaster with prim decorum. He poured a finger of whiskey into each. Joanna accepted her drink and held it close, grateful for something to do with her hands.

"All right, now I think we can get down to business." Charles lifted his whiskey in a brief toast to the onlooking paintings and knocked it back, leaning his chair at an alarming angle as it squeaked in protest.

"Well, as you know, I'm taking over for your previous agent, Mitch," Joanna said. "His father has suffered an unfortunate medical emergency."

"All the more fortunate for us lonely Hench boys, so that we may entertain such a lovely, *lovely* lady visitor as yourself." He shook his empty glass in the air. "Gus! Another round. More for you, Joanna? I'm buying." Charles winked.

"Thank you." Joanna examined the man's face. Was Charles flirting with her? She wore her smile like a mask. "I understand that you have several acres of land to sell, in addition to this house and the outbuilding. Have you determined your asking price yet?"

"No." Charles sighed and looked toward the window, where the last of the day's sunlight was turning orange and dusky. Joanna saw his mouth work, as though he were ruminating over his next words. "You're not from around here, are you? Not a local? You don't look it."

"No, I'm from Phoenix, originally. This is my first visit to Sunshine, and I must say, it's a very special little town."

Charles guffawed and turned away from the

window to stare directly into Joanna's eyes as a drop of whiskey dribbled down his chin. He set his glass down hard, and wiped his face with an open hand.

"Special, *horseshit!* It's a dump, darlin', and it's okay to say so. No one in their right mind stays if they can go. Only reason the Henches are still here is…well, tradition, I suppose. If you can even call it that. Or maybe it's just plain stupidity."

Joanna squirmed, grinned widely, and tried to think of something to say.

"It's okay, darlin'. The Hench family's ready to move on, and you're here to help, so let's get to it. Enough with the pleasantries. Where do we start?"

5

An hour later, Gus walked Joanna to her car. It had been an exhausting meeting. Charles was hard to read. He was alternately lecherous and resentful, yet he never made a pass at her and he didn't send her away, either. He drank half of the bottle of rye whiskey during the meeting, and showed no signs of slowing when she left.

As Joanna unlocked her car, Gus lingered a few steps behind her, prying a rock from the earth with the toe of his boot.

"Sorry 'bout Da'. He's had a hard time of it lately, and isn't much used to outsiders any more. I mean, you know, visitors."

"It was nice to meet him, Gus. I hope I can help your family." Joanna paused, then took a deep breath and asked the question that was on her mind.

"Have you thought about where your family is going to live when you sell this land, though? I don't understand why you're selling at all. You own this property free and clear. I know you have a brother who lives here with you, and an elderly aunt who probably doesn't want to move. The place seems to fit your needs, and from the statements I've seen, you don't need the money. So why sell? Why do you want to leave?"

Gus glanced away, scanning the darkening desert hills as if expecting the arrival of some waiting predator. He didn't answer, but shifted his weight back and forth, looking alternately scared, and guilty, and sad.

"You really ain't from around here, are you?" His unusual drawl became more pronounced.

"No, I'm really not. Is there something I should know? If there is anything problematic about the land, you need to disclose before you can sell. That's the law."

"Oh, no, the land's fine, just *fine!*" Gus grinned, uneasy. "It's the neighbors, I guess. Good neighbors are so important, you know."

"Yes…" Joanna said. As soon as the sun had disappeared over the horizon the temperature had plummeted. A cold breeze swept dust from the ground and caused the dry shrubs to tremble and shudder. Joanna folded her arms, trying to stay warm. Gus had something to tell her—that he *needed* to tell her—but he was frightened. What could he be afraid of, standing outside his own house next to a harmless city girl in the beautiful Arizona dusk? He looked down at the dirt and shuffled his feet like a shy young cowpoke, occasionally flicking his eyes up toward the hills.

"So…then you really ain't never heard of the Cutters?"

6

The year of 1929 closed not with a roar, but with a sharp cry of pain and confusion. The country's broken economy had moved some folk out of their homes and into diaspora: they migrated to far places on rumors of prosperity and opportunity. Often, their journeys ended in blood—by mishap, mischief, or murder.

On an arid hill west of the Hualapai reservation, a wagon breached. It rattled down the mound to come to a rest at the bottom, where its sullen mule put her head down and exhaled in a deep snort, sending up twin puffs of powdery sand from the barren desert floor.

The stopping point seemed a totally arbitrary choice. The area had no distinguishing features other than a tiny creek a quarter mile to the north. Low, sloping dunes created a late sunrise and an early sunset, and offered some minimal shelter from the wind. There were shrubs and a few trees. That was all.

"Here, Pa? But there's nothing around. Why here?" Abigail wrinkled her nose and yanked on the yarn hair of her doll. "I hate it."

Ardell Hench jumped from the wagon bench and landed heavily on the ground. He straightened his back and lifted his chin, smelling the air, squinting at the distant mountains.

"Yes, Abby. Here. This is it. Get your mother."

Abby climbed into the back of the wagon. Among the baskets of flour, piles of moth-chewed clothing, cook-pans, blankets, the last few potatoes, and a canister of water, lay her mother. She was pregnant to bursting.

"Mama! We're here. Pa says come see."

Abby gripped her mother's arm to help the woman rise to her feet and step down from the wagon. This late in the pregnancy, her mother seemed like a priceless and delicate vase, apt to shatter to pieces.

"Here, Ardell? Why?" she asked.

"Because," Ardell said.

He had been born in New York City. After his father packed up and left for a lady in Chicago, his mother found employment in a laundry. It was hard work for low wages; not enough to feed them both. As a young boy Ardell learned to work the streets, liberating pocketbooks from tourists. The pair had earned a meager living until his mother died of consumption. Ardell traveled to Boston looking for work, then to Nashville, Tulsa, Austin, and Albuquerque. He had married, and remarried. He had three or four children in two or three states.

"Because I say so, Carla. We're here because I'm tired of moving around. I want to rest my bones. No one will move us on from here. No one wants this desert, not even the damn Indians. I bought it cheap. That makes it ours, and ours alone. That's enough for me, and it's going to have to be enough for you, too." Ardell started untying ropes from the wagon with quick, decisive movements.

"Where you at, girl?" he called.

"Here, Pa," Abby replied, stepping out from behind the mule. "Just petting Honey. She's awfully tired."

"Stop foolin' around, girl. Unpack the cookware."

7

Joanna sighed, spreading the pictures she had taken of the Hench homestead into a fan on the motel bed. Every picture was ugly. It was an ugly house on an ugly piece of land, desirable only in the eyes of the owner. Her job was to listen to the client's needs, sell the property, and take her fees—but she wished she could talk Charles out of the whole thing. He wanted twice what Joanna thought he'd get for it. He'd be lucky to sell it at all.

What Gus had told her about the neighbors wasn't encouraging, either. With his lip curled in disgust, he had described an incestuous family hidden away in the nearby foothills, who only came out at night and probably ate their own young. She didn't believe a word of it, but it wouldn't do for Gus to be gossiping like that to prospective buyers. She had nodded and listened to his story, wide-eyed with sympathy, and made a mental note to talk to Charles about putting Gus to work in the back pasture whenever new clients examined the property.

The last two snapshots Joanna had taken presented the house as a dark silhouette in front of a glorious sunset. From a distance, they captured some of the charm of the structures without showing most of the weathering. Artistic, if not informational—and somewhat pleasant looking. The red glow of the approaching twilight evoked a mood of peace and rest, and simpler times. It was the best she could do for now. She plugged her iPhone into her mini-printer to create the physical copies insisted upon by the local paper for real estate listings. Settler Times didn't even have an email address; she'd have to drop off the pictures in person at the press office tomorrow morning. What a pain in the butt.

As the little printer worked, she ran through her mental notes on the layout of the Hench House for the listing text. There was a large entryway, and a parlor. The kitchen was not very big, but it was equipped with cabinets and updated appliances which would be included in the asking price. A dining room, almost as ostentatious as the parlor, opened from the kitchen. It was across the hall from a great-room, which was the home's most unique asset. There was a fireplace, plenty of room for a sofa set, and an old upright piano. The second story was all bedrooms, with one large bathroom. Charles had shown her the stairway to the basement, but had not taken her down. She suspected he did not trust the ancient wooden steps to support his prodigious weight.

When the printer was finished, she set the pictures on the dresser and walked into the bathroom, stripping off her dusty jacket and sweaty blouse. She hated the uniform.

If her thirteen year old self could see her now, she'd be disgusted. Skirt suit, clunky three-inch wedge heels, sensible makeup. Ugly but serviceable. That's how she felt these days, inside and out.

As warm water filled the bathtub, she drifted back to the photos on the dresser. Her phone camera had not adjusted well to the uneven light, and the last picture she took looked grainy and underexposed. She would have to take a better picture for internet listings, but this one was at least interesting. The last rays of the sun reflected off one of the two upper windows of the house, creating a bright gleaming eye and a wink. The porch was spacious but bare, and would require some potted plants and flowers before showing. Maybe she could get Gus to install a two-seater swing. Wide stepping stones designated a path down the gentle slope in front of the house, forming a walkway sturdy enough to survive winter downpours.

Joanna decided she'd try to get some better pictures tomorrow, see if she could check out that basement, maybe even walk the perimeter of the property. She'd brought boots and slacks, just in case. Might as well use them.

There was the outbuilding to examine, too. The second structure—which Charles called the "barn" but which looked more like a glorified storage shed—had fewer windows, and several holes in the roof. It also had a stepping-stone path, but instead of starting at the front door the stones led away from the back of the building toward a dip in the ground. Joanna had not noticed the second path during her initial tour of the property. She squinted at the picture, bringing it close to her face. An archaic wooden hatch was set into the desert floor, encircled by a ring of rocks and small boulders. A few feet away, a skinny post with an illegible sign stuck out of the ground at an angle. Perched on top of the post was an enormous black bird, head cocked to the horizon in dark silhouette.

8

"You never mentioned an extra cellar. What's this?"

Joanna handed Charles the picture. They were sitting in the parlor again, Charles drinking from his glass of whiskey while Joanna nipped delicately at her own, trying not to swallow much of it. She held each drop on her tongue, letting it burn her taste buds before it trickled into to her empty stomach. If she'd known she was having whiskey for breakfast, she would have made a greater effort to eat something earlier. It was ten o'clock in the morning.

"Oh, of course. The old root cellar." Charles leaned back and tried to cross his legs, holding the picture out for Joanna to take back.

"For food storage? Must be ancient."

"My grandfather built it in his early years, as protection against the summer heat for whatever meager sustenance he could coax from the barren soil. Before we got the power line, you know. Now I'm not sure what's down there anymore. Mostly junk, probably. Hasn't been opened in ages."

"Well, we should take a look. If it's a hazard, it should be filled in before listing the house. If it's stable, we can advertise it as a feature. You know, something that brings character to the property. It adds some history which we can include in the listing, maybe even an interesting story if you can think of one. Some investors like that kind of thing. I'd like to go check it out before I leave today, if you have the time to show me."

Charles folded his hands in front of his mouth and peeked at Joanna over the top of them. "Tell you what. I'll send Gus this afternoon, see what's down there. No need for you to go tramping around in a dark, nasty hole. Could be dangerous. I promise a full report," Charles vowed, placing his meaty right hand over his heart and bowing his head.

"That's fine. But have him take some pictures, will you?" Joanna set her glass on her coaster, and picked up her briefcase. "I have to drive home this evening. Is there anything else you need from me before I get back to the office and start working on your listing?"

"Actually, there is something. Gus might have talked to you yesterday about, uh…our dirty laundry. Did he mention our troubles with the neighbors?"

"The Cutters, yes. He seemed quite agitated. Do you think they are going to cause problems while you are on the market?"

Charles chuckled. "Well, that's just the thing. I aim to keep them in the dark about the sale until all's said and done. They don't read the paper and they don't talk to the town people, so I'm hoping they won't find out until we're quit of this place. But if they do find out…and especially if any of them try to talk to you…"

"Yes?" Joanna asked.

"Just be careful. Don't say anything you don't have to."

"I can handle myself, Charles, but thank you. I assure you I will practice perfect discretion. I'm going to do my job and sell your house, not engage in gossip with the locals. I know what I'm doing."

Anger flushed red on Charles's face. He set down his glass. "All right. Shut your mouth up for a minute and listen to me. I'm not just telling you to watch your words, I'm telling you to watch your ass. Those Cutters—they're dangerous, and they're crazy. Most of what Gus probably told you was true, and he doesn't know everything. We're moving because of them, if you haven't figured it out, and if they find out what's going on they'll explode out of the hills like an ant farm flushed with hot water. If you can't handle this, then we'll find someone else who can. Understood?"

Joanna stared into his eyes and clenched her jaw, suppressing an avalanche of retorts before spinning away toward the door without a word. She nearly made it out of the parlor without opening her mouth, but with her hand on the knob, she stopped. The heat, the surreal landscape, and the strange solitude of the desert had tired her out. It was too much. Her indignation flared into rage and she whirled back toward Charles in a fury.

"I'm not your servant, Mr. Hench. I'm a realtor, and I'm the best chance you have at selling this remote patch of dirt. I'm ready and able to do so, but I won't be treated with disrespect by you or anyone else," she said in a single breath. "I don't know the Cutter family, but they're not *my* problem. I don't believe half of what I've heard about them, but even if it's all true, I don't care. You don't strike me as a coward, Mr. Hench. So we can either focus on the business at hand and get this all over with, or you can find yourself another realtor to scare with your boogeyman stories."

Joanna's heart sank. What was she doing? He was a client, and she needed this job—but she wouldn't be treated like a child. The arrogant patriarch would have to decide. The jeweled clock on the hearth ticked away tense seconds as they measured each other, waiting to find out which direction they were headed.

Charles frowned, furrowing his eyebrows, then finally offered a gracious smile. "Very fiery, Joanna. You're absolutely right. I apologize. You know your business, and you're a tough young lady. I'm merely concerned, as a father would be for his little girl. I hope you can see that. Just be careful who you talk to, that's all I'm asking. Do we have a deal?"

Joanna shrugged. This didn't feel like a win. His apology was slathered with condescension. She suppressed her anger, and forced a conciliatory nod.

"Deal. I'll call you tomorrow for your final approval when the listing is ready, Mr. Hench. Have a good day."

9

After putting her briefcase in the trunk, Joanna leaned against the convertible and took one last look around the property. Despite its squalor, she felt confident she would sell it. A jackrabbit poked its ears out of a hole in the hillside. It examined her, wiggling its nose and cocking its head, before ducking back into the earth.

Joanna shaded her eyes with her hand and squinted at the door to the root cellar. What was really down there? Of course she didn't believe Charles was telling the truth. There was something about it he didn't want her to know. She would probably never find out, and she could accept that, but she hated being lied to. A good realtor should have the complete trust of her clients.

A black crow landed on the signpost next to the cellar door, re-creating the exact scene she had taken a picture of. The bird cawed, an ugly rasping sound, and flapped twice without alighting. It was a ratty old thing. Several of its feathers were missing the tips, and many more were broken and bent. How could it fly with such damaged wings?

Joanna heard the soft crunch of shifting gravel behind her. Someone was walking up, maybe Gus wanting to say goodbye. She thought he probably had a little crush on her. It was sweet.

Before she could turn, a cracking sound exploded inside her head like gunfire. Her vision was splashed with red and yellow fireworks, and the ground rushed up to smack her cheek. Sharp pebbles dug into the side of her face as tickling droplets of blood ran down the back of her skull. Someone rolled her over, powdering her head wound in the dust. White puffy clouds overhead looked blurry in the blue sky, brushed with pulsating streaks of blood and adrenaline.

A masked face appeared overhead, then was gone just as quickly. Had it been framed by a crop of red hair, or was that part of the fireworks show? Distant rumbling grew louder, rushing in until it was on top of her, running over her, smothering her like a dry summer storm. The thunder was black and sounded like catatonia.

Joanna closed her eyes, and floated away.

10

"Harrison. Drink with me."

Afternoon light refracted in the parlor's segmented glass windows. Shards of sun, redirected by the paneled glass, bounced off the fine crystal glassware, speckling the wall and floor with tiny drops of rainbow light. It was a beautiful effect.

Charles poured whiskey.

"Yes, sir." Harrison took the glass and sniffed, inhaling the scent deep into his lungs. High quality hooch; could mean good news, or bad. The farmhand sat in an exquisite armchair—a weed in a bed of roses. "What's the occasion, boss?"

"We're selling, Harrison. The whole property. Which means you're out of a job, sorry to say. I wish I could have given you more notice, but I'd be happy to write you a letter of recommendation. You've been a real help around here the last few years. A *real* help." Charles raised his glass in a half-hearted toast before knocking it back.

"N…no! No sir, please don't. Don't leave me behind." Tears welled in Harrison's eyes. "I got nowhere else to go. I mean, I got no family. Brother died two months ago, and Mum's been gone five years. You don't even have to pay me, but please let me come with you."

"I'm sorry, Harrison. I don't know where we'll go from here, so it has to be just family. You understand. We'll be moving quick and quiet." Charles shook his glass in the air, and Harrison refilled it with a trembling hand. "*You know why.*"

"Yes, sir. I know. You'll have to move fast, to avoid interference from the cursed ones. I can help. I can-"

"Anyway, this might be an opportunity for you, Harrison. You don't want to get stuck out here forever like us Henches did. The desert dries a man out. You should find yourself a girl, Harry. Get out of Settle. Don't settle for Settle!" Charles smacked his knee and hooted. His nose turned purple-red as he shook and guffawed.

Harrison stared, his whiskey forgotten, pleading with red bloodshot eyes. "Don't make fun, sir. You know I can't get a girl."

"Just keep trying, kid. There has got to be a girl out there just like you. Look in alleys, under rocks, behind saloons! Hah! Be fearless, son! God helps those who help themselves. Like I said, I wish we didn't have to let you go. I really–"

Brakes squealed outside. The scrape of tires skidding along the graveled road was followed by a crash of splintering wood. Shouting followed—more excited than hurt—and the laughter of young men, whooping with excitement. Charles began throwing his weight back and forth in his chair, trying to gain the momentum to stand. "What the *unholy* fuck was that?" he yelled.

Harrison stepped to the window to take a look, then ducked quickly as a gun was fired. The shot came so close to his head the slipstream following it tousled his hair before the bullet exploded a stained glass lamp next to Charles's chair.

"Cutters, sir. A whole bunch of them," Harrison said, with his back pressed to the wall.

One of the voices outside was amplified by an electric megaphone, making it supernaturally loud. "Waddle your fat ass out here, Charles! If you can fit out through the front door, that is! Come on, doughboy!"

"Come on, Hench. Here piggy piggy! Heeeeeere piggy piggy piggy!" The robotic voice moved around the house, circling toward the east side.

Charles displayed surprising agility as he scampered along the floor on his toes and knuckles, staying below the level of the window sill. He crawled under a table, breathing heavily, and made wild gestures at Harrison to join him there.

"What are we going to do, boss?"

"Shut up, let me think." Charles put his hands on his face and wiped his cheeks, clearing sweat from the bags under his eyes. "What the fuck is he doing? Why now? *Dammit!*"

The megaphone had completed its circle around the back of the house and was approaching again from the other side. "We figured out your plans to cut-and-run, chickenshit. You coward! Your father would slit his wrists if he was still alive today! Ashamed of his chickenshit son!"

Another shot rang out, and a second-story window shattered. Someone upstairs screamed.

"We already caught your realtor-bitch, Charles! We stuck her in the hole! This is the end! Come out and face it like a man!"

People were fighting in the kitchen. The legs of the big wooden dining table screeched as it slid across the linoleum. Something—Abigail's old cookie jar, probably—was shoved off the counter, and it shattered on the floor. The screen door slammed open, then slowly squealed shut. From the side of the house came the sound of boot heels being dragged through the dirt. The footsteps stopped when they reached the front of the house.

"We got one of your panty-stains out here, piggy! You better come out, or the piglet is gonna get yoo-than-ized!"

Harrison popped his head up just long enough to peek out the window. "They got Marcus, boss. Sat him up execution style."

"That Harry the hare in there with you, Charles? I seeeee you, harelip! Roll the big pig out out the door and maybe we'll let you run, rabbit!"

"Maybe I should go out there, boss. Maybe I can get Marcus–"

"Marcus is dead." Charles leaned his head back against the wall and shut his eyes.

"But boss, we gotta–"

"No. He's already dead. And so are we."

11

It was cold and dark in the small room. Had she left the air conditioner on all night?

The air danced with slipstreams of purple mist.

Joanna shifted, unable to get comfortable. She was laying on a blanket which had balled up under her, and her back ached. The mattress as lumpy, made up of only a tattered sheet and a few rough coverlets which were spread over something hard.

Had she fallen out of bed? She had no memory of driving home. But she'd checked out of the motel this morning…And then what?

Blinking in the gloom, encouraging her eyes to focus, she reached out to both sides, waving her arms. Where was the *lamp?*

A thin shaft of blue-gray light, so bright it looked solid, pierced the center of the room. Thousands of tiny dust-motes danced in it, lovely and twinkling. The spot of floor illuminated by the light was covered in natty carpet. As Joanna's eyes adjusted, she saw decaying shelves on a wood paneled wall and a rusted bucket with a mop leaning in it where her lamp should have been.

This wasn't her room.

She bent her legs and leaned forward, trying to stand. The world swooned drunkenly around her and she fell back on her butt into the pile of blankets, her limbs numb with exhaustion. She was injured. She had been hit. Someone had hit her. Her head throbbed: when felt the back of her scalp, her fingers came away matted with loose hair, sticky and dark with drying blood. The wound was still wet, but the bleeding had stopped.

Her attacker had…red hair? No one she had met on this trip had red hair.

She explored the back of her head again, pressing gently. A massive, slow wave of agony rose and broke on her skull, and she moaned. She blinked her eyes hard, trying to stay conscious through the pain. "No passing out. Stay awake, Jo," she whispered.

When the tide began to ebb, she again examined her surroundings. The pale beam of dusty light was coming through a tiny hole in the ceiling. It was bright but looked natural, like moonlight. As her vision improved, she saw antiquated wooden cabinets piled high with glass jelly jars, stacks of paper and fabric, countless odds and ends. Shelves lined the walls holding books, figurines, taxidermied rats, fancy pens and ink-pots, mirrors, a huge assortment of items all coated with grime. Every flat surface was hidden under clusters of knick-knacks and junk. On a wall in a distant corner she saw a large green rectangle covered in faint slashes and circles: a chalkboard. None of the items in the room seemed to relate to each other.

"Hello?" Joanna called out. Her voice was a harsh whisper. She cleared her throat and tried again.

"Anyone there? Hello?" There was no answer.

Sleepiness was creeping up on her again. She closed her eyes, and let herself drift away from the pain into strange dreams.

12

Through the 1930s, Hench Valley was beset by roving packs of coyotes, violent monsoon thunderstorms, and rightfully furious Hualapai Indians. It was no place to try for a fresh start; certainly not an ideal location to raise a young family. A less stubborn man would have given up and moved himself back to civilized territory, but Ardell refused to abdicate. He had staked his claim, and as he liked to proclaim on a near-daily basis, Henches never ran from a fight.

The closest town was a little bump in the road called Gleason. There was a market, a bar, a chapel, and not much else. The pastor sermonized on Sunday afternoons; morning services had been bumped back a few hours to allow for farm hands' hangovers, ensuring the pews were full. On Mondays, Wednesdays, and Fridays, the chapel also held classes for children aged five to sixteen: reading, writing, 'rithmatic. The land was dry but plentiful, and corn would grow if it was tended carefully. Cows did alright, too. Gleason was tired, hot, and hungry, but it was positioned at a busy crossroads which allowed for just enough trade to keep everyone alive.

A few years before the arrival of the Hench clan

there had been some excitement: the discovery of gold in the hills, followed by a brief rush of prospective miners who brought with them cash and crime and big ideas. When the veins were soon discovered to be filled with nothing but pyrite, the prospectors left and took their excitement with them.

The years following the rush saw Gleason dwindle to the point where its people lived in nearly tribal conditions, huddling together in lean-tos and trapping rabbits for food. Just before the town died out for good, it hit the lottery and got connected to a railway. The station changed Gleason from a miserable hovel into a struggling town, bringing in enough prosperity to rebuild its crumbling downtown—but it was still a rotten place to live. Some luxuries became a little easier to come by, like licorice candy and real east coast whiskey, but few people who came through on the train decided to hop off and stay.

On his plot outside the town, Ardell built a tiny house out of crooked planks brought back in the wagon from Gleason's meager lumber yard. As the years passed, he learned how to turn a profit with his cotton crop and dairy cows, earning a thin living by selling to the traders at the train station. As soon as he was able, he expanded the house, adding a kitchen for Carla and a private bedroom which would, in the distant future, become Charles's garish parlor.

As the Hench family's wealth grew, Carla's health deteriorated. She bled too much when she gave birth to a son soon after they settled, and although she survived, her strength never fully returned. Even as Carla declined into frailty, Ardell's wallet thickened from a bumper crop of cotton. The next time an artist came through on the train, he commissioned a painting of himself and his wife which he hung with pride on the freshly painted planks of the bedroom wall.

Ardell doted on his son. Jason grew up strong and lean, tempered by the desert heat. He learned how to help his father with the crops and cattle by the age of six. With the cows, he displayed an astonishing rapport—somehow able to keep them obedient during milking and calm in bad weather. After a powerful storm in the winter of 1936, two dairy cows went missing. Jason led his father through the mud and weeds into a shallow valley between nearby hills, directly to the missing livestock. When Ardell asked how he knew they were there, Jason replied with a cryptic, sideways smile. "I could feel their fear."

Carla succumbed in 1939. She spent her last week coughing up blood. Ardell was terrified her condition might be contagious and barred Jason and Abigail from entering her room. Jason never saw her during the final few days. His last words to his mother were spoken not to her face, but at her graveside—something for which he never forgave his father.

After her mother's death, Abigail retreated to the kitchen and rarely emerged. She spent her days cooking and cleaning, speaking in a low voice only when spoken to. Wearing her mother's apron, she put her head down and worked until her fingers were capped in thick calluses.

Ardell donated most of Carla's belongings to the church. In his pain, he scoured the house clean of her essence. Her clothes were given to the poor, and her most personal items hidden away in the depths of the root cellar. The only memory of her he kept close was the painting he had commissioned, but he installed a curtain over it, shrouding his pain.

Ardell had little patience for grief. In a bullish effort to move past it, he forbade his children from crying in his presence, and started visiting the town more frequently to "socialize" with the locals. Every time the train pulled into the station he lingered nearby, ready to help women with their bags, find them a place to stay. There was a hole in his heart, and it was his determination to fill it without delay.

And so in 1940 Ardell married Lona Cutter, a wild and red-maned runaway daughter of a Swedish dairy farmer. In 1941, she gave birth to twin boys, each with a shock of red hair already growing on their crowns when they emerged from her womb.

Lona named them Cary and Drake. They were clever and healthy, and had nothing to do with Ardell's grief. He obsessed over their every need, putting the past from his mind. Abigail tended to the house, and Jason tended to the stock. Hench Ranch was not filled with happiness, not exactly, yet it enjoyed a rare stretch of both prosperity and peace. Briefly, Hench House thrived.

13

Pulsating blotches colored the darkness behind Joanna's closed lids. Her consciousness began to return, along with her headache. The pounding waves of pain had dimin-ished to a background hum with occasional sharp stabs whenever she tilted her head. She stretched and arched her back, then straightened her legs—too quickly. They stiff-ened in agony as cramps ripped through her calves and thighs. She grabbed at the blankets on either side and held on for the ride, clamping her jaw down on a scream as tears squeezed through her shut eyelids. After an eternity the muscles relaxed and she lay exhausted, gasping in the stagnant air.

Joanna cracked her eyes open just wide enough to get a blurry idea of the shapes in the room. The room had become brighter since she fell asleep. The light sent a needle of pain ricocheting through her forehead. She blinked the fog from her vision and forced her eyes wide open, trying to ignore the concussion hangover. From somewhere above the hatch, a crow called out in triplets; *caw caw caw, caw caw caw.*

Nothing in the room had changed except the light. The ray coming through the hole overhead was now yellow midday sun. She sat up and stretched—carefully this time—touching her toes, turning her head from left to right, working out her stiff neck. When she wiped her face with her fingertips, she discovered grit had accumulated in the corners of her eyes. How long had she been unconscious in this abandoned place? The air wasn't cold, but she pulled a blanket over her shoulders for comfort.

Now, how could she get out of this pit? Maybe if she stood on top of one of the antique dressers she could reach the hatch…

"Monster."

The voice was low, dirty, filled with accusation. It came from one of the distant corners she could not see clearly, where the long shadows of the looming furniture met and faded into one another.

"Monster, monster." Shuffling.

"Who's there?" Joanna's voice trembled. "Please don't hurt me."

There was a lurching movement at the edge of the darkness—a gray shroud draped over pale skin, low to the ground, crawling. A small object rolled through the layers of dust on the floor and came to rest against Joanna's leg: a green apple, vibrant in the gloom. On the skin, an intricate drawing had been carved. The cuts which exposed the soft white flesh of the fruit were rapidly browning, caked with dust.

Joanna picked up the apple with a shaking hand. When she turned it so the stem pointed towards the hole in the ceiling, the carving resembled an odd face with two distinct eyes, a shallow scrape that could be a nose, and a crooked mouth. The delicate features were very small, making the fruit appear as a giant, malformed head.

"What is this?"

"Monster."

"Yes, monster." Joanna agreed. "Who are you?"

The voice moaned, yearning, as though it had waited years for the question to be asked, for the opportunity to be noticed, acknowledged, and accounted for.

"I…teras."

"Is that your name? Come out of the shadows. Why are you hiding back there?" Joanna no longer felt afraid. If this creature had meant to hurt her, it would have done so as she lay sleeping.

"Monster."

"I'm not a monster! You don't have to be frightened. I won't hurt you."

The voice laughed ruefully, and Joanna froze. Had she misjudged again? The realization of her vulnerability struck her. She assumed she was in the root cellar, but she didn't know for sure. She had lost blood, and her muscles still felt torn from cramping. Judging by the light, she hadn't eaten in…well, nearly twenty-four hours, not counting Charles's whiskey. She wasn't even sure she could stand.

The laughing thing shifted in the darkness again, then grew brighter as it moved toward the light. It swayed to the left, then lurched toward her, dragging something behind it—a large, round appendage, leaving a trail in the dust. It pulled itself forward with its other elongated arm, grasping at the soft dirt. Horror paralyzed Joanna as the creature became visible. It stopped a few feet away and raised its head, gazing directly into her eyes.

Its skull, misshapen and huge, was draped with a cloth that formed a makeshift hood over its face. The eyes looked normal, except for their enormous size; each was two inches across, from corner to corner. The dilated pupils were ringed with brown so dark it was almost black. The nose was absent, but for a hideous ridge of soft flesh over two gaping nostrils. The mouth sagged on one side, leaking a brown stream of saliva carrying traces of old food and the stench of decay.

Joanna screamed in shocked horror, and the monster cried out in harmony. As she again lost her fragile grip on consciousness, the screams faded away and darkness settled over her mind once more.

14

When the sun rose the next day, the remaining associates of the Hench compound included four family members, two farmhands, and one geriatric cur named Ugly Earl.

Marcus had talked Charles into buying the pup back in the late '90s from some kids selling mixed-breed hounds out of a milk crate at the side of Sunshine Highway. The dog was stupid but loyal, and in his youth had been a pretty good ratter. Whenever Gus's thickheadedness got under Marcus's skin, he'd take Earl out for a hunt. At least he had an excuse to be stupid, being a crossbreed mutt. Ugly Earl and Marcus became best pals, so when Marcus didn't fetch him for his morning meal, the dog went looking for him.

Ugly Earl tottered out the back door just after dawn and wandered across the yard, blinking in the early light. He paused near the small cactus garden to the right of the porch and squatted, straining, before continuing on across the yard in search of his old friend. Earl—deaf as he was—had slept peacefully through the events of the previous evening curled up on a burlap sack, so finding the stiffening remains of Marcus in front of the house came as a shock. Earl paused, licked Marcus's ear in an attempt to wake him, then trembled and sniffed around the body. When he had made his diagnosis, he squinted at the dunes, scenting the Cutters in the distance, then gazed back down at Marcus. He was an old dog with a long memory, and he had smelled that other herd before—the pack from the deep desert. Their smell meant death. He sat back on his haunches, pointed his wrinkly old nose towards the heavens, and howled a low eulogy for his master.

The solemn sound echoed in the hills and woke Charles from his uneasy slumber on the parlor floor. The two families were at a stalemate. One of the Cutters had tried the front door in the early hours before dawn and received a gut full of bullets for his trouble, courtesy of Harrison. Aside from Marcus, none of the Hench clan had been taken yet. Harrison remained hunkered down with Charles in the parlor. The other farmhand, Ezra, had called down the stairs soon after the beginning of the siege to assure Charles the rest of the family was safe.

Harrison had stayed awake all night on watch duty. He sat under a table across from the south wall, below the level of the windows, listening and occasionally making rounds on hands and knees through each room on the first floor.

Charles groped for a shard of a mirror which had been shattered in an early barrage of gunfire. He picked it up delicately with his first finger and thumb, keeping the sharp edges away from his pink fingertips, and held it up next to the window he was leaning under. In the reflection he had a clear view of the tangled mass of limbs and sun-faded denims that was Marcus. Next to the pile sat Ugly Earl, caught up in his stupid lament.

15

Joanna knew she was dreaming.

For one thing, her head wound was gone. And she wasn't in the root cellar, either. Also, she was naked.

And she was nowhere at all.

On all sides, including above and below, a vast expanse surrounded her floating body. Slipstreams of purple mist looped and played in the void. In the distance—an extremely great distance, she sensed, measured not in the simple terms of human language but in those of vast space and time—the sound of wind grew gradually louder. Joanna felt no breeze, but the sound was of whipping air; perhaps of something cutting through it. Something very fast. It was far, far away for now, but she could sense it was headed directly toward her.

Behind her in the void, something exhaled a deep breath. She whipped her head about, trying to spin herself in the void, but could find no purchase in the mist. In the corner of her eye, she saw the silhouette of a massive figure. Thick horns, like those of a bull, protruded from its head.

"Who are you?" she asked. Her words disappeared into the darkness like smoke in the wind.

The distant object that raced toward her in the void wailed, a long slow dirge like an old dog's howl carried over the unimaginable emptiness with perfect clarity. It was the sound of grief.

But the sound wasn't in the void. It was outside, in the daylight.

Joanna woke up. She found that the cries were real: somewhere above, an old dog was crying like a widower at a funeral. And the creature in the root cellar was echoing the mourner but softly, in perfect unison.

16

The Cutters awoke to the sound of an ancient dog singing a raspy dirge made hollow and haunting by the echoing effect of the desert hills. Ethan, who was on second watch, scurried toward Samuel, keeping his head below the level of the protective dunes.

"Boss! Boss, it's their dog. I think the whole group is wakin', might be a dust-up soon. Saw somethin' move in the window. On yer guard, sir."

Samuel grunted and glanced around the make-shift camp, counting heads. None were missing from his contingent other than that idiot Levi, who had tried to rush the front door against Samuel's explicit orders. Three men, two women, and one boy all lay drowsing fitfully on the desert floor. During the night they had occasionally whimpered in their sleep. A soft group—most of them too young to remember the really savage feuding of the old days—they had not been eager to follow Samuel onto the battlefield. However, they were encouraged when Marcus was brought down, and he had seen the zeal in their eyes when they realized the rest of their quarry was trapped inside their own stronghold. He had promised them more blood in the morning. They had brought only a single pack full of food and water with them, just enough for a couple days; Samuel did not expect this final showdown to last any longer than that.

He rolled from his back to his belly without raising his head, and peered over the low dune which protected their camp. They were situated about fifty feet from the main house on the south side, near the gravel driveway leading back to Sunshine Highway. The Cutters had approached from their own territory in the east, but had deviated just a bit south before engaging Hench House. Samuel had only been thinking of a view of the road, but luck was on his side and he got a bonus; they arrived at the right time to shut down that nosy realtor bitch and stuff her in the hole. Samuel let the boys have some fun with her car, but then they had laid low, watching the front and back, trying to encourage the Hench clan to waste bullets. The siege was a strategy game which would end in short order after one side or the other ran out of ammunition.

Samuel gripped his gun and slithered higher onto the rise, digging into the dirt with his elbows. The Hench mutt was moaning over that rat-turd Marcus, just as if the cocksucking boy hadn't killed one of Samuel's very own sons a few years back.

"Wakey, wakey, Charlie Brown," Samuel muttered, lining up the sights on his gun and squeezing the trigger.

Ugly Earl was cut off mid-howl. He yipped once and crumpled, coming to rest with his chin on the small of Marcus's back. His legs moved for a few seconds in a gentle lope, creating lopsided dog-angels in the dust before he finally laid still.

"Ought not to 'ave wasted the round, boss," Ethan mumbled. "Just a dog."

"Not just a dog, Ethan. I blew a hole in their confidence. They'll answer, I reckon. Wait and see." Samuel chuckled.

Samuel was right. A shadow appeared in a second-story window, and three quick shots followed an aggrieved sob as the new addition to the small pile of corpses in the yard was noticed. Dust puffed up on either side of the Cutter camp, and one wild bullet punched a hole through a lanky cactus a few feet to their right.

"Toldja," Samuel cackled. "That's one bullet to their three. You gotta get in their heads, Harl! We can't stay out here all week, don't have enough water. Let's get this party started!"

Samuel let out a whoop and gripped his megaphone, holding it straight up into the air. As he pressed buttons at random, car alarms and air raid sirens disrupted the stillness of the dawn.

17

The morning raid was exhausting but resulted in no major casualties. Samuel called a medical cease-fire around noon to gather his soldiers and tend to their wounds. Charles's idiotic manchild, the one called Gus, had stood too long in the window and been shot, but Samuel thought he had probably just been clipped in the ear. One of his own boys had fired a lovely shot that crashed through the southeast bedroom and shattered an old cremation urn, powdering the room with ash—no injuries inflicted, but demoralizing all the same, so Samuel counted it as a point in his favor. He hoped the ashes had been Carla's.

Ethan Cutter ducked in time to avoid a bullet from Harry the Harelip, but sand from the impact of the bullet on the hardpan shot up into his face. His eyes watered for an hour as Samuel chided him for being a crybaby.

Samuel was furious at the slow pace of the offensive, but kept himself under control with a mighty effort. The raid had been arranged hastily. His sisters could not handle the shotguns so they held the revolvers, but they did not possess the skill to send any bullets home at long range. He had one good rifle which he kept for himself, leaving the two shotguns to Ethan and Eugene. They would run toward the barn and hunker down behind the realtor's car, baiting the Hench cowards to waste ammo, then fire wildly at the side of the house, filling the walls with shot—and the Hench household with calculated terror—before scampering back to the camp behind the dunes for water and reloads.

As the day warmed, the energy drained from the

camp. Searing heat withered their ambition, and they began to bitch and whine. Samuel alternately barked orders and threats but he could tell he was losing them. Finally he took the women aside. He tugged on their skirt, pressed his fingers to their lips to let them know they must keep quiet, then crawled with them into the sliver of shade behind the tall cactus.

"How you girls holding up?"

Dahlia frowned. "It's hot, Sammy. Can't we just leave it for now and come back tonight?"

"Shut up, *Dolly*," Daria hissed. "This is important. Right, Sammy?"

Samuel smiled, gracious and compassionate. He crouched so he was just a little higher than them, forcing the females to gaze up at his face. He looked them over. Could he count them as two soldiers, or only one? Attached neatly at the hip, they lived in symbiosis, never physically apart yet constantly at odds with each other. The twins overheated rapidly and required more water and food than their independent siblings did. Their difficult existence was a struggle no single-bodied person could comprehend, and Samuel could never decide whether they were an asset or a liability. But the sight of them squatting in the dirt, each gripping a huge revolver in opposite hands, presented a bizarre and terrifying vision. More flash than function, perhaps, but every Cutter family member was entitled to their chance to take out a Hench, and Samuel intended to ensure his arachnoid sisters their moment of glory.

Samuel made a decision: he was going to tell them.

"I'm going to let you girls in on something, now. I've been approached by the Lord our God in a vision, and I was tested. And I passed the test."

"Sammy! How wonderful!"

"Yes. He came to me disguised as Satan himself, a

being with horns who lived in a mist of evil. But I passed
the test, and He shared with me the secrets of the universe.
Then, He told me what we must do. He told me the *truth,*
praise God."

"Ooh, Sammy," the girls gushed.

"Our family is very important. You know it is. The
Lord and I, we talked about how the Hench family was
fixin' to cut and run. About how we can't let that happen.
They want to break tradition, to bring shame to their family and ours. And in doing so, they may well destroy the
whole dang *world.*"

"Bastards!"

"Cowards!"

"True words, sisters. You speak truly. This valley
is ours by rights, having been cast out unfairly. Our own
people squat in mud, huddling in the dark shadows of the
hills, and we come here now only to reclaim our birth-
right! So we may bring our children out of hiding and live
in our ancestral home. By the Lord, our cause is just! But
these traitors seek to keep us down!"

"Devils!"

"Shitheels!"

Samuel headed into the home stretch of his
sermon. "Let's end the feud today. Here and now! I know
you're tired and hot; we all are. But I need your help, girls.
I can't do this without you. I need you to keep the true
family together, united by our pure blood and the willing-
ness to sacrifice it for our kin. Will you stay? Will you help
me?"

Samuel opened his arms and bowed his head, just
as Jesus the shepherd had welcomed the weakest sheep to
his flock.

The drama worked. His conjoined sisters leaned
forward and embraced him, each placing a pointy chin on
one of his shoulders.

"We're with you, Sammy."
"We love you, Sammy."

18

The howling—both from above, and inside the pit—was cut short by a shot from a gun.

Joanna was jolted awake. Instantly panicked, she sat up and looked for the beast with the huge wet eyes and tree-branch arms. The room was brighter now, but the corners were still in shadow. She fumbled in the dim light for something to hold; a weapon, anything, until her hand overturned a shallow bowl, dumping its contents. Her instinct screamed that she must run, but there was nowhere to go, so instead she grabbed the bowl and held it in front of her chest.

"Where are you? Show yourself!" she screamed. "I'm tired of this! Either come at me or go away and leave me alone!"

The room was silent. She turned her attention to the items that had been in the bowl, and found an odd assortment: a bandage, a small white pill, a fresh apple—this one was red—and a plastic lighter. And, laying in the dust, a cigarette.

What kind of monster leaves its victims care packages?

"Uh…thanks." Chastised, Joanna put the items back into the bowl and swallowed the aspirin dry. She chased it with a bite of the apple.

Shuffling from the corner of the room. This time, the creature approached more carefully, keeping its head down. As its asymmetrical form neared Joanna, the light illuminated its scaly skin and stringy hair. It reeked of mold and dark places; a dank, cemetery smell. It eased fully into the light, moving with gentle caution as though

Joanna were an injured bird that may try to take flight on a broken wing and bang itself senseless on windows. It raised an open hand and splayed its long fingers into a "stop" gesture.

"Safe."

It was the first word the creature had said that Joanna understood, other than "monster." But what did it mean?

"I'm safe here? You're not going to hurt me?"

The creature didn't reply. Instead, it sat cross-legged a few feet away and pulled a slender white stick out of some hidden pocket. Another cigarette. As Joanna watched in disbelief, it put the cigarette in its mouth and sat, patient, as if waiting for her to perform some expected trick.

What else could she do? She picked up the cigarette from the bowl and put it in her mouth, then sparked the Bic and offered the creature a light. It kept its enormous eyes closed as her hand neared its face, as if out of courtesy for Joanna's revulsion. This creature was a grotesque; why, then, did Joanna feel as though she were the one being tamed?

She lit her own cigarette and leaned back against the cabinet behind her, trying to appear relaxed while keeping a close watch on her new friend.

The creature spoke. "Christian."

"You're Christian? Um…I'm Catholic, I guess. Not really practicing, though…"

"No, name."

No name? Joanna frowned, and the creature waited.

"Oh! Your name is Christian. I'm Joanna."

They sat for a while in quiet, taking drags on their cigarettes, exhaling gorgeous swirls of smoke into the slender ray of light. Joanna could hear some distant shouting, and a car alarm. And…an air raid siren? Made no sense.

Another minute passed, and she heard the faint pop-pop of gunfire. What the hell was going on out there? Whoever had hit her over the head was still doing their dirty work, apparently. She'd have to sneak away. If she could get to her car and call the cops, she might have a chance. Maybe her purse and the phone inside it were still in the convertible's trunk.

Joanna finished her cigarette and snuffed it out in the dirt.

"Well, I have to get going, Christian. Thanks for the smoke. I haven't had a cigarette in about a decade, but I feel like I earned that one. But if you don't mind, I'm going to get a move-on. Not that I haven't enjoyed my time in your…*lovely* cellar…" Joanna looked toward the overhead hatch and started to rise to her feet.

Christian reached out and grabbed her arm, forcing her to sit back hard on the pile of blankets. He fixed her eyes with his and they were fully open now, liquid and dark and filled with fear.

"Cutters."

"Yeah, I figured that out. But I'm not staying with you in this stinking pit. No offense."

Christian's face contorted with annoyance. He pointed at the hatch. "Death."

"Hey, you underestimate me, Chris. I'll be okay. From the sound of it, they're down the road a ways. I only have to make it to my car. I have a phone."

"Foolish."

"Well, maybe so and maybe no. But I'm leaving either way." Joanna rose to her feet, wobbled a little, then tried taking a step or two. Other than sore muscles from cramping, her legs were uninjured, and the roar in her head had quieted. There was a wooden ladder leaning against the wall that looked tall enough to reach the hatch.

Joanna bent over and tightened her boot laces. She was ready.

"He's in here," a voice said from outside. The slender beam of light was blocked from above, and the room blinked into darkness.

A voice began shouting, directly over the hatch. "Hey! Hey, freak! You down there? The exterminator's here, so all you little nasties better take cover! We're comin' for ya!"

As the hatch door swung upward, the cellar filled with light. Joanna leaped aside and landed on her stomach next to an antique wardrobe. She tucked in her feet and made herself small, trying to blend in with the heaps of junk. The dark silhouette of a hand waving a gun and a head wearing a baseball cap appeared against the square of blue sky in the opening.

"Where you at, freak-boy?"

Joanna saw Christian move quickly toward a corner of the room which was draped with thick curtains. The man over the hatch saw him too, and fired two quick shots after him. Christian let out a howl, then collapsed bodily to the floor, grasping at the hanging fabric and squirming in agony.

"Gotcha, you rat! Too easy!" The hatch slammed shut. Footsteps crunching on gravel moved away from the opening.

The silence returned. Joanna scuttled over to Christian and paused, desperate to aid him but still overwhelmed by her revulsion at his mutated body. She couldn't touch him.

Joanna felt helpless, and ashamed.

Christian coughed, and sat up. He turned and looked at Joanna with a hideous, toothless smile.

"Deceit."

"You were pretending!" Joanna plopped down on

the floor next to him. "Damn it, Chris! Don't scare me like that again."

19

The twins grew up strange.

Drake and Cary were fearless boys, with near-insatiable curiosity. They explored Hench Valley at a young age with Jason following closely behind, keeping them safe. The party adventured through pebbled dunes and cactus-man forests, tracking coyotes and examining the winding tracks of snakes and learning how to tell species apart by the trails they left behind. Despite the time they all spent together, Jason never developed a brotherly relationship with the other boys. The twins communicated almost telepathically, in a silent language made up of subtle nods and darting eyes. Jason watched them with his arms crossed as they hunted squirrels and rabbits with Ardell's .22 long rifle, and dutifully cheered when one of them brought a rodent down. But what they tended to do next with their prey Jason could never understand.

They would skin and gut the small creatures, making ammo satchels and wallets out of the hides as normal boys liked to do—but they also had a preoccupation with the entrails. The twins would dissect the bloody organs and then jar them like jelly, hiding them away in their room under the floorboards. From time to time, Jason retrieved and disposed of the stinking containers before Ardell and Lona could discover the mess. When Jason asked them about their disgusting hobby, they would only say that a magical bull appeared in their dreams and told them to do it.

In 1948, when Jason was nineteen and the twins were seven, he taught them how to ride. Drake took to it immediately, sitting deep in the saddle and keeping his heels down, bending his young filly to his will. Cary was more hesitant. He leaned forward nervously, yanking on the reins every time he felt himself slipping. It was one of the only differences between the brothers. Drake shouted instructions to Cary from the fence: lean back and stay loose, hang on with his knees and not his hands, move with the horse if she spooked, stay calm. Cary showed an uncharacteristic flash of anger towards his twin brother, barking back that he was fine and Drake could go to hell. Fear showed plainly on Cary's face, as well as shame.

Cary wanted to give up on riding, but Jason wouldn't let him. By the time the boys were nine, Jason was dragging Cary to the pasture a couple times a month, refusing to give up, insisting that until Cary could ride it was like he was crippled. Drake tagged along for the entertainment, enjoying the rare sensation of being better at something than his identical twin.

Jason brought along Fiona, a three year old appaloosa with a calm disposition. Cary didn't like any of the horses, but if he had a favorite, it was her. A swirl of black spots dotted her white hide like leaves whipped up in a gust of wind. She rested her soft muzzle on Cary's neck, and he endured while she tasted his hair and salty shoulders. Fiona was patient with Cary as he trembled atop her, gripping her mane, trying not to look down. She was a sweet young mare, uncommonly mellow for her age. Cary grew to love her, in a way, but he still never really trusted her. Despite her gentle personality, Fiona's size and strength terrified him.

One blistering August afternoon, Fiona stepped into a nest of rattlesnakes. As a mass of venomous cords writhed and darted beneath her hooves, she reared and screamed, showing her yellow teeth and the whites of her eyes. Cary gripped the saddle and held on, his worst fears abruptly become real. Fiona trampled the nest and bolted with tiny black whips clinging to her forelegs as Jason and Drake chased her into the desert. She eventually tripped and rolled in the sand. In his panic, Cary was clutching madly to the saddle as he was crushed under her weight. The boy's neck snapped and he died quickly. When Drake found him, the heels of Cary's boots were still clumping and rattling against the desert floor as he convulsed in his death throes.

Fiona died a few minutes later, when Drake—his young face a grimace of grief and rage—put the .22 to the horse's staring eye and pulled the trigger.

20

Joanna and Christian sat together on the blankets for hours, listening to the shouting and gunfire coming from outside the hatch. As the day wore on, the sounds became less frequent, then ceased. Neither of them attempted to open the hatch. Whoever was out there assumed the cellar's inhabitants were dead, which meant they were safe, for now. The slender beam of light coming through the hatch turned gold, then amber, as the sun began to set.

Joanna had been in the hole for a day and a half, at least. Would anyone be alarmed? She lived alone in a studio apartment. She didn't talk to her neighbors. As a realtor, her time was mostly her own, and her office mates would simply assume she was working with a client. It might be a week before she was missed.

Joanna's stomach growled.

"Eat," Christian said, offering her another apple and a bag of peanuts.

"Where do you get this stuff, Chris? Do you go shopping? Don't take this the wrong way, but it doesn't really seem like you ever leave this hole."

"Charles."

"Oh, Charles brings you food? That's um…nice of him. Does he make you stay down here?"

"No, job."

Christian had a job? Joanna tried to visualize him in an apron, stocking shelves at a local supermarket, and couldn't do it.

"What do you do? If you don't mind me asking."

Christian sighed, and a tiny drop of spittle flew from his lower lip to land on the carpet. Joanna, disgusted, tried not to make a face. She would never get used to this creature…but, somehow, she kind of liked him, too.

"Family, first."

It was another of those phrases Joanna could not exactly decipher. Did he mean that it was important to put family first? Or did he work for his family?

Christian saved her from asking what he meant by tugging on her sleeve and moving in his slithering, graceful way across the room towards the chalkboard. Tall bookcases created a library atmosphere in this section of the room, where he clearly spent most of his time. As Joanna neared the chalkboard she glanced at the book bindings: Advanced Condensed Matter Physics, Aristotle's Nicomachean Ethics, Sun Tzu's The Art of War. The walls were full of shelves crowded with textbooks.

Every inch of the chalkboard was covered in mathematical scribbles, dizzying in their complexity, with arrows connecting different algorithms and computations. It must have represented countless hours of work. Christian pulled himself up onto a tall stool next to the board and used his shirt sleeve to clear a space in the middle of the mad array of numbers and letters and lines.

"Whoa, hey! You're erasing all your stuff! Hang on, you're messing it up…" Joanna watched in amazement as Christian scrubbed a wide empty circle in the center of the board with reckless impatience. He picked up a piece of blue chalk from a tray at the bottom, and wrote a name at the top of the empty space; *Ardell.* He drew a short arrow next to it, then another name; *Carla.* He drew an angled arrow coming down from the names and wrote *Abigail.* Then he drew a second arrow and wrote *Jason.*

"Hmm, okay, what is this? Like a family tree?"

Christian nodded. Then he picked up a piece of red chalk and drew a quick, bold line through Carla's name. "Died." He added a new name, *Lona,* to the left of Ardell's name, and more lines which pointed to a pair of names, *Drake / Cary.* "Twins."

"Drake and Cary were twins, huh? That's really neat, Chris. I used to know a couple of girls who were twins, back in college. They were both redheads. One of them was really annoying, and the other one…"

"Shh," Christian stared at her. "Important."

"Sorry, Chris, I just…okay. Sorry." Joanna shut her mouth.

With the blue chalk, Christian added *1921* above *Ardell > Carla* and *1940* above *Lona > Ardell.* Then, he picked up the red chalk again and slashed a red line through Cary. "Died."

"Wow, that sucks!" Joanna said. Christian shot her another look. "Sorry, sorry. I'll be quiet."

Chris drew a thick vertical line separating Lona and Drake from the rest of the family. "Cutters. Banished."

Joanna opened her mouth to speak, then shut it again.

Next to Jason, Christian wrote > *Olivia,* and below those names he drew another pointing arrow, this time with the names *Charles* and *Christian.* "Twins."

Below Drake, Christian wrote *Samuel,* then with the blue chalk wrote in large letters at the top of the separated side, *Cutters.*

"You mean you're all related? You, Charles…and

those guys out there with the guns? This whole thing is some kind of massive family feud?"

Christian sighed. He added one more name, beneath Abigail; *Grace.*

"Job."

"What's your job, Chris?"

Christian lowered himself carefully from the stool and shuffled into the darkness. Joanna followed. At the end of the room there was a hallway which resembled an old mine shaft. Irregular wooden boards held up the earth on both sides of the narrow walkway. Roots and stones protruding from the dirt were visible between the panels. The thin air smelled dewy and mineral, and the temperature was several degrees cooler.

"Wow, your place is bigger than it looks. Where are we going?"

Christian pulled a keychain LED flashlight from his pocket and clicked it on, washing the space in a cold bluish glow. As he maneuvered down the hallway, the light bobbed and rocked with his uneven gait, causing the shadows to sway in time with his movement. At the end of the tunnel the earth between the wooden panels on the left fell away, leaving only the planks of the fence, through which a warm light was shining. Behind the boards was a small cavern.

"Caregiver." Christian pointed toward the open space.

Joanna stepped up to the fence and peered through. The little cave was carpeted in a similar fashion to Christian's living room, but the walls were packed dirt instead of paneled. Old furniture was hidden under piles of clutter and books. A lamp shed amber light on the earthen walls through a stained paper shade. In the center of the open space was an enormous bed, and sinking gently into it was a mound of strange flesh and crooked limbs.

Adult arms draped over each side, but a third, childlike arm was curled on a round belly. The hands were covered in smooth sleeves of skin, never fully developed, useless. Fat legs curled under the torso in an unspecified position, seemingly without bones. As Joanna observed, her breathing slowed, and cold dread filled her up. She prayed the mound would not wake, would not look towards her with whatever it had for a face.

"Grace," Christian sighed. Then he winced, and ventured a halting sentence; "There, but for the grace of God, go I."

21

Abigail stopped smiling when her mother died. The girl rarely spoke, and when she did, it was in a whispery mumble directed down toward her battered shoes. She swept the kitchen twice per day, cooked meals for the family and farmhands, and aged slowly. As she neared thirty years old, she appeared only eighteen but for a dull and timeworn weariness in her eyes. Jason invited her along whenever he made a supply run into town, but Abigail refused every time. The farm was her entire world, and she would never leave it.

Drake also stopped smiling. With his twin gone, he seemed lost, always alone even when surrounded by family. He was distant and confrontational, never happy, and openly blamed Jason for Cary's death. Ardell pulled Drake off of Jason more than once, prying a weapon from his fingers, sometimes locking him in the root cellar until he had calmed. Lona sided with Drake in blaming Jason for the accident. The Hench family's solidarity began to crack as a rift formed between them.

Soon after Jason turned twenty-one, he married Olivia Tomsen, a quiet and waiflike girl who made Ardell's lonely heart ache for Carla. In his enthusiasm for the match, Ardell rented Gleason's little chapel for the wedding, and hosted the event with gusto. Nine months later, Olivia gave birth to twin boys.

Ardell was as overjoyed as he had been when Cary and Drake had been born, and once again he threw himself into the infants' care. Charles was born healthy and strong, but Christian's body was twisted all wrong, and his eyes were too wide for his head. The doctor gave him three weeks to live, but Christian paid that no mind and instead grew up as strong as an ox. His bent body caused him some pain, but made him powerful in unexpected ways. Olivia loved her boys equally, and seemed to take extra pride in Christian's determination to thrive. Jason built a small home for his little family with his own two hands, right in back of Hench House so his family could have their own space while still working on the ranch. Ardell heartily approved, and picked up a hammer to help as often as he was able.

Drake's mind was clearly unhealthy, but no one—not even his mother—knew how to help him. He had taken to collecting dried-out bits of desert creatures and turning them into a kind of mad taxidermy, attaching all the wrong parts to each other. He hid his handiwork in the root cellar: a coyote with a rattlesnake tail, a crow with the teeth of a mountain lion, a rat with twelve legs. Drake found these creations amusing and spoke to them often, seeking their advice and enjoying their mute companionship. Lona thought him a brilliant artist, and spoke often of moving to Phoenix to enroll him in an artist's college. Her ideas sent Ardell into manic fits of laughter which further tore their relationship apart.

Drake was a constant menace to Jason and his young family. He stole food from their kitchen, woke the babies up at night, and one time Olivia walked into the bedroom to find Drake hovering over the boys close enough to feel their breath on his cheek. Olivia screamed, and Drake ran. Finally, when he was twelve, Ardell could no longer overlook the boy's hostile nature, fearing he would someday lash out directly at the young twins and harm them. Drake's obvious madness and Lona's unfailing loyalty to him was frightening to Ardell, who still felt love for his wife in a complex tangle of emotions he could not understand. He was a simple man, pragmatic and hard-working, who was confused by the depth of the abyss of grief into which Drake and Lona had plunged. Cary was dead: people died, especially young people, all the time.

Ardell contacted a psychiatrist in San Francisco who claimed he could help the pair, and train tickets were purchased. Arrangements were made for Drake and Lona to stay in a comfortable sanitarium and health spa during their treatment in California, but they never arrived at their destination; they disappeared the morning before their planned departure. Ardell launched a halfhearted manhunt. After a day of searching, they were found several miles to the east of Hench Valley, living out of an old wagon. Mother and son would survive on their own, they said, refusing to return to Hench House. Ardell washed his hands of them, wounded at their refusal of his generosity. The way he saw it, so long as they stayed away from his grandchildren, they could rot in hell. No harm done, in the end.

What Ardell did not take into account was the loneliness of his daughter. He didn't understand Abigail's self-imposed seclusion any more than he could understand Drake and Lona's desperate grief. As she aged and closed herself off from the outside world, Ardell spoke to her less, uncomfortable in the face of her pain which was a constant reminder of his own. He waited, and hoped she would come back to him some day. As the years passed, her solitude and obsession with cleanliness bordered on madness; she was no longer in the world, but orbiting somewhere outside it, a dismal satellite watching from a shadow as everyone else went on with their lives.

Late one night after teaching the boys their lessons, Ardell walked into the kitchen to find Abigail on her back with young Drake on top, furiously driving himself into her by the firelight. Ardell howled and ran for his rifle, but Drake disappeared over the hills, running for his life. Ardell wanted to pursue him into the desert but the farm-hands talked him down, and eventually got him drunk instead.

Drake never again reappeared at the Hench farm. Nevertheless, his actions had a permanent effect, as Abigail's belly began to grow. As she neared term with the bastard child in her womb, she looked happy for the first time in years. Silent and majestically maternal, she smiled as she served supper to the men of the house. She glowed in her pregnancy, utterly feminine and fulfilled, despite Ardell's fury.

22

"You want me to climb in *there?* No way, Chris."

Christian pointed at the narrow tunnel and nodded. It was round, about eighteen inches across and two feet tall, centered in the wall at waist height from the floor. He shrugged and smiled in his crooked way, with the right side of his face scrunching up his cheek as the left side lay lax and drooling.

"Safe."

"Really? You sure about that? Because it looks dangerous as hell to me."

Christian shrugged again. "*Safer.*" He turned toward a wooden school desk and took some items from a drawer. "Here. Light. Water."

He offered Joanna an LED headlamp and a plastic bottle. In his voluminous pockets he stashed a second bottle and two apples before stretching an elastic-belted lamp around his head.

"Seriously, Chris? There has to be a better way."

A loud banging noise erupted from somewhere above the wooden hatch. A drunken shout thundered through the small cavern. "Hey, who's still alive down there? I hear you! Come out and play!"

"They're back! But why? They think you're dead!" Joanna whispered.

"City-bitch! Come on out, honey! I promise we won't hurt you too bad. We're gonna treat you *so good,*" the voice said. Someone laughed.

"Oh my god," Joanna said.

"Now." Christian switched on his headlamp and pushed Joanna toward the hole.

The passage was awkward, taller than it was wide. The floor of the shaft was smooth and worn; well-used. It was packed hard and picked clean of sticks and rocks. The sides were rougher, cut into the earth, sprouting hairy roots that reached into the crawlspace like skinny arms. Spiders had connected the roots with intricate webs in a lattice that made the ceiling low. Brushing the top of the tunnel would sweep it clean of spiderwebs and dead bugs.

"I...I can't go in there."

"Can."

"No. I'm not afraid of those guys, Chris. Really, I'm not."

"*Will.*"

Joanna peered down the hole. It was inky-black from beginning to end. The dim light from the root cellar faded after only a few feet, giving way to stifling darkness almost immediately inside the entrance. The headlamps cast a weak circle of light that was effective only in show-ing how just many insects populated the tunnel.

"You don't get it, Chris," Joanna whispered. "You've been down here for…god knows how long. I'm claustrophobic. You know what that means? It means I'm scared of…fuck that. I'm *terrified* of this shit. I can't do it. I'll freak out. I don't even know what will happen. I got stuck in an elevator in Las Vegas once…" Joanna laughed nervously. "I mean, it wasn't even stuck. I thought it was stuck. It was a slow elevator, it stopped at the twentieth floor, and something…it was probably computerized or something, it took like five extra seconds to open the doors, and I was already banging on the walls. I almost pissed my pants. And this…Chris, can't you see the *spiders?*"

The wooden hatch door squeaked open. Daylight poured into the cellar, illuminating the filthy antique bookcases and shelves buried under a century of old-west dust.

"Yoo-hoo, babe. I see you! Come on out, we won't hurtcha! You wanna ride back to town?"

Christian's head whipped toward hers and he looked Joanna in the eyes. She saw his entire face, now fully out of the shadows, and noticed for the first time the careworn wrinkles framing his limpid eyes, his compas-sion and fear. He winced, and frowned, and Joanna knew something was about to happen.

Christian spun Joanna around, placed his hand on the back of her head, and shoved her toward the hole. Her knees hit the dirt wall beneath the opening, but she felt her hips being lifted, and her legs thrust in. Christian shoved her rudely ahead as he climbed in after her.

"*Move!*" he yelled. "Ignore spiders!"

Joanna's arms buckled and she fell to her elbows, but Christian was unrelenting, prodding her in the ass with his gnarled knuckles as he crept in behind her. Tiny roots scratched at her face as she moved forward, digging her hands into the dirt and pulling herself through the passage. She tried to keep her head down to avoid snagging the webs she knew were overhead, but her sore back tired of that quickly. A spider crawled across her forehead and down her cheek. She smacked at it and it popped between her fingers, leaving a smear of guts across her chin.

She felt a hand on her ankle. It closed tight and yanked her to an abrupt standstill, throwing her to the floor of the passage. In the darkness, she heard only her own heavy breathing. "Chris? What is it? Is that man following us?" She realized she had never turned on her head lamp, and switched it on.

Christian didn't answer. He was facing away from her, struggling with something. Joanna heard scuffling, then the soft thud of earth collapsing. Sand and pebbles shifted, dirt fell. He grunted, then hissed in pain. Someone shouted near the opening, and Joanna heard crashes that sounded like bookcases being tipped over. Christian was kicking at someone in the tunnel opening. When he made contact with the heel of his boot, his opponent fell backwards into the cellar.

Joanna craned her head back, bracing her shoulder blades against the tunnel wall. She had just enough room to turn her head and shine her headlamp on Christian's back. He was working frantically, scraping madly at the ceiling and scratching in the mud, bringing chunks of dirt down.

He was burying them alive.

"Chris, what the fuck are you doing that for?" Joanna burst into tears; she knew the answer. "There has to be another way. Those guys will leave us alone eventually! You can't just trap us in here. *Please.*"

Christian didn't reply. The cave opening narrowed,

then disappeared as he frantically scraped clods of mud from the walls of the tunnel. He grasped a thick root and pulled hard. The wall behind it gave way, and a small avalanche collapsed the tunnel behind them with dreadful finality. When the dirt stopped sliding, silence fell in the cavern and all was still.

The opening was sealed: they were entombed in the earth.

23

On the day Grace was born, the desert was searing and still. Even before the lunch bell rang, heat mirages rose on the horizon, blurring the line where the blue sky touched the scorched hilltops. Cows and horses sought the scant shade beneath scrawny wasteland trees, and smaller creatures hid deep in their holes. The day was too hot for foraging in the sun; the animals would wait to eat until twilight soothed the desert and brought relief to the blistering sands.

In the heat, Abigail labored. She was quiet during the delivery, crying out only at the end when the tiny beast's large, misshapen head—a head which would never grow hair, nor feel a complex emotion or produce a rational thought—appeared between her mother's legs. Like her uncle Christian, the girl was a pretzel of a newborn, broken and bent. Abigail cradled the baby to her chest and whispered her name with zealous love; *"Grace."*

She was doted upon even as she grew and twisted into a creature which would increase in size but never become a fully thinking person. Perhaps the girl's dependence on Abigail made her devotion to her daughter even stronger: a baby which would never grow up, never grow out of her need for her mother's caring embrace, would never leave home and abandon her mother to solitude in her old age. In her vulnerability, Grace belonged to Abigail forever and ever, and their mutual need for each other was absolute.

The baby's father would not stay away after her birth. Drake could see Grace was an aberration, but nonetheless he tried time and again to steal her from the Hench household and take her to Cutter-owned lands. Christian devoted himself to protecting the child, and after Drake's break-ins increased in frequency and aggression, Abigail conceded to Christian hiding Grace away in the cellar to care for her there. She mourned the loss of Grace from her bedside, but Abigail would rather see her girl locked safely under the earth than removed from Hench territory. And so Grace grew underground, curling and pale like a strange root, as Christian read to her from books she would never understand.

After Grace's cradle was moved to the cellar, Drake gave up on her and focused on starting his own family. He purchased a healthy young girl from an elderly Asian man who passed through Gleason station on a cold Thanksgiving morning. Samuel Cutter was born the following year. Drake had hoped for twins, and blamed the girl for her failure to provide them. When she died after childbirth, Drake did not mourn her. What little love he had remaining after his lifetime of grief was given to his son. Samuel grew into a strong young man, and had daughters of his own—a magical set of twins who were joined at the hip.

Abigail aged and hunched, wearing deep tracks in her kitchen floor where she paced between cooking and cleaning. She visited Grace once a week to pop sweets into her mouth, fetched by Jason from the town market. Eventually, the day came when she could no longer descend the ladder into the root cellar, and her happiness retreated again as it had after the death of her mother. Grace was close by, almost under Abigail's feet—yet she was also very far away.

Ardell's heart gave out before he could marry a third time. Christian dug a burial chamber in a branch off the root cellar, which would be expanded over the years to hold many more bodies as the feud between the two families grew into a violent war. After Charles inherited Hench House, he converted Ardell's old bedroom into a combination parlor and war-room where he held business meetings over countless glasses of rye whiskey. He developed into a shrewd businessman, abandoning farming in favor of more illicit trade opportunities which could generate enough income to keep the growing Cutter clan at bay with hired men and guns. He led the family like it was an army, a general who was single-minded in his determination to exterminate the enemy, never doubting his righteous cause even though he had not personally witnessed the genesis of the feud. Gleason changed its name to Settle and established itself as the capital of Settle County, its success due in part to generous donations from the Hench family. The Cutters and Henches fought decade after decade, until between their lands ran a never ending river of bullets and blood.

And in this way, many years passed.

24

"Slow, now. *Very* slow," Christian whispered. The tunnel was old and fragile; spills of earth tumbled from the walls as they crawled along.

Joanna inched through the passage, crushing clods of dirt under her palms. Dry roots and wet worms squeezed between her fingers. She kept her breath deep and even, concentrating on the in-out movement of her lungs to ward off her fear as she moved through the hole. Her mind would occasionally wake to the horror of the close passage, causing chills of adrenaline to ripple up her back and scalp. Each time, she clenched her jaw shut and closed her eyes, refocusing on her body's careful movement through the darkness: calm, calm. Cool as a cucumber.

If she gave in to panic, they would likely both die.

Joanna's arms ached, and her knees were deeply bruised. She no longer even attempted to brush the spiderwebs from her hair. How much time had passed? Impossible to guess. Christian followed close behind as they crept. At some point, he tugged on her ankle and whispered a word: "Rest."

Easier said than done. Joanna slumped back onto her heels, but she could not sit up comfortably under the low ceiling. She leaned against the side of the hole, bringing her knees near her chin and placing her feet on the opposite wall, allowing her arms to stretch out to either side. When she arched her back it popped three times, loud as a BB gun in the noiseless cave.

"How long is this tunnel, Chris? Where are we going, anyway?"

Christian didn't answer. His long fingers hid his face, and his body was trembling. When he looked up at Joanna, she could see the grime on his face was streaked clean where tears ran down his cheeks. His sobs were whimpering and soft, wracked with helpless grief. The trickling tears appeared small and delicate, out of proportion with the size of his monstrous eyes.

"*Grace,*" he sobbed.

"Oh my god, Chris! I'm so sorry. I didn't even think…They probably won't even find her." But Joanna knew as she spoke the words that they weren't the truth. Having failed to catch their true quarry, they had doubtless tortured and killed Christian's helpless niece. She reached out to touch his shoulder, and after a brief internal struggle, finally managed it.

"*Failure.*"

"No, Chris. You did what you had to do. There's no way you could have saved her. It's not your fault."

He didn't reply, but bowed his head again, wiping his muddy face with his rough sleeves. Joanna watched his back heave and shudder as he mourned, surely not for the first time. How many relatives had he lost to the Cutters throughout his life? Joanna tried to imagine the depth of his sadness, and could not.

"Chris…I'm sorry. But we have to keep going."

Christian nodded his head. Joanna resumed her crawl, and noticed the air in the hole had become thin. She had to take long, deep breaths to get enough oxygen; not good. Despite this, she was calming, feeling more in control.

She would get through this.

Christian retched. He stopped and coughed from deep in his lungs as spittle dripped from his lower lip.

"What's wrong? Chris?" Joanna turned, wrenching her cramping neck to whisper to him.

"Hurt."

As Christian leaned back Joanna saw a hole in his shirt gape open, caked with blood and dirt. A cut in his pale belly oozed and dripped, spattering the dirt floor.

"You got stabbed back there? I didn't know that guy had a knife! Why didn't you say anything? We have to hurry! We have to stop the bleeding…get you to a doctor…"

"Can't. You go."

"Fuck that! Come on, soldier! Right now!" Joanna grabbed the neck of his shirt collar and yanked. He yelped with pain as blood gushed from his side.

"Sorry! I'm so sorry. But, Chris…we have to get out of here now. You're bleeding out! I won't let you die in this hole."

Christian nodded. "Go."

25

As Joanna and Christian crept underground, Abigail and Gus huddled in the corner of an upstairs bedroom, away from the shattered windows. The floor was littered with books and knick-knacks that had fallen as shelves had collapsed from the walls, weakened by the intermittent blows of shotgun fire shaking the house. Burning pellets from the guns had pockmarked the ceiling. Abigail sat on the floor and rocked gently, plugging her ears with her fingers whenever the Cutters opened fire.

"Aunty Abby? Where's Da'? What should we do?"

Abigail didn't answer. She had been through this so many times. She had lived her entire life on this battlefield. And she would hide, as she always did. The Cutters always tried, but they had never broken through the line. First Ardell, then Jason—until he was murdered by the bastard Samuel—and now Charles would protect her. Christian would protect Grace, and Charles would protect Abigail. It had been this way for many years, and it would not change today.

"Pray, Gus. For your father."

"All right, Aunty." Gus dutifully knelt before her and folded his hands in front of his nose like a little boy in Sunday school.

"Dear God," Gus began. "Please save Da', and me, and Abigail, and Harry, and Grace, and Mar…Marcus…" His voice began to hitch. "I mean, please let Marcus into Heaven. He was a good brother, and I'd sure like to see him again some day. Amen." He wiped tears from his eyes with clenched fists.

"Good boy, Gus. Marcus sees you, and he loves

you, and you will be with him again some day. Now fetch us some water from the pitcher."

The stairs creaked, and Charles appeared in the hall outside the door, breathing heavily. He climbed upstairs only when necessary, as a general rule. He labored through the doorway into Abigail's room, cheeks flaming.

"Hunker down, Abby. Come close, Gus. It's all over now, for sure! *Shit!*" Charles choked and sobbed. "That bastard Harrison. He went over. God damned traitor! He's with the Cutters! Looks like Ezra cut 'n run, too. They weren't family, but still…"

Gus's face wrenched with grief. "Good ol' Harry? No, Da'! He'd never!"

"Well, he did, Gus. You got to learn you can't trust anyone. You can't…" His voice trailed off as he realized the desperation of their situation. Marcus was dead. Harry was a turncoat, and Ezra, the new farmhand, had run off. Abigail was ancient and frail, and Gus was thickheaded. Christian and Grace were still in the underground, probably dead.

Charles took stock. He had his rifle, and enough bullets to hold the hallway for now. But the three of them would never survive a lengthy siege.

Gus wept in the corner, until Charles lumbered over and cuffed him on the ear.

"Man up, Gus. Be like Marcus. Think! What would Marcus do right now?"

"He'd…he'd…protect you, Da.'"

"Would he cry, Gus?"

Gus sniffed hard, sucking snot up into his nose and wiping his eyes. "No, Da.'"

"So then, are you done?"

"Yes, Da.'"

Charles sighed. "Good. Now, boy, listen up. We're probably done for. But we'll take a few of them with us, anyway."

Gus darkened. "I'm going to kill Samuel. He killed Ma'. He killed Gran-dad. I'm going to kill him back."

Charles laughed a deep, belly-shaking laugh. The odor of rye whiskey rode out on his breath. "That's right, son! Maybe you'll get your chance yet. Use this, if you get the opportunity." Charles handed Gus his knife; a relic which had once belonged to Grandpa Ardell.

"Now, let's block up this hallway. They'll be here soon."

26

Harrison approached the dunes with his hands in the air. "Peace! I want to talk to Samuel. Don't shoot!"

"Stop right there!" Ethan appeared from behind the rise. "Drop your gun. Now! And move slow!"

Harrison picked his gun from his pocket and held it between his thumb and first finger, moving it away from his body before dropping it to the dirt.

"That's all I got!"

Ethan stepped toward him, keeping his gun aimed. As Samuel watched from his rat hole, Ethan patted Harrison down.

"He's clean, boss."

Samuel signaled to the twins to stay low and walked out from the dunes, keeping his eyes trained on Harrison until the dropped gun was in his own hand.

"Well, well. Harry the Harelip. If you're here to negotiate, you can tell Charles we're not interested. He dies today, along with what remains of his family. This day ends in blood."

"Not here for Charles. He fired me just afore you showed up, the fucker. I come to join your cause."

Samuel smirked. "What makes you think we'd have

you? You're no Cutter, and you're no Hench either. You're just a lost little lamb. Did Charles get tired of your ugly face? That why you're here?"

Harrison would not be baited. He swallowed hard and winced, fighting off tears. It would not do to cry in front of Samuel Cutter.

"The family was all I had. But they were gonna leave me! They were gonna turn me out. I ain't got nowhere else to go. So if they don't want me, then I guess you can take me. I can fire a gun, and I can cook, a little. And take care of things…" His voice trailed off. Samuel stared at him with a steady, predatory gaze that made Harrison's skin crawl. He searched for more to say.

"What if I-"

"Fine," Samuel said. "But you have to prove yourself. You were with Hench for too long for me to just trust you right off. You have to do something for me."

"Anything, boss," Harrison said.

"We think the sewer rat is still alive. Christian. Bring him to me."

"Yes, boss," Harrison said. "Should I-"

"Dead or alive. I don't fucking care."

27

The tunnel felt endless. A large beetle—perhaps a cockroach—skittered into Joanna's pant cuff and halfway up her leg before she could swat it away. She leaped forward, her stomach flip-flopping with revulsion as she pummeled the bug through her clothes with her clenched fist. She felt a crunchy pop, and goo seeped through the cloth.

Christian breathed heavily behind her, wheezing with pain. Joanna tried to move slowly so he did not drop behind, but her fear was screaming at her, telling her it was definitely time to panic, hurry up, get out of this pit before it collapsed.

The tunnel narrowed further, at times brushing her shoulders. What would they do if it simply ended? There could have been a collapse since the last time Christian came through here. What would it be like if Christian died behind her, his body blocking the only way out as the battery in her headlamp faded away and she slowly suffocated, her screaming throat filling with dirt as the final cave-in began…

Joanna shook her head and slapped her face, shocking herself out of the horrific vision.

"Shut up," she whispered to her unruly imagination.

"Jo?" Christian said, worried.

"I'm fine. How long is this cave? Are we going to run out of air?"

As Joanna finished her sentence, a wooden door came into view. It was archaic and hand-made, fitted perfectly to the shape and size of the passageway.

Joanna fought back a cry of relief. She reached for a black iron latch.

"Wait," Christian whispered. "Listen."

Joanna pressed her face close to the door and peered through a knothole. The view was of the kitchen in Hench House, from underneath the dinner table which was pushed against the wall instead of in its normal place in the middle of the room. She remembered asking about this little wooden door on her tour of the house with Charles; he had told her it was an old-fashioned wood storage cubby, leftover from the days when the house still had a potbelly stove.

The kitchen was a mess—broken glass, pieces of a shattered appliance—but it was empty of both Henches and Cutters.

"It's clear." Joanna flipped the latch and pressed

gently on the door. The hinges were stiff with disuse, but they opened quietly. She crawled out from the hole and breathed deep, leaning against the wall under the table.

Christian followed her with less grace, bumping to the floor and uttering a tiny whimper as his wound gaped and spilled fresh droplets of blood from between the folds of his bulky shroud. He panted and pressed the heel of his hand against his stomach.

"Wait here," Joanna whispered. She crawled through the room toward the cabinets, leaving a trail of dust. The house was still, but eerie and expectant as though recently vacated. It didn't feel safe.

Joanna found a kitchen towel and filled a small bowl with water from the sink, then returned to Christian. His wound was angry and red around the edges, with a thin line of yellow pus was forming in the middle. Not good. Joanna wiped it clean and pressed the towel over it, then pushed Christian's hand onto the towel, wordlessly showing him where to hold it in place to slow the bleeding.

After Christian was cared for and resting against the wall underneath the kitchen table, Joanna slid over to the doorway. The hall between the kitchen and the parlor was empty. A board creaked overhead, and Joanna heard low voices coming from an upstairs room. So someone was home, after all. But were they Henches, or Cutters?

Joanna crept up the stairs, keeping her back to the wall. As soon as she was high enough to see across the floor, she turned around and peeked through the banister posts in the direction of the voices. The bedroom doors were all closed, the voices muffled.

No choice: she'd just have to knock.

28

Gus was ready.

He knew he wasn't smart. He was good at taking care of the house, fixing leaky pipes, patching the roof. But he was never good at books, and common sense wasn't his best skill. A disappointment to the family, he was. This was his big chance. He would save his Da', save his Aunty Abby, and prove his worth for once in his darned life. He lay in wait by the door, tense and poised with Grampa's knife in his hand. Someone was approaching from the hallway.

Gus crouched, muscles tight like a snake coiled and ready to strike. He felt powerful, ready. Pride filled his heart. He was responsible for the family, just like Da' always was. There was a soft knock on the door, then a brief pause, followed by a louder knuckle-rapping. Aunty Abby sat on the floor with her fingers in her ears, and Da' sat beside her with his rifle ready. Gus glanced back, nodded to his Da', and backed up a step, holding the knife out in front between his family and the intruder.

A moment of silence passed. The person on the other side of the door turned the handle. It was time.

Gus brought his boot up and kicked as hard as he could at the door. He felt it connect with something soft on the other side, and the intruder tumbled to the floor.

"Got him!" Gus shouted.

He was in the hallway in a flash. Leaping and stabbing with his eyes squeezed shut, his knife found the intruder's flesh and he drove it in deep, shouting with triumph.

A woman screamed.

"Gus! Get back! *Get off her!* It's fucking *Joanna!*" Charles struggled to his feet and charged across the room. He grabbed Gus by the nape of his neck and yanked him up off the floor with a single movement, crying out,

"Abigail! Help me!" Gus scurried backwards down the hall, staring gape-mouthed at the bloody knife sticking out of Joanna's leg.

Charles sank to one knee, narrowly missing Joanna's arm. Abigail appeared behind him with a handful of cloth strips and, somehow, a large bowl of warm water. She was an old hand at field medicine. Joanna felt her head lifted and placed on something soft—Abigail's lap. Then Abigail leaned forward and placed her pointy elbows on Joanna's shoulders, pressing down with all her ancient strength.

"Ready?" Charles asked.

Abigail nodded. Strands of her thin hair tickled Joanna's face. She was going to faint…

Charles yanked the knife from Joanna's leg, and her screams began anew. Joanna's muscle cramps earlier in the day now seemed like a faint childhood memory, akin to losing her first tooth, or bumping her head the first time she was too big to run under the dining room table. Leg cramps were a tickle, a dream. *This* was what real pain felt like.

After the knife was removed, Abigail tended to Joanna's wound with stunning speed and efficiency. She grabbed the knife, cut through the fabric over the wound, and stripped the leg bare. Bandages made from strips of torn cloth were tied tight, halting the gush of blood.

Abigail appraised her workmanship, frowning. "That will have to do until we can get my sewing kit. It's downstairs. Charles, will you go-"

Men shouted in the parlor. Glass shattered across the floor as someone swept Charles's crystal highball glasses off the desk.

"Too late, Abby. They're here. Get back into the room. Gus! Get up, you useless lump! Help me!" Charles gripped Joanna's ankles, and Gus caught her under the armpits. They moved her into Abigail's room, then slid a rolltop desk in front of the door as a makeshift barricade.

"No! No, you can't! Christian is downstairs!" Joanna cried. "We have to go get him!"

"Dammit, why didn't you say—it's too late now! They're coming!" Charles was panicking.

"You can't just leave him! We have to get him. They'll kill—"

Joanna tried to stand. Just bending her knee was agony. She grasped the window sill and pulled one leg underneath herself, then the other.

Charles sat down and shook his head, distraught with indecision. "To get him, we'd have to leave Abigail. Do you really expect her to defend herself?" Abigail was once again sitting in the corner with her bloodied fingers jammed in her ears, rocking gently forward and back. Gus continued to frantically stack furniture.

"There has to be a way." Joanna was sobbing. It wasn't fair. Christian had saved her—he had risked his life to save her, maybe even sacrificed it, if that wound became infected. He wouldn't have been stabbed if he hadn't pushed her ahead of him and let her escape first.

She had to find him.

More shouting from downstairs. They were ransacking the kitchen. Had they found Christian? She hoped he was still huddled under the table, hoped he was still alive. Christian, who spent his entire life caring for his family, had been left behind by them.

Joanna knew what she had to do.

She grabbed a handful of Abigail's field dressings and wrapped them around her hand before popping the remaining shards of broken glass out of the broken window, cleaning the edges. When it was clear, she sat on the ledge and brought both of her knees up to her chest with a gasp of pain as the hole in her leg yawned. She then spun around and tucked her feet out the window. Twisting in the window frame, she rolled onto her stomach and dangled her legs, trying to find a foothold on the porch overhang below.

"Joanna, what the hell are you doing? You'll kill yourself!" Charles rushed toward the window. "Get back in here!"

"Christian—your *brother*—is still down there. I'm going to get him." She found a narrow ledge with the toe of her boot and lowered her weight onto it, transitioning from the window sill to a strip of wooden trim. The foothold was flimsy, and the wider porch roof was still a few feet lower. Now what?

A sudden crash relieved her of further indecision. The wooden siding broke, and her own weight tore her hands from the sill. Her face scraped the side of the house until she turned over and tumbled down the thin overhang on her ass, sledding swiftly toward the final drop. In the moment before she shot over the edge, she found a hole in the roofing and grasped it to slow her descent. She had just enough time to twist to the side and angle her fall so she would land on her good leg.

Despite her effort, it was not a graceful landing. Her knife wound gaped, gushing blood as she landed. She clamped her jaw shut, tamping a howl of pain down to a low moan. As soon as the stars cleared from her vision, she crab-walked backwards, dragging her injured leg to hide in the shadows below the porch.

The only good news was that she was still alone. Her tourniquet was soaked with blood and coming loose. She pulled the knot tight. When she touched her face, her hand came away wet; her cheek was bleeding from being dragged down the outer wall. Everything else was sore, but intact. She sat in the lee of the porch, catching her breath. So where was she now, exactly?

Her best estimate was that she was around the corner from the front door, but on the wrong side from the kitchen. The parlor would be behind her now.

So, where were the Cutters?

Shouting and banging erupted from upstairs, as well as a thin scream—that was Gus, not Abigail. So, the Cutters had found the barricade, and the last remnants of the Hench family. Joanna could hear wood boards cracking, bring pried away. The Cutter boys were working to remove the door.

Maybe that meant they had not found Christian yet. Their noise and excitement might cover the sounds of her entry. She would just have to hope.

As she crawled out from under the porch and stood, balancing on her good leg, a shadow fell across her path.

"Well, hello, honey."

Granger's smile was broad, gap-toothed, smug. "Nice to see you again, city girl." He stepped toward her and swung his arm. The butt of his gun struck the back of her aching head, and the world went dark again.

29

The air in the void was thin. Her wrists ached.

And the object was closer.

She didn't know how she knew that, but she knew. She couldn't see it—it was still too far away for now. But the thing was a million miles across, traveling a million miles an hour. Nonsense numbers in a meaningless void, and yet they terrified her.

The Demon with the horns—the term "Demon" sounded so trite and smacked of a religious experience, but that was the only thing it resembled—had moved close to her side in the void, showing itself more clearly. It wanted to talk, this time.

"Who are you?" she asked.

"Monster," it said.

"No shit."

The object in the distance started its keening wail. How far away was it? A million miles? A billion? And yet its approach was so eternal, so inevitable, it filled her with dread. It was larger than the world, the galaxy—and when it arrived, all would end. She knew.

"All right, let's try this: what are you?"

"The great terminus," the Demon rumbled. "But to you, all that matters is that I will bring about the end of eternity, and you cannot stop me."

"Why would I want to? That's not my job. Anyway, everything dies eventually."

"You misunderstand. You are on the cusp."

The statement, so mildly delivered, gave birth to a deep terror in Joanna greater than any she had ever experienced. Was she to bear witness to the end of existence? Her hope, to which she had clung so doggedly, weakened.

"Get out of here!" someone cried. "You will not harm her!"

Joanna lifted her head—it was heavy, god, so *heavy*—and saw another figure in the void who stood between her and the Demon. It was nebulous, made of mist, yet gave an impression of no-nonsense propriety. Not unlike a butler.

The distant object rushing toward her was screaming. It was far still, but moving closer, and was aimed at her. And it was incredibly massive.

Something was coming; something big.

And then she woke up.

30

"Why are you helping them? What are they to you? You're no Cutter—Chris showed me the whole family tree. You aren't on it." Joanna blinked hard, trying to focus, trying not to faint again. Her head, much abused over the last few days, felt concussed.

Granger had bound her wrists with rope so tight her hands were turning white. He had dragged her to the dilapidated little building Charles had called the "barn." The whole structure leaned alarmingly backwards, as though shocked by the events occuring in the yard out front. The stalls and center walkway were mostly empty except for some old horse ties mounted to the supporting posts by metal rings, to which Joanna was now bound.

"You're asking me? Why're *you* helping the damned Henches? You got even less a stake in this than I do. I'm on Sammy's payroll! You should've gone back to the city while you still could, little girl. Now you've gone and picked a side in a very nasty dispute."

"I…it didn't start out that way. But I met some of them, and then the Cutters attacked me. I never really got a chance to leave."

"Well, sucks for you. Samuel has an interest in you."

"Let me-"

"Don't even say it, hon. You know I'm not letting you go, so don't ask. You got nothing to offer me, but Sammy will hook me up. So just leave it." Granger tapped a text message into his phone. "And will you look at that, he's on his way now. You sure got his attention."

Joanna hung her head. Behind her was a heap of straw five feet tall, rotting in the humid air. When they had entered the barn, mice with pink tails had fled the sound of their footsteps to hide in holes burrowed deep into the dirty pile. The barn smelled like a basement overgrown with mold: stale, damp, and forgotten. Ancient clods of dry horse manure were piled in the corners, too dessicated to attract flies.

The hooks Granger had attached to Joanna's wrists extended her arms to either side. Her hands didn't hurt yet, but it wouldn't take long for them to start aching, and numbness would follow soon after. She had to escape before that happened or she'd have no hope of getting the ropes off before Samuel showed up.

Granger pulled a lighter and a pack of smokes from his shirt pocket. He smiled crookedly at Joanna.

"Cigarette?"

Joanna glared.

"Aw, sorry about that. Guess that'd be tough when you're all trussed up like a Christmas goose. Next time, perhaps."

He bit the end of a cigarette and drew it from the pack with practiced ease. As he cupped his hands to light the tip, flickers from the lighter's flame reflected on his face. Joanna watched him squint his eyes in pleasure as he inhaled the smoke.

They waited together in uncomfortable silence.

"Damn, where's Sammy at? I can't wait here all day. Damn store's locked up an' everything."

Granger leaned in the doorway and crossed his legs, creating a dark silhouette that made him look like a lonesome cowboy looking out over his herd. Joanna quickly glanced around for a way out of her situation. There was a pitchfork in the corner of one of the horse stalls, a rusted-out wheelbarrow down at the other end, a decaying leather halter on a hook. Nothing especially helpful, and nothing was within reach anyway.

Granger reached into his back pocket and withdrew a switchblade. He flipped it open and etched a clumsy "G" into the door frame, revealing a layer of cleaner wood underneath the carved lines.

That was it, then. Her only chance would be to get that knife.

"Let me go," she said.

"Now honey, I *just* said to shut the fuck up. If I didn't say that out loud before, I'm saying it now. Nothing you say is gonna change your current situation, so keep quiet and you'll improve your chances of me not punching your face."

"I said, let me go."

Granger whipped his head around. "Di'n't you hear me, bitch? I said keep quiet!"

"Let me go!"

"Alright, you're a fighter. That's how you want it. Let me see what we got in here."

Granger's eyes fell on the leather halter. One tar-sticky corner of his mouth curled into a smile. "You want to disobey like an animal, well then that's what I'll treat you like. You got a horse face—let's see if this fits ya."

"Let me go now, you *asshole!*"

"You don't talk to me like that!" Granger glowered, showing his patchwork teeth, and took long, angry strides across the barn floor toward the halter. "*I'll let you-*"

Joanna's foot shot out and struck his shin. She managed to get her toe hooked under the bottom of his pant cuff and twist it around, causing him to tumble hard to the floor. As soon as he was down, she planted her heel hard in his ear, landing with all her weight. There was a sickening snap, and Granger began to writhe, moaning with his lips pressed onto the concrete floor.

His knife was still gripped in his right hand, the side closest to Joanna. She drug her heel across the floor, hooking his hand, trying to work the knife loose. His grip on it was surprising; even in his half conscious state, his hand kept a tight hold on the hilt.

She stomped again, bashing the heel of her boot on his fingers. The knife clattered out of his hand and slid a few inches across the floor—in the wrong direction.

Joanna gasped, and her eyes shot wide open with dismayed shock. The knife had almost moved out of reach, but she held her breath and strained against the ropes, pointing her foot until she could pin the tip of the blade and drag it forward. Her hands had started to go numb, but were not so far gone they did not scream with pain as she pulled. Her wrist bones felt loose in their sockets. Blood trickled down her leg, sticky on her skin. She held her breath, and dragged the knife across the concrete.

Granger continued to moan low. She wished he would just pass out so she didn't have to listen to him.

The knife was right under her feet—in her possession now, technically—but how would she get it up to the ropes?

Joanna wanted to scream with frustration. It was right there, exactly what she needed, against all odds. But how could she reach it? Without hands…

She braced the toe of her left boot under the heel of her right and began to push. Her laces were tied tight, but it would have to come off. There was no other way.

Her right foot throbbed as the blood flow was blocked by the tightening boot, but she pushed harder and harder until her skin chafed and the tiny bones in her foot crackled under the strain. Joanna took a deep breath, closed her eyes, and pushed.

The boot slid off simultaneously as the tiny bone on the outer edge of her foot broke with a wet crunch. The pain was intense, but secondary: she didn't have time for it. Her toes were intact, and she wasted no time gripping the knife between them.

She began to swing her leg back and forth, loosening the tendons, then threw it up onto the rope connected to her right arm. Exhausted muscles in her back and her butt screamed; she hadn't stretched her body so far since gymnastics class when she was eight years old. But it was done.

She had planned to pass the knife off to her hand, but her fingers had checked out. They weren't even tingling anymore, just dead. Her foot would have to do most of the work.

Joanna took a deep breath and see-sawed the knife against the rope. Every time she cut deeper, she nearly dropped the knife. By the time the rope began to fray, cramping had settled in to the arch of her foot and her calf with long screaming spasms. The clean white interior of the rope began to show; she was making progress, but it was so *slow.*

Halfway through, she had to bring her leg back down to rest. She was losing blood flow to her foot. If she didn't give it a rest, it might go numb, and she'd be stuck again. But the ropes were old and brittle; maybe it was already enough.

She pulled hard. The fibers held at first, but then she felt a tiny tear. The rope ripped slowly, agonizingly… until finally it gave.

Joanna was free. She reached for the knife on the floor, but her fingers hadn't gotten the message yet. She jammed them in her mouth, warming them, then shook her hands in the air, trying to flex her fingers.

"Wake up, wake up…" she whispered.

A long, aching cramp brought her hand back to life. It felt like a thin hot blade was being inserted into her wrist and driven up through her palm. Ignoring the pain, she continued to work her fingers, curling and straightening until sensation returned to her fingertips.

She tried again for the knife, and was able to

grasp it loosely between her thumb and first finger. It was enough.

By the time she was free of the other rope, Granger had begun to stir.

31

Three Cutter men shouted in excitement as they searched the bottom floor of the house. They overturned chairs, flipped furniture, and smashed all the glass to pieces. Two of the men were young, no more than about twenty years old. One of the men—the one barking orders—was older, nearly the same age as Christian.

So, Christian thought, this was the great and terrible Samuel.

He'd never seen the man in person. Samuel was scrawny, like most desert dwellers, and his skin was scored with deep wrinkles. His faded vest, buttoned over a filthy white undershirt, might have been brown once but was now sun-bleached orange. Grey slacks—frayed, but still nice enough to seem out of place—and leather moccasins completed his ensemble. Blue, piercing eyes watched over his men in the intense manner common with psychopaths.

Christian watched, holding his breath, as they guzzled beer they found in the refrigerator. How could they not see him? He tucked in his feet, hid his face under his hood, and waited until they tired of trashing the kitchen and finally headed for the stairs. He lurched toward the back door on three limbs, holding his left hand to his side, hoping he wasn't leaving a trail of red drops behind him like bread crumbs. As soon as he crawled out the back door and closed it gently behind him, he turned to see Harrison walking up.

Christian immediately knew something was wrong. Harrison's face was twisted, resolute, making his old harelip scar flare prominently. A tire iron swung at his side. Beads of sweat popped on his upper lip and forehead and soaked his armpits. The hand gripping the tire iron was clenched tight, showing white knuckle bones through the skin, his nails digging into his palm. The man had murder in his eyes.

"Peace," Christian tried, raising his long arms. He had nothing else to offer.

"Shut it, slug," Harrison replied. "Samuel sent me. I work for him now. I don't want to kill you, because I don't want to carry you. You're to come with me. Run, and you die."

No choice; Christian wasn't built for battle. He struggled and rose to his feet, then followed Harrison around the corner to the front of the house. The front door was swinging shut just as it came into view, and Christian caught sight of Joanna's hair. She was alive! His eyes darted to Harrison, but the man was squinting at the horizon, looking for Samuel. He hadn't seen her. There was still hope.

32

Joanna ducked through the front door just in time to avoid being spotted by a man she did not recognize coming around the corner holding a tire iron. She hunkered down beneath the window, in the same place Charles had used the mirror that morning. She heard two sets of footsteps crunching in the dirt—one of them was dragging, injured—then stop in front of the porch. The uneven gait was very much like Christian's.

A voice said, "We're just gonna wait here. Samuel's killing your brother right now, you know that? And Abigail, too. *Exterminating.* Serves you all right, too…" He trailed off, muttering. Joanna looked through the window in time to see him cuff Christian's face, splitting his lip. Christian flailed into the dirt, using the opportunity to look toward the house; there, in the window, he saw a face. Joanna. For a moment, their eyes met.

"Freak blood. Great. Fuckin' disgusting." The man sneered, wiping his hand on his shirt.

Christian sucked on his lip, filling his mouth with blood before coughing on the man's shoes, spraying red droplets from his toes to his knees. The man jumped backward, hissing with revulsion, and tripped over his own feet.

It was Joanna's chance. She couldn't shoot the man with the gun she had taken from Granger or she would risk alerting every Cutter in the area to her location. He would have to be taken down the hard way. Ignoring the pain in her leg, she sprinted from the shadow of the porch and tackled him, pinning him to the ground.

"Chris! Now!"

If Christian was surprised, he did not show it. He struggled to his feet and kicked the man with one of his huge boots, burying it in his ribcage. He kicked again as the man curled in pain, a single blow to the head. Streamers of spit and sweat flew from the man's face and soaked quickly into the desert floor as he passed out.

"Quick, let's move him inside. If we leave him here, we'll get spotted by Samuel and his posse. We have to hide," Joanna panted.

They each grasped one of the man's arms, and with a great deal of effort they moved him into the kitchen and stowed him under the table. They could hear the sounds of the ongoing siege upstairs. Samuel hadn't broken into Abigail's room yet, but he was getting close.

"Dead?" Christian asked.

"Just unconscious, I think. Who is this guy, any-way?" Joanna asked.

"Harry the-" Christian started, then paused. "Harrison. Turncoat."

"Chris, go outside and find somewhere to hide. You're hurt. I'm going to see what I can do about Samuel."

"You, too." Christian frowned. "Who hurt you?"

"Gus, but it was an accident. And after that, someone who works for Samuel. Don't worry about him, he's tied up in the barn."

Christian's eyes flashed as a slow smile worked its way across his face. "Wow! Good job, Jo!"

"Hah. Thanks, I guess. But yeah, I'm hurt too. And you...I'm worried you're gonna lose a kidney." Joanna turned toward the hall.

"Not your battle." Christian was resolute.

"Maybe, but-"

Before Joanna could finish her sentence, Christian tumbled to the floor. The effort of pulling Harrison into the house had torn open his wound; blood dripped from his shirt. Joanna helped him back up, while Christian muttered, "Fine, fine..."

"Wait." Joanna stooped under the kitchen table and took Harrison's gun from his pocket, then handed it to Christian. "Take this. Try to get out the back, Chris. Find somewhere to hide, and I'll find you later. I promise!"

Christian gazed at her, sad and tired. The gun looked wrong in his hands; he was a gentle monster, not a fighter. He was much older than she, and wiser, too. But sometimes he still seemed like a child. Joanna kissed him on the forehead, and whispered, "I'm so glad you're okay, but we're not safe yet. You have to trust me. Now go!"

She didn't wait for a reply, but began to make her way up the staircase as she had done before, with her back pressed to the wall. She heard Christian crawl toward the back door. When she was halfway up, the kitchen door clicked shut. Good.

She peeked through the banister again, with her eyes at the same height as the second story carpet. Samuel's two young men were working on unlocking the door, while the ringleader himself stayed back. Two or three bullet holes studded the door; Charles had fired at them, but must have been wary of wasting ammo on unseen targets.

What was she going to do? She had never fired a gun before in her life. It looked like the revolver she was holding had three bullets loaded, but did she have time to fire them all? Even if she managed to take out the Cutters, Gus had almost killed her last time she had approached the family unannounced. Would Charles finish her off if he didn't know she was coming to his rescue? She grimaced in frantic indecision.

One of the young men became impatient. "Samuel, let's just do this!" he whisper-yelled. He didn't wait for a reply, but shouldered the blockade roughly, popping off the old doorknob and forcing the door open an inch before the weight of the stacked furniture slammed it shut again.

Charles fired two quick rounds through the door, and the man crumpled.

Joanna didn't hesitate. She bounded up the last few stairs on all fours, leaning to the left to take some weight off her injured leg, and took aim at the remaining young man. She prayed to whatever god might be listening that it didn't have a safety.

It didn't. The gun kicked back more strongly than she anticipated and she stumbled heavily onto her bad leg, but the bullet went home, striking her stunned target above his left eye.

Samuel charged at her, roaring with surprise and rage at the sudden shift in advantage. He started straight towards Joanna, but knocked her aside and leaped down the staircase, taking several steps at a time. He fled into the desert alone, leaving his megaphone and his empty gun behind in the sand.

Joanna grinned and called through the bedroom door, "Charles! I'm home!"

Gus hollered and whooped with joy.

33

"*None* of you have a car?" Joanna asked Charles. Christian had joined them upstairs in Abigail's room to make plans. They were finally all together, the remaining members of the Hench family: an army of five against an unknown number of enemies.

"Nope, never really saw the need for one. Got no animals to care for these days, so no need to haul feed. Gus walks to the market for us, and none of the rest of us get off the property much. Had an old truck 'til a few years back, but it broke, and the nearest mechanic is clear out in Redstone. So, we couldn't get all the way out there without the truck, you know, and it was broken…"

"Okay, I get it. Maybe the rental will work long enough to get us all into town."

"Joanna," Abigail said. It was the first time she had spoken since helping bandage Joanna's leg.

"I don't suppose…you've seen my daughter. Her name is Grace."

Joanna looked to Christian, who hunched in his seat, heavy with guilt and regret.

"I'm sorry, Abigail." Joanna said. "She-"

"She died, Aunty. I'm sorry, I'm so sorry," Christian wept.

"I thought so," Abigail said.

The room fell silent. Joanna looked from one family member to the next, desperate; she had to allow the family to grieve, but time was so short.

For the first time in days, Hench Ranch was calm. The only remaining Cutters on the property were dead by gunshot wounds. Samuel had fled, but he would be back, and probably soon. He hid in the desert, licking his wounds and preparing for his final assault on the property. The convertible, if it worked, was their best chance to get out before Samuel returned, desperate and furious by his previous defeat.

"I'm going to look at the car," Joanna said. "If it still works, we're all going to leave, okay?"

No one answered.

Joanna swallowed her impatience and went downstairs. From the front porch she scanned the surrounding desert, squinting in the direction of Samuel's camp in the dunes. All was quiet.

She remained alert as she inspected the convertible. Samuel's men had ransacked it, as expected. Her purse was gone, along with the cell phone inside. The car had been slammed into a fencepost in front of the house and sustained heavy damage to the front end.

Too bad she hadn't purchased the optional extra insurance.

The fender was drooping, and she could tell it would scrape on the front tire, but maybe it would work long enough to get them to town. After working it back and forth until an internal clamp snapped, she was able to pull it away from the frame. Hinkel's Rent-a-Car would certainly never rent to her again.

The keys were still in the ignition. Charles and Christian appeared on the porch, holding each other up with their arms slung over their shoulders. Gus loomed behind them.

Joanna sat in the driver's seat, and experienced a moment of disconnect.

The car was just so weirdly normal, with its out-dated CD player and the keychain with the blue plastic fob printed with "Hinkel's Rentals: We Make You Move 513-9927." The last two days had either been the worst nightmare of her life or a fantastic adventure. Maybe both. All she wanted now was a long bath, some scented candles, and a big fat glass of wine.

She closed her eyes, took a deep breath, and turned the key.

Nothing.

Joanna's eyes welled up. It wasn't fair. She would have to make the walk back to town. On her wounded leg. No other option. She'd get help, somehow, there had to be a police station somewhere…

"Joanna. Drive," Christian called from the porch.

"Chris, I can't! Don't you understand? It's broken! That asshole Samuel and his crazy little clan smashed it! I…" Joanna trailed off.

The car was still in (D) for "Drive." Oh.

She shifted the car into "Park" and tried the key again. It jumped to life.

"Oh thank *god!*" she yelled, then buried her face in her hands and laughed with tears running from her eyes.

34

Samuel crouched in the narrow shade behind the cactus with the remains of his resources. He watched the Hench group stumble from their house with red, drooping eyes that spoke of exhaustion and grief but also a certain defiance. It was the look of people who were tired, but thought they were winning. The Pig-King Charles and his monstrous brother had been wrung out by the desert, dried up and drained, but were still unbroken. Gus, the slack-jawed jackass, was simply vacant. Abigail was not to be seen; perhaps they had left her behind so she wouldn't slow them down.

The realtor-bitch was fresh, lively. She didn't belong here, and Samuel had not accounted for her when he made his invasion plans. Even as her tears streaked the dirt on her cheeks she looked strong, like her heart was filled with some strange purpose. Despite her ugly professional clothing and innocent demeanor, she looked dangerous. She had the might of Babylon at her back, and could rain hell upon them all if she made outside contact. The Lord had warned him about her, but too late. He would have to improvise.

Samuel watched the family from behind the dune, feeling helpless. He wasn't wounded, but he was alone. Well, the twins were here, but they hardly counted for much. He had taken their guns from them, but they had already wasted most of the ammo.

"Sammy? Sammy, where's Ethan?"

"Keep your damn mouths shut, now! Ethan took a bullet. The plan's changed."

The twins said nothing, but Samuel could hear them quietly sobbing. Ethan had treated them like dogs, but the soft hearted little fools still wept for him. Probably had thought he loved them, wanted them. Well, they would be his only mourners. The man's voice had been grating, and his personality about as fun as a crabby snatch.

The city woman was sitting in the car. She had some trouble with the ignition at first—how like a woman!—but then she got it started, and screamed some kind of strange war cry.

"Okay, time's up, girls! It's your turn! You got to run fast! Go get that car, you hear me? It's your big chance to make me proud!"

They hesitated. "Sammy, we're the only ones left.

Maybe we should-"

"*What?*"

Daria, the more assertive of the two, wore the defiant expression of a petulant child. "We should go home, Sammy."

"Let them keep their ugly old house," Dahlia piped in. "I like Cutter Camp better, anyway."

"I can't believe what I'm hearing." Rage lent Samuel's voice a trembling vibrato. He raised his shaking hands, clenched, ready to crush a windpipe in each fist. "I don't give a dusty fart what you think! You go now, or I'll make sure you'll wish you had!"

Then, with a mighty struggle, Samuel softened his demeanor. This was part of it; the end of the show, the blowoff.

"You know I love you girls. Do you love me back?"

The twins nodded.

"And I know you love God. I know better than to even ask if you do."

They nodded again.

"And you know He came right up to me with this plan, don't you? You know because I told you. I saw Him, in the purple mist, and He told me. So even if you don't care about disappointing me any more-"

Dahlia gasped. "Sammy, no..." Daria said.

"I hope you won't let Him down."

"Never!" Dahlia said.

"I'll be right here, looking out, shooting at them with my gun. See? Because I'm always looking out for you. And when you get back, we'll all go home together and have a little party like we did when you were girls. Does that sound okay, my lovelies?"

Dahlia and Daria needed no other encouragement. They loved Sammy, lived for Sammy, craved his approval. They rose up from behind the dune, their arms stretched skyward, their faces steeled. They had already prepared for battle, tying their middle legs together (Daria's right, Dahlia's left) with bound leather straps so they could run in tandem across the desert hardpan with speed. Middle legs, outer legs, middle legs, outer legs. They had practiced at this, and their swift approach with arms outstretched was the stuff of nightmares.

Charles spotted them from the porch, and his mouth gaped with terror. Gus pointed into the desert and cried out in alarm, but Joanna didn't have time to turn her head before the twins were upon her. A tornado of limbs beat her shoulders, pummeled her body, caught in her hair. The girls were a giant Frankensteinian spider, pieced together out of a jumble of parts stolen from two whole women. They ripped at her clothes, trying to pull her from the car. The dual-bodied creature was five feet tall, six feet wide, and had twenty scratching claws.

Joanna punched the door lock down and gripped the steering wheel in terror. The car was the only protection she had. If she was pulled over the door and into the desert—into Cutter territory—they would rip her to shreds. She slammed her elbow into the right twin's nose, breaking it with a snap like a mussel shell. The women issued a wailing harmonized howl, high and manic and guttural under a flow of streaming blood.

The twins reached deeper into the car and sought a stronger grip around her midriff. Joanna planted her feet on the floor beneath the brake and gas pedals, trying to root herself inside the vehicle while Charles and Christian lumbered down the porch steps, calling out her name. The women improved their grip at her waist, clutching the waistband of her slacks with their fingers.

"Gus! Help her, damn you!" Charles hollered as he and Christian limped across the sand.

Gus paced on the porch, clenching his fists in fear

and indecision. He wanted to help, more than anything in the world—but it seemed like every time he did, he always made things worse.

"I cain't, Pa!" he said. "I'm cursed! I don't wanna get you all killed!"

"What the hell are you talking about, boy?" Charles boomed, reaching for the fighting women with his massive arms.

Just as Joanna was beginning to lose the battle, the women were yanked backwards. Charles and Christian had finally made it to the car and were prying them off of her—but the women's hands held tight, and were taking Joanna with them.

Joanna hugged the steering wheel to her chest and yelled, "Try again! *Pull now!*"

With all their strength Charles and Christian gave a mighty heave, prying the twins off of Joanna. In the tug-of-war, she felt a rib pop.

The hard-earned victory did not last long. The con-joined women spun and scratched like cats at the mens' faces before turning and once again lunging for Joanna, enraged and relentless.

Gus reached a decision. He screamed, a warbly battle-cry that confused the twins more than it frightened them. He sprinted from the porch, whining with fear, and hugged the women in his gangly arms. He clung like a spiderweb, unwilling to harm the women but unable to let go. While they were distracted by Gus's bizarre ambush, Joanna squirmed from their grasp and scrambled away.

In the melee her foot landed squarely on the gas pedal.

The car lurched, finally toppling the fence post that had blocked it, and careened toward the house. As Gus and the brothers held the twins, the car door tore away from the womens' hands, spinning them to the desert floor. The women screamed in pain and fury like banshees with strands of Joanna's hair still woven through their fingers.

Seconds passed like minutes. Joanna stomped the floor again and again, unable to find the brake pedal. In the final moments before the car slammed into the porch, she ducked into the passenger seat and put her arms over her head. Timber splintered as the front wall of the house rocked above her, and a deep rumbling began in the depths of the structure. The few remaining intact windows shattered as the building swayed sickeningly to the left in slow motion, then to the right. Planks of siding popped off with little puffs of white dust. The motion of the house above her in its final moment was dancelike, mesmerizing.

"Jo! *Out!*" she heard Christian yell.

His voice broke her hypnosis. She opened the car door and tumbled to the dirt, crawling away on hands and knees toward the fence where Christian and Charles leaned, huffing with exhaustion. The conjoined women had surrendered; they lay bleeding in the dust.

A tremor vibrated under their feet as they watched the house list further left. A pale face appeared in an upstairs window, looking down into the yard in sad confusion before the house fell in on itself: Abigail. Gus spotted her and screamed, then sprinted toward the house before Charles could stop him.

As Gus skirted past the car on the porch, planks of wood broke apart with splintering bangs. The porch cracked upward around the car lodged in its center, and shards of glass trickled down through the crumbling tinder. Gus was crushed by the door frame before he made it into the house.

The following crash was enormous, blowing dirt and debris like shrapnel. As the house foundered, Joanna heard something else in the din; a thundering bellow of anger and frustration. The shadow of a huge horned figure appeared for a fraction of a second—just a blink in the dust—before retreating again into the void.

The Demon from her dreams. But how could he be here?

After the house completed its collapse, a further fall occurred; a snaking line of dirt collapsing away from the back of the house like a long tail. The tunnel. Then, with a soft rumble, the root cellar imploded.

"Abigail! Oh, god…" Charles sank to the dirt in grief. "Gus."

Christian didn't look aggrieved. He looked furious. His huge, liquid eyes narrowed, and his mouth opened wide enough to show his jagged, broken teeth. He clenched right fists, with his head bowed. A knife appeared in his left hand from a deep pocket.

"Chris. No," Joanna said. "If you kill them-"

"I won't kill them," he growled.

"They're victims too, Chris," Joanna said.

Joanna couldn't see what he was doing as he crouched over the conjoined women, but a thick pool of blood appeared like a dark shadow under his stooping figure. They women screamed. She wanted to stop him—Christian was a gentle soul, and he did not deserve to live in regret, but the image of the twins looming over her, grabbing at her with fearsome bloodlust, gave her pause. Maybe they deserved to die.

When he stood, Joanna saw Christian had not killed the women but instead had cut them apart where they had been joined at the hip. She was shocked. This assault seemed almost more devastating than their murder would have been. It was more personal. He had changed them, fundamentally; but why?

"You are cast out, once again," Christian said. "Alone, in every way. No longer a part of any family, and no longer a part of each other."

"Chris, they might still die. They're bleeding out."

Christian shrugged, and threw the knife into the sand near the pooling blood.

The act of separating the twins freed something in him. He wanted more. He wasn't calmed, or redeemed, or satiated. His revenge hadn't given him closure, but brought instead a sense of power and purpose. Christian stood up straight, his muscles tight. If anyone had touched him in that moment, he would have unwound like a spring. Joanna and Charles watched him in apprehensive silence.

"*Samuel!*" Christian said, scanning the horizon. "Samuel," he said again, tasting the name in his mouth. The distant silhouette of a man was moving up the hills, over the dunes. He was leaving a clear trail in the sand.

"It can wait, Christian," Charles said with odd tenderness. As he spoke, he gazed toward the remains of Hench House, his home and his castle—now nothing more than a pile of smoldering lumber and bones.

"We all need to rest," Joanna said. "Chris! Please."

Christian finally exhaled, and seemed to deflate. He sat down heavily next to Charles. Christian's madness subsided within the embrace of his brother.

Joanna tended to the sisters, who had fallen unconscious from pain and blood loss. The wounds were large, but Joanna thought they were probably not fatal as long as she could stop the bleeding. She bound them in long strips of cloth pulled from their skirts. Tonight or tomorrow, when they awoke and found themselves no longer a single, but double—what would they think? Joanna could not imagine what their reactions might be.

Hench House was a tomb which would stand in memory of the family until the desert wore it away. The roof lay like a canopy covering the collapse, gently draped over a mound of graveyard dirt. Abigail and Gus had died along with the house, and Grace was buried in her own bed deep within the earth: a tulip bulb that would never bloom.

Christian sighed—a low, moaning breath, from deep within his chest—and bowed his head. He looked more tired than anyone Joanna had ever seen. His hand dug into a fold of his cloak and found his cigarettes and lighter.

The three of them smoked, waiting for the night's approach, and sipped from Charles's pocket flask of rye whiskey. The house occasionally issued pops and bangs. Sunlight reflected off shards of broken windows and lamps, making them glitter and sparkle, casting odd reflections on their vigil. A green-scaled lizard dashed past, pausing to cock its head and examine the group with a black rolling eye until a loud crack from the house scared it toward the hills. Once the wreckage finally settled, Hench House would quickly be claimed by wildlife, a new refuge for the tiny desperate creatures of the desert.

In the quiet, Joanna had time to consider the vision she had seen during the house's collapse. The Demon from her dreams had been present while she was awake—he was not just a thing of her imagination, then. He had flickered out of view quickly, as if exhausted. And he seemed infuriated, frustrated; like someone who had crafted an intricate plan which had failed.

Every possible interpretation of the vision filled Joanna with dread.

35

Evening arrived. The sunlight angled and cooled, transforming into musty orange beams cutting through the lingering dust cloud from the collapsed house. The daytime animals quieted; desert loons stopped chirping, rabbits stopped digging. Night animals awoke and left their dens, issuing howls and strange screams from the cover of the growing shadows as the prey animals tucked themselves away into their nests and holes.

As the sky purpled, pinpoint stars peeked from the darkness to illuminate the snaking paths of the wild desert predators. The moon rose while the sun still lingered in the sky, and for a while both were visible. Full and pregnant, the moon's glow turned the dirt to silver specks as pretty as sand in an hourglass.

"Time." Christian rose to his feet. He began to struggle toward the hills, casting about, trying to spot Samuel's footsteps. Deep grooves trailed behind him as he dragged one of his feet sideways, pulling it along like an anchor.

"Christian, you *can't*. You're too badly hurt. We need to go to town and get some help," Joanna said. "I'm hurt, too. We can all go together."

"Joanna, I'm sorry, but he's right," Charles said. He had been uncharacteristically quiet as they sat watching the house sink into its final resting position. The destruction of the building had shaken him, destroying his bombastic self-assuredness. Charles's power had disappeared with the ranch. Now, left with no place in the world, he deferred to Christian.

"It's time for the Cutter-Hench feud to end. If we leave now, just run away and leave the desert behind us, then we'll never come back. It will never be concluded. All the pain, all the deaths…for nothing." Charles watched Christian limp toward the dunes. "And there's one more thing, Joanna. This feud between our families—it's who we are. For generations we have been consumed by this battle, for better or worse. That's probably a bad thing, but it's beyond us to change it now. We have no choice. It ends tonight, one way or the other."

Joanna sighed. "Fine. I get it. But we should try to find some weapons. We need protection. Samuel's not going to give himself up without a fight…"

"No. This is not your battle, Joanna. It's a Hench family affair." Charles gave her a long look before trailing Christian into the desert. His lumbering bulk faded into a grey shadow in the twilight. He followed in the rut created by his brother, gradually gaining on him. Without pausing in his lurching steps, Charles turned his head in the darkness and called back to her once more.

"Go home, Jo."

Joanna was stunned. Charles was right; it wasn't her battle. What was she doing here? She could have found a way to leave any time after escaping the root cellar. She wasn't a member of either of the feuding families. Her job and her apartment was waiting for her in the city, where she belonged. The game was over, Samuel had won, and it was time for her to leave.

Except, it wasn't. She watched the two brothers march slowly, resolutely, into the desert. The one in front, monstrous and malformed, was her unexpected friend. The one behind, massive and gruff, shared more heart with his brother than he imagined. To her great surprise, she realized cared for them both as much as if they were her own family.

Her leg was hurt, but she could walk on it, and she was probably still in better condition than either of them. Would she really leave them now?

No.

Joanna looked around in the dim light until she found Christian's knife, and picked it out of the sand. The sisters lay sleeping fitfully. There was nothing more she could do for them now. She positioned their arms so they would be holding hands when they awoke.

By the time she was ready, the brothers were approaching the upper ridge of the hills. She closed her eyes and breathed in, drawing the rapidly cooling wind deep into her lungs, then followed the line of footsteps into the darkening desert.

36

In single file, they stumbled through the moonlight: Samuel, Christian, Charles, Joanna. Christian's wound had closed enough to stop trickling blood, but his pain was enormous. The cut gaped and oozed if he moved too swiftly or fell down, spattering blood on the desert sand. Joanna's leg weakened as she hiked, until it became numb and swollen. The hand she had pulled from Granger's rope throbbed, and her arm felt loose in its socket.

Charles was uninjured, yet Joanna feared it was he who was in the greatest danger. He gasped for air, in constant pain as his ankles twisted in the sand and his swayed back struggled to support his wagging belly. He sweated heavily, dripping from his face and chest, and he shook his left arm often as though it were sore. Joanna ached with sympathy for him, and dreaded to imagine leaving him behind if he suffered a heart attack. Would Christian be able to march on as his brother lay dying in the desert behind them? There was no way they could carry Charles all the way back to town. Whether Joanna and Christian pressed on or turned back, they would have to leave him, and he would be a feast for the coyotes that were already beginning to yip in excitement as they stalked the exhausted convoy.

The night grew cold. Crickets chirped from the cover of dry bushes and dark rocks that looked like crabs burrowed in the sand. At Joanna's back, the day had receded in a glorious splash of purple as white puffy clouds crept across the sky, chasing each other into the west, continuing their flight below the skyline toward California and the ocean beyond. The evening breeze picked up, evaporating the sweat from her skin. It felt wonderful, but Joanna was sure that in a couple of hours she would be thinking back on the warmth of the afternoon with longing.

Christian pulled up his headlamp, which was still hanging on his chest like a necklace, and switched it on. Joanna remembered she was still wearing hers, too. It washed Charles's broad back in unnatural blue light. Joanna was shocked to see how much he was struggling. His gait was uneven; he lurched to the right with every step.

"Christian, break," Joanna called softly. "We have to rest."

They regrouped and sat near a large granite boulder pockmarked with erosion. The moon had risen until it was directly overhead, nearly full and bright enough to show all its spots. Christian sat in the lee of a stone shaped like a pillar, and pulled his hood over his head.

"Look. Someone's been here," Charles said.

The rocks they sheltered next to were covered in colorful drawings: animals, flowers, stick figure people engaged in battle and lovemaking. Some spots were just swirls upon swirls of spiraling paint. Tucked away under the boulder was a stash of beer and whiskey bottles—thirty years old at least, maybe more. Poetry wound through the drawings in a meandering scrawl. At the bottom, a signature was barely legible: "Jack."

Charles procured his flask.

"One for the road," he said, and swallowed. He raised his flask to the paintings. "And one to you, my friend, whoever you were. To Jack."

Joanna and Christian declined whiskey, but Charles didn't complain about drinking alone this time. He indulged with a crooked smile, his eyes squeezed shut.

He drank as one does at a wake, with a sense of the great shift that had occurred in the world as he knew it. He drank with the knowledge that this forced march marked the end of his old life, with no guarantee he would ever be able to begin anew.

"Christian," Charles said between sips. "Do you remember Penny?"

Joanna saw Christian's black hood turn toward Charles. "Yes. Long ago."

Charles chuckled. "A thousand years at least, feels like. Wonder where she is now, my beautiful Penny. Probably married some rich boy. She'd deserve it, that's for sure."

Christian sighed. "Deserved better than you."

"That's for damn sure!" Charles huffed. "Joanna, I wish you'd met this girl. You'd have liked her. She was tough, and pretty, too—like you. And she liked me, can you believe it? I damn near asked her to marry me."

"Was she Gus's mom?" Joanna asked.

"Gus's mom, she…died young. No, Penny was our mail carrier. This was twenty years ago. I was thinner then—not a lot, mind you, but I could make it up the damn stairs without risking an infarction—and I pitched some pretty good woo. Every day I'd wait for her, holding flowers or some such crap behind my back, damn near out of my mind just to see her smile."

"What happened? Why didn't you propose?"

Charles leaned back, lowering himself to the desert floor. He stretched, extending his arms over his head, groaning in relief as his spine popped.

"Thought about it. For a long time, too. She was too good for me, but she really did seem to like me. I even baked her cookies, that's how crazy I was about her. Damn, but they tasted awful…"

"And? What happened?"

Charles sighed. "I couldn't ask her to become a

Hench. It'd be no different from drafting a young soldier directly to the front fucking lines. I could never ask a lovely girl like her to join us in this god damned feud. I lost Gus's mother in a pointless gunfight; I couldn't put another outsider in danger, ever again. After I realized that, I knew I would always have to live alone, or move away from the ranch. I suppose I could have left with her, just married her and taken off—but Abigail, and Grace, and Christian…I couldn't abandon them. Just couldn't do it."

"Oh, Charles. I'm so sorry."

"You understand? Do you see why it has to end this way, and why it has to end tonight?"

"Yes."

Charles tipped the flask over his upturned face and dripped the last bit of whiskey into his mouth as he gazed up at the stars. A drop trickled over the corner of his mouth, down his cheek, and onto his earlobe where it hung like a pearl.

Without turning to face her, Charles asked, "Why are you here, Jo?"

Joanna felt hurt by the question, but could not have explained exactly why.

"I want to help."

"At the risk of your life? Really? A few days ago we were strangers to you. Who in their right mind would get knowingly wrapped up in this shit?"

"I…I just…" Tears welled in Joanna's eyes. She wiped at them with frustration.

"I'm not trying to call you out, Jo. And, Lord knows, I appreciate all your help. I just wonder how bad things must be for you at home for this shithole to look better than going back there. But a hell of a lot of people have died over the years, and I don't want to lose you too. My conscience can't take it."

Joanna sobbed. "My home isn't bad! It's just…

it's just that nothing *matters!* I thought I was going to be a lawyer, but the college loan debt scared me, and I quit school. And I was going to get married and have kids, but then that didn't work out either, and then I started selling houses and…"

"Is being a realtor so bad?" Charles asked.

"That's not the point! My life is *meaningless!* I'm invisible—no husband, no kids, no close friends. I'm just… average! I'm not really important to anyone in the world. I don't even have a pet cat! I guess I just saw an opportunity to help someone for once, to make a difference, and suddenly that chance mattered to me more than anything else. Your life, for all its problems, is connected to something greater. You know your ancestry, you have family, your existence matters. You have purpose. I want it too."

"So we're a charity case for you?"

"It's more than that. It sounds awful when you say it like that."

"Charles," Christian said. "Shut up."

"Sorry, Jo," Charles said. "We're grateful, of course we are. Tonight ends an ancient feud, and you may well be the sole survivor. Maybe you can write a book about us some day."

Christian stood. "Hurry."

Joanna had never felt so weary, but she took away Charles's flask and helped him to his feet. He groaned deeply, painfully.

Joanna almost asked if he was sure he was ready to go, if he perhaps wanted to rest a little longer, but stopped herself. She knew this path was his only purpose now.

They resumed their march: Christian, Charles, Joanna. Samuel was no longer visible ahead in the dark, but his path was obvious in the moonlight.

After another hour of walking, they heard sounds ahead. Christian clicked off his lamp and motioned for Joanna to do the same. They huddled in a shallow gorge just outside a low place in the wastes that glowed with camp-fire and commotion; a valley community, nestled between bald desert hills.

"There. Cutter Camp," Christian whispered.

37

The first thing Joanna noticed on their final approach—after the deceptively homey atmosphere provided by the bonfires—was the stink. Fume-laden smoke reeking of rot and refuse was lifted on a hot breeze, rushing out of the camp and up the hillside. Dilapidated human-waste compost canisters were clustered on the far side of the camp, flanked by burning trash middens lining the north and south sides. A small cultivated field was situated near the center, supporting a struggling crop of alfalfa hay and country corn. Wooden pens housed scrawny dairy cows standing in a stratification of moldy dung. The scene was far removed from the bustling settlement Joanna had imagined when she first looked up from the desert toward the camp to see the cozy bonfire flickers rising between the dunes.

The place was not lively. Movement could be seen just inside the flaps of a collection of patchwork tents which faced inward on the east side. A low murmur of whispers rose from all sides; the voices of people who had been told to keep silent under orders, or threat of harm. Joanna could not tell how many residents were in the camp but she could hear an occasional cry, a sharp word, something heavy being dragged through the sand behind the tents.

"Chris? This a trap, isn't it?" she muttered.

Christian didn't answer. He scanned the camp with his preternatural eyes, and Joanna wondered for the first time if he had superior night vision. He had spent many years alone in the cellar. It would make sense for him to be unusually well adjusted to the dark.

"Never actually *seen* it before," Christian whispered. He was fascinated, viewing for the first time this place he had heard stories about for his entire life.

Charles huffed a derisive chuckle. "It's a dump. Me and the boys specced it out about twenty-five years back, and it's about the same now as it was then. It's amazing they're still alive out here—and it actually looks like their numbers have grown. I wonder how Samuel managed that."

"Where did all these people come from?" Joanna whispered.

"Haven't the faintest. Should've just been Sammy, some hired hands, and whoever is left from his side of the family. Couldn't be too many. But it looks as if he's assembled a small army, somehow."

"What do we do now?" Joanna asked.

"Go slow," Christian whispered.

He shuffled over the dune, keeping low to the ground. As he tiptoed toward the edge of the camp with his head up and his eyes wide, darting from tent to tent, Joanna crept behind him. Charles stayed behind to catch his breath on the hillside, leaning back with his great hands folded atop his heaving belly.

A sound from the right—footsteps. Joanna whipped her head around, but whatever approached was coming fast with the light behind it, creating a confusing silhouette. The figure slammed into Christian without slowing, rolling over and over with him through the dirt.

The camp stopped holding its breath. A war cry rose up from one tent, then was echoed in another. The entire population of the camp burst forth, exploding into movement and noise with a single purpose.

Tarps were torn asunder, crates were flipped over, and torches were lit. A horde of people, dressed in rags and armed with sticks, swarmed from the shadows of the camp.

"Children!" Joanna gasped. "Oh my god, they're all *kids!*"

They called out with shouts of excitement and fierce cries, thrusting their crude weapons toward the stars in the sky with the fervor of ancient tribal warriors.

Whoever was wrestling with Christian was pummeling him. Joanna sprinted toward the pair and aimed a kick at the attacker. The enemy cried out and turned belly-up on the hardpan—and Joanna was struck with guilt.

The fighter was just a boy, about eleven years old. His shirt was tattered, with large holes through which Joanna could see crudely drawn tattoos covering the skin of his belly and chest. He looked up at Joanna and snarled like a cornered beast. As he assessed her, his eyes squinted with hatred and rage, but no fear.

"Children! My children! Bury them!" A voice boomed like that of a prophet.

The girls screeched and the boys shouted triumphantly as they charged at Joanna and Christian, striking them with their small fists, hanging onto their clothes, hitting the back of their knees with sticks until they were forced to the ground. The children screamed in victory and leaped onto Joanna's arms and legs and stomach, pinning her in the dirt. Christian and Joanna shoved and fought, but the horde was unlimited; every time one child was shaken off, another appeared in their place. They were outnumbered—but more than that, how could they fight back against such an enemy? A tiny girl squealed with glee and drove her pointy knee into Joanna's thigh.

Under the assault in the flickering light it was impossible to take a count of the children, or even see their faces clearly. All Joanna knew was that some were very young while others were teenagers, and there were dozens of them. As they crowded over her, she noticed some of them appeared strange. One tawny-headed boy had a face which was lopsided, mashed to the left, with one eye too high on his forehead. A girl pinched Joanna's arm with a hand that had only three large fingers, like a little bird's talon. A young lady without legs screamed in Joanna's ear and pulled at her hair.

"*Enough!*" cried the loud voice.

Samuel stepped out from behind the tents, his arms open wide. His shoulders were draped in a shawl knit from colored scraps of fabric, studded with dried desert flowers and crumpled bits of glittering trash. Bottle caps, human finger-bones, and teeth dangled from the edges of the garment, clinking against each other like wind chimes.

The children froze in place, keeping Joanna and Christian pinned under the collective weight of their small bodies. Each issued from their throat a soft wail, moaning in a high singsong tone with either fear or pleasure as Samuel examined their work.

"How do you like my family, Christian?" Samuel smiled. "They are just like you, don't you think? You must love them as much as I do. Beautiful little monsters!"

"So many…" Christian gasped.

"I've been busy creating an army of the unloved, the unwanted. Some of them I sought out in the great world, in the orphanages—the imperfect children of Babylon, you see. The damaged. They would have spent their lives condemned and alone, but I rescued them. I have become their father and their savior!" cried Samuel, throwing his arms up in the light of the bonfire.

"Savior Samuel!" Several of the children cried out, "We love you!"

"Yes. And they who are particularly blessed—those brought into being by my own seed—why, they are directly related to *you,* Christian! How lucky you are to discover your family is even larger than you imagined! *My children!*"

Those who had not cried out before did so now. The entire camp yelled in unison, "Father Samuel! We love you!"

"I know it, my children. And whether you were taken in from ungrateful Babylon—as I brought you out from the soulless cities beyond the desert, the unknowable lands, the great beyond—or fathered by my own magnificent seed, you are all equal and beautiful in mine eyes. And I know you will all serve me, even when my requests are difficult to understand, because I am your light and your shepherd."

The fanatical youth bowed their heads and tightened their grips on Christian and Joanna, remembering fully their devotion to their father.

"My children, my loves," Samuel sighed. "Now. *Tear our enemies to pieces.*"

Christian and Joanna felt their bodies being pulled by scores of small hands. Sharp jolts of pain shot through Joanna's shoulders as her arms started to dislocate. Teeth bit at her neck and legs, tiny feet stamped on her ankles. Five children sat on her chest and stomach, crushing the air from her lungs.

"My sisters!" Samuel's voice boomed as he turned his attention to the tents. "You women who are born of my mother and have been granted the holy wombs! You who designed my beautiful creations that now grace our enemies with their touch! Join me to watch our children in their holy mission!"

Two women stepped from behind the tents and fell to their knees behind Samuel. More women could be seen crouching in the shadows. If they were mothers, they were unwilling ones. Scars marked their faces, and their tattered skirts were crusted with blood. Broken and sobbing, they knelt in the dust in Samuel's shadow.

"Children! Stop now!" Samuel cried. The horde paused in their assault to look up at their leader.

Samuel tilted his head with an attitude of grace and welcoming.

"Relent now, Christian, and join us. We will soon see if your lady here has the same gifts my sisters possess." He turned his attention to Joanna. "Do you want to try your hand at expanding my army of exquisite little beasts, my love? Will you join us, or will you die?"

Joanna couldn't respond; a child, its face indeterminate under layers of mud and filth, had jammed her mouth full of rotten straw.

"Fuck you, Sammy!" Christian yelled, struggling mightily with the pile of limbs weighing him down. But he was loathe to harm them. They were too delicate, too soft…and too much like *him*. They were unique and beautiful, and not to blame for this madness.

"*Samuel!*" Another voice echoed from the darkness beyond the bonfire's glow, as loud as the prophet's and filled with fury.

It was Charles. He stood on a hilltop, looking down into the camp with trembling rage and loathing. The light from the fires made his face glow like a second moon in the sky; anger had twisted his expression into a grimace.

"This was it? This was your great plan? You would sacrifice *children*? You're madder than your mother!"

"Look, my children," Samuel addressed the camp. "Your Uncle Charles. He insults your grandmother, like a coward. Impotent, weak, and at the end of his life, to be sure. I brought him with me tonight, all the way across the desert, as a gift for you. Tonight, you will taste his flesh!"

Charles screamed and descended into the camp like a runaway freight train, his massive legs powering his bulk down the hill, impossibly fast for his size. Drops of sweat sprayed in his wake. His stomach bounded and lurched as he took aim for Samuel and charged directly towards his target.

Samuel looked surprised, but his expression soon turned to amusement. He stepped nimbly aside with a bullfighter's grace while pulling a thin knife from a hilt on his hip. As Charles thundered past without slowing, Samuel stabbed. A bright red slash appeared on Charles's leg, and he howled in pain. His gait began to lurch as blood poured down his leg, soaking his shoe.

Charles slowed and chose a new target, turning his momentum toward the pile of children atop Christian and Joanna. His face contorted with wrath and regret as he struck them, hurling aside the ones who refused to give up their assault.

Christian and Joanna helped each other rise from the sand and stood back-to-back, ready to defend themselves from the army which was already beginning to collect itself. Some children lay on the ground, crying and cradling bent limbs. Unhurt fighters circled with their hands out, reaching to grab and pull and break bones.

Charles turned and ran for Samuel again, and once again Samuel stepped aside with grace, this time carving off Charles's left earlobe. Blood poured to the sand, and the desert sipped it up like wine.

"The desert is eager for your blood, and the fires hunger for your flesh, piggy!" Samuel laughed. "My children will eat pork tonight!"

"Charles! Stop! You can't beat him!" Joanna screamed.

"Won't…let…him…win…" Charles huffed. Each breath he drew in wheezed and whined; his throat was closing, his chest collapsing. He turned toward Samuel one more time.

On Charles's third pass, Samuel plunged the knife into his gut, burying the blade to its hilt. Charles stumbled and dropped to his knees like an ancient circus elephant, shocked and exhausted.

Samuel circled his conquest to face him. "Die, Charles. You are nothing but a pig, and you shame your family. The Cutters won today, do you hear me? I want you to understand that before my children eat your flesh and the desert dogs gnaw your bones."

Charles did not reply. A thin line of drool dripped down his chin and created a dark spot on his shirt. He leaned forward, appearing faint. With his massive hands, he pulled the slender knife from his stomach. A fount of blood followed. He pressed his left hand to the wound as Samuel circled, seeking a view of Charles's face during the moment he died. He leaned in.

Charles lunged forward and planted the knife deep into Samuel's knee. Samuel crumpled to the dirt next to Charles, howling enraged epitaphs.

"Fucking pig! Mother fucking-"

The women from the shadows were upon Samuel the moment he fell. More sisters ran out from the tents, screaming like furies, to beat him with their fists.

"No more! No more Father Samuel!" they cried, as tears of rage and relief streamed down their cheeks.

The children were stunned. They watched, mouths agape, as their family turned on itself and tore itself apart. In their fear and confusion they forgot Christian and Jo-anna and stood stunned, the youngest ones clutching each other tight.

Christian roared. He rushed forward with his hand gripped on Joanna's wrist, charging toward the circle of children at its thinnest point. He slowed his lumbering gallop only to push an older boy to the ground and to dodge a teenage girl who grabbed for his neck. He lunged forward until he broke the line, running clear of the children before letting Joanna go and looping back to bear down on Samuel.

Samuel had pulled his knife from his leg and was slashing wildly at the sisters.

"Bitches! Get off me! I am all you have! I am your savior! Get off me!" he screamed. "Children! To me! To me!"

The child army rushed toward Samuel and the sisters, although whether it was their intention to help the flailing man or the vengeful women was unclear. They clustered around the group and Samuel thrashed indiscriminately with his blade, slicing the cheek of one boy and cutting deep into the arm of a sister. The children screamed in terror and they changed their course, scrambling to escape the madman.

Samuel regained his feet amid the tumult and speared his knife through the eye of one of the sisters. It was his final act. Christian rushed behind Samuel, moved toward him with quick and measured steps, and wrenched the knife from his hand. In a single swift movement, Christian slit Samuel's throat.

"Monster," Christian said.

Samuel raised his arms toward the bleeding children and tried to speak, to issue a desperate command. But his blood pooled in his mouth, and he tumbled to the ground like a sack of old bones. Peace fell over the camp. The children, sensing a monumental shift, suddenly were no longer soldiers but simply children again.

A girl began to sob, gently. A sister took the girl in her arms.

"It's okay, my angel," she said. "Cry, now. Cry out all your tears."

38

"Whatcha doin?"

A little girl with green eyes and a harelip stared at Joanna as she worked.

"What are those holes for?" the girl asked.

"They are for Father Samuel and Uncle Charles, so we can bury them," Joanna answered.

"What for?" the girl asked, tilting her head to peek around Joanna at the graves.

Joanna leaned on her shovel. "What's your name?"

"Carrie." The girl, a brave soldier only three days ago, now felt shy. She looked down at her ragamuffin shoes.

"We bury them so they can be at peace, Carrie. So you don't have to burn them with the trash, like you used to do with your dead. So they aren't eaten by the coyotes. And so that we can honor their bravery, and their humanity, and remember them in the best possible way. Understand?"

The little girl nodded. "I like that. Thank you, Joanna."

Joanna smiled. The work of the last few days had been sad and exhausting, but also fulfilling. It was work worth doing. The children were underfed but still strong; they worked tirelessly under Christian's patient direction, cleaning out the compost systems and raking out the trash middens. The desolate campsite was slowly being scrubbed clean and transformed into a true homestead.

Later in the day, Joanna approached Christian. "Chris, they'll never let you keep these kids out here, you know. Once the police find out what's been going on, they'll shut this place down. Maybe you should just move on, try to get them into foster homes. They need education, health care…"

Christian shook his head, looking sad. "Maybe. Later. For now, they need family. And love."

"That's true," Joanna replied. "For now."

Christian looked over his little flock in the valley with pride: a happy, hardworking family. He loved his cousins already, and they had accepted him without question. Christian looked like them, whereas Samuel had looked down on them. Samuel had been a thorn in an infected wound that Christian had washed clean, and they worshipped him for it.

"Chris, I have to go."

Christian gave Joanna a look of such sorrow she almost took it back.

"My life isn't here, Chris. This desert is still like an alien planet to me. I'll admit it's beautiful sometimes, but it's like Mars out here. Seriously. The valley may be home-sweet-home to you, but I'll never really be comfortable here."

"Stay. Please." Tears filled Christian's eyes like ponds overflowing.

"I wish I could. But I need warm baths, and cell phone reception, and lattés."

Christian smiled, but shook his head. "No. You're tough."

"Yeah, I guess I am, sometimes. Kinda. But I can't live my life out here. I just-"

"Go." Christian stretched his long arms around Joanna and embraced her, holding her tight. Joanna squeezed him hard, feeling no repulsion at his angular limbs, coarse shock of hair, and lumpy frame.

"Go home, Jo. Go with love."

The next morning, Joanna hoisted a pack full of water and scraps of food to her back. The children swarmed around her, calling out her name, touching her with their hands, little fairies granting their blessings. Christian watched, and smiled his crooked smile.

He pointed west and said, "Walk west. Five hours."

Joanna squinted into the sunlight and fixed her sight on a jagged mountain peak which hovered over the distant town.

"Careful." Christian held her hand briefly, squeezing it. "Goodbye, sister."

"I'll see you again, brother. I promise," Joanna replied, kissing his cheek.

She half slid, half climbed down the rocky hillside at the west edge of the camp. When she reached the bottom, she turned and looked up to find a crowd of waving children. The smallest ones pressed close around Christian, clinging to his robe, their upturned faces happy and excited.

Joanna turned her back to the camp and started her journey.

But she wasn't going home. Not yet.

39

"You can't actually hurt me, can you? Not directly."

Joanna knew she was sitting in a cave near the Cutter compound, but she also was aware she was drifting in a void. Her mind was in two places at once—it was fascinating, but her head was pounding. The pain throbbed rhythmically as she confronted the thing she now knew was twisting the natural progression of her life. She had to know why. This time, she had called out to him as she drifted to sleep and he had appeared, just as she thought he would.

The Demon circled her, seething.

"You are somewhere else. Not in the real world," Joanna said.

"Nonsense. All worlds are real."

Joanna pressed on. "You have to reach people in my world through their dreams, have to manipulate them by working on their subconscious. You can't be here physically."

"Fool."

"You messed up the whole Hench family, destroyed their lives just to set a trap for me."

"Trivial."

"Why do you look like that? Like…like a bad Halloween costume?"

"Does it frighten you?"

The Demon swiped at her with a massive claw, but it entered and exited her body like vapor.

"Why me? What's so special about me that you desperately want me dead?"

"Nothing," the Demon hissed. "You are meaningless. Insignificant. Empty. Useless, pointless, and hollow."

Tears rose in Joanna's eyes. It wasn't the answer she expected.

"Stop it. Stop saying that."

"Inane. Absurd." The Demon grinned.

"N…no…"

"*Worthless.*"

Part 2

THE RED ROAD TO VEGAS

Marie regarded her sandaled feet, wiggling her toes. Her shoes would never last—they were exactly the wrong kind of footwear for a long walk.

Her right arm and ear burned. To the west, the sun boiled toward the horizon over distant Los Angeles, Hollywood, and cool blue expanse of the Pacific Ocean. California: the birthplace of dreams and wealth and glamor, if you believe the magazines. She closed her eyes and felt California—the whole *idea* of it—gently tug at her; its celebrities, palm trees, hints of salt spray on the coastal breeze. But the same visions which attracted her also frightened her. Marie wasn't a glamor girl. What would she do with herself around such luxuries? Her hair was brown and straight, her eyes were brown and dull. Boring, boring. And, of course, her teeth…

Oh god, what would they think of her teeth?

To the east, Las Vegas. It held her left hand in a gentle grip, smiling, coaxing her with fantasies of wealth and dubious fortune. It was another citadel of glitz and lights and artistic passion like Los Angeles, but perhaps more forgiving. It was a newer town, and in the last few years it was really coming into its own. The glittering city was a bastion of humanity in an unforgiving desert, rebellious and unapologetic; a tempting enough scandal, even for 1959. Marie had heard rumors they built a new hotel every day. Las Vegas was almost exactly one hundred miles away, but the stories she had heard made it feel so much closer; the thrill of the stage, the music, the show. High rollers and lowlifes—but where could she fit in?

In either direction, the road was red; almost the color of brick, but just a little brighter.

Which way should she go?

A crow circled overhead, cocking its eye at her, examining her for signs of exhaustion. Marie was tired, but she wasn't dinner for the vultures just yet. Her family home was to her back, and she planned to leave it there. She was far enough from the compound that her father's shouts and her mother's bawling were no longer audible. The decision was hers now; she was eighteen, a fully grown woman. It was time for her to take the first step toward her new life.

Marie looked to the west. She couldn't see California, of course, blocked as it was by the hills which surrounded Zzyzx Valley. But she could sense it there, beckoning her with glitter and magic, promising so much. She recognized the deception.

Las Vegas was a trap, too, but at least that city was more honest about it.

She waved at the sun, having made her decision, and turned her face to the east.

2

Within two hours, Marie was walking in twilight. The breeze cooled her skin as the sun dipped behind the jagged desert hills that had always reminded her of her own broken teeth. In a few minutes, she would be walking in the dark. Her departure from home had happened so quickly she had not thought to bring food or a flashlight. She at least had the presence of mind to bring a backpack containing a jug of water and her life savings—forty-seven dollars and twenty-two cents.

Marie plodded along the side of the highway with her arm jutting out directly to her side, her thumb stuck up. She wasn't naive; she knew hitchhiking as a lone woman was a terrible risk. But her sandal straps had begun to fray, and the hot pavement was melting the tread from her soles. She could not continue on foot day after day; finding help would be necessary, and she must take her chances. Most of the people along Highway 15 were families on vacation anyway, not the type to take advantage of a young girl traveling alone. Cars sped past with the tops down, blasting jazz and rock-and-roll. A noisy blast of air smacked Marie in the back each time they went by, parting the hair at her neck with an increasingly cold chill.

She was only three miles from Baker when her first ride slowed and pulled over. Marie jogged to the car, wincing at her sore feet and back as her pack scraped against her sunburn.

"Las Vegas?" she asked the driver. He was an older gentleman, driving with his windows rolled down. Remnants of grey hair like Brillo pads were stuck behind his ears, wildly fluffed out by the intense winds of the highway.

"Nawp, just s'far as Baker, darling. But I'll take you there if you like."

"I'm thankful, sir," Marie replied, settling into a leather car seat. Her swollen feet hurt even worse once she was off them; they throbbed in time with her heart beat.

Jackrabbits dashed from the sides of the road as the car sped along the highway. One skidded to a halt atop a boulder and looked back at the car with a big round eye, much like the crow which had examined her on the highway.

"I'm Pete. I'm a chef—well, a glorified burger flipper, really. Work at the Bun Boy. It ain't prestigious, but I been there twelve years already, and Baker's a pretty cheap place to live, so it suits me fine. So now you know all there is to know about me. What's your name, girl?"

"Marie. I'm from Zzyzx Town."

"Oh *really*, now?" Pete's head whipped back and forth between the road and Marie. She kept her face forward, not sure what to expect; what had people heard?

"Yes," she said.

"That fancy health resort with the hot springs? Well, isn't that a hoot! I didn't know anyone lived out there full-time. Although I suppose someone would have to, to take care of the whole place. The owner your pappy or something? I met him, once. Last name of Sterling? Springer?"

"Starling." Marie didn't want to talk about her father. "What's Bun Boy?"

Pete frowned, and Marie knew she'd already made a mistake.

"What you mean, 'what's Bun Boy?' You know, the restaurant. Hamburgers, french fries. How is it you live as close as Zzyzx but you've never been to the Boy?"

Marie shrugged. She wasn't sure how much information she should be sharing with this stranger. She was eighteen, and an adult, sure. But she was also a girl. Would her father come looking for her? Maybe, if he was angry enough. And some well-meaning people would surely hand her over if he did. Baker was too close to home.

"Oh, yeah," she said, feigning recognition. "I just forgot. I've been there plenty of times."

"Of course you have," Pete beamed. "If you'd like, I bet I can sneak some french fries out the back door for you. Soon as I start my shift."

"Thanks," Marie said. She fell silent, watching the sinking sun's reflection bounce and jiggle in the side mirror.

"Here's our exit," Pete said, steering the car towards Route 127, Death Valley Road.

3

Thirty minutes later, Marie was seated on a greasy towel by the back door of the Bun Boy, savoring her first-ever french fry.

It burnt her fingertips until she cooled it with her breath and popped it into her mouth. The salt burned a tiny cut inside her cheek she didn't even know she had, and her eyes watered at the tastes and textures of crisped potato and lard. Pain and ecstasy all at once. Father had never allowed foods with unnatural quantities of salt or fat. The pictures of french fries she had seen in magazine ads had never looked especially appealing to her; she realized now those ads only work on people who know what they're missing.

She ate half the fries, then pressed the paper clamshell box shut to keep the rest for later. The grease and salt was incredible, overwhelming, and filling—far more so than the simple breads and jams her mother made. After she placed the box in the bottom of her pack, she turned her face to the main street. She needed a place to spend the night.

Again, east or west?

The sun was down now, and the street lights had flickered on. The Bun Boy had a matching motel right next door, aptly titled Bun Boy Motel. It looked abandoned, but she could see people moving around behind the tattered curtains in the rooms.

Down the street a brilliant sign read "Royal Hawaiian Motel" in lights as bright as she imagined the Las Vegas Strip would boast. The main building was lined with bowing palm trees, and featured a beautifully sloped roof like an island cabana. Festive paintings of flamingos and coconut drinks decorated the walls near the parking lot. It was lovely, but clearly out of her price range.

Marie walked down the street to the east, away from the Royal Hawaiian. A dark corner would have to do. She had brought the greasy towel Pete sat her on behind the restaurant, hoping he wouldn't mind. She was sleeping rough tonight, and would need all the padding she could find.

Several buildings down the main road were abandoned, each one dark and ominous. Spiders infested them all, no doubt, but she could handle spiders. A greater concern was rats, which could be dangerous in large numbers when hungry. Could be snakes, too. She knew what a bad bite could do to a body. But no matter what happened now, she couldn't return home. Nothing would be worse than that, not even dying alone in one of these derelict, stinking buildings.

She picked the one which looked most recently abandoned; a medical care center for mothers and children. Perhaps the building would attract less vermin, having previously been neither an eatery nor a motel. The ground-floor windows were broken, and Marie found it simple enough to step through a large window frame near the front door. She tip-toed through the lobby, feeling broken glass crunch under her thin sandals, and found a small room which still had an examination table inside. No one would find her here; the private exam rooms had no windows. When she closed the door, the room was shut up tight.

As she stretched out on the examination table, Marie tugged Pete's greasy towel up to her shoulders and exhaled long and deep, trying to calm her thoughts. What would she do tomorrow? And would father show up?

The events of the day had been shocking, but not entirely unforeseen. Marie had been laying money by for two years, waiting for an opportunity to come along which would allow her to gracefully leave her father's compound.

That opportunity had never arrived; she had ended up simply using a raging argument between her parents as an excuse to make her exit. Her hopes had always been that a man—a dark stranger, preferably, both handsome and kind—would arrive at the health spa in search of her father's snake oil cure-alls. He would find her instead, fall madly in love with her, and whisk her out of the desert. But most of her father's customers were dumpy middle-aged women, looking for miracle solutions to sagging flesh and papery skin. They couldn't help her any more than her father could help them.

So, she had made her own opportunity. Her parents' argument had been trite, certainly less substantial in subject matter than their past fights. It wasn't about money, or the resort, but about coffee. Her mother had drank the last of it, and her father was upset. A simple thing that spun out of control like so many other disagreements in their household. No one was beaten bloody like previous events; no broken bones or teeth this time. Still, the fight had taken a cruel turn, and Marie's mother was left sobbing and confused, as usual.

There were so many other things they could fight about which were more important. Father was an unabashed con man, and his fake remedies often took the place of real treatments which many of his customers no longer sought after consulting him. Marie felt sure some people must have died as a result of the false hope her father offered. Mother was weak and selfish, insensitive to the pain of others, while thinking herself a tortured soul. On top of everything else, she had ignored what Father did to Marie, which made her as bad as him.

Marie hated them both.

Mother, and her crocodile tears. Father, and his medical interests. Marie ran her tongue over her shattered teeth. The two in front were most intact, with only a bottom corner missing from the left tooth. Her canines were dull but solid. Further back in her mouth she felt points and valleys like shattered stained-glass windows, sharp enough to cut into her cheeks when she ate if she wasn't careful. Several molars were missing entirely, for which she was grateful. The gaps didn't hurt any more, healed up for years now. Marie wondered what her father had done with those missing teeth. Were they in a jar somewhere?

She was so tired, and turning the day's events over and over in her head would never bring sleep. Frustrated with herself, she flipped onto her left side and yanked the greasy towel up to her ears. Deep breaths, clear mind. She thought of the remaining french fries in her pack and her stomach rumbled—but no, those were for tomorrow. Think of something else.

Her imagination drew a picture of an open green field. Butterflies, a flurry of orange and yellow, bobbed in the shade of a huge oak tree in which a grumpy owl snored. A soft breeze kept the summer sun from scorching the swaying grasses. White clouds passed overhead, creating moments of shade during which ladybugs buzzed skyward to introduce themselves to the butterflies. In the distance, the horizon was covered in a thin veil of purple mist.

Marie slept.

4

Pete felt good about helping out the girl. Foolish of her to travel alone, of course, but she didn't seem to be afraid of anything in the world. And she stared at everything so odd, like she'd never seen neon signs or mailboxes or any of the other regular things you see on a city street. When he offered her french fries she thought hard for a minute before nodding. What kind of teenager hesitated so long before accepting french fries?

When he stepped out the back door to check on the girl during his break, she was gone—along with his best rag, which he'd given her to sit on. Oh, well. He had bigger problems.

Anna was being a real pain in the ass tonight. She was fifteen years his junior, yet she was his boss since her daddy owned the place. She was an okay worker when she wasn't too hungover, and Pete didn't mind her much. But tonight she was antsy, and snapping like a firecracker at Bud, the other chef—and it wasn't just her.

Everyone was on edge. The coffee bar was filled with solo eaters, twitching inside their coats like there were fleas on their skin. Without knowing why, they sought refuge and company tonight. They had left their homes to wander into the light and drink from their cups as a community. Something was in the air; everyone could feel it. It was like when the Santa Ana winds kick up, bringing with them the tiny zaps of static electricity that surprise you every time you get shocked by a door handle, no matter how many times it happens.

It was hot tonight, but not too hot. It was dark, but there was a moon, and it wasn't full, either. Something else was going on. Maybe there was going to be an earthquake.

"Order up!" Bud shouted, his voice unusually shrill. "I said, order is the fuck *up!*"

"I heard you the first time, jackass!" Anna hissed.

"Then why didn't you *get* it the first time?" Bud snapped.

"Easy, partner," Pete said. "You okay?"

"I don't know, Pete. I just don't feel right tonight. I think maybe I'm coming down with some kinda bug. The flu, maybe."

"It's not just you. I don't feel good either. Can't quite put my finger on it."

"You think…maybe it's those test sites? You know the ones. The nuclear stuff they do out in the desert. I heard they zap those ions or whatever and if it gets airborne, it can mess you up just by floating in on a breeze. That's what happened in Japan, remember? I wonder about that a lot."

"I don't know, Bud," said Pete. "But if it was that, I think we'd all be a lot sicker by now."

"Maybe, maybe."

Pete's skin twitched like bees were scuttling up his arms looking for a place to sting. Goose-pimples popped on his shoulders and raced down his back, making him feel hot and cold at the same time.

Something was happening.

The lights in the Bun Boy flickered off, then on again. The fluorescents emitted a buzz and a hum, straining at the intermittent electricity. Then the lights clicked off for good.

The whole town was out. Under the light of a half moon, the population stumbled into the street from bars and late-night diners, muttering with unease. Power outages were not uncommon in Baker; the system was old, cheap, and sun-cooked. It often overheated in the peak of summer, and every outage seemed to weaken the grid further in a cycle of decay. Repair and replacement would require funds the poor little town had no hope of procuring.

"All right, everyone go home. Bun Boy's closed until tomorrow," Anna called out.

"No shit," a man grumbled, eliciting snickers from some of the other patrons.

Most of the crowd shuffled toward their homes, walking slowly in the pale light. A few walked in pairs, but most were out alone tonight. The refuge they sought from their unease had been disrupted, and tempers ran hot. Two fistfights erupted among the bar patrons within minutes of the power loss. Anna quickly shut herself and the crew inside the restaurant.

Then the air became heavy.

The atmosphere was like a bag of water lowered onto the shoulders of the town. The weight was from something invisible, unknowable. It was accompanied by a low twang, felt as much as heard, thrumming like a powerful electrical current. It hurt not the ears but the bones, a deep hard bruising. Several people fell to their knees, groaning. Some died immediately.

A female tourist in a flowered dress shuffled down the street, crying *What? What?* while yanking her husband along behind with her hand locked on his wrist. Blood trickled from his ears, disappearing in the collar of his red western shirt.

An elderly man lay on the sidewalk with his legs bent. His bones were cracking, splintering under the pressure of the sky. From his mouth fell his teeth, one by one, as the pressure broke them from their moorings.

Inside the Bun Boy, Pete could feel the weight but was able to move around enough to dash toward the back door of the restaurant. It was better in the back rooms. He could still hear that twanging sound, and the air was hard to breathe. If the back rooms were better, he thought maybe the walk-in freezer would protect him entirely.

The freezer was lined with thick metal sheeting and was as dark as the devil's asshole. Pete rammed his shin on a beer keg and hopped, hissing and cursing, until he stumbled over a side of beef that sent him tumbling to the floor. He checked his pockets for matches but found none. Waving his arms in the dark, he found a crate of beer and sat on it, blocking the door. In the dark he hid, shuddering from cold and shock.

Someone pounded their fists, screaming.

"I saw you run in there, Pete! Let me in!"

Pete pulled the beer crate aside.

Anna slipped through the door and spun around to grasp the handle and slam it shut. In the brief moment of light from the dining room, Pete saw her cheeks were streaked with black mascara tears.

"What the hell is going on out there?" Pete asked.

"I have no idea. But those who aren't being crushed somehow are suffocating now. I tried to help...I couldn't..." Anna slumped to the floor, wiping tears from her face before they could crystallize in the cold.

Anna's whispers were loud in the dark. "You think it's those nukes they got in the desert? That's what Bud was talking about earlier. The whole night felt strange, you know. It's like we all knew. Something was in the air..."

"I know. I felt it too. But my brother said they stopped testing years ago."

"I just don't know, Pete. Maybe...maybe it was Japan."

They fell silent, imagining what was happening outside. Pete's chest ached with guilt, knowing people were dying while he cowered in a freezer. But he couldn't save them, could he? Certainly if someone knocked, he would let them in. Definitely...

No one else knocked. An hour passed, then two.

"I'm getting too cold, Pete. Like I'm going to faint. I have to get out."

"Fuck," Pete sighed. "I know, me too. Let's do it."

"God, I'm so scared," Anna said.

"Me too. But you stay here a minute, let me take a look."

Pete pushed the door open.

The lights were still out in the diner. When Pete stepped out of the freezer he felt the atmosphere press on him again, but it was less heavy than it was earlier.

"I think it's letting up."

"Okay."

Anna stepped out of the freezer, rubbing her arms with her hands. She walked up close to the glass windows overlooking the street and gasped, covering her mouth with her hands.

Bodies were crumpled on the street and sidewalks. They lay like dropped piles of laundry in every direction. Some held each other tight, either hugging or fighting in their final moments. Blood pooled under the corpses, soaking into the pavement.

One man had sat down on a planter next to a hedge, then fallen back into it; his brown loafers were visible, sticking out of the hedge. The street sign for the liquor store across the street had disappeared under the frame of a Chrysler that had smashed into it and become hung up on the pedestal. Its engine was still running, but with a lopsided rattle—it sounded sickly. Small black lumps littered the grass and picnic areas; birds, fallen from the sky, all dead or dying.

"Oh my god," Pete whispered, sinking into a vinyl bench seat. "What have they done?"

5

Marie woke up with a dry mouth and aching hips. She had been sleeping with her jaw hanging open, the slumber of the exhausted. She'd probably been snoring, too. Good thing her father hadn't been around for that, he would have mocked her relentlessly.

She'd been dreaming, too. Someone had been talking to her in the darkness. Had been offering her something she didn't trust, a dangerous exchange. He said she was the closest one to—something. The end of the line. She was to be the first one at the last stop before Voidsville.

And if she wanted, she could take advantage of his one-time offer to end the world. All she had to do was make sure the train reached its destination. Then she turned around to look at the speaker, and noticed his horns—massive, thick and oily. Her dream-screams woke her up, rasping quietly in the examination room.

A terrifying nightmare, and nonsensical to boot. She thought it was probably about her father. He had always loved talking about the devil and his sinful temptations; it was one of his favorite topics.

Marie rolled off the examination table and landed with her feet atop her sandals to avoid touching the filthy floor. As she shuffled her feet into the straps and pulled on her pack in the dark, she wondered what time it was. The room had become stuffy overnight, and she had a moment of claustrophobia; it was high time to leave this nasty little cave.

As she entered the lobby she could see the sun was up, but it looked more like evening than dawn. The light was colored all wrong—the solemn hues of dusk, not the optimistic yellow of a new day. Marie wondered if she had slept through the entire night and all day, too.

As she exited the building through the broken window, she stopped short. Five feet in front of her lay a body. Had it been there last night? It was right in the path she had walked, but she didn't remember tripping over anything in the dark.

Perhaps he was drunk. Marie had never tried alcohol before, but her mother had told her of its evils—how it could make you sleep deeper than you should.

"Sir? Or ma'am? Can you hear me?" Marie called out.

The figure did not move.

Marie moved closer. The man's eyes were crusted open in a distant stare, and a wet trail of bloody spit traced the edges of the mouth, leaking out of the corner. Dead, then, and recently.

What should she do? If she reported the body to the police, they would start asking questions. Marie couldn't afford to linger here; she had no doubt her father would make at least a cursory effort at finding her, and Baker was only seven miles from Zzyzx Town. She had to move on immediately.

"Sorry, mister," Marie said. "You're just going to have to wait for someone else to find you."

She made her way toward the street, and found another body laying out in the open, right on the sidewalk. This one was twisted, her mouth open in a scream—she had died hard. Her eyes had flown open, long black eyelashes starkly visible against white, drained lids. A tongue that was just beginning to turn leathery sagged out of her mouth. The body's bones looked slightly warped, as if someone had gently stepped on them, pressing with the ball of their foot until they were splintered just enough to be unusable.

She counted six more bodies in her vicinity. They didn't look real; it had to be a prank, prop corpses for some sick practical joke. But no one jumped from behind a building crying out "Surprise!" The town was silent; no people, no power, no animals. It was as if everyone had played a game of "Ring a Ring o' Roses" and all fallen down, but forgotten to get up again.

The air was heavier than usual, like it sometimes felt in the heat of midday. It wasn't unbearable, but it was all wrong for the time. The sun was a half-inch off the eastern horizon; about 5 o'clock, or so.

"Marie!"

The shock of hearing her own name called out among the carnage startled her badly. The voice was shouting, but muted; it rang from behind a thick pane of glass. Pete was pressed up to the windows of the Bun Boy across the street, staring at her wide-eyed through the glass.

Marie waved, a weirdly normal gesture for a girl surrounded by bodies. But what else was there to do? She walked toward the restaurant, weaving a path between the woman on the sidewalk, a teenage boy in the middle of the street, and three little piles of dead sparrow. Pete danced toward the door and held it open for her, beckoning.

"Marie! You're alive! How did you…uh…" Pete paused.

"I don't know, because I don't know what happened. Why are all those people dead?"

"My god, Marie. Your teeth! What happened to your *teeth?*" Pete said.

Shame roiled Marie's stomach. "They were like that last night. They've been like this for years. You just didn't notice in the dark."

Pete looked unsatisfied, but let it go. "If you say so, honey."

"So? What happened?" Marie asked.

"We don't know," Anna said. "We hid in the freezer when it happened."

"When *what* happened?"

"It was like…the sky suddenly was heavy. No, more like the air pressure went up. A lot. I don't know how else to describe it," Pete said.

"But it's over now," Anna said with a feeble shrug. "I guess."

"So did this happen everywhere, or just here?" Marie asked.

The real question was, did her father die too? The idea filled her with panicky, guilty excitement.

"No idea. Power went out right before it all started. No radio, no television."

"So what do we do now?" Marie asked.

A small pile of dark clothing in the street caught Marie's eye. No, not clothing; it was a huge black crow. One wing jutted up into the sky, fractured in the middle. The animals had died, but there must be others alive somewhere; animals in caves, maybe. And other humans who had sought refuge in enclosed rooms, just like Marie had.

"We have to find more people. Maybe someone knows what's going on," Marie said.

"We should head to the resort! Out to Zzyzx! Maybe your papa pulled through," Pete said.

Marie's shoulders stiffened. "I just left there, I'm not going back."

"You're runnin' away from home? I kinda wondered about that when I picked you up. Didn't want to ask, though."

"It's not running away when you're eighteen. I can do what I want. And I'm not going back there," Marie said.

"Alright. Well, the next decent town to the east is Nipton. I'll drive us there," Pete said.

"I got a sister in Nipton," Anna said. "At least, I…"

"I'm sure she's fine, honey," Pete said.

Anna's face wrenched with realization. "So many people dead. And for what? We don't even know…"

"Oh hon, come here," Pete said, wrapping his arm around Anna's shoulders. She sobbed, drenching his shoulder with tears and snot.

Marie stepped outside.

The street was silent. No birds chirped, no locusts sang. A gentle, hot breeze quivered the trees. In the distance, Marie's ear caught a low twanging sound, a deep reverberation as if the earth were an instrument that had been strummed and had not yet stopped moving. Marie looked up to the sky and listened. Did the twang grow a tiny bit louder? The change in volume was gradual enough that she could not be sure.

"Pete!" Marie called out. Her voice echoed a single time among the buildings in the stillness.

He stepped through the doorway, leaving Anna weeping softly in a plastic diner booth.

"Do you hear the noise? In the distance, like a hum," Marie said.

Pete's face became distant as he focused on the sound. "Yeah, I do. It's like…a vibration, almost."

"Keep listening."

As they stood quietly, Marie saw a squirrel dash across the street at the intersection. So, some creatures had survived, then. Just like she thought. The ones who had been able to burrow had survived.

Pete's head shot up and he fixed his gaze on Marie's face, but he wasn't looking at her. He was looking through her, focusing on the distant sound.

"Oh my god. It's getting louder. It's coming back. The…the earthquake thing. Airquake. There's going to be another one."

"I think so too," Marie agreed.

"Get to the car. We can't survive in a freezer. Maybe we can find a town with something like an army bunker, or a bank vault."

"And people. We're still alive, so there must be other people alive somewhere," Marie said. "I hope."

6

Marie sat shotgun. Anna stretched out in the back seat of Pete's car, sniffling and wiping her nose with a soggy tissue. They had stuffed the trunk with water jugs, hamburger buns, and crackers—everything else in the restaurant would have required cooking or refrigeration.

"Ready?" Pete asked. Without waiting for a reply, he turned the key in the ignition. "Let's burn rubber!"

Nothing happened.

"Shit," Pete said. "Sorry, hon. Guess the starter's out."

"I have a car," Anna said. "It's out back."

"It's not the starter," Marie said. "It's the airquake. I think everything that's electric or any kind of machine is messed up. The vibration, you know? The buildings all look like they're leaning, too. I think it kind of knocked the whole world out of alignment."

"But we have to get out of here!" Pete said. "The sound is getting louder. We have to find better shelter."

"We'll have to use the freezer again, this time," Anna said. "Or Marie's examination room at the urgent care. How long do you think we have until the next shock?"

Pete cocked his head, listening. "I don't remember exactly how loud the first one was—had my mind on other things—but I think it's getting close. An hour, maybe less. That's just enough time to get to Nipton, if we had a car. Damn it!"

"Okay. The freezer is probably too dangerous," Marie said. "We could get stuck in there and suffocate if the door gets jammed. Let's use the exam room. Bring some lights with us if we can. Not matches, they use too much oxygen. I wonder if flashlights still work?" Marie said.

"Got one in the trunk. Let's find out," Pete said.

Half an hour later, they were crammed into Marie's makeshift bedroom from the night before. Pete's flashlight worked, but it was dimmed, as if its energy had been drained. By the time they took shelter, the twang was loud enough to be heard without concentrating on it; it permeated the air, caused the sand to dance on the desert floor and the windows to rattle in their frames. Anna was terrified. Her skin was the color of fresh paper, and her eyes were wide and red.

Marie wasn't frightened. It was a wonder. She felt unease, confusion, and worry. But not fear. Her father must have already pulled most of the fear out of her over the years. Nothing could terrify her more than the sound of his approaching footsteps. Marie felt calm, among friends, and sheltered. No problem.

At least her father had done that small favor for her. It may not have been his intention, but he had taught her how to be brave. May he rot in hell.

As the airquake neared, the thrumming could be felt inside the examination room to the point of discomfort. The wall Marie leaned against began to vibrate so hard it hurt her back, so she tilted forward and rested with her elbows on her knees.

"This place is shaking apart," Pete said. Cracks had begun to form where the walls met the ceiling, and hairline fractures crept down the walls. Wooden rafters in the ceiling creaked and popped under the strain.

"Hope it holds. Didn't even wake me up last night," Marie said.

"This one feels stronger," Anna said.

The flashlight flickered out.

In the darkness, Pete felt panic begin to rise in his chest. He breathed deep, focusing on his lungs. In, out. A foam ceiling tile broke and struck the nape of his neck as he hunched forward.

"What was that? Everything okay?" Marie asked.

"Fine," Pete gasped. In, out. Breathe.

And then it was over. The walls stilled, the air relaxed. The rattling and creaking subsided in weakening bursts.

"We should get out of here. This structure might not be safe any more," Pete said.

When they opened the examination room door, more ceiling tiles fell to the floor. Pete swept a pile of them aside when he pushed the door open. The door squealed on its hinges as loud as a cat, and scraped against its frame.

"Hear that? Building's not square any more," Pete said.

"What's that mean?" Anna asked.

"Out of square; crooked. Probably going to fall down. We need to get out right away."

7

Jeff sat in the corner on the floor of the safe room, taking short nips at his ARMY labeled water bottle.

"Come out here and help me," Dr. Andersen called.

"With what?"

"I'm taking measurements. Just jot down some numbers for me, will you?"

The safe room had withstood the vibrations better than the rest of the building. The entire USGS campus was cracked and rattled from the event which was not an earthquake.

"Why are you bothering with that? It wasn't a quake, it's not our department. Earthquakes don't crush people with thin air."

"I'm a scientist, and so are you. It's our job to at least try to discover the truth. Come into the lab."

"I'm an *intern,* and I haven't even graduated yet. I guess I never will, now that the world's gonna end," Jeff said.

"Just shut up and help me. What else do you have to do, other than cower in that government-issued mouse-trap?"

The computer was dead. Its green light was blinking, but the mainframe was skewed out of alignment as if stepped on by Godzilla. Jeff scribbled notes and numbers onto a messy stack of grid paper attached to his clipboard.

"I'm getting readings from the ground. Not exactly earthquakes, but it's still some kind of seismic activity. It's more like a reverberation. Like the plucked string of a guitar."

"You mean it's still going on?"

Dr. Andersen frowned at the seismometer. "It is. But it's not shaking. It's like…harmonics."

The seismometer cracked with a loud plink. Stress fractures appeared in its metal casing as the device rattled itself apart.

"What in the *Sam Hill?*" Dr. Andersen shouted.

"Doc! Come on! Get back in the safe room!" Jeff yelled. The reverberations were growing louder. Jeff's ears were buzzing, like they did after he saw Elvis Presley in concert last year. He had spent the next two days nursing both a hangover and some permanent ear damage.

Dr. Andersen lunged for the safe room door, but the knob wouldn't turn. "Did you lock it?"

"No! I just closed the door!"

"It's jammed! Like it's wedged shut!"

The building warped and swayed in the massive sound. Its walls leaned and tilted and cracked. The safe room door cracked neatly down the center.

As Jeff died in a tumble of fracturing bones, the sound filled his whole mind; the harmonic thumping, rattling his brain, streaming blood from his ears and nose and tear ducts. It was the loudest thing he could imagine. Louder even than the screaming girls had been when the King took the stage.

8

The town of Baker was worse for wear. The Royal Hawaiian sign had collapsed, sending shards of shattered plastic into the street. The Bun Boy Motel had withstood the shaking a little better—or perhaps it was just harder to see the damage amid its preexisting dilapidation.

Several windows had busted out of the Bun Boy's storefront. The liquor store across the street was seeping liquid through the front door; Pete could only imagine what it looked like inside, all those glass bottles.

"Okay, we got to move on right away. I'm open to ideas, if anyone has any. The freezer in the Boy is still intact, but Marie's right—I'm terrified about the possibility of us suffocating in there. Using it for shelter should be considered a last resort."

"We have to get to a bigger city," Anna said. "Maybe find some other people. But we can't just wander down the highway or we'll get caught outside in the next quake. I can still hear that sound. It's going to keep coming back, isn't it?"

"I have an idea about that," Marie said. "Was it just about twelve hours between airquakes? Maybe *exactly* twelve?"

"Sounds like a natural phenomenon. Maybe a space thing. That's kind of comforting," Pete said.

"Not really," Marie said. "It's a lot easier to deal with people than with the planets. If it was being caused by another country or something, like a new weapon in the Cold War, then negotiation would be an option. But if this is some kind of cosmic change…"

"Then we're fucked," Pete said. "You're right."

"It's like an echo bouncing between buildings. Except the second airquake was stronger than the first. But I bet they won't all be the same. The sound seems quieter now. The next one might not be as bad. Maybe."

"And it might be huge! Shake the whole planet down!" Anna said. "Who cares what's causing it? We have to find a way to leave here now or we'll die just like everyone else!"

"Keep calm!" Marie snapped. "We're working on it, Anna. I know you're scared, but we have to keep our heads."

"No, actually she's right," Pete said. "We can debate the cause later. The clock is ticking, yeah? So we need to come up with a plan."

Marie looked up and down the main street. They were in the middle of the desert, in a town that was being gradually shaken to death. They couldn't stay, but if they left they would be without shelter. And without shelter they would die in the desert, in puddles of their own blood and broken bones. So, they needed shelter they could take with them. Like camping.

"A tent! A metal tent, though. Like…a dome," Marie said.

"A what?"

"We need a tent without windows, made out of metal. We'd have to drag it along with us, but I think we could do it."

"And where the hell would we get something like that?" Pete said.

Marie considered. "Can you weld?"

9

Anna was the one who found the Volkswagen Beetle on the outskirts of town. It was banana yellow, and mostly rust-free. Pete gutted it, using a blowtorch to sever it from its working parts. He tore out the seats, valves, brakes, and steering column. After severing the engine from its moorings and detaching the undercarriage, they lifted the shell away from its guts and tipped it onto its side in the desert sand. Pete rolled the chassis into place and reattached it to the top. When he was done, there was nothing left but the body, floor, and wheels; a hollowed-out bug shell.

"It's coming back. The airquake; it's getting close. There's going to be another within the hour. Not as big as the last one, I think," Marie said.

"All right." Pete nodded, wiping his hands on his pants. "I'm not done yet, so we'll have to use the freezer. We'll just have to hope it holds together one last time."

It did, but the metal walls warped and creaked. Rivets popped from the edges where the panels connected, and near the end of the shaking one of them broke loose. It would not survive more than one more quake.

As soon as the vibrations ebbed, Pete went to work cutting rounded metal panels to weld into the window frames of the car. He attached strips of metal over every crack and hole, finishing each joining with caulk. When he was done, he had a hollow, rolling cabin with sealed metal windows; a portable shelter. It wasn't pretty looking—Pete was a cook, not a handyman—but he did a thorough job.

"How will we move it?" Anna asked.

"It's got wheels. We have to pull it. Let's look around for some chains," Marie said. "Is there a hardware store in Baker?"

"Are you serious? How far do you want to go? That thing must weigh a ton, even without the engine and stuff!" Anna said.

Pete sighed and arched his back, which popped loudly.

"Far as we have to," he said.

Marie had brought a bottle of root beer from the Bun Boy. She gripped it by its neck, and grinned at Pete.

With a theatrical swing, she smashed the bottle on the fender. "I christen thee '*Shell On Wheels!*'"

Pete laughed. "That's a damn stupid name, girl!"

"Yeah, well, too bad. It can't be changed now, it's

permanent. I already broke the root beer," Marie said.

"Here." Anna approached with a bottle of green nail polish. "I think I remember how to write in script." She painted the name on the driver side door in swooping cursive. "Now it's official."

"Pete, be honest with me and don't spare my feelings," Marie said. "Is this crazy? Do you really think this is going to work?"

Pete stretched again, looking toward the horizon. Twenty-five years ago, he had left his parent's Texas home to move to Las Vegas. His head had been frontloaded with stupidity and confidence, a result of being an absolute killer in the small local card games. He was going to be a big man, make his fortune at the tables, live off of gambling full-time. It never occurred to Pete that not everyone in Las Vegas would play fair. He ended up broke as a joke, but he landed on his feet—in Baker, not Las Vegas. The closest he ever got to wealth and glamour was a peek in the windows of celebrity limousines when they stopped over for gasoline.

He gave their chances at surviving the next day equal odds; considerably better than his chances had been at making it big in Las Vegas as a wet-behind-the-ears, twenty-two year old drifter who didn't know better than to take loans from sharks. It was time to set out again. He survived last time, he'd survive again. Probably.

"I think so, Marie. But there's only one way to find out," Pete said. "Next airquake should be in about six hours. We'll have to test it. I'll sit in the Shell, you two take the freezer just in case it doesn't hold."

"No, I want to do the test. You and Anna take the freezer," Marie said.

"Hell no, girl! This is my handiwork, I'm doing the test run."

"It was my idea, Pete. Also…just, please. Let me do

this. Don't argue. Please," Marie begged.

Pete frowned. "Why, though?"

"Don't worry about it. Look, I'm not scared, ok? It's going to be fine, I just know it."

"Yeah, I noticed that," Pete muttered. "All right. But if it gets bad, you try to run in, join us in the freezer, okay? We'll pull the Shell right up to the back door of the Boy, get it as close as possible."

"Sure," Marie said. "I promise."

10

Marie sat in the Shell, swaddled in an old blanket. She wasn't cold, but the covering made her feel safer. The shelter was holding; it rattled and creaked in the air pressure from the quake, but no cracks appeared in the seams or in the new metal window-shades. Pete had done a good job.

The car swayed nauseatingly until the event ended. Marie tumbled out the door, dripping with sweat, just as Pete and Anna burst from the restaurant entrance.

"You're okay, honey? You're okay?" Pete shouted. "Show me your ears."

Marie tilted her head to the side as Pete brushed back her hair. "No blood."

"I feel okay. It's really hot inside, though," Marie said.

"I was worried about that, but I don't think we have a choice," Pete said. "God damn, this might actually work."

"When are we leaving?" Anna asked.

"As soon as possible," Marie said. "The Demon warned me…"

"What? What did you say?" Pete asked, his eyebrows raised.

"I…nothing. Sorry, I'm pretty tired. I'm just a little

loopy. Need to get out of the sun."

"Go ahead and get some rest. I'll hook up those towing chains you found. Anna, see if you can find anything else we might need. But remember, whatever we bring with us will add to the weight of the Shell. The only really heavy thing we should be bringing is water."

"I know where there's a well. I'll take care of it." Anna walked past the restaurant onto the playa, taking a wide roundabout path to avoid the flyblown bodies in the street which were beginning to rot. When the wind gusted stronger than a breeze, it picked up the odor and swept it into their faces.

"Let me take one last look," Marie said, heading toward the urgent care center. Sooner or later, she knew they'd need medical supplies. The center should have plenty to gather—provided the whole building didn't come down on her head. It skewed madly to the left, now.

"You should be resting, Marie."

"I'll be fine. I just need to cool off. I'll be okay inside."

"Be careful in there. That building looks like it's been whacked upside the head with a baseball bat."

Two hours later, the group was ready to leave. They'd have ten hours to move east before having to stop and take shelter inside the Shell. Marie calculated ten hours at three miles per hour—an optimistic pace, considering they'd be towing a car on foot the whole time—would gain them thirty miles.

As Anna returned with filled water jugs and bags of food, Pete finished attaching the tow chains.

"Wrap this around your shoulders, Marie."

Pete held up two loops of chain bound tightly in strips of building insulation. "Anna, you too."

The chains fit like a backpack. Marie had never owned the kind used for books; she'd been home-schooled, and her books never left the little classroom area her mother had prepared for her study sessions.

"Comfy," she said.

"It won't be for long," Pete said. "But I think this is our only way out of here, and we can't stay. Savor this moment, girl. This is going to be a hard trek. Wish I could do all the pulling myself, but I'm just not strong enough, even on the flat stretches."

"Oh!" Marie said. "I just thought of something…"

"I know. I'm worried about it too."

"What? What's wrong?" Anna asked.

"Hills. The road east is uphill. I'm not sure we'll be able to pull the Shell up a hill, even a little one. It's a hell of a lot harder than going on a flat surface."

Anna set bundles of bread and crackers on the floor of the Shell next to the water jugs she had scavenged. "We're going to have to try," she said. "I think the freezer is about to fall in. We need a city, somewhere with resources…and maybe a bank vault. Or a big bomb shelter."

"Maybe we shouldn't go east, though. What if we go west instead? Toward California?" asked Marie.

"Just as many hills that direction, I think," Pete said. "Doesn't matter which way we go. But we're a lot closer to civilization if we go east. About ninety miles to Las Vegas, if we even need to go that far."

"You think that's possible?" Marie said. "Ninety miles?"

Pete hiked his set of wrapped chains onto his shoulders. "It's a long shot, I know. But we may as well give it a try. There's nothing left for us here. Everyone ready?"

Marie nodded. They stood in a row in front of the Shell; Anna and Marie on either side of Pete, who leaned heavily forward on his chains like a working steer.

"Let's move out!"

11

The Shell was easy to move, at first. On the straightaway, it glided along like a well-oiled curtain runner. When they hit their first low rise, beads of sweat appeared on Marie's forehead, and a vein began to bulge in Pete's neck. Anna's legs burned. But they crested the hill, and took a brief rest at the top before gently easing the Shell down the other side, leaning backwards against it as they crept downhill to keep it from picking up speed.

"Alright. Tough, but not impossible," Pete said, huffing at the bottom of the hill. "We're okay for a while now, anyway. It goes flat here for a good spell."

"Who's that?" Marie said, pointing.

A mile down the road, the silhouette of a person was wavering in the heat lines rising from the asphalt. They stumbled back and forth, from one side of the highway to the other, holding their head in their hands.

"Another survivor! Out here? How?" Anna said.

"We better ask," Pete said. "Let's go!"

As they neared the lurching person, his features came into view; his hair was wild, caked with dirt. His pants were so tattered below the knees, his exposed shins were burnt and bare. When they came close, he whipped up his head and moaned, long and low like a wounded stray dog at night.

"Careful," Pete said. "I don't think he's right in the head. You two stay back. I'm going to go say hello."

"I'm coming with you," Marie said.

"No, you stay here. He could be dangerous."

"No." Marie slipped from her harness and stood next to Pete. "We go together. Anna can stay behind with the Shell."

Pete looked down at Marie, saw the expression of resolve on her face, and shrugged. "Okay. Just be ready for anything—and that includes running back this way, you hear? If I run, you run."

"Same to you, Pete," Marie said. She kept her eyes fixed on the staggering man in the road. "Let's go."

As they approached the man, he tilted his head to the side and watched them carefully, as if trying to judge whether they were an illusion. He uttered a high, questioning wail, daring to hope they were not figments of his imagination.

"Hello, mister," Pete called out. "Are you okay?"

The man stumbled toward them, then tripped over the strips of fabric dangling from his tattered pants. He tumbled to the hot asphalt, skinning his hands. Wincing and muttering under his breath, he rubbed his palms together to soothe the pain and grind the sand out of his cuts.

"Can you talk?" Marie asked.

The man pointed at his head. A rusty trail of blood ran from his ear canal down his neck, into his shirt collar.

"N…no. Maybe," he said.

"You got stuck outside, didn't you? During the… thing that happened. The shaking."

The man shook his head, and pointed out into the desert. "Mine."

"Yours? What's yours?" Pete asked.

"No. *Mine*," the man said. "Halloran."

"He means the old mine shaft," Marie said. "He took shelter in the Halloran mine shaft, but he couldn't get deep enough. So he got hurt, but he's still alive. I think something bad happened to his brain."

The man grinned and nodded eagerly, but winced and held his head as the sudden movement caused waves of pain. A fresh drop of blood ran from his ear and drew a red stripe down his neck.

"What's your name?" Pete asked.

The man couldn't answer. He curled into a fetal position on the burning pavement, scraping his skin wherever it was bare to the ground. He moaned in pain. Something was broken inside.

"Let's just call him Halloran," Marie said.

They turned back toward the Shell, leading Halloran. When they were close, they helped him sit inside. As soon as he was in the shelter, he blacked out—either from pain or relief, Marie couldn't tell. Another fresh drip of blood started from his ear as he fell back onto a pile of rags.

"This is a bad idea," Anna said. "We don't know this man. He could be dangerous."

"I'm not sure he's going to make it, anyway," Pete said. "Look at him. He looks like he walked off the front line of the war. Couldn't hurt us if he tried."

"Even so," Anna said. "I don't like this."

"I get it, Anna. But we can't leave him out here," Marie said. "Let him sleep a while in the Shell with the doors open. Maybe he'll come to."

The group rested in the shade of the Shell, sipping warm water from glass jugs.

"How did you know about the mine shaft?" Pete asked. "I've lived in the area for decades and I've never heard of it."

"When you are a kid stuck in the desert with nothing but a lot of books to pass the time, you read a lot. I'm home-schooled. And by that, I mean I am self-taught. My mom couldn't be bothered to actually teach me anything past basic reading, so I read every book I could get my hands on and learned as much as I could. So I could leave someday."

"Leave home? You didn't like living in a resort?" Pete asked.

"There was nothing there for me."

"So you studied history? For fun? Poor kid," Anna said.

"One of the books I had was full of maps of California. Topographical maps, historical maps. All kinds of stuff." Marie looked worried. "That's how I know we've got hills ahead of us. Big ones."

"Well yeah, everyone knows about those. Driven over them a thousand times," Pete said.

"I haven't," Marie said. "I've never left Zzyzx before."

Anna stared. "What do you mean, never? Now that just can't be right, honey. Tell the truth."

"Never mind. Let's go," Marie said, rising from the sand. "I think we have about eight more hours before the next quake."

"Why don't we wait until the sun goes down?" Anna asked. "It's too hot out here."

"Water," Pete said. "We'll run out if we don't find more soon. We have to move as quickly as possible or we'll run out of resources. The clock is ticking."

"I'm so tired already," Anna groaned, picking up her chains.

The tall hills inched closer.

They crept across the desert for two hours before Halloran moaned loudly and banged on the ceiling of the Shell.

"Guess he's awake. Let's see how he's doing," Pete said.

"Careful," Anna said, backing away from the Shell.

The inside of the car was oven-hot. When Pete opened the door, Halloran tumbled out onto the dirt, breathing heavily. He rolled onto his back and gazed up at Pete, then touched his hand to his lips.

"Thirsty?" Pete asked. Halloran nodded.

"Pete," Anna called from twenty feet away. "We

don't have that much water. We should save what we have."

"We've no more right to it than he does," Pete said. "Show some sympathy, hon."

After Halloran swallowed three massive gulps of water, his eyes cleared and he become more conscious. He looked calmly from Anna, to Marie, and to Pete with monk-like calm. Nodding at no one, he leaned on the Shell, using it to rise to his feet.

"Good! Feeling better?" Pete said.

In response, Halloran shuffled to the front of the Shell and picked up one of Marie's shoulder chains. He looped it around his right shoulder, and nodded again.

"He's going to help us," Marie said, picking up her left shoulder chain.

"You sure you're ready, man?" Pete asked. "You've been through hell."

Halloran didn't reply. He swayed in place but didn't fall down.

"All right! Move out!" Pete hollered, hauling his chains onto his shoulders. "Let's get a few more miles before sundown!"

And on they walked.

12

The next quake was due an hour before sunset. The group of four huddled around a bonfire, sipping water from paper cups. Halloran fell asleep immediately, curled into a ball near the Shell, hugging his shins.

"Why's the road red?" Anna asked. "I mean, I always knew it was red, I grew up out here and it's always been red. But I never really wondered why. Marie, was that in one of your books?"

"It's clay, taken from the hills. Easier to use local resources than try to ship in black asphalt from the big cities. Cheaper," Marie said. "I read about it in my 'Nevada History' book."

"Clay, huh? Guess that's why it's so full of potholes. The roads out here have always been pretty bad. They seem to just melt away every time it rains," Anna said.

"If you ask my dad, of course, it's red because of the sin," Marie said. "The effect of immorality in Las Vegas. The blood of the gamblers and prostitutes, mixed in to the very path they followed to leave Babylon. 'The road to Las Vegas is awash in the blood of the weak', he always said. It ran like a river, right next to our home, and if I dipped a toe in, it'd pick me up and carry me all the way to Hell."

"I'm starting to understand why you left," Pete said. "That's a blackhearted thing to say to a child."

Marie smiled and grimaced. "That's nothing," she said. "Mom said he just wanted to keep me safe, but I knew the truth. He enjoyed scaring me. He also-"

"What was that?" Anna said, gripping her blanket to her chest.

Beyond the glow of the fire a twig snapped, and a small tumble of sand spilled down a rocky hill. Red pinpoints of light popped up and stared down into the camp, reflecting the light.

"A bunny rabbit," Pete said, chuckling. "Critters that were able to burrow deep in their holes survived the quakes. I wonder, though. They might be damaged, like Halloran."

"I saw a squirrel yesterday," Marie said. "It seemed fine."

"We will take our lessons from the small creatures in these times, in the end times, in the time when time folds back." Halloran spoke in a distant, soft voice, staring directly at Marie. "He knows you. The one with the horns. He told me to tell you to tell me about the pendulum."

The phrase "end times" chilled Marie. She had

heard such words from her father on so many occasions she had eventually learned to discount or ignore such speech. But hearing it from this broken man, after the events of the last couple of days, made them feel real. Her hands shook.

"The one with the horns?" Marie whispered. "Was he-"

"None of that talk, now," Pete said. "Whatever has happened is a natural phenomenon, not a biblical catastrophe. I bet the quakes will taper off. And even if not, we'll adapt. We'll figure it out."

"No," Halloran whispered, and went back to sleep.

The group lapsed into silence, staring into the fire. Marie was stunned.

"Time for us all to turn in," Pete said.

"But we only have a little bit of time left until the next quake," Anna said.

"Catch a nap, if you can," Pete said. "You too, Marie."

"No, I'll take the first watch. You've been working hard, fixing up the Shell. I'll stay up, and wake you all soon."

"No, Marie. You-"

"Pete, no. You aren't the leader of this team, and you aren't my father. I don't need a father. Please, let me take this shift. And try to accept that we are all equals here, however difficult that concept may be for you."

Pete's mouth fell open. "I…Well, I know that. You don't have to tell me…" Pete bowed his head. "You're right. I guess my instincts have been kinda kicking in. I feel protective, you know?"

"And I appreciate that, Pete, we all do. So much, you have no idea. But we all have a place on this team, and none of us is at the front. We all pull together," Marie said.

Pete nodded. Marie took note of the position of

the moon, using her hand to measure its distance from the horizon.

"One hour of sleep. I'm leaving us a half hour buffer, just to be sure," Marie said.

"Th…thanks, Marie," Pete said.

"Thank you," Anna said.

"You," Halloran echoed, in between snores.

The group slept, while Marie watched the moon sail between the stars.

13

Mr. Gibson really hated the son-of-a-bitch who ran the resort.

He delivered water to Zzyzx Town four days a week, pumped from a local well directly into a five-hundred gallon tank he had mounted on his truck. He had several customers on the outskirts of Baker, mostly the old and infirm who could not drive out to obtain their own water due to illness or frailty. Mr. Gibson kept his prices low and his delivery schedule consistent, and he earned a good enough living to get by.

But Starling, he was a real pain in the patoot. Wanted his water delivered first thing in the morning, before anyone else was attended to. Wanted the whole tank each time, but would only pay half per gallon what Mr. Gibson normally charged. And he got away with it, because the quantities still made it worthwhile to deliver—just barely.

As he did most mornings, Starling appeared right on schedule to personally overlook the transfer of water. He crossed his arms and watched Mr. Gibson feed the hose, turn the spigot, open the pump. He sniffed and grunted, and spat in the dust. A distasteful man. And all the locals knew there were no real hot springs in Zzyzx

Town. No water at all, hot or otherwise, except what Mr. Gibson delivered on Mondays, Tuesdays, Thursdays, and Fridays. The pools had to be drained, washed, and refreshed regularly, especially since it sat warm and tepid for so many hours. What a damn waste.

He had just finished the transfer into Mr. Starling's open holding cisterns when the air began to vibrate. Fine ripples fluttered the surface of the water; they bounced off the sides of the tank, collided with each other in the center, and receded back to the edges in oscillating waves.

"What the fuck is that sound?" Starling shouted. "That your truck doing that?"

But the sound grew and grew. Mr. Gibson pressed his palms over his ears and squinted, as though the air had filled with thick fog.

"Get in! *Inside!*" Mr. Starling yelled, waving his arms. He led Mr. Gibson through a side gate and down a long hall lined with green doors, from which customers were poking their toweled heads.

One cried out to Mr. Starling, "I demand to know what's going on here! I demand that the sound stops! I demand-"

"Gibson! In here!" Mr. Starling unlocked a grey door halfway down the hall. A wooden plaque said "sauna" in carved script. It was a small, damp room without windows. Mr. Starling pulled the heavy door closed behind them, shutting out the growing noise. A tiny trickle of blood ran from his nose, spattering his lavender silk shirt.

"I can still hear it," Mr. Gibson said. The twanging sound that had rattled his teeth was still audible, but muted. In the hallway, a man screamed something about demanding a refund and tumbled to the floor, scraping the door with his fingernails as he went down.

"What…"

"I have no idea. Never happened before. Hope to Christ it isn't my fault somehow," Mr. Starling said. "Can't think how it would be. Must be military. Japan, most likely, the bastards."

"Your nose is bleeding, Mr. Starling," Mr. Gibson said.

"Judd," Mr. Starling said, taking a fluffy white towel from a teak wood box with brass hinges. "We're in a situation, I think. First names to save time from now on, yes?"

"Frank."

"As you say, Frank. Now tell me, does that horrendous sound seem to be getting any quieter?"

Frank tilted his head to listen. He heard screams still, but fewer now. Did everyone run away? Or was it worse…

"Perhaps."

"Not gone though, not yet. I think we'll just wait here a while."

Frank noticed his hands were shaking. A stress response. He had been too surprised and shocked to realize how terrified he had been. Now, he felt a funny feeling in his throat.

"Mr…I mean, Judd. Pretty sure I'm gonna puke."

"Damn it. Alright, here, use this." Judd handed Frank a water pail with a bar of soap still sitting in the bottom.

After Frank filled it, Judd draped a towel over the top and set it in the corner. "You done? That's the only bucket in here."

Frank nodded, wiping his mouth. "Sorry."

Judd pressed his ear to the door. "Think it's quieter now. Let's take a peek."

When Judd cracked the door open, it moved only five inches before running up against something heavy. "It's jammed. Help me push."

Together, they were able to shove aside the body of the fallen customer until the opening was wide enough for them to squeeze through. Fresh blood still trickled from the man's ears and nose. His tear duct ran red, filling his open eye. He was dressed in a white robe embroidered with "Zzyzx Resort," which was caked with an unspeakable mess.

"Oh hell," Judd mumbled. "Oh *hell,* I hope this wasn't me, somehow."

"I'm sure it was the military. You know, out in the desert," Frank said. He wondered to himself, why was he trying to assure this man? He didn't like Mr. Starling… Well, *Judd*…and didn't care what became of him. But something about the man's demeanor just demanded service.

"Better check on your wife," Frank said. "She in the owner's wing?"

The Starlings' private suite was in a separate building on the other side of the compound. It was older but in decent repair, and surrounded by dancing topiary. Mrs. Starling had always favored the leafy flamingos most of all, with their cleverly bent legs made of painted wooden stakes which supported the shrubbery making the main body. A small family of them occupied the corner garden near the front door.

Mrs. Starling had collapsed outside the entryway, just a few paces from her beloved flamingos. The ground nearby was littered with items spilled from her purse; a red and white pinwheel mint, a book of matches, and a melting tube of red lipstick. Judd held back and waited for Frank to diagnose the situation. Even before he took her pulse, Frank knew she was dead; her eyes were open wide and crusted dry. He knelt and pressed his fingers to her neck so Judd would know an effort was made, but nodded and backed away quickly.

"She's gone," he said. "I'm sorry, Judd."

"I can still hear the sound. That weird vibration, it's still in the air," Judd said.

"Yeah, I know it. That thing might happen again. We were okay last time, I guess 'cause we shut ourselves away," Frank said.

Judd frowned. "Frank…I saved your life, you know," he said, looking Frank in the eyes.

Frank's skin crawled. He owed Judd now, didn't he? Owed him big. A terrible situation to be in, to be sure.

"Thank you. I surely am grateful for your help," he sputtered.

"I'm sure you are. But that's not enough. I need your help now, you know. We need each other. So you have to stay with me, you hear?" Judd said.

"I guess so. I guess that'd be okay."

Judd stared at the lump that was his wife. He did not cry. His face looked exalted, excited. Beads of sweat, not from the heat, formed on his forehead.

"I am beginning to understand what has happened here. I have been waiting my entire life for this day, and it has finally come." Judd's eyes flew open wide, showing the white, and looked into the sky. "It's happening, and within my own lifetime! The Christ is *returned!* And the devil will come from the east, as it is ordained! Oh, hallelujah! We will rush to meet him!"

"Sir? It seems to me more likely that-"

"Frank Gibson! I can save you. I have resources and means, both on earth and in heaven. I walk with God, and I can keep you alive, son. But only if you're a believer. Do you believe?" Judd's voice raised to a shout in the hushed resort, echoing off the buildings.

"I…have to go check on my truck. On my house, and…and my family."

"Now, Mr. Gibson, I know you don't have family. I

know your wife already passed on some years ago, and you got no one else to check on. I have a suspicion your truck won't currently be working, neither; I heard our generators click off as soon as the air started to go all funny. Praise the Lord! My water fountains are off, and the compressor's shut down, too. The Lord hath spoken; our technology is useless in this, the afterworld. You do as I say, now, and He may have pity on you ere the end."

Frank considered. He was not a religious man, but *something* had happened, and that was a fact. Maybe Judd had the right of it, or maybe he had gone mad. But either way, Frank suspected Judd couldn't survive very long alone. If Frank left him now, it would be like…well, like murder.

He nodded.

"Good," Judd said. "Now, I also happen to know you have experience in car repair. So help me take a look at this truck over here. If we can start her up, it might just keep us alive and get us out of here, to boot. Hallelujah!"

14

"My car!" Halloran cried out.

They were making their way around a sharp curve, pulling the Shell along the outer median for the greatest visibility around the blind turn, when a vehicle came into view. Halloran dropped his chain harness and lurched forward, stiff-legged, toward a cobalt Packard parked at an angle on the side of the highway. Physically, the man seemed fine, but his balance was still off—his inner ears were imbalanced, and blood still trickled down his neck from time to time. He lurched and lunged for the car like a drunken man returning home after a night at the bar.

"Some things," he said. Ducking into the back seat, he pulled out several items; a blanket, a sack lunch in an oily paper bag, and a rope. He tossed them onto the pavement, grinning.

"Let's try it." Sitting in the driver's seat, he dug around in his pocket until he found a Packard fob. But when he turned the key in the ignition, his smile drooped.

"Nothing," he said. "I thought, maybe…"

"Too bad," Pete said. "Wish I knew more about cars. Don't suppose you do, Halloran?"

"No," he said. "I sell magazines."

"We'll have to leave it here, then. I'm sorry, man."

"I ran when the sound started to make my ears bleed," he said. "I left her here. Had seen an old gold mine a mile back. Ran and ran and ran to it."

"Good thinking," Anna said. "And you're talking better now, too. Do you remember your name yet?"

Halloran shook his head.

"No matter," Anna said. "Give it some time."

"Well, grab what's useful," Pete said. "And we'll move on. Five more hours until the next airquake, by my reckoning."

In addition to what Halloran brought from the back seat, they salvaged from the trunk a gallon of water, a small tank of gasoline, a book of matches, a leather jacket, and a stack of women's fashion magazines. Pete and Halloran loaded the items into the Shell.

"What're those magazines for?" Anna asked. "They're heavy. Do we really need them?"

"Guess not," Pete said. "We'll leave 'em." He moved the stack to the side of the road.

"Wait," Marie said. She pulled one magazine from the middle of the stack, a random choice. "I want one. Just one." The cover featured a glamor girl wearing the brightest red lipstick Marie had ever seen. The woman had glimmering blue eyeshadow and a drawn-on mole under her right eye. Marie thought she was fabulous and ugly and gorgeous all at once. She rolled up the magazine and jammed it into her backpack.

"Okay, we ready?" Pete said.

"Let's go," Marie said.

The hills were starting to become more steep. If they had not found Halloran, the incline would have been impossible to climb while towing the Shell. As it was, all four needed to rest every half hour to catch their breath and drink water. The going was slow. When the time came to stop and take shelter, Pete packed rocks behind the Shell's tires to prevent it from rolling backward down the hill. As they sat in the Shell waiting for the sunset air-quake, the air grew thin. The temperature crept up and up with the volume of the twanging in the air, until both were overwhelming. As soon as noise began to recede, they burst from their shelter gasping and pouring sweat. The warm evening air outside felt cool compared to the dark oven of the Shell.

"Oh, god. Oh no," Anna said. She covered her mouth with her hand and pointed at the rear end of the Shell. "What do we do about that, Pete?"

The back left tire had ruptured during the quake. The rim was already cutting through the heat-softened rubber, sinking into the red asphalt like lava.

"We're dead. That's it, we're dead," Pete said.

15

"Can we at least turn on the vent?" Bryce asked.

"The air conditioning doesn't work. I didn't fix up anything that wasn't necessary." Stefan downshifted and tapped the brake, letting the car coast at 30 mph.

"I know the air conditioning doesn't work, I just mean the fan," Bryce said.

"Didn't fix it. Just crank down the window," Stefan

said.

They were already thirty miles from the shop, and Stefan knew it was a big risk. It was like sailing out to sea in a leaky boat to escape a fire burning its way down the shoreline. The tool closet they had sheltered in during the quakes had started to crack, though. The car he chose was in good shape, and luxury, too—an almost-new Cadillac, brought in two days ago by a casino owner and his wife. They had broken down on their way to their second home; a cottage in Long Beach, California, they told him. At the time, Stefan had given them an estimate of a $150 repair, done in forty-eight hours or less. Just as their car was finished, the couple died in the airquake, banging on the glass door of the shop. They had fallen with their foreheads pressed together, laying in a mixed pool of blood.

Bryce was the auto shop gopher, and just a kid—sixteen years old. He sold soda pop at the counter, drove into town to pick up parts that had been shipped out from the city, and cleaned greasy fingerprints off cars that had been repaired and were ready to be returned to their owners. The boy's drunk daddy had beat him to a pulp last Christmas, and Bryce had showed up at the shop with an eye like a fig, purple and mushy with bruises. He spent the next two days straight in the shop working double shifts, sleeping in the tool room at night. He cleaned every grease stain, greeted every customer—anything to convince Stefan to let him stay. But Bryce's daddy was found dead soon after, behind a bar in State Line. Coroner said it was a heart attack brought on by excessive drinking. Bryce never had to go home again. And he never even cried for his daddy, the poor kid.

The Cadillac began to shake.

"What's wrong? Is it happening again?" Bryce asked.

"No, I think it's the alignment. We'll be okay for

now, but it'll have to be fixed as soon as possible so the tires don't wear out," Stefan said.

Fixing up the Cadillac had been a challenge. The shaking had warped it, somehow, throwing everything out of alignment with everything else. Even now, the cab didn't feel square. But at least the engine was top quality. None of the Packards or Oldsmobiles on the lot would have stood a chance of starting up. But the Cadillac had pulled through, just barely, with a lot of work. Stefan could tell it wouldn't last long. They would have to find a new place to shelter, and fast—the car already felt like it was pulling itself apart. It wasn't really just the tire alignment; the whole vehicle was twisted and loose. But he didn't want Bryce to know that, just yet.

"What's that over there? A gas station?" Bryce pointed at a dark square on the horizon.

"Yeah, I think that one's abandoned. I've noticed it before, driving by. We could try it out," Stefan said. "Maybe the restroom is enclosed enough to shelter us. Worth a try, anyway."

Stefan pulled off the highway and parked the car next to the building. The Cadillac shut off with a window-rattling shudder. There was a finality to the motion that worried Stefan; would it ever turn on again?

The rest stop was empty, dried out and full of sand and spiders. The restroom was enclosed with no windows, but it had one vent at the bottom of the door which had been busted out. Bryce got caught up in an old spiderweb that wrapped around his head and clung to his hair.

"Help me move this," Stefan said, shoving a vinyl bench seat across the floor toward the restroom. They moved it into the little room and wedged it against the inside of the door, blocking the low vent. Stefan clicked on his flashlight and jammed toilet paper into the gap under the door.

"Not much protection. Hope it's enough," Stefan said.

Bryce sat on the bench and hugged his knees up to his chest. "Gonna die anyway, might as well be here."

"Don't talk like that. Go to sleep if you can."

"No way," Bryce answered, his eyelids drooping. Stefan turned off the flashlight and sat in the corner near the sink, listening to the incoming twanging drone; when it got loud he could feel his eardrums rattle, ready to burst. He draped his jacket over Bryce's sleeping head and pressed his hands over his ears until the sound faded away like the angel of death passing them by one more time.

16

"I found it!" Marie called out, pulling on the knob that released the Volkswagen's front hood.

Inside the storage compartment Pete found a spare tire and a wrench, in addition to a pile of greasy rags and an old bottle of soda pop.

"I was so concerned with stripping the car, I forgot to check the trunk," Pete said. "Nice thinking, Marie."

"Is it any good?" Anna asked.

Pete lifted the tire from the compartment and bounced it gently on the asphalt. "Seems fine. We still have a problem, though. No jack."

"No problem," Halloran said. He had been standing away from the group, with his eyes focused on the horizon in a distant, thoughtful daze. His mind seemed to be crawling back from the brink and healing itself, but his cognition was still weak.

"What do you have in mind?" Anna asked, skeptical.

"Gather rocks. Big ones. And wood, if you can find any," Halloran said. He showed them how to stack the largest stones they could find on the ground behind the busted tire until they touched the underside of the Shell.

"Now dig," Halloran said, scooping dirt from underneath the tire with his hands.

"Oh! I have a wooden bowl," Marie said, understanding. "We can use it as a shovel."

Slowly, the Shell settled onto the stack of rocks as the dirt was cleared from under the busted tire. In a few minutes, the tire hung loose over the hole.

"Very fucking clever, Halloran! If you ever remember who you were before the airquake, I'd love to know," Pete said.

Halloran said nothing, but smiled as he spun the tire iron, loosening the bolts with practiced ease. "Done this before," he said.

"How long until the next one, Pete?" Anna asked.

"Not long. Maybe an hour. We'll stay here for now, camp again. But we're getting low on water. We can't spend the whole night here, can't spare the hours."

"Done," Halloran said. He started pushing dirt back into the hole. When it was full, he kicked the rock stack out from under the Shell, and it settled heavily on the ground. The new tire was four inches deep in the soft sand of the freshly dug hole before it stopped sinking.

"Great, now its stuck again," Anna said.

Halloran picked up a chunk of wood and jammed it under the front of the tire. "Pull it together, and I'll push from behind. We should be able to get it right out. Ready?"

"Let's give it a try," Pete said.

They rocked the car forwards and backwards until it ran up out of the hole. As soon as it was out, Marie heard an approaching sound; a car on the highway.

"Pete! Do you hear that?"

Almost before she was finished asking, a box truck had crested the hill and zipped past the Shell at sixty miles per hour.

"Holy hell! They're really moving. How, though? How'd they get it working?" Pete asked.

"Well, they're gone now. Didn't even slow down," Marie said. The open window of the box truck had left behind a strange odor that tickled at the back of her brain; a familiar smell, of a certain brand of cigar.

"Forget about it. We should just keep moving. Come on."

As they picked up their chains, Marie froze.

"What's that?" she said.

A high-pitched bark, confident and excited. But it didn't sound quite right.

"A coyote. Sounds like there's just one," Anna said.

"No such thing," Marie said. "There will be a pack of them. Normally, I don't think that would be a problem. They're scared of humans. But that bark…it sounded funny. It sounded…"

"What?" Pete asked. "What do you mean?"

A small, fierce animal dashed from behind a small rise near the highway. It screamed as it ran, blood crusted in the fur inside its ears. Pus ran from its eyes, staining dark streaks on its cheeks. The sound it made as it moved toward them reminded Marie of the twang of the airquakes; poking at your eardrums like a cotton swab jammed too deep—or maybe like the whistle of something moving quickly through the air. Marie put her hands over her ears, but it didn't help.

It leaped into the air, launching itself at Halloran's face without hesitation. Halloran fell to the ground, striking his much-abused skull against the desert hardpan. He screamed and scraped at the animal's eyes but it chewed his flesh with mad determination, tearing at his cheeks with sharp fangs. Its companions circled the Shell and howled, adding to the din of Halloran's screams.

Marie picked up one of the rocks from the stack under the Shell and brought it down hard. It broke the coyote's spine with a loud snap, but even then the animal continued to scrape weakly at Halloran's face. He rolled over, pitching the coyote into the dust, and grabbed it with his hands. In a swift motion, he twisted the coyote's skull from its spine with a wet crunch. The rest of the pack fled—but Marie knew they would be back.

Halloran collapsed to the dirt, heaving. His breathing was obstructed by blood pouring from his nose into his throat. He coughed, coloring the sand red. When he rolled over and turned back towards the group, Anna screamed.

His nose was badly broken, mashed all the way to one side. One eye hung out of its socket and lay on his cheek, staring down at the dirt. It looked burst, like a soft boiled egg someone had mashed with a spoon. His lips were split, and the skin of his face was shredded into flopping flaps. The white point of his cheek bone jutted from the flesh under the deepest cut.

"Get water," Marie said. "And the blanket."

Marie gently rinsed Halloran's frayed face as he screamed, kicking his heels on the ground. The wounds were deep and were already beginning to flare red with infection. Pete had removed the ruined eyeball, severing it from its mooring with his pocket knife. Marie pressed the empty eye socket shut after rinsing it with a cup of precious water. Mercifully, Halloran fainted.

"He won't make it," Pete said. "You know he won't."

"Maybe not," Marie said. "But we have to try."

"Do we?" Anna asked. "We didn't start out on this trip with him. Never should have picked him up in the first place. And now we've used up almost all of our water!"

"If the coyote hadn't attacked him, it would have

been one of us. You should be glad he was here," Marie said. "Be grateful you still have your whole face, and shut the fuck up."

Anna sulked into the cab of the Shell, whimpering.

"The sound, Marie. It's loud. We don't have much time, and we're going to have to lift him."

Marie wiped Halloran's forehead with the last clean corner of the blanket. "Okay, let's do it. Should we ask Anna for her help?"

"Do you think we can do it without her?" Pete said. "I think she's overwhelmed. She's acting childish, which is out of character for her. I mean, she's my boss. Or, she was, anyway. All I'm trying to say is she's acting funny, and if we can do this without her, that'd be my preference."

"I'll try, Pete. But I'm tired too."

"I know, honey...I mean, *Marie*. I know."

Marie gripped Halloran's ankles in her hands and began to breathe deep.

"One...two...three!" Pete said, lifting under Halloran's armpits with a grunt. As they shuffled toward the Shell with Halloran swinging between them like a hammock, Marie heard another bark. It was far out in the desert this time, but the sound filled her with dread.

"Pete," she gasped. "Did you-"

"Yeah, I heard it."

"Anna!" Marie shouted. "Can you open the door?"

No answer.

"Anna!" Pete boomed, briefly losing his grip on Halloran's torso before hoisting him again with his knee.

"Go away!" Anna screamed from inside the Shell. "Just go away! We're all going to die anyway!"

"Set him down," Pete huffed. Marie lowered Halloran's legs to the dirt.

"It's locked," Pete said, trying the door. "Anna! We have to get inside before the next quake. Please, we only have a few more minutes!"

Anna didn't answer. Marie heard a sob from within, deep and mournful. As if in response, a coyote howled—closer, this time—and then another joined in chorus. The pack was converging.

"Anna, open the fuck up!" Pete yelled. Halloran stirred; he was beginning to wake.

"Can't smash a window, they're all steel. Can't go through the back, the engine's there. Is the hood still popped?" Marie asked.

Pete's jaw dropped. He sprinted to the front of the Shell and threw open the lid. "Thank god I cut through the back wall when I pulled the steering! Can you climb all the way through, Marie?"

Marie stepped into the storage compartment and ducked through the opening at the back. She was immediately struck with something like a paper towel tube—it was her glamour magazine, rolled up tight. Anna hit her on the head with it over and over until Marie grabbed her wrist and twisted it, making her scream with rage.

"Bitch! Don't you touch me, you little bitch!" Anna shouted. Ignoring her, Marie scooted to the door and unlocked it. As she pushed it open, she saw Pete's face twisted into an expression of terror.

"They're here, Marie. The coyotes. Help me with him!"

As they hoisted Halloran into the Shell, Anna curled up into a tiny weeping ball at the back of the car. They slammed the door shut just as a pack of five coyotes descended on the Shell, flaring their noses in excitement at the stench of fresh blood.

"They're right outside," Pete said, breathing hard.

"They're brain-damaged, I think," Marie said. "Like Halloran."

One of the coyotes launched itself at the Shell,

hearing their voices. It yipped in pain as it cracked its head open on the metal door. The rest of the pack raised their voices in madness and triumph as it tumbled to the dirt and writhed, growling, under the side of the car.

The Shell began to tremble. "It's a big one," Pete said. "Like the first one."

They rode it out, listening to the cab creak around them. Pete eyed his welding work with worry, but it held tight. Anna moaned and sobbed softly. Halloran came to briefly during the quake, screamed once, and fainted again as blood pooled in a renewed rush onto the floor under his head.

After the quake passed, the coyotes were silent. Marie and Pete cracked the door. Small furry piles decorated the landscape; the coyotes had survived the previous quakes, somehow, but this one had been large enough to take them all out. One of them still twitched, its little foot digging a shallow channel in the sand.

"That's just as well," Pete said.

"I guess," Marie said. "I feel sorry for them, though."

Pete grunted. "Too sorry to eat meat tonight?" He pulled his knife from his pocket.

Marie's eyes widened. "I hadn't thought of that. I guess…"

Pete's white teeth shone in the setting sunlight. "Can you stomach it? Helping me carve one up, I mean. Or have you had your fill of blood today already? I'd understand."

"No, I'll help. I can do it," Marie said.

"I know you can," Pete grinned.

17

"Your wife," Frank Gibson said. "You want to bury her

before we leave?"

Judd Starling glanced back at the shaded overhang behind his wife's beloved topiaries. Her body was beginning to attract flies; he could hear them from where he stood, in the utter silence of the dead resort.

"Nah. She's fine where she's at. Never lifted a finger a day of her life, see no reason why she should be bothered to move now she's dead." Judd threw a pile of blankets on top of their food provisions in the back of the box truck.

Frank shrugged. His surprise was nonexistent, but he still felt a pang of disappointment in Judd. Surely, his wife was worth the minor consideration of a decent burial. They'd been together for years—since before the Depression. One time a few months ago she had pulled him aside to chat, and told him about all manner of things; her sister's new beau (too effeminate, and Mrs. Starling had her suspicions), the boy who delivered the newspapers on Sunday (dark-skinned, so she always kept a close eye until he was gone), and the details of her long, unsatisfactory marriage. The woman had seemed lonely, but Frank had difficulty pitying the woman. Her own choices had put her here.

None of his business.

"Damn shame, though. She was trying to catch pregnant, and thought she might actually have done it. She was pretty long in the tooth for having another, but we weren't sure. Might have finally got that boy we wanted all these years," Judd said.

Frank stared. "I'm so sorry, Judd. That must be-"

"No matter." Judd pulled himself into the passenger seat of the truck. "This heap all fixed up and ready to move on outta here? This place is going to rot, and soon. Going to smell to high heaven once the sun gets to work on those bodies."

Frank slid into the driver's seat without a word,

but with a feeling of foreboding in the pit of his stomach. This would be a long trip. It was like working at a job you hate, without ever being allowed to clock out. Like slavery, he supposed. But now Mr. Starling held all the cards; the truck was his, the food was his. He claimed to know someone in Las Vegas who would take them in—a casino manager. And he'd have access to a vault in which to ride out the air storms.

Judd's callous response to his wife's death brought Frank's grief over his own to the fore. It had been years, but the pain still crashed in his chest like a thunderhead. She had loved to drive, and their road trips had been long and adventurous. Their list of conquests included the Grand Canyon, Crater Lake, and even a journey all the way to the beaches of Corpus Christi. They'd made love at night on a towel in the sand, and watched the sun come up.

And now she was gone, replaced by fucking Mr. Starling, carnie that he was. Frank figured he'd get himself to Las Vegas then give him the slip once he sussed out the situation in the big city. By the time they got there—a three hour drive, if they were lucky and the truck held itself together—he knew he'd be frustrated with Mr. Starling enough to murder the man, and he didn't want to add that evil act to his long list of troubles.

"How I figure it, we've got at least five hours until the next…you know, air pressure thing," Judd said. "If you don't drive like a pussy, we'll get to Vegas in three. You up for the challenge, daddy-o?"

Judd grinned. He knew all the right buttons to push. He knew how to light a fire under men's asses, how to singe them just the right amount so they hitched up their skirts and ran but didn't quite burn to death. He'd push Frank hard to get them to Vegas, then ditch him before he headed over to the Golden Pot. Literally, if necessary; Judd had left better men in ditches, the good Lord knew.

The truck rumbled to life. "She lives!" Judd hooted. Frank popped the clutch and eased the truck forward, listening close to the sounds coming from the engine. It rattled and clanked, but seemed solid enough. It only had to go a hundred miles or so.

"How the heck did you fix this piece of shit, Frank?" Judd asked, biting the tip off a cigar. "It barely worked *before* all the shaking started."

"It weren't easy, sir," Frank said. "Everything was shook out of alignment. The pistons were-"

"Anyway," Judd said. "Cigar?"

"No, sir," Frank said. "Thank you, sir."

"No need to call me sir out here, Frank! Mr. Starling will do just fine."

"Yes, sir," Frank said.

18

"It's done," Stefan said to himself in the warming morning sun. As he had feared, the Cadillac had breathed its last when it issued death rattles outside the abandoned gas station. He hadn't woken up Bryce yet; might as well let the kid sleep. No harm in it. They weren't going anywhere, and in eleven hours, maybe ten, the next quake would probably bust their brains apart.

The storage closet had cracked during the morning quake. As soon as Bryce had fallen asleep, Stefan had checked the walls with his flashlight; large gaps had appeared, too big to patch. No way the building would survive another shaking, even a small one. It'd come down around their ears, crush them under the weight of the gas station roof.

Maybe he should let it, and stop worrying about it.

It might be a better way to go than letting the blood pour from their ears and noses and eyes while the delicate grey matter in their brains was scrambled.

But Stefan couldn't let it go. As he sat in the driver's seat of the dead car his thoughts were dark and his hope was nearly gone, but he didn't want to fail Bryce, and he wasn't the type to give up.

A rabbit poked its head up from behind a granite boulder. It had survived by burrowing deep into a hole. Maybe it had even closed the earth in behind it, caved in the path for protection. Some of the animals, it seemed, had an instinct for surviving all external dangers.

Could he dig a hole?

No way. Not with his bare hands—even if he found something to dig with, he could never dig a shelter large and solid enough, with a door that closed flush, in the next few hours. And even if he did, their water was nearly gone. And even if it wasn't...

They were done. He wished they'd died in the initial event. Surviving this long had made him feel useless hope, made him believe there was a reason he still lived. Maybe that reason was keeping Bryce alive, or maybe there was a future for him somewhere else. Somewhere the earth wasn't shaking itself to pieces.

He heard a rumbling sound in the distance. Too soon! The last quake had only been a couple of hours ago. Was the pattern broken?

But no, it sounded like an engine. A car—and it was *working*.

A box truck crested the hill with the rising sun behind it, reducing it to a black square against the sky. It was rattling and shaking, on its last legs but running all the same.

Stefan threw the Cadillac's door open and sprinted through the dust, waving his arms. "Hey!" he screamed. It bothered him to show such desperation, but he was unable to stop himself. "Please! Help! There's a kid with me! You have to help us!"

The truck pulled to the side of the road, then abruptly returned to the middle. It swerved again to the shoulder, and Stefan noticed there were two men fighting over the wheel. The driver was trying to pull over but the passenger was striking his head with an open hand, waving around a lit cigar and screaming in his ear.

The box truck zipped past. Apparently, the passenger had won the fight.

Stefan knelt in the sand and sobbed.

19

"Anna, we can't do this without you. Please come out." Pete gently knocked on the Shell's door.

Even with Anna's help, the going would be slow now that they had hit the foothills. And Halloran wouldn't heal; Marie could tell. His face had puffed up with infection, and he rarely became lucid enough to speak. They wet his lips with drops of water every couple hours, but it was the most they could do. The remaining ounces of water had to go to the pullers; for now, that was Pete and Marie. Anna sat in the Shell and stared at the floor, at Halloran, and at the empty water bottles.

"She's in shock, Pete. There's not a lot we can do about that." Marie hoisted her chains onto her shoulders. "Let's just get as far as we can. Nothing else to do."

"Bullshit! She's gonna help us whether she likes it or not. No water or food for flakes." Pete yanked open the door of the Shell and leaned in.

Anna screamed. Her shriek was followed by a high moan from Halloran that dissolved into whimpers.

"Pete, please. She's in a childlike state of shock. Let

her rest," Marie said.

"*Dammit!*" Pete slammed the door on Anna's sobs. "We can't afford this. Don't have the resources to be wasting time. Hot as hell in there, too. Don't know how she can stand it."

"We can stand here arguing and wait for the coyotes to come back this evening, or we can get as far as we can. Pete…I can't pull alone."

"Your shoes, Marie. I know there's a hole in the heel. Your poor toes, hon…the skin, it's shredded off. That's one thing we can help, at least," Pete said. He poked his head into the cab again, softer, quieter than last time.

"Anna. Do us a favor, love. If you have to stay in here, then go ahead and stay. But please, give us your shoes."

When Pete returned to Marie he was holding a pair of sensible waitress clogs, size 7. Marie was a 7.5, but she squeezed her feet into the shoes and cut a small slit across the top of the toe, making a little extra room.

"I guess they'll work okay," she said.

"Good," Pete said. "We got flat road for two or three miles. Let's cover that, at least. Ready?"

"Ready."

By the time the road became steep again, the shadows were growing long. Even before the bottom of the sun touched the horizon line, Marie heard coyotes yapping in the distance. So a few had survived; perhaps they had a deep den, or were using one of the mines for shelter like Halloran did. By now, most of the small creatures that had dropped dead during the first airquake would be starting to rot. The coyotes must have gorged themselves, at first. Now, the food supply was turning bad, and they would have to become brave or starve.

Marie's knees ached. Her head throbbed with the pressure of constant pulling. Worst of all were her shoulders; it felt like her arms were being worked from their sockets. Deep purple bruising had set in from her biceps to the bottom of her neck. The skin wasn't rubbing off yet, but it would before long, and then she'd be at risk for infection—just like Halloran.

He didn't have long, now. Halloran had retreated into a deep coma, his breaths long and slow but for an occasional gurgle. Anna wiped his face occasionally, wet his lips when they became caked with spit, and kept his head cushioned with a blanket. She had stopped crying, but had not yet fully checked back in to reality. The last words she had uttered had been her screams at Marie, when she had driven her from the Shell during the coyote attack.

"Stop," Pete gasped. "We're done. Two percent grade for the next few miles at least."

Marie dropped her chains.

"End of the road, hon. Can't do it, not the two of us. Maybe not even if Anna comes to her senses. Might could have done it with Halloran, but if he isn't dead yet, he's wishing he was. We tried. We tried."

Marie picked up rocks from the side of the road and jammed them behind the front tires to stop the Shell from rolling backward. Pete slumped to the side of the road. Deep wheezes issued from his lungs, a worrisome sound.

"I'll build a fire," Marie said. "Maybe we can lure Anna out for a while before we have to hide from the airquake."

"Sure, hon, you do that."

Marie stepped nimbly down the slope at the side of the highway, watching for sinkholes and listening for coyotes. All was quiet, for now. But she knew she should hurry. She smashed a prickly dry tumbleweed to bits for kindling, and scooped it up in an old cactus husk. A dead tree supplied her with a small amount of solid wood. She was able to gather enough for a one hour fire, maybe two. It would have to do.

As she picked up her haul and cradled it in her arms against her chest, she spotted a rectangle on the horizon; a man-made shape, not a mountain. A building.

She dropped her firewood and trotted back to Pete, who was sprawled in the middle of the highway, half asleep.

"Pete! I think there's a rest stop ahead!"

Pete rolled on his side and farted. "Whoops, sorry Marie. What was that?"

"A rest stop, or a gas station. I saw it on the horizon. Looked about a mile away—guess that means it's probably actually two or three. But it's not too far to walk to. We should check it out."

"In the morning, sure," Pete said.

"We should go now. We're out of water."

"I know, Marie. But, don't get your hopes up too high. And the coyotes…"

Marie sighed. "Yeah, okay. You're right. In the morning."

20

Stefan's ears were trickling blood.

Before the quake arrived, he had tried to patch up the little room the best he could, using wedges of wood and torn rags. He jammed them into the cracks near the ceiling, using a screwdriver to pack the patches tight.

"I don't know if it'll hold, kiddo, but it's all we can do. I'm so sorry."

Bryce had nodded and curled into a fetal position in the corner of the room. When the quake was over, Stefan's ears tickled and leaked and his head buzzed with shrill tinnitus that echoed the frantic ringing of the quake.

They had survived, but it had been close, and they both felt dizzy.

Bryce's eyes seeped pink tears. It felt like when he had fallen out of a tree when he was 9 years old. The doctor had told him his head was "concussed." He hadn't been climbing any trees lately, but his head was spinning after the quake much like it had in the days after the fall—pounding and unsettled in a way that made him nauseous.

Stefan's brain was popping and crackling like a tree right after a lightning strike; he prayed he would not have a seizure. He'd had them as a child, his mom said, and he had been nervous about them coming back ever since. Most of them happened before his adult memory started, but he still had vague recollections of waking up with his father's hands pinning his shaking shoulders to the floor, and the taste of the wooden ruler his mother had put between his teeth.

The morning quake had been stronger than last night's. Their strength seemed to be somewhat random, like gusts of wind in a storm. But one thing was consistent, at least; the timing was always perfect. Every twelve hours the air grew heavy, right at six o'clock on the dot.

The last quake had shaken loose not only Stefan's wall patches but the foundation of the building itself. It groaned and leaned, and wide gaps had opened as the quake was winding down. Its usefulness as a shelter was done.

Stefan had no idea what to do with his last remaining hours. Sitting and waiting to die was a nightmare, worse than if the building had simply collapsed on them during the quake. He had no pencil and paper to write his last will and testament—and who would read it, anyway? Bryce had fallen into a deep sleep, a reaction to shock. Stefan felt lonely, but knew it was kinder not to wake him. So he was left with his thoughts as the world wound down.

He walked out to the highway, kicking stones, wiping at his tickling ears with his shirt sleeve. He felt a spidery, crawling sensation in his ear canals; they were coated inside with drying blood. The sensation was deeply uncomfortable.

His final hours would be spent rubbing at itchy ears.

Other than the swerving box truck, no cars had passed by on the highway since Stefan and Bryce had arrived at the gas station. A skunk, bloated and flyblown, lay on the shoulder a few yards to the south. Its swollen eyes had popped from its skull in the heat.

The sudden appearance of two human figures awash in morning sunlight on the ridge startled Stefan badly. He jumped and ran several paces up the highway—toward the skunk, which filled his nose with its spicy odor—before he got his own feet under control and stopped. If they were wanderers, they could be dangerous.

One of them was large; a man with a wagging beer belly. The other was smaller and looked like a woman. She waved.

Friendly! Stefan whooped and waved his arms over his head like an island castaway, and jogged toward the people. The pair were burnt and bruised but very much alive, and in good spirits.

"I'm Stefan! And I'm sure glad to see you!" he called out.

"Marie," the young woman responded. "And this here is Pete. But how'd you get all the way out here?" Marie asked. "This place looks like it's been empty for years. And most cars don't work any more."

"I got one working. That old Cadillac, there," Stefan said. "But she crapped out on me yesterday afternoon. If you all don't have a car, how the hell did you get here? Nearest town is well…Baker, I suppose. You from Baker?"

"And proud," Pete said. "We brought our shelter with us. You'll see, we'll show you. Couldn't get a car running. Automobile work isn't really my forte," Pete smiled. "I'm a short order cook, for all the good it's worth during the damned apocalypse."

"We have two more with us," Marie said. "Well, one more, I guess. Our friend was attacked by the coyotes. He's dying…or maybe dead, by now. And Anna, she's a little sick in the head at the moment."

"She get caught by a quake? Bryce and I got shaken up pretty bad this morning. Can't believe we pulled through, actually."

"Not exactly. More like a panic attack. She watched the coyotes tear up our friend," Pete said. "She's not handling it well."

"I see. Understandable. But say…you have shelter, I think I heard you say," Stefan said. "Bryce and I, we're in a bad way. You see…"

"You're welcome to come with us," Marie said.

"Oh thank god," Stefan exhaled. "I was afraid to ask, but this place is done for. Whole building's about to fall like Berlin. So here it is, the million dollar question: you all got any water?"

Marie fell silent. Pete shook his head.

"A cup or two left, maybe. We were hoping you had some."

Stefan slumped. "I see. Out of the frying pan, into the fire. Well."

"Let's head to our shelter," Pete said. "That much we can do for you."

By the time they had woken Bryce and returned to the Shell, Anna had pulled Halloran out of the cab and laid him in the sand. He had died in his sleep. Anna was shaken, but actually seemed calmer now that Halloran had passed. His tortured breathing and spasms of pain were done.

"What happened to him?" Bryce asked.

"Coyotes," Pete said.

Bryce gasped.

"Don't worry, boy. The quake got them," Pete said. "Popped their eyes out like-"

"Pete!" Marie said. "Shush!"

"We should bury him," Anna interjected, speaking for the first time in over a day. Her voice was dry, raspy with thirst and fear.

"I wish we could, but we can't. We can't afford to waste the energy or the time. If we don't find water today or tomorrow, we're as dead as him," Pete said.

"I don't understand," Stefan said, looking over the Shell. "You have a car? You said you couldn't get one working."

Marie picked up her harness and looped the chains over her shoulders, wincing at their touch on her bruised flesh. "More like a carriage than a car. And we're the mules. It's not the best, but the Shell is a tank—it can withstand the airquakes. We've not been hurt at all since Pete cobbled it together. And we've come quite a few miles. Heading all the way to Las Vegas, if we have to. Although I hope we'll be able to stop sooner."

Pete picked up a chain harness and held it out to Stefan. "It's odd, and it's hard labor, but it works. Still want to join us?"

Stefan looked at Bryce, who sniffed and nodded, wiping crusted blood from the corners of his eyes.

"We're in."

21

Frank had been raised to never hate a man. Hate his actions, sure. Hate the evil he does, if he does it. But always keep a spot of compassion in your heart for the *man,* as his behavior was likely the result of an unfairly difficult life.

But Frank couldn't help it this time. He despised Judd Starling, loathed him. Wanted him dead.

Frank's jaw ached—a common side effect of being blindsided by a cowardly son of a bitch.

He wanted to pull over for the crying man by the side of the road, but Mr. Starling fought him on it. Said they didn't have the resources to support a third wheel. Frank had tried to pull over anyway. Mr. Starling wasn't his boss, or even his customer any more. But Judd had actually grabbed at the wheel and stopped him. If Frank hadn't given in, Judd would have crashed the truck. They careened out of control for a moment, until Judd popped him in the jaw with his elbow and screamed at him to keep driving. So Frank had.

He felt awful about it. He'd even considered waiting until the bastard was asleep, then driving all the way back to the curve in the road where they'd seen the man. But starting up the truck would likely wake him, and it wasn't really less sinful to leave Judd behind than it was to leave the stranger, if you live by the Bible. So he stayed, and built a fire as per Judd's instructions.

When the time came, they waited together in the back of the box truck for the next quake—the nighttime one that came around sundown. They sat in silence, in the dark, listening to the quake sing its ghostly song. Frank thought again of the man from the side of the road; was he dying now? If he was, did that make Frank an accomplice to murder? He whispered a short prayer, just in case God was aggrieved. Frank expected to meet him soon enough; it wouldn't do to have anything left undone.

Anyway, the box truck seemed to be holding. The cargo area was flimsy, but put together just well enough to keep their ears from bleeding. The sidewalls flexed and wrinkled, warbling like an old saw, but they didn't crack.

"I know you're thinking about that man, but you'd best put him from your mind. He won't be the last beggar we come across, and if we pick up one we might as well get them all. And then we *all* die, like beggars. Understand?"

Frank nodded. He didn't agree, but he nodded anyhow. "The truck is running rough. I don't know how long it'll last. Might just be the heat, might be something worse. How far do you judge we still are from State Line? We may want to swap out vehicles as soon as we find another one with cargo space."

"We'll get there tomorrow, I believe. If we don't stop for beggars, that is." Judd shifted his weight to his left butt-cheek and farted, then spat into the fire. "You sleep now, you hear? For an hour, just 'til the quake. Then I'll sleep for a few while you keep watch, and then we'll go before the sun's up. Keep the engine cool as long as possible. Right?"

"Yeah. Sure," Frank said. He balled up his jacket and lay his head on it, but kept his eyes cracked open. He watched Judd grimace in the firelight, and wondered if the man was thinking of leaving him behind. Frank himself had considered it—to backtrack and find the stranger they'd passed, sure—but he also wondered if he couldn't just do better on his own. And why was Judd keeping Frank around anyway? Surely the man could drive the truck himself, so why was he sharing his resources? In case the truck broke down, probably. Judd was the worst kind of man; both greedy and clever. Some time soon, Judd's need for Frank would pass, and then…

Frank knew he was in danger.

He closed his eyes. Only had forty five minutes left to sleep, and he needed every second. He had to trust Judd wouldn't crack him on the head with a rock in his sleep. Or, rather, he had to trust Judd's greed and his need.

What else could he do?

22

Marie had the dream again; the third one in the last two days. It woke her up each time she had it, interrupting her sleep.

Purple smoke curled around her ankles like snakes. In the distance, she could hear an airquake approaching fast; twang, twang, twang. Satan's guitar string plucked in a rock-and-roll rhythm, distorted and low.

This time, she could see more plainly the thing which swung overhead; it was a great pendulum, thousands of miles from top to bottom, affixed to nothing. The ball at the bottom was the world, swinging back and forth, screaming in the wind. A thousand miles it swung forward, then a thousand miles back, and every time it hummed past her head the air vibrated, tousling her hair and rattling her teeth.

Underfoot was the moon, but smaller than it should have been. White dust powdered the laces of Anna's overworked boots. As the earth zinged by, she saw the tides changed with each swing, on a massive scale; water covered entire coasts and ate the land, then retreated and gave it back on the next pass.

The pendulum was swinging and singing; twang TWANG *TWANG* while the oceans swallowed and regurgitated the land.

She felt a tickle on the side of her neck, and when her hand came away it was covered in blood. Her ears were bleeding.

A figure appeared in the mist. It was male, and horned, like an old god. It stood in the path of the pendulum, and when it swung close he caught the earth in his claws. It crumbled to dust and fell through his fingers.

Someone in the distant dark, a voice she did not know called her name. *"Marie…"*

Marie woke up.

23

"It's done, Judd. It won't start. Not now, and not ever again."

The engine was cold after their rest. It didn't even try to turn over.

Judd punched the dashboard. "Just what the fuck are you playing at, Frank? You said this heap of shit would get us to State Line at the very least. Are you trying to mess with me?"

"Look, I don't really know what was wrong with it in the first place, any more than you do. The quakes throw everything out of square, you know that. I hit some things with a hammer, realigned what I could with the tools I had on hand. I made no guarantees about-"

"Shut the hell up! You've killed us both out here! Soon as we run out of water…"

Judd grunted and kicked open the passenger door. He strutted to the front of the truck. "Pop it! Pop the *goddamn* hood!"

Frank dutifully released the hood latch, knowing Judd wouldn't have a clue what he was looking at and was likely to come away from the engine more furious than before.

It was time to think seriously about how to handle the man.

There was a rope behind the driver's seat. Frank dug through discarded fast food trash and empty cans until he found it. He held it loosely at his side like a cattle herder sneaking up on a wayward calf.

"What the *hell* is wrong with this cocksucker?"

Judd screamed. He picked up a rock and hammered the cold engine with it. "Work, you shit!"

Frank waited.

As expected, Judd came tearing around the fender a minute later, rock in hand, his face purple with rage.

"What good are you anyway, you fucking yo-kel-necked-"

Frank aimed for the man's temple with his fist and struck true. Judd tumbled to the ground like a sack of potatoes, an insult gurgling in his throat.

"Sorry, Judd. But you're just not pulling your weight," Frank said, turning the man over onto his bulbous gut. He tied Judd's wrists tight, then sat him upright as the man grumbled and seethed, ejecting insults and threats with upper-class outrage.

"Kill you! First I'll sue you, and then I'll kill-"

"No, you won't. Just settle yourself now. I'm going to take a look at the truck—and I thank you for trying to do the work yourself with your little rock, there, but I'm quite a bit more qualified. I doubt I can fix it, but I'll do my best to ascertain the trouble. You just rest a bit now, sir."

Judd ground his teeth, and the sound sent a shiver up Frank's neck. He heard a molar split with a tiny *pop*.

Frank had won the battle; he took this as a sign of the Lord's approval, and was grateful.

The truck's engine was cracked. It was incredible it had lasted as long as it did—again, by the grace of God. The shudder it had made when Frank turned it off the night before had been foreboding, though, and he'd well known it at the time. He had expected Judd to last a little longer, though, before totally losing his cool. Shame about that. Excessively comfortable men often don't deal well with change, or fear.

"Okay sir, the engine's quit on us for good, but we can still use the back for shelter. So if you work with me, I'll help you get situated in the cargo hold. Whenever you're ready."

"Untie me, you bastard! Untie me or-"

"Alright now sir, you're going to have to concentrate. I have plenty of rope, and if you are thinking of biting me I'll have to wrap it around your head instead of just your hands. Gags are uncomfortable, and I assume you've never experienced that before so I'm going to tell you right now that it's not something you want. Understand, sir?"

Judd snarled, but stayed quiet. Frank helped him to his feet and sat him on the back of the box truck. He scooted backwards on his butt until he was leaning against the front of the cargo hold, away from the light of the cresting morning sun.

"Alright, good. I'll join you shortly, sir."

They had stopped in the middle of nowhere. Until the truck gave out, their progress had been steady and optimistic. They hadn't bothered seeking out any additional resources, anticipating only their arrival at State Line the next day. There was nothing to be found in the area but red rocks, dead cacti, and a couple of distant bunnies Frank knew he had no hope of capturing for food. A Twinkie wrapper flipped and danced in the breeze along the side of the highway before tumbling into a dry creek bed.

Then, a sound in the distance—rumbling, but not like the twang of the airquakes; it was thunder.

To the west, a huge grey thunderhead whorled in the sky over the hills. The cloud rose up over distant California on its way in from the Pacific Ocean, and it was headed straight for them, bloated with water.

Containers! Frank scrambled. He found an empty Coke can, and created a quick funnel with a foil hot-dog wrap he found in the ditch. He set out an old 7-Eleven cup he found behind the seat, and a broken styrofoam ice chest with three good corners. He dug a crater in the sand and lined it with a black trash bag, praying it didn't have any holes. Even after the first drops started he kept working, setting out bits of trash and digging pits in the sand.

Water, a gift directly from the Lord! Frank wept.

24

"It's raining! My god, it's actually raining!"

"Catch it! Quick!"

Anna crept from the Shell. She reached toward the sky, letting the fresh drops streak down her sweaty skin, trickling on her scalp. She smiled.

"Get the jugs. Make some funnels from those paper plates. Hurry!"

The little camp scrambled as the rain fell cold, hard, and fast. The downpour only lasted for fifteen minutes, but it was enough to catch some water and rinse the sweat from their skin. It felt like a miracle.

When they had set out all the containers they could find, Marie stood and spun in the rain, feeling the drops strike her sunburnt skin. Her father had always hated the rain; it was bad for business. And when father was unhappy, Marie tended to suffer. But he was gone now, and she was free to be herself; to be happy.

Marie smiled as she danced, but she didn't part her lips. She may be free, but she was not undamaged. Her smile scared people, made them gasp and raise a hand to their mouth in shock or empathy.

Judd Starling had fancied himself a dentist. He didn't any any formal training, yet he was determined to discover new dental techniques he could market as a unique feature of the resort. He tried chemical compounds, tools, and deep soaks on Marie's teeth, justifying his research with the often-repeated claim that she had "soft teeth" and required special care.

So she learned to smile with subtlety. The corners of her mouth curled sweetly, and her eyes half-closed; thereby, she kept her pain hidden away.

Halloran had had nice teeth. Marie regretted they were forced to leave his body at the roadside, but before they left she had created a tiny cross out of twigs and twine to stick in the dirt behind his head. The coyotes would eat him, but that couldn't be helped. She knew Pete was right; if they didn't hurry, they'd end up just like him—except there would be no one to make a twig cross, or say words of remembrance over their bodies at the side of the road.

But for now, she smiled in the rain.

Bryce, who acted curiously boyish although he was nearly the size of a man, laid down in the soft mud and sprawled like a starfish. He stuck his tongue out at the sky, but only caught a few drops.

As the rain ceased a strong wind picked up, battering their hair and rocking the Shell. They tumbled inside, soaking wet and excited. Anna arranged the water jugs in a neat row at the back of the shelter then combined their contents into a single jug, careful not to spill a single drop; a gallon and a half remained. Considering the labor required to pull the Shell uphill, it would last them a day, maybe two.

25

Chester Norton stumbled along the rainbow paths that led through the gumdrop forest.

Never could he have imagined a day when his idyllic wonderland would be strewn with corpses. They were beginning to rot, and he didn't have the energy to bury them, nor the emotional fortitude to ask any of the park guests to do the work. Many of the survivors were just children. And anyway—what was the point?

He figured it was likely the end of humanity. If it were not for the access tunnels under the carnival rides, he wouldn't have been able to save the handful of people he did. There were two whole families still alive, plus a small cluster of teenagers, most of whom were still too shocked to communicate very well. The older kids' parents, he assumed, were dead, mingling with the general population of decaying bodies scattered across the grounds.

The fresh food in the park was turning almost as quickly as the corpses, so he bypassed the restaurants at King Arthur's Food Court and instead made for the vending machine plaza. Without electricity, he'd have to smash the machines open—but that didn't matter any more, did it? His insurance company was very likely shut down, if the rest of the world looked anything like his poor little park. He didn't expect a visit from the Coca-Cola representative any time soon, either.

The park wasn't overly full when the tremors hit. He'd been having an off season—well, no, strike that. It was time to be honest with himself; the amusement park had been a bust. His dream had been to open a rest stop that was something more than a couple of bathrooms and a collection of dusty park benches. It was to be an exciting break from the highway, halfway between Baker and State Line. Road-weary parents could stretch their limbs and sip lemonade while the kiddos burned energy playing tag and riding the mini roller coaster. He had even designed a custom mascot, Curioso the Clown, to pose for family pictures. Spared no expense.

The park did okay, actually. The numbers it pulled on weekends would have been enough to get by in the city, but it just wasn't enough to justify the high cost of electricity and the water that had to be trucked all the way out to the desert site. He was proud of what he had accomplished but even if the apocalypse hadn't happened, he would probably have shut down within the next year or so.

The blue path he was strolling down turned purple. He was almost to the end of the rainbow.

Chester's shoe landed on something soft that popped like a big pea pod. When he looked down and lifted his foot he retched; it was a man's hand, wearing a hefty silver ring. The fingers had burst under Chester's heel, spraying little streams of dark, curdled blood across the purple concrete. The hand jutted from a bush that couched a large man's body, twisted with rigor mortis.

Chester quickened his pace, scraping the heel of his shoe on the pavement with every other step, trying to focus on his task and not on the bodies surrounding the path. If he thought about them too hard, he'd go mad. He needed to get crackers and chips from the machines, as well as cigarettes to calm the adults and candy to calm the kids. Water, if there was any left, and Coca Cola if there wasn't. He wished he had extended the underground tunnels all the way to the vending machines. The food courts didn't have the same electricity and mechanical requirements as the rides, so the extra work hadn't seemed necessary at the time of construction.

He dreaded the walk back, past the man with the silver ring.

The machines were locked tight, but Chester made quick work of their glass panes using a glittery rainbow-painted rock from a nearby planter. After smashing the doors, he kicked out the clinging shards of glass with his heel, which was still drying after his encounter with the corpse on the path. Crackers and cigarettes. He had to make sure he left enough room in the opening for his hand to reach in without getting cut open. He didn't want to end up like little Jimmy.

Poor Jimmy. The boy had fallen and hit his head

on the first day, and ended up with a raging infection from the cut. His entire head was swollen up. They'd given him aspirin, but it hardly made a dent in his fever. The kid was going to die and they couldn't do a damn thing about it. At least his parents had already gone during the first quake. Maybe the boy would get to meet up with them soon. Chips and candy.

"Chester?"

Someone had followed him. Someone young, with a sweet, gentle voice and green eyes.

"Sally! What are you doing out here? You don't want to see all this…all these…"

"I want to help, Chester. You didn't have to come alone. I brought a bag you could use."

"Thank you, Sally." Chester scooped handfuls of snacks and candies into the burlap sack she held, picking chunks of broken glass out as he found them.

"There's another path back to the tunnels," Sally said. "I figured it out on the brochure map yesterday. It's longer, but we don't have to go past the…the man. That you stepped on. I saw…"

"Okay. We'll go another way, if you want to. But it'll be longer, and probably not any nicer, you know."

Sally nodded. "I know, Chester. But I'll be brave enough, if I'm with you."

They wound their way back to the tunnels via Carnival Town. Clown statues which had once seemed whimsical to Chester now looked terrifying, laughing and exulting over an orgy of tumbled bodies. A young girl with harlequin face-paint slumped over her knees in the shade of the Tilt-A-Whirl ticket booth. Her hands were still loosely pressed to her bloody ears. Sally sniffled, and buried her face in Chester's lapels as they walked past.

"We just need to take a left at Lollipop Lane, and when it ends we'll be in the employee area. Less people.

Won't be as awful, I promise," Chester said.

Chester felt Sally nod against his chest. She was a lovely girl, but only sixteen. He hoped her growing attachment to him was daughterly, and not something else.

The backstage area was better…and worse. There were fewer bodies here, sure—but more of them wore faces Chester recognized. Buster lay slumped over a lunch table, still wearing his tool belt; he'd been hired straight out of vocational school, hand-picked by Charlie to maintain the machinery. He was young but bright, and handsome to boot. Helen, a plump hen of a woman who baked spiced cakes and raspberry tarts for the employees during the holidays, lay like a log in the middle of the walkway. Chester gingerly stepped around her body, guiding Sally without letting her look up from his jacket. Helen's nose was caked with blood; it looked exactly like the innards of one of her famous raspberry tarts.

As they neared the entrance to the tunnels, Chester heard sobbing. One of the young ones was crying again. How long could they last like this? None of this was Chester's fault, and the people hiding here weren't his guests any more. They were refugees from a terrible calamity, just the same as he was. Even so, he felt responsible for this lost flock. And sooner or later, no matter what he did, someone was going to snap. There would be hysteria, probably followed closely by violence. That's just how people were.

Then, all hell would break loose.

26

Something hunted Marie in the dark.

It was horned, and tall. Like how her father had always described Satan, but scarier. Much more dangerous, and much more real.

Every step it took cracked the earth beneath its

hooves. The ground reverberated, ringing out with the sound of the airquakes. The creature's horns were massive twisted cones scraping the sky. Eyes like glowing embers scoured the desert for Marie as its hooves flattened the sand dunes. It was beautiful and dangerous, wearing the form of a man with an athletic physique yet adorned with all the hideous features of one of her father's Demons.

It was coming for her. But why?

Overheard, Marie could see a million stars. Under her bare toes, as always, was the soft desert sand. To every side was darkness. And, in the darkness, a monster which sought her yet did not want to destroy her. It wanted something else.

"What are you?" she asked.

The creature froze, as if stunned by being addressed. Then it spoke. "Armageddon."

"Why?" she asked.

"Nature," it answered.

"What does that mean?"

"Inevitability, and chance. Your luck is bad."

Marie squinted in the dark. "Can you tell me what the quakes really are?"

"Yes."

Marie waited. The creature seemed to be struggling to stay in place, as if it was being pulled away, tugged by unseen forces. Three shadows danced behind him, smoky and amorphous.

"All of life is stuck in a repeating eternal loop of pain and destruction. I can tell you how to stop it."

"Okay," Marie said. "So tell me already."

"At the end of the universe, time swings like a pendulum. When time reaches its final point, everything becomes still for the smallest fraction of the shortest moment. It is like the crack of a whip; the end breaks the sound barrier, and for a moment all is calm. Then it swings back the other way, filled with energy and thunder. Your world—all of the worlds—will end soon. And then they will be reborn, as they always have throughout eternity."

"So 1959 really is the end of the world?"

"No. Time will end in 2019. When it does, *all* of time will end unless the pendulum swings. All of time, no matter what year you think you are in when it happens. It will collapse like a chain reaction. Understand?"

"No."

The Demon snarled. "Then stop asking questions."

"And the airquakes?"

"A symptom of the slowdown of time. All times have symptoms of the end now, simultaneously. All times that are near the end are sick, although they are not all the same."

"That's nonsense. What does all of this have to do with me?" Marie asked.

"Nothing," the creature said. "And everything. Your position in the stars is a coincidence, but without your hand, the reversal cannot take place. Everything would simply end. Forever."

"What am I supposed to do? How do I stop that from happening?"

The creature moved close, pressing in on her space. He came near enough for Marie to smell him—ashes and sulfur and the zing of adrenaline fear.

"I propose that you do not, Marie. Either way, your life will cease. The universe is not blessed by its arrangement; it is cursed. Help me end its suffering."

Marie woke up. In the distance, a coyote cried. She was safe in the Shell.

She thought about telling Pete and Anna what had happened, but in the end she didn't tell anyone else about the dream. Pete would have laughed it off, dismissed her experience as simple night terrors. And it wasn't really a dream, was it? It was far too real. And anyway, it was for her, and only her. There was no way she could convey to anyone else in the group the experience of talking to the creature in the void, and there was no reason to try. And if what the creature said was true, it sounded like she had a big decision to make—a decision that was hers alone.

The weight of it bore down on her shoulders, doubling the effort she made to help pull the Shell. For a while she thought she was hiding the burden well, but she caught sideways glances from Pete and Anna and knew they had caught on that something had changed in her. The world was ending; that was the source of the quakes. And it had something to do with her—a sad, dusty hermit of a girl from the middle of nowhere, on her way to the middle of nowhere. How could she have any hope of making the right choice?

If Demons existed after all, did it mean her father was right? And if that strange religious world of his did exist, just where the hell were all the angels?

She trudged on, pulling the Shell, but she started to feel disconnected from the team. Where were they going? Did they really have any chance at walking all the way to Las Vegas? It now sounded like a silly child's fantasy.

Marie fell silent, and stopped vocalizing her opinions. She let Pete build the fires at night and keep track of the airquakes. Anna stepped up a little, working to stretch the remaining food and water they had left. Stefan and Bryce caught rabbits to eat, and found an old plastic keg of water at an empty rest stop which they boiled and strained for an hour before deeming it safe to drink. The world spun on around her, but Marie was no longer exactly part of it.

The others noticed, but they didn't say anything. To them, Marie had taken on the air of someone otherworldly; she was quiet, and wise, and patient. The group became her flock, asking for her opinion when it was needed and usually getting an answer better than anything they came up with themselves. They tried to let her rest, as she often seemed tired and distant, but she would not have it; she worked hard, always at one of the center chains, and never cut a shift short. She was no longer sure they would reach their goal, but she was more sure than ever that they had to try.

If the world didn't end before they got there.

27

"Chester," Sally whispered. "Chester, I'm scared."

She tip-toed to Chester's cot and delicately lifted his blanket. He slept in his clothes, she noted. Too bad.

He was sleeping near the edge of the cot, so it was easy to slip in bed behind him. Carefully, she cradled his body in her own, and reached around his belly with her hand. She could feel his breathing, rising and falling, and she slowed her own to match it with his.

"What-"

"Shh," Sally whispered. "I just want to sleep with you."

"What! Sally, no." Chester tumbled from the cot and pointed at her with an accusatory—and, he hoped, fatherly—attitude. "It's inappropriate. You're just a kid!"

"But-"

"No." Chester stood and straightened his shirt. So, Sally really was smitten with him. A hellish development. "Listen, you just stay right there. Take my cot, and go back to sleep. I'm going to go check on the park."

"Let me come-"

"*No.*"

Chester stepped out into the crisp air. The sun was not quite up, but there was enough light to illuminate the dark blue roller coaster against the powder-blue sky. Morning dew created a watery sheen on the giant clown hat that formed the roof of the milkshake hut. The coyotes were quiet, retired for the night; daylight would arrive soon, along with the morning quake. He scanned the tunnel flooring, and the hinges on the doors. They still held, but were working loose with each quake, and not in a way that could be fixed with simple tools; the wood was splintering. The whole place was rattling apart.

They had two days left here, maybe three, before the tunnels started to collapse for real. Then what?

"Papa," a child said.

It was Simon, in his cowboy pajamas and brown socks, trundling out of one of the joining tunnels while rubbing his eyes with his fists. The six-year-old had slept most of the time since the first quake. He only woke up long enough to nibble candy before crying himself back to sleep.

"Good morning, Simon. Your papa's not here right now, but if I see him, I'll let him know where you are. Okay?"

"*Find* him," the boy demanded, groggy and grumpy. Simon's parents were, without doubt, among the dead on the rainbow paths. Chester wasn't really good with kids, for all his grand ideas about entertaining them. He didn't have any family of his own. Perhaps that's why the park had been such an appealing idea in the first place. It was an opportunity to bring joy to children, even if he had none.

"Okay, Simon. But first, have something to eat, okay?" Chester offered him an Abba Zaba—his last one, and his favorite, too.

"I'm tired of candy. That's all we've eaten for days," Simon said. "I want a hot dog."

"Yeah, well, I want some god damn whiskey,"

Chester muttered. He pocketed the candy bar and walked out of the tunnels; he was running out of things to say to the younger children. The piles of vending machine treats were starting to lose their appeal, and Chester had little else to distract them with. Time was running out.

He stood a few feet out from the doorway and stretched, reaching for the sky with his fingertips. His back popped like distant gunfire. A warm breeze picked up, bringing the scent of rot, stronger now than it was on previous days. He had to get everyone clear of this place, but how?

The parking lot was tidy and well-graveled, and still filled with an assortment of family sedans—none of which worked. He had tried every one that had keys still hanging from the ignition, which had accounted for most of them. He wasn't a mechanic, but the cars wouldn't even *start* to start, which seemed like a pretty fatal problem. They were as dead as everything else.

A sudden burst of laughter coming from the western horizon jolted him badly. None of his tribe could possibly be all the way out there, could they? But on the street he saw a car, and it was creeping slowly forward. A working car!

28

"Join us," Marie said. She knew it was what the carnival man wanted, but he was afraid to ask. The invitation was a mercy, saving him from his reluctance to impose on their group.

"Oh thank you, thank you!" Chester said, clasping his hands. "But we won't all fit in your vehicle. There's twelve of us, including a few kids."

Pete frowned. "Do you have a safe place to hide from the quakes? I can help put something together for you, but it will take a couple of days."

"We've been hiding in concrete tunnels under the park. I had them put in when I was building, for storage and ride access. They're holding for now, but I wouldn't give them more than four or five more quakes."

"Should be enough," Pete said. "Got a blowtorch?"

"Maybe, in the tool shed. But, say…" Chester said. "Um."

"What is it, Chester?" Marie asked. "Just say it."

"Do you know what's happening? Have you heard anything? Was it the military? Is it…you know, everywhere? The death, and the shaking. We've been so closed off here…"

Pete glanced at Marie. He had a feeling she knew something, although he could not take a guess at how. He had been at her side since the beginning, and had spoken to everyone he had. But she seemed different, recently. More withdrawn, older, wiser.

Marie said nothing.

"We have no idea. I'm sorry, Chester. But we're as in the dark as you are," Pete said. "We're heading to Las Vegas, and we think maybe we'll get some answers there."

"Right," Chester said. "Well, the roller coaster repair shop's this way, should have plenty of tools. Let's see what we can find."

Pete set up the group with two family wagons, carving the metal window panels from the doors of other cars. He gutted them with Stefan's help, while Bryce kept the smaller kids busy far away from the bodies littering the park. The children played in the sun and enjoyed their new jobs, helping Bryce collect bits of trash; cups, empty popcorn bags, discarded bags and cardboard boxes. What specific purpose they'd serve, Bryce couldn't have said. But it kept the little ones busy, and might be useful if the rain returned.

Pete had the new shells completed in a day and a half, with enough time left to line them with tarps and fabric gathered from the park. He refitted the original Shell with new tires, and added more bedding. When they were done, they lined up all three cars on the highway to form a bright caravan; the yellow Shell led in front, followed by a blue Crosley station wagon and a brick-red Ford.

"It's a parade!" Sally giggled.

"Next quake will be here in half an hour," Chester said. "Sun's starting to go down. Everyone back to the tunnels. We'll ride it out and then hit the road, get a couple hours in before the coyotes turn out."

"Marie?" Pete said. "That sound okay to you?"

"Yes, Pete. That will be just fine."

She had let them all work without comment over the last couple of days. The Demon visited her again, with more information which left her bewildered and irresolute. He had told her something about three women of fate. She couldn't remember exactly; sometimes what he said was difficult to retain after she woke up, but he would never speak to her outside the dreams.

Marie retreated further into herself, but tried to hold to on the outside world, too; these people needed her. They felt it too—the coming end, and her importance in it. Often they would shout out plans and ideas on how to proceed or gather resources, but they would always wait and ask her opinion before they began. She wasn't sure their deference was entirely deserved, but she understood they needed a leader, preferably someone with a slight air of mysticism. She accepted the job.

"What do you think of the caravan, Marie?" Pete asked.

"It's wonderful, Pete." Marie caught his eye and offered him an appreciative smile. "Good job."

Back in the tunnels, Anna examined Marie's shoulders. The bruising was deep; Marie's bones ached.

"You need a rest, honey. It's been days, and I'm worried you're going to do some permanent damage to yourself. You're too young for this kind of labor. There are enough of us now to take shifts pulling."

"No," Marie said. "I won't quit. I-"

"Marie," Pete said, taking her hands in his rough paws. "Listen, now. Your spirit may be willing, but your body is tired. It's your turn to take advice from us. The rest of us will all be taking shifts, and you have to as well. You hear me?"

Marie bowed her head. "I hear you, Pete. Thank you." She was at risk of drifting away from the world, forgetting the limitations of her flesh. But Pete would remind her to eat, and wake her from sleep when she didn't wake up on her own. He kept her grounded.

29

Ernie sat with his eyes squeezed shut and tried to remember the light. It had been days since he'd seen it.

He missed his wife. She had very independent ideas—really a bit of a know-it-all—but Ernie found her endearing. Her rules were simple but strict: no cigarettes, alcohol, or fried foods. Somehow she had got it in her head that they were unhealthy, no matter what the TV commercials or even the government said about them. She was a health nut, and a little bit crazy, but he loved her.

A year ago, she had caught him smoking in the attic. A terrible row had ensued, followed by a promise: he would never smoke, ever again. Not anything, even cigars. His wife had only stayed with him because of that promise, and it was one he intended to keep. She said he had to stay strong and healthy to see their kids graduate from college, which meant quitting entirely. Not just a pack a day, or even a butt at lunchtime.

Nothing. Kaput.

So, he quit. He felt better, sure, but sometimes the cravings got so strong he started ransacking pockets he already knew were empty for one last cigarette; surely he'd left one somewhere; a backup, an emergency smoke for when nothing else would soothe the nerves. Some days, he felt he'd die if he couldn't find one.

He chuckled. The sound was flat as shale as it bounced off the walls of his tiny prison. See, if he hadn't quit, he'd probably have a lighter. And maybe if he had a lighter, he could find a way out of this hole.

Maybe quitting had killed him after all.

The building had collapsed around him as he worked in the basement, sorting boxes of old paperwork. There didn't seem to be any leadup to the collapse; a low hum, maybe, but not that grating rumble like you hear before a big earthquake. First thing that happened was just his head hurting a bit. Then, before he could run upstairs, the stairwell collapsed, and the concrete walls followed soon after. It was the strangest thing.

No rescue crews were on their way, from the sound of it. The rubble overhead had been silent and still since the event, other than an occasional low vibration from somewhere above every few hours. Ernie hoped it was the approach of a digger. Didn't quite sound like one, though.

The air was getting thin. That was what scared him more than anything else. If the building collapsed the rest of the way, then he'd die quick. If he passed out from thirst or hunger, he'd just slip away in his sleep. It was the thought of suffocation that filled him with dread— dragging useless air into his lungs, heaving until the last moment came as he was wracked with cramps that shot through his body like electric eels on cocaine.

Ernie's fingertips throbbed. Maybe it was best he

didn't have a light. A few minutes after the collapse, he had momentarily lost his cool. He didn't remember much, but he knew that he had screamed his throat hoarse. His hands had clawed streaks of blood onto one of the concrete walls—and left behind a fingernail, too.

Since then, his thoughts were mostly of the past. Good times: the bright summers when the kids were out of school and the whole world was full of sunshine. He had taken that brief chapter of his life for granted, and longed for it now with a deep thirst greater even than his need for water. He dreamed of days like when his little boy was born, and a year later, the girl. He'd thought the newborns a little ugly at first, but didn't tell the wife. Then, after a single hour cradling them in his arms and caring for them, looking into their eyes, he knew they were the most beautiful sight he'd ever seen. Miracles, they were.

He heard a sound above his left shoulder, and nearly jumped from his skin.

Scuttling, like a small animal—a rat.

Great, now he had rats.

Then the thought pushed its way to the front of his mind, and his eyes flew open in the dark. A rat! A rat was a living creature, one that needed air and water—and if he was hearing it now for the first time, it had entered recently. Somewhere, there was a hole. That meant the air wouldn't thin. And, more than that, somewhere past the hole there was probably water, and food too.

The sound stopped, but for the first time in days he felt a crumb of hope. He sat still, so still he could feel his heartbeat, and waited for another sound.

30

"How far, Pete? Do you think we're going to make it?" Anna asked.

Pete stood and stretched his back as he did ten times a day, listening to the pops that sounded like the crackling lard from his deep fryer back at the Bun Boy. It wasn't the first time today someone had asked him that same question, as if he was supposed to know. But, as always, he did his best to give an answer, neither to the positive or the contrary. He couldn't afford to give false hope, but he didn't want to risk losing the whole team to despair, either.

"Still too early to tell. We found some more water, sure, but we picked up a lot of people, too. And even aside from the use of resources, more people means more trouble. More chances for someone to get greedy, or mean. You know."

"I know," Anna said in a soft, thoughtful voice, remembering her panic attack from the first days of the trip.

"Don't worry about it, honey. You've toughened up. You're one of the leaders of this group, and I trust you. I want you to know that."

"Thanks, Pete." Anna smiled with tired eyes. "That means a lot. Really, it does."

The newcomers from the theme park were a weak and frightened bunch, even without accounting for the children. In truth, some of the children were better behaved than their guardians. One middle-aged man— Reuben, his name was—tried briefly at the beginning of the journey to take over the caravan. He was a politician, he said, and therefore a natural born leader. He challenged Pete, and nearly took a swing at him. The tense moment was defused by Marie, who asked in her subdued voice that everyone remain calm. And for some reason, it worked.

But Marie wasn't quite *Marie,* any more. She still clumped around in Anna's boots, still had the same sweet smile that showed off her jagged, broken teeth when she forgot to keep her lips pressed shut. But there was a sort of unrealness to her, like she wasn't entirely attached to the world any more. Pete was sure it was connected to the airquakes, but he didn't ask her about it. She had mostly stopped speaking.

Marie approached him, as though she knew he was thinking of her. "Pete," she said in a voice grown distant and sweet. Angelic, sort of. "Pete, I want to let you know something."

"Yes, hon? What is it?"

"You're not going to like it," Marie said, smiling. "I already know you won't like it, but you have to stay calm about it, okay?"

"Why? What's wrong?"

"Nothing. But during the next quake, I want to try something. I am going to sit outside the Shell. I'm going to ride it out."

"What? Marie, no! Absolutely not!"

"Pete, you know I've changed. I'm not quite…in tune with the world any more. Yes, that's it exactly. The world vibrates, like music, with its own tune. I'm singing a different song now, and I don't think the quakes will hurt me any more. Understand? It's like…a different wavelength."

"I suppose I understand, kind of. But I don't see the point of trying it. Why take the risk, Marie?"

"Because I have something else I need to do; a task even bigger than crossing the desert. Something to do with the quakes. And I need to find out if I have the strength to do it."

"I know you're right. I know you've changed, and something is going on that I can't hope to understand. But can you at least tell me a little about it?"

Marie considered. "I could, but it wouldn't help. It would make it worse, I think. Can you trust me?"

Pete sighed. "Do me one favor, Marie. Please."

"Anything, Pete."

"We're maybe ten hours from the state border. The next quake is in an hour, but if you will join us in the Shell this time, I'll say nothing against your experiment during the next one. But let it be tomorrow. I expect to find something at the border town, but I don't know what. Could be good for us, could be bad. I'm hoping for shelter and supplies. Can you wait until then?"

"Yes, Pete. I don't know what difference that makes, but if that's what you want, I'll do it." Marie's voice grew more faint. "I'm going to go to the Shell now and sleep. I'm…tired…" Marie swooned, and Pete caught her in his arms. She regained her balance but was weak, swaying like a thin birch tree in the wind. Pete wrapped his arm around Marie's shoulders and pulled her into a hug. He nodded and bowed his head, as tears squeezed from his crinkled eyes. "Okay, Marie. Okay."

31

"State Line, Nevada," little Simon read slowly. The sign was weathered but readable. "We're in Nevada! We made it!"

Pete squinted at the distant town creeping over the horizon and called back down the line, "Welcome to the Silver State, everyone."

Reuben, the politician, grunted. He dropped his chain harness and swiftly strode toward the town, muttering "I got a man to see. Good luck, assholes."

Pete watched Reuben hop a short wooden fence and make for a group of low buildings set apart from the casino. "No loss there. What a pain in the ass he was."

"Pete," Marie whispered. "You did it."

"Well, it's not Vegas, Marie. It's Nevada, though, and we're about forty miles from the city. If we can find food and water here, and not too much trouble, I think we'll make it the rest of the way."

"This place looks like it's in good shape, Pete. Do we really need to keep moving?" Anna said.

"We'll see."

The buildings at State Line had hairline fractures, but were mostly intact. The most promising building, a country club called The Redwood Room, looked freshly painted and clean. Signs pasted to the awning advertised "Gambling" and "Live Floor Shows." A row of shiny cars lined the front walkway.

"It was a busy place," Pete said. "So…"

"Dirty inside. Bodies," Chester said. "That's just as likely as anywhere we go, though."

"Yeah. You want to go in with me?"

"Well, 'want' is a strong word. But sure, I'll accompany you. Let's see what we've got."

Pete and Chester approached the front door. They pulled their shirt sleeves over their hands and used their fists to clear dust from the glass.

"No good," Chester said. "Too dark inside to see anything. Think the windows are tinted, too. Swanky joint."

"All right. Let's just do it, then." Pete put both hands on the metal push-bar and leaned. It barely moved an inch.

"That's odd. It locked?"

"Don't see why it would be. Here, help me out."

Both of the men threw their weight against the door and it slid open, leaving a thick brown streak along the floor. There was more than one body blocking its path: several people had rushed the inward-swinging door, crushing against it, and had died in a small pile as the blood ran from their ears. Several of the bodies had broken limbs.

"Fools were in such a rush to leave, they just about killed themselves before the quake did," Pete muttered, holding his shirt sleeve over his nose. "For all the difference it made."

A maelstrom of flies rose from the twisted limbs, buzzing like tiny chainsaws. They were so bloated and logy with excess food they thumped clumsily into Pete's head as they circled in the room.

Chester coughed. "This place is rotten, Pete. Too many bodies. It's too late; they've already had a chance to fester in this enclosed room. Never get the stench out."

"God damn, but that's the *worst* thing I've ever smelled." Pete stepped backwards out the door, gagging. Chester followed, pulling the door shut behind him.

"We need water, food. What do we do?"

Pete walked around to the back of the building, but found only locked doors.

"Let's try the next one."

Two buildings over was a smaller slot-machine lounge called Primm Casino. It was less glamorous than The Redwood Room, but also less populated with rotting corpses. Chester and Pete donned rubber gloves from the maintenance closet and moved five bodies from the casino main floor out to the open desert behind the building. Pete half-heartedly kicked sand over the corpses, but it was a job poorly done. He was just too tired.

When the room was clear, Chester peeled off his gloves and chucked them into a gilded trash can behind the bar. "All right, that gives us enough room to set up camp. Not too bad in here. But this place doesn't appear to have a restaurant, and we need food."

"Only one thing we can do," Pete said.

"Ugh, no. I think I know what-"

"We're going back into The Redwood. But we'll prepare, as much as we're able. Make some masks, somehow. Block some of the smell. Cloth sacks over our heads to keep the flies off."

"God damn. Pete, that place is crawling."

"Yes it is. But we really don't have any choice, you know."

"Yeah," Chester said. "I know. We going in after the next quake?"

Pete fell silent, remembering the promise he'd asked of Marie.

"Yeah. After the next quake. Depending on…well. Yes, after the next quake."

"Pete. Pete! Who's that? Is that Reuben, coming back?"

Chester pointed at a man lurching across the gravel parking lot. The cuffs of his pants were tattered and he seemed exhausted, but his eyes were alert. He was battered and worn, but in his right mind, at least.

"Hi there," Pete called out. "We're just looking for water, not trying to do anyone any harm. I'm Pete."

The man rasped, "Judd. Judd Starling."

From the distant Shell, a thin wail drifted. It ended in a sob.

"That was Marie," Pete whispered to Chester. "Oh god, oh no. I think he's…this man is her *father*."

32

Ernie waited until the scuttling sound moved close, then made a mad grab in its general direction. He was blind in the dark, but his ears had grown sensitive enough to hear every tiny footfall the rat made inside its hole, and his hand struck true. The creature screeched and writhed in his palm, but he gripped it tight even as he felt its chiseled front teeth pop through the skin on the side of his hand.

He desperately wanted to kill this animal which

had invaded his space and probably shat on his floor and had its run of the whole damn place. He wanted to maybe eat it, or at least sip some of its blood, to survive a little longer. The strength of his desire to do so surprised and dismayed him. He wanted to eat a rat; what was happening, here? Had he lost his mind?

He stifled his urges; he had a plan.

From his pocket he withdrew a string he had worked from the lining of his pants. Actually, it was several threads, all pulled from various articles of clothing, doubled and tied together. It would have been longer if he hadn't doubled it, but he was worried about its strength against the fear of the rat. It was only about ten feet long.

Using his free hand and his teeth, he tied the string around the top of the rat's tail, right where it met the hair. He pulled the knot tight enough to make the creature squeak with pain and rage.

"Shut up, Gerald!" he screamed at the rat.

Yesterday, he'd blacked out. When he woke up he had named the animal after his old boss, Gerald McCoy. He had been unconscious when the designation happened, of course—but he arose from his nap with the sure knowledge that the rat's name was Gerald.

Yeah, he was definitely starting to get a little weird.

Ernie was right on the edge of losing his cool again, but he couldn't afford that right now. This might be his last chance.

After giving the knot one final tug, he set the rat on the concrete block to his left, close to where he had first heard it making noise a day and a half ago.

Gerald wasted no time in running off, scrambling up a pile of concrete chunks and frayed wires. It clawed up planks of wood, making tiny scraping noises which sent shivers up the back of Ernie's neck. Six feet up the wall, it entered a hole. The string in Ernie's hand tugged a little, and he moved toward the sound of the rat, giving it as much slack as possible.

The hole was small, but when Ernie pressed his face up to it he could smell fresh air. There was also the smell of rat droppings, and—just faintly—rotting food. The fissure was an umbilical to the outside.

So, he had a lifeline. But unless he made the hole a lot wider, all he could do was *smell* the outside world. Of course, there was a good chance shifting the rubble would bring the entire building down on him. But now, after days in the dark, that prospect didn't seem so bad at all. Either he got out to the light, or he got out to the darkness. Either way, he'd be out.

Ernie couldn't hear the airquake happening outside. He could feel a strange vibration in the soles of his feet, but it wasn't strong enough inside the cavern to worry him, or make him consider the possibility of danger. Under his shoes, it was just a little tickling—a slight vibration, and the air felt strange. But in the back of his brain, a tiny alarm sounded; something was out there, and it might not be too good. Might be dangerous.

He ignored it. What choice did he have? Ernie got to work.

33

Marie focused on the sound of her own breathing. She sat with her mouth open, panting in the heat. The closeness of the humid air, already ninety degrees at sunrise, pressed in on her as she waited for the atmosphere to start trembling. As she waited, she worried. Not for her own welfare, but for those she led. If she died now, what would become of them? The morning had not gone especially smoothly.

Pete had not handled it well. He put on a brave face until she actually opened the casino door to leave, but he lurched toward her at the last moment, trying to pull her back inside. He had shouted something frantic about how she would die with blood pouring from her nose and ears, and for no good reason. Pete believed Marie when she said she had a purpose which could not be fulfilled unless she could endure the quakes without shelter; he had grown to respect her judgement. But still, he felt a deep dread that Marie would simply die, and he wouldn't be able to save her. Letting her experiment with her life while he hid in a shelter ran against his instincts.

Anna and some of the others had talked him down, backed him away from the door. Eventually they coerced him into the casino's vault, where they could ride out the quake in safety. Marie's guilt over Pete's anguish was sharp, but she was steadfast. If she couldn't do this, the world would die. She was sure of that now.

Last night's dream had told her. It had been a roaring storm of chaos and noise; white noise which was not soothing but instead rattled your skull and muddled your brain. The Demon who had spoken to her before was there, and under his arms he held two bodies; a middle-aged woman with blood streaming from her hair, and a younger woman wearing a purple skirt covered in little lighthouses. As Marie watched, the young woman looked up at her and opened her mouth to speak. But instead of words, a small bird flew from her throat and was swept away in the storm.

A third woman had walked up behind the Demon—she was barely visible past the Demon's massive form—and lingered a moment before taking his tail in her hands and yanking it with all her strength. The Demon tilted his head back and roared, not in pain but in anger, and threw the middle-aged woman directly at Marie. As the body struck her, Marie woke up.

She was in a dark casino.

All around her she saw the sleeping forms of her family, her friends.

As she blinked the sleep from her eyes, she had felt sad that her first experience with the glitz and glamour of the Nevada gambling culture was dead and cold. No twinkling lights for her, no rings and bells and "jackpot!" cheers. The shiny silver dollars the slot machines still held in their bellies offered no thrills. What use could they possibly have in a dead world? Skipping-stones?

The rest of the group was still asleep except for Stefan, who was on night watch. She had looked around the room in the dim light of the cresting moon coming from the window. Children, some parents, and a couple of teenage boys who had eyed her coyly at first until they eventually caught sight of her broken teeth. Her original partners, Anna and Pete, whom she had come to love as her family.

She was almost a child herself, and on her own for the first time. What right did the universe have to demand she sacrifice her life for the first people she had ever cared about?

From the casino vault she had heard a faint moan, and a deep snore which she recognized very well; her father.

Her boogey-man. The sound of his voice made her teeth hurt.

As she sat now on the hilltop waiting for the sun, she thought of her childhood. Her mother was caring but vacant, drifting away whenever she sensed pain or danger. And most pain and danger came from her father.

He'd never laid a hand on Marie in any kind of sexual way. He hadn't been bad like that. But he was relentless in his desire for fame, success, immortality. His health resort had not been a place for Marie to live, but simply to exist. It wasn't for her. It was for him, as everything in the whole world had always been.

She had lain awake so many nights with the exposed nerves in her teeth throbbing, terrified to move her tongue or even breathe too hard lest she brush a freshly cracked tooth and cause an electric shock of agony to jolt down her spine all the way to her toes. He gave her pills to dull the pain, but they didn't work well because he wouldn't give her more than half a tablet due to her young age.

For a while, her front teeth had looked fine. Father had managed to clean them with a new solvent he concocted, and they were shiny and white for a single summer. Then, they began to erode. The solvent ate at them and they wore away like chips of ice under warm water. Father tried to replace them using coyote teeth, very innovative, but it was no use. The transplants wouldn't take. He finally obtained two human incisors—Marie didn't ask where he got them—and performed another transplant, so she could bite into food again. The incisors eventually took, but the rest of her teeth still gnawed inside her cheeks like a saw.

And now he was here, in the little town behind her, sleeping safely in a casino vault, surrounded by stacks of useless cash. Was it somehow the Demon's doing?

Father had acted unsocial, and the group had locked him up. He was hurt in the head, like Halloran had been. And he kept rambling about someone named Gibson, how he'd gotten the better of him, bashed his head with a rock. Most of it was gibberish.

When the morning airquake came they'd all have to crowd into the vault with him for a while, but Marie wouldn't be there. She'd be sitting on her hilltop outside, under the sun, waiting for the end—or the beginning, perhaps. If she lived, perhaps she would finally understand what she was meant to do next.

34

"What's she doing?" Bryce asked.

"She's just sitting on that little hill out there. Like she's meditating or something," Stefan said.

"We have to get into the vault," Chester said. "It's time. Pete?"

Pete stood at the door, his eyes fixed on Marie's back. "I'm coming," he muttered, touching his fingers to the glass. "Be safe, Marie."

They pressed into the vault, forcing Marie's foolish father to the back as they pulled the door shut behind them. It couldn't be locked from the inside, but the younger men grasped the pull-handle and leaned back, keeping it tight long enough for the quake to pass. When the door stopped vibrating in its frame, they cracked it open and peeked outside. A window in the lobby had cracked and a slot machine had vomited its coins, but the large room was otherwise unchanged.

"It worked," Chester said. "This place can protect us."

"Let me out. Let me out!" Pete shouted from the back. "I have to check on Marie!"

They exited the vault, gasping for fresh air. Pete lurched, wide-eyed, across the casino floor toward the doors.

"Not you," Chester said, pushing Marie's father back into the vault.

"But I can't even breathe in there! Please, Gibson! You gotta let me out!" Judd yelled.

"I'm not Gibson, I'm Chester. Anyway, you're staying put for now. Maybe we can talk about it later, but now's not the time."

Judd stood on his toes, peeking at Pete over Chester's shoulder. "What's going on with Marie? Why's that ugly man so worried? What happened to my daughter?"

"We're about to find out."

"She's my daughter! You can't keep me from her! She's *my-*" Judd screamed, but Chester cut his words short with a threatening wave of his fist. Judd retreated to the back of the vault.

Pete lost no time sprinting across the street in front of the casino. He climbed the little hilltop with huge strides, calling Marie's name. She had fallen over, and her hair had fanned out on the hilltop like a spray of wild grasses.

Pete cradled Marie in his arms and pried her eyes open with a clumsy thumb. "Marie! Marie, can you hear me?"

"Pete!" Anna called from the bottom of the hill. "Is she bleeding? Did her ears leak?"

Pete didn't answer, but crouched over Marie, pressing his fingers to her neck for a pulse. Tears ran down his cheeks.

Marie took a deep breath and opened her eyes. "Pete. I'm okay. It's…so good to see you again."

"Oh, thank god! Will you come inside now? Please?"

"Yes, Pete. But I'll need your help. Do you think you can help me?"

"Of course I can, Marie." As they made their careful way down the hill toward the casino lobby, Anna saw Marie's hair had turned white.

35

Marie had learned much in her dreams, yet she did not know exactly *what* it was she learned.

A woman with aged eyes who was not yet old

stood in a battle stance in the desert at night. She was unarmed, and wearing a professional looking off-white silk blouse and black slacks with tattered cuffs which were tucked into sensible boots. From her manner of dress she was unprepared for the situation she currently found herself in, yet she was confronting it with a measure of strength and poise that Marie admired.

Her friend was dressed in a large black cloak which concealed his body, but Marie could sense the person was twisted and misshapen under the folds of fabric. As she watched on from atop a small hill near the scene, the cloaked figure pushed back his hood to reveal a strange, mashed face which conveyed compassion despite its un-usual configuration. He crouched near the woman in the silk blouse with his left arm extended, shielding her from an angry, wiry man standing near a central bonfire.

It was night; the perimeter of the camp disap-peared into darkness. Marie could make out a ring of short people, childlike and gaunt, standing at the perimeter of the light cast by the fire. The tribe watched the standoff with fear and fascination, but Marie could not tell who they were rooting for.

A massive man lunged like a stalking animal from beyond the circle of onlookers. He was furious and red, his face twisted into a knotted expression that spoke of a lifetime of betrayal and pain. The woman in the silk blouse cried out, *"Charles! Stop! You can't beat him!"* but the huge man was undeterred, and charged at the wiry man with all of his strength. He was not to succeed; the wiry man plunged a knife deep into the fleshy belly of the fat man, who collapsed into the dust.

The wiry man knelt and said some words Marie could not hear, but his speech was ill-timed. The huge man pulled the knife from his own body and thrust it into the wiry man's knee. It was not a fatal blow, but it was a crippling one.

The vision began to fade, and Marie felt herself moving away from that time and place. In the final moments before she lost sight of the fight she saw that the wiry man's knee injury may in fact have proved fatal, as the scores of onlookers rushed at him and pulled him down to the ground.

Marie expected to wake on the hilltop, but instead she found that she was in a dilapidated house—no, some kind of motorhome, like the kind some people took camping. The young woman and the middle-aged woman from her other dreams were here; they were the pair she had seen when she was in the void with the pendulum. The Demon had thrown the older one at her—and she saw that he was here too, his unfathomable presence made all the more implausible, almost comical, by his mundane surroundings. The hulking beast filled an entire doorway at the end of the room, emanating power and rage and lust with his presence. Marie went unnoticed by all three, including the Demon; he was fixated on his prize.

The younger woman stood near a table in the middle of the room. There was something strange about her; she was dark and shadowy, almost a ghost. Marie could not imagine what that meant. She was present and visible yet fading swiftly from the light, changing more into a hazy silhouette of herself with every passing second. Down her neck ran a long vertical gash, like a fault line between her head and her spine.

The Demon stepped toward the middle-aged woman, who was incapacitated with terror. He gripped her wrists in his massive claws and pressed her body to the wall. A voice spoke—it was too loud to be human, loud enough to shatter glass, yet she did not hear it with her ears. The sound bypassed her senses and appeared directly in her brain, a complicated voice interlaced with screams of agony or rapture from a million souls. It was the Demon's true voice, the way it was heard outside of dreams. The voice said, "*Come, bitch.*"

The younger woman screamed with rage, and charged at the Demon.

Marie woke up.

She was on the hilltop, and Pete was cradling her in his rough arms, calling her name.

36

Anna leaned back, watching the stars twinkle. Most of the rest of the group was sleeping indoors, but the casino still smelled bad to her—faint cigarette smoke, with an underlying odor of rotten meat. She found a ladder to the roof and camped there instead, safe from the smell and from brain-damaged wildlife that might come wandering through town. No coyotes up *here.*

She sipped wine from a crystal balloon glass she found in the VIP lounge. It was the best she'd ever had, and she didn't think it was just because the last couple weeks had been so hard. It was really good stuff; the label was scrawled with gold letters she could not decipher. Looked French.

It was a beautiful night.

The absolute silence of the little town was eerie. There should have been night creatures; owls, or coyotes, or even crickets rubbing their legs in the dark. But the only wildlife was the flies, most of which had probably migrated over from The Redwood Room.

Still, it was beautiful. The best night since Baker.

To the west, a light flashed. Anna's tired brain initially assumed it must be the headlights of a car cresting the low hill near the town, but when she looked closer she realized the movement was closer than that, and the light was all wrong. It was the dancing of firelight, not the steady beam of lamps. And it wasn't moving, except to engulf a small building at the edge of town.

Anna jumped to her feet.

Shouting from below; questions, alarm. An unknown person was running with a torch in hand from one building to the next, screaming, mad. They smashed windows, lit curtains, threw bottles like Molotov cocktails, with the clear intent of destroying all of State Line.

Anna rushed down to the main casino. The next few minutes were a blur; the front door was pushed open and a torch flew inside and landed on the carpet, throwing sparks. Children cried, and the parents in the group shoved them out through windows, climbing over tipped slot machines to escape the rapidly spreading blaze. Anna covered her mouth with a cloth and helped guide the group to safety. Outside, she counted heads, but kept coming up short.

Someone was missing.

"Marie!" Pete screamed in the noise of the fire. "Where's Marie? She sleeps deep! Has anyone seen her yet?"

Anna didn't hesitate; didn't even think. As she ran back into the casino, she worked methodically, first dropping to the floor under the thickest layers of smoke, then calling Marie's name, working her way across the singed carpet. The fire had almost reached the bar, which was loaded with flammable liquids; Anna didn't have long.

She found Marie pinned under a tipped slot machine, semi-conscious. The girl seemed to be still asleep, somehow, even in the noise and the panic. She wasn't hurt; just asleep. When Anna tried to rouse her she struck out with her fists, yelling, "*I told you I won't, you'll have to kill me first. I won't help you.*"

Anna braced her feet against a poker table and

dragged Marie towards the door until the movement woke her, and they were able to help each other through the flames. Anna pushed Marie ahead, hurrying her, but as they reached the glass door she felt her hair catch fire.

Reaching hands pulled Marie through the door to safety. It was the last vision Anna saw before the fire engulfed her body.

Pete watched Anna disappear into the flames, screaming. It was too much for him. He spun on the group, demanding to know who started the fires, shouting, pointing. His rage and exhaustion drove him into a fury.

A laugh from behind the crowd pierced through his accusations. Reuben the politician stood there, stripped naked, holding a lit torch. Blood streamed from his ears.

"Burned it! Cauterized the wounds! He told me to do it! The devil made me do it!" Laughing, he touched the torch to his hair. In seconds, his body was immolated, and he died where he stood.

37

Judd Starling was at the end of his rope.

The group of losers and miscreants led by that greaseball Pete had tied his wrists together and tethered him to the rear of the ugly yellow car they hid in during the quakes. They let him in when they had to, but not before blindfolding him like the cowards they were. He hadn't helped matters, of course—probably shouldn't have bloodied that Stefan fellow's nose, broke it most likely— but the ruffian had laid hands on him; practically asked for a pounding.

Judd missed Zzyzx Town. Never should have left. Frank had talked him into it, practically forced him out of his own home. Frank was dead now, with a bad case of splattered brains, but that didn't really help Judd's current situation much.

As the stupid mules pulled their empty shells across the desert, he stumbled along behind, fantasizing about Mrs. Derringer. She'd been a regular, and a rich fool to boot. Blonde, svelte, and pathetically dumb; Judd's favorite kind of woman. She'd had a penchant for the baths, and being of European descent did not balk at reclining topless in the salt soaks. As of Zzyzx's massage and bath customers were men, he never received a single complaint.

He thought of her now, allowing his mind to wander at will as the balls of his feet began to wear through his shoes. She had greeted him one time with a kiss on the cheek. He had inhaled deeply, enjoying her scent; hair that smelled like lavender flowers and, just faintly, of the special eau de toilette he had left in her private rooms. His chest had swelled that she had deigned to use it, although she could not have known he was the one to leave it there specially for her. In any case, it showed she approved of his refined taste, and thereby…

"Move it!" Stefan barked behind him, picking dried blood from his nose with a dirty thumbnail. "You're lagging, and it's making the pull harder. Pick up your feet, asshole."

Judd snarled, and Stefan kicked at his sore leg with his boot. "Faster! You won't be an anchor on my watch."

"My feet hurt. My shoes are wearing through," Judd said, adjusting his pants. His tender memories of Mrs. Derringer had given him an inconvenient woody.

"All our shoes are wearing through. It's the heat. You're not special, and I'm not letting you ride inside. I know that's what you want."

"Wouldn't dream of it," Judd sneered. "I want to ride on top."

"Shut up."

Judd could tell the group's patience was wearing thin. They thought they had it made back at State Line, before that loose cannon of a politician burned the whole town. Tempers were running hot and Judd was fairly sure he could use that to his advantage, if he kept his eyes and ears open.

Stefan walked up to Pete and paced him. "How close, you think? Another day?"

"Actually, maybe tonight," Pete said. "Although we won't be able to tell how close we are if it's dark. Strange to think of that. Glittering, sparkling Las Vegas—dead as a doornail."

"We should camp, wait to approach until tomorrow even if we're making good time. No idea what we'll find there. Marie?"

"Yes," Marie said. She had been walking next to Pete, and Stefan hadn't even noticed. She glided like a spirit these days, even in Anna's oversized boots. As she paced the Shell, footfalls which should have scraped and thudded on the red asphalt made no sound, as if she wasn't quite touching the earth. Her hair which had so recently turned white was now streaked grey with ash from the fire, and cropped oddly where it had been burned away.

"Tomorrow will be the day. Tonight, we rest one last time in the desert. Las Vegas might be…bad," Marie said. "Stefan, lead out in the front. I know your pulling shift is supposed to be next, but I need you scouting. I'll talk to Chester about taking your spot. Pete, speak to the families. Tell them what the plan is. See if you can find any last candies for the kids. They're tired of it, I know, but they won't refuse it and it still seems to help calm them down a little. Soda pop too, if there's any left. Cigarettes for anyone over fifteen. Use the rest of what we have to make everyone happy. Because tomorrow we either restock, or…"

"Or we're done," Pete said. "End of the line."

"Yes," Marie said.

"What you talking about, little girl?" Judd said. "They all listening to you, now? Why, that makes them even stupider than you. Never thought it possible!"

Marie walked with her head down while Pete bristled on her behalf. He knew she didn't want him to defend her, but it took all the strength he had to keep his mouth shut. A frown creased his face.

"Girl. Girl. Girly. Marie. Mare-bear. Mare. Mare. *Marie!*" Judd shouted.

"*What!*" Marie yelled, whipping her head toward her father, suddenly grounded. Her boots scraped against the asphalt.

"Well hello, honey!" Judd said. "So, you and that big fella—you fucking him yet? That why he's following you around like a sick puppy, right? Sure can't think of no other reason why he would be. You're dumb, and you're ugly too. He must be desperate. Oh, by-the-by, your momma's dead. Don't recall if I mentioned that before. Fat cow's head exploded, how about that! Probably because you run away from home, Mare. Broke her fat heart. God's wrath upon you both," Judd giggled.

Marie was done. She spun and strode toward her father, her boots clumping on the red clay and her face twisted into an expression of pure hatred far removed from her normal radiant countenance. The caravan slowed and stopped, watching.

Judd did not realize how much danger he was in until the moment Marie grasped his throat in her hands and squeezed. He could feel his neck bones grinding together under her fingertips. His eyes bulged in their sockets as tears dripped from the corners.

"Marie," Pete said. "Don't do it. It won't make anything better."

Marie released her father's throat but stayed close, staring into his eyes as he tried to look away. Judd could feel her hot breath on his neck. Would she tear his throat out with her pointed teeth? He understood now that she could.

His knees weakened under her judgement; she emanated sheer power and rage beyond her means. She was his daughter, and yet she was not; he tried to match her gaze—but then she smiled at him. It was not sweet, or daughterly; her grin looked like a shark's maw, ready to tear his face off without remorse. It was both threat and accusation. He glanced away, unable to meet her piercing, loathing stare. Who was this creature? Not his daughter. Something else; yet perhaps still partly of his own making.

She released him from her presence. Proceeding down the line, she called out to the caravan.

"Move on! Let's go, everyone! We approach our destination!"

Judd walked on in silence. He was broken, but not beaten. He felt for the item he had hidden in his front pocket: his wild card. It was still there, unnoticed. Soon, it would be the instrument of his freedom. Little Marie had been changed by her journey, that much was apparent. But she could still be rattled, hurt. Timing his escape at the perfect moment would be critical.

He had only to wait.

38

Marie dreamed. She sat on top of the Shell, conscious of her beloved ones who crowded together in the cab below—minus one. Lovely, frightened Anna, who had saved her life. A wholly unexpected act of bravery. Was Marie deserving of such a sacrifice? She swayed and sang under her breath a song she did not know and had never heard before; "*when you're close to me, I can feel your heart beat, I can hear you breathing near my ear…*"

Something ventured close, as the purple air popped and buzzed in the airquake.

"Who are you?" she asked. Hot breath on the back of her neck created goosebumps that raced up her scalp and down her arms. Tiny searing breezes whipped in her hair, in her ears, reminding her of the flames that took Anna. The Demon was at her back, reaching his arms out to embrace her.

"Bad luck," he replied.

"I don't accept that. Who are you, really? Tell me. I know you want to. The satisfaction in your voice betrays your pride."

The Demon moved away. She felt the cool night air again on her skin. But the creature didn't leave. He was bursting with information he desperately wanted to tell her in his arrogance, even if telling her would weaken his position.

Finally, he relented, giving in to his base desire to brag.

"An ancient energy. An original being of power and lust and all the forces of existence. I will usher in the end of all things, because it is my greatest purpose. I wanted your help, and you refused. You are now in my way," he hissed, blasting Marie with a puff of scalding air.

"Me? What did I do to stand in your way? All I did was refuse to help, and you tried to kill me."

"Not just you, Marie. The three who wish to reverse the pendulum. I would see it fly off its axis, to free the universe from its eternal prison."

"But why do you harass me? Why *me?*" Marie asked.

"Bad luck," the Demon said again, with amusement in his voice. "And this time, I'm telling the truth."

"He's not," someone said. "You are dishonest as always, Demon." The speaker was ethereal, not-quite-there, like a ghost. Over his arm was draped a neat towel, embroidered with initials; "MJP."

"Who are you?" Marie asked.

"No one, quite literally. Your spirit animal, perhaps?" the creature tittered.

"No one and nothing," the Demon growled.

"Oh, am I stealing your thunder?" The spirit asked.

"You can't. You're nothing but a simulacrum. You aren't real."

"I'm as real as you are, you silly cow," the spirit replied.

"Enough!" The Demon swept his great paw through the spirit and it disappeared into a puff of mist. "I am finished with you!"

He turned his attention back to Marie. "Wake now, and leave my realm!"

"But I-"

Marie opened her eyes as the airquake subsided. In the distance, the last of the coyotes yipped and howled as it died.

39

Pete and Bryce were up front, pulling the Shell with Marie and one of the teenage boys from the amusement park. The rock formation beside the final curve of highway before Las Vegas came into view looked like a beached whale, its nose almost touching the red road.

They could see a dark string of squat buildings in the distance, shimmering like an illusion in the heat which bore down upon the valley. More structures came into view as they turned the corner; strip malls, movie theaters, markets. In the valley basin to the west, sprawling ranches sectioned out the plains. To the east, small houses not much larger than shacks dotted the landscape.

"I thought…I thought it'd be bigger," Marie said.

"It sparkles more at night," Stefan said with a tinge of apology in his voice. "Or, it used to."

"Welcome to the last bastion of the wild west," Pete grunted. "It's not much to look at, but it's fun after sundown. If you're of a certain frame of mind."

Marie gazed into the valley with disappointment. She had expected too much—an oasis of pools, fountains, and trees. Perhaps some local philanthropists who welcomed wandering refugees in from the unstable environment. She knew her hopes had been unrealistic and she had tried to keep them in check, but the final sight of the squalid, dusty town in the distance filled her with despair. Dry, dismal, and vacant. It was hard to imagine anyone surviving here.

"It'll be okay," Pete said, his voice strained. "We just better keep moving. That was the plan, wasn't it?"

"Yes. How far is it? A few more miles, I assume, even though it looks so close…"

"Twenty, at least. I know it looks closer, but I've driven through here before. We've quite a hike, yet."

"*Twenty?*" Marie gasped. "But it looks like only…"

"It will be fine, Marie. We planned for this," Pete said. "Give Chester your harness. It's time for a shift change. And keep your chin up."

As Marie paced the Shell, she read the signs on the sides of the road: "$5 Divorce in 5 minutes or less!" and "Parson's Dude Ranch! Singles Welcome!" One sign proclaimed "Faro and Roulette Players Drink For Free!"

By the time they drew close to the first row of buildings, the sun had already dropped behind the mountains which ringed the valley, draping it in premature dusk. They had encountered no one on the road, but passed several cars with sun-baked bodies slowly decomposing on melting vinyl seats.

Marie read every sign. "Palm Resort and Casino! Best A/C In Town!" "Night Owl Nude Review - Live Dancers!" "Steak Dinner 30 Cents With $20 Casino Chip Purchase!"

They stopped for the night to shelter and rest. As they prepared for the final stretch in the morning, melancholy gripped the group. Marie hadn't been the only one with high hopes for this place. It was the end of the line, and their fates depended entirely on what they found here. They could not reasonably travel further; there was not much to be found east of the city anyway. This would be their last home, no matter what happened.

Picking up their chains for the last time, the caravan was sluggish in their despondency. By the time they reached the center of town, the sun had started to set. Massive dark signs with dead neon tubing perched atop the largest buildings; Flamingo, Golden Nugget, Pioneer Club. The structures were squat and sad, and many of them had crumbled.

"Might as well stop here," Chester said as they reached the center of the strip. "This is as good as it's going to get."

Pete strode to the middle of the thoroughfare and shouted, "Hello? Anyone here?"

His voice echoed among the buildings.

"The next quake is imminent," Stefan said. "Let's just shelter in the cars and look around more after, okay Pete?"

Pete frowned. "I thought I heard-"

"After. No matter what you heard, we got to take care of our own people first. Everyone's tired. Let's get them into shelter."

The group piled into the cars. Marie stood outside

and stared at the buildings, trying to swallow her disappointment. Had their struggle been for nothing? What was it all for?

"Marie? You coming?" Pete called out as he herded Judd into a car.

"No, Pete. I'll be fine. You go ahead. I'll see you soon."

"It might not be safe, Marie. I don't mean the quake. I mean…there might be people who've been affected by the quakes. Or animals, like the coyotes. I'd just as soon not leave you alone here."

"The coyotes are all dead. All the animals are dead now, I think. I haven't seen a rabbit in days."

"You're not helping your side of the argument, Marie."

"Pete, you're running out of time! Go! I'll be fine."

The air began to quiver. Pete hesitated, glancing toward the hills.

"*Go!*" Marie shouted again.

Pete slammed the Shell door behind himself with the strength of anger. Marie tried not to be hurt by his frustration; he was only trying to protect her, after all. But she had never asked for that, had never needed it. She sat on the hood of the Shell, wondering if the quake would bring another dream. As the vibrations intensified, she closed her eyes and opened her mind.

But Pete had been right; Marie heard a sound that was not part of an airquake or a vision. It was in her own space and time, here and now. A low moan issued from a collapsed casino across the street. Someone was there.

Marie walked toward the cracked slabs of concrete and chunks of splintered wood, feeling the street rattle under her soles as the quake intensified.

From a narrow hole in the concrete, she heard a scream of surprise and anguish. "Hello? Is anyone there?"

she called out. The trembling air created a vibrato in her voice.

"Help," a weak voice cried. "I'm…I'm *bleeding!* My eyes…Why…"

"You need to find shelter!" Marie said, kneeling near the hole. "Move further back if you can! Get away from the opening!"

A pale hand covered in bloody cuts was thrust through the hole, desperately clawing at its edges.

"Who are you?" Marie asked, her voice hitching with pity. She already knew she could not help this man.

"I'm Ernie. Have you seen Gerald? Who are-" But his voice was cut off by a high scream of pain. He screamed over and over, his cries becoming garbled as blood filled his throat. Marie grasped his hand; if he was to die, at least he would not go alone. Halfway through the quake the reaching hand went limp, and the man died with a guttural sob.

Marie wept, mourning the stranger she could not see as his hand cooled in hers. Then she cried harder… and harder. She cried for herself, for her friends, for her mother and for the entire world; it was really the end. She had let herself believe there was a chance Las Vegas was untouched, somehow. That there would be healthy and happy people here, ready and willing to save them all. But it had been an impossible dream, and her heart felt torn open as her eyes poured streams of precious tears—even as she cried, she knew it was water she could not afford to lose in this arid hell.

She kissed the dead man's hand, tasting the salt of her own tears as they wet his scraped skin. "I'm sorry," she whispered, to everyone. To Ernie and to Anna and to all the people she had led on a desperate trip to nowhere.

As soon as the air stopped shaking, Pete threw open the door of the Shell. Behind him, the rest of the group cautiously emerged from their cars. They had heard the man's screaming. Stefan and Chester had used all their combined strength to prevent Pete from bursting forth to find Marie during the peak of the quake. He was covered in sweat, and upon seeing Marie's sobbing face embraced her, holding her so tight she could hardly breathe.

Marie wondered what she had done to deserve such love, such devotion. She had led them into the middle of nowhere to die.

"I'm fine, Pete. I'm okay. I promise."

40

The small crowd circled the Shell, waiting to hear Marie speak.

She stood on top of it, in front of the backdrop of the setting sun. Before she opened her mouth, she had no idea what she planned to say. She simply knew something must be said, and no one but her could do it.

"Everyone, I…" she started. But her voice fell silent. So many people watching her, a young woman from nowhere, a castaway from her own family and from the world. Why did these people follow her? She was the least of them.

"We're with you, Marie," she heard Pete say to her right. But that was just the problem, wasn't it? They were with her; looked to her for answers. It turned out that she had none.

"We made it," she managed. "All the way to Las Vegas. It's not as…nice as I'd hoped. Maybe we can find some water somewhere. I'm sure we can, if we try."

The crowd shifted and muttered. Was that all? They needed congratulations, comfort, hope.

Someone cleared their throat. A child coughed. In the distance, winds rushed down the mountains with a sound that normally would never have been audible over the hustle and bustle of downtown Las Vegas in the evening.

"Is that all?" A voice called out. It was a mocking voice, cruel and remorseless. Her father's voice.

He had worked his wrists free as everyone was distracted by their new surroundings. And he had a gun.

"Where the hell did you get a gun, man? Put that thing away!" Pete said.

"Reuben. Remember Reuben? Before he got his head squeezed by the quake in State Line and developed a hankering for arson, he and I had a little talk. Did some business, like men do. Gun's been in my pocket since State Line. Couldn't hardly wait to show you, but I wanted to hold out and see Las Vegas first. Now we're here, and I'll be taking my leave. I'd just love for you to try to stop me," Judd said, waving the gun.

"We're not going to stop you," Stefan said. "Please, just leave now, and never come back. We'll let you go, as long as you don't shoot. Right, Marie?"

"You little idiot," Judd said, pointing the gun at Marie. "You've let all these people down, you know. And still, they follow you. They don't even realize that you've killed them all."

"No," Marie said. "No…"

"It's *all your fault*, Marie."

"Don't you talk to her like that!" Pete shouted, striding out from behind the Shell. Judd swung the gun toward him and fired once, hitting him in the leg. As Stefan ran to his side, Judd fired two more shots. The first one missed, but the second created a tiny hole in the side of Stefan's head.

The crowd scattered, taking cover in the stinking casinos and ruins. Some panicked and ran straight into the desert. Little Simon hid in the rocky hills and never found his way back out. Bryce ran and ran, looking for the rest of the children, but never found any of them. Sally clung to Chester as he had a heart attack in his terror; she sat by his side as he died, as the young always do for the old. Judd shot her dead as her tears fell on Chester's shocked face.

Marie wailed with grief and rage as she watched her friends fall.

"It was all for nothing, Marie," Judd said. "You ran away for no reason."

"Why? Why are you like this?" Marie cried. "I'm your daughter. Don't you feel any love for me at all?"

"Love, Marie? The strong don't need love. Love is a crutch, and I'm disappointed in your weakness for it. You aren't my daughter."

Despite her hatred for her father, his words hit like a hammer to her chest.

"I should have had a son."

Marie nodded. She knew it to be true. "All my fault," she whispered.

Judd giggled. The sound of it shocked Marie to her core.

"And this is your fault, too," Judd said. "And now you'll be all alone." He placed the barrel of the gun in his smiling mouth and pulled the trigger.

Marie sat on the roof of the Shell in the empty street, surrounded by a dead city.

"*Alone.*"

Part 3

THE BIRDHOUSE KEEPER

1988 was the first year of the great North American Drought.

It would last until 1990. Of course, we didn't know that at the time; what we knew during the long arid summer was that the backs of our legs stuck to the vinyl seats in our old station wagon, our ice cream cones dripped faster than we could eat them, and Phil Collins was the greatest musician of our generation.

Bird and I celebrated her twentieth birthday sitting in our car, eating french fries. She nibbled the crispy tips of each one before folding the middle in half and stuffing it into her mouth, chewing slowly with her eyes half-closed in pleasure.

I couldn't coax her inside the restaurant; it wasn't one of her better days. She withdrew from the outside world a little more each year. I knew Bernadette was different as soon as she was born, even though she learned slower than other children. As a young child she had trouble pronouncing her name, to the mocking delight of the other school children. She found "Bird" easier to say, so that's what stuck.

Every mother thinks their baby is special, so of course my opinion is biased, but I really mean it; she was extraordinary. Everyone could see it. When she was an infant she was quiet and calm, with a gaze which sort of looked right *into* you. That changed as she grew older and became afraid of so many things; loud sounds, bright lights, strangers. But she was always brilliant, in her own way. Her teachers and doctors told me she had some kind of disorder, but I never saw that it mattered much so long as I could make her happy. She was just Bird; my daughter, my love, my soul. And she was a wonder to me.

As the evening swept away the heat of the day and the streetlights flicked on one by one, I lit a single birthday candle stuck in the bun of Bird's hamburger. She swallowed a wet mouthful of french fries before carefully blowing out the flame. Thunder rumbled in the distance; we would have to drive home before finishing our food. Bird hated thunder, and there was nothing else in all of nature like New Mexico dry lightning.

"Time to go," I said, turning the key in the ignition. Our old station wagon rumbled and rattled when it was cold, but always started. Most reliable car I ever owned. She was a little shaky sometimes, but never quit on me entirely, and I could usually fix things on my own when something went wrong. She could have lasted us a few more years, at least.

Bird dropped a french fry between the seats.

"You'd better get that, Bird. Or we'll get ants in the car."

"Yuck!" said Bird, fishing between the center console and her seat with her fingers pointed like scissors. "Got it."

As I pulled out of the parking lot, I remember seeing a car grille through my side window. It was stuck through with brown leaves and twigs lifted in the hot winds pushed ahead by the coming storm. The distinctive blue oval with Ford in silver script slammed into my side of our car without slowing. If they had been going any faster, I might have died. As it was, I hit my head on the inside panel near the door pretty hard. Bird screamed, seeing blood gush from my hairline, down my shirt, soaking my jeans. I tried to reassure her I was ok, but my words felt all wrong in my mouth. Then the world went watery and purple, and slipped away.

The next thing I remember is Bird looming over my hospital bed, pleading silently with puffy red eyes. Her hand gripped mine, slick with tears. Just a concussion, the doctor said.

Maybe so.

But a few days later I blacked out in the bathroom, and that was the beginning of what I really want to tell you about. That was when the seizures started. And I think that's when I visited the changing house for the first time.

2

Our sturdy little house on Blossom St. was walking distance to the One-Stop Mart, the flower shop, and Pavio's Italian Restaurant. I could do most of my shopping at the One-Stop, which was owned by the oldest woman I have ever met; Barbara was 102. Behind the counter she sipped whiskey from an Atlantic City souvenir cup and cursed like a sailor. I suspect she sold cigarettes to the younger teens, but I never caught her in the act. Barb kept her prices on basic necessities low but the trade-off was your personal time; you couldn't make a purchase without listening to a repeat of one of her sordid war anecdotes, a complaint about her effeminate brother, or a gruesome description of her latest pet's health troubles. I think she must have originally opened the store just to maintain a steady flow of avid listeners for her lifetime collection of tales and grievances.

The flower shop, Rosebuds on Blossom, was in its third iteration in that exact location. In the late '70s it had been owned by a sweet Chinese couple who sold it to pay for college tuition for their son. He dropped out and returned home, and the whole family left town soon after. The next owner was Jim Swift, a leftover hippie who, I suspect, entered the flower industry via his interests in buds of a more illicit type. His kids eventually forced him into some kind of rehab in California and sold the shop to its current proprietor, the very proper Miss Edna Hamm. From the east coast originally—New York City, Barbara informed me with an indelicate sneer—she seemed resentful to be living in our tiny artistic community. Under her ownership, the store carried more silk and imitation plants and fewer of the fresh flowers which were difficult stock to maintain in our remote area. She didn't have a single friend in town and she couldn't have been making much money, but she stuck around anyway, pushing her monthly sales in the newspaper and making regular appearances at city council meetings. I would sometimes drop in for a bunch of carnations for the dinner table or a new succulent plant for the front stoop, and found her service to be quick and efficient but her personality charmless. Weird looking eyes, too.

Next to the flower shop was Pavio's, which was Bird's favorite Italian restaurant. To be honest, it was the only Italian restaurant in town so there wasn't much competition, but even so it really was pretty good. I don't know why the place was called Pavio's; the owner was a massive and gentle man called Salvatore, and I never asked him about the restaurant name. But he could craft a mean deep-dish pizza, and the pasta he served—on the week-ends only—was hand-made from scratch.

Two weeks after the car accident, I was standing in our kitchen, staring into the refrigerator. Two eggs, sweet pickle relish, leftover mashed potatoes—almost definitely rancid by now, but I was afraid to lift the lid to check—and one rapidly browning banana. Nothing for dinner.

Mother of the Year, I am not.

"Maman, spaghetti tonight! Pavio's!" Bird begged.

"It's Thursday, honey. Salvatore won't have any spaghetti until tomorrow. But I can cook some if you want. I'll have to run to the store."

Bird frowned, but nodded her approval.

My car was still in the shop for repairs, but I'd been told by the mechanic that it didn't look good. Due to the age of the car, it was most likely totalled. He was still wait-ing for the insurance company to process the claim. So I was on foot, and my trip to the store was limited by what I could carry on the walk home. My list included fresh tomatoes for pasta sauce, paper towels, spaghetti noodles, and a bottle of chardonnay for my evening wind-down. Bird could have helped carry more, but she wanted to stay home and watch television. I said she could, as long as she washed the dishes. Come to think of it, I don't think she ever did her chores that night.

Later that evening, I was very glad I had thought to buy wine.

I could leave Bird alone in the house for a few hours at a time—long enough to run errands or go see a movie. She was careful and self-sufficient when she was on her own, unless something unusual happened. The day

I walked to the store I was on my way back to the house when I heard an awful howling; you could hear it all the way down the street. Over the howling, in a higher pitch, I heard a familiar wail; Bird was crying. When I stepped through the front door I entered a house of horror. Bits of food had been mashed underfoot in the entryway, screams rang out from two directions, and the faint scent of blood lingered in the air. In the coat closet I found a dog, trembling in fear. It took me twenty minutes to sort out the situation; a loose dog with an open leg wound had found its way into our back yard. Bird had panicked, not because she was afraid of the dog but because she desperately wanted to help it and didn't know how. She was always trying to help, but often became too overwhelmed by her anxiety and empathy to know what to do. So she had locked the problem away in the safest place she could find, which happened to be the hall closet; the terrified animal had pissed all over my winter boots and smeared blood on my long coat. But I couldn't be mad at Bird. She was bawling, locked in her room. I didn't see her again until the dog had been safely picked up by its owner.

Both her fear and her courage were wildly unpredictable.

In those days I worked from home as a tailor, hemming pants and making simple bespoke dresses so I wouldn't have to leave Bird alone for too long. My studio dominated the living room, which was lined with wheeled clothing racks and sewing machines in various stages of disrepair. My workhorse machine was an old Singer from the late '70s, an oily and temperamental beast. When clients visited, Bird hid in her room under the covers until they left, but she was always full of questions later; what did they look like? What did they want sewn? She inquired in short, one- or two-word sentences. *Lady or gentleman? Cuffs shortened? Dress hemmed?* Her distaste for strangers did not trump her fascination with them.

The day I fell unconscious in the bathroom started out normally. We made breakfast together in our little kitchen—I cooked the eggs, Bird toasted the bread—and as we ate we watched reruns of Bird's favorite show, *Cheers*. She loved Sam Malone and his winning smile, Carla with her scrappy comebacks, and even snobby Diane as she whisked around the bar with her flowing skirts and golden hair. Bird's absolute favorite, however, was Norm; she seemed to be drawn to the sad kindness that swam in his tired eyes.

As we sat together and watched the characters on the screen deal with the problem of the day—I think it was the one where Coach got a second job managing a little league club—my ears began to ring. The light coming through the windows was suddenly too bright, too white. Thin streaks of lightning flared from the edges of my vision as it narrowed to a dark and distant point. Paralyzing dread rose up within me; not a fear of anything in particular, but simply a roaring tsunami of pure terror from deep within my brain. Sweat dripped from my forehead, wetting my shirt collar. I stumbled to the bathroom, hands and feet numb as fence posts. I had no idea what was happening to me, but I didn't want Bird to know anything was wrong.

I rinsed the sweat from my face with splashes of cold water at the bathroom sink. In the mirror I saw my eyes were bloodshot and my skin was the matte non-color of blank newspaper. My blouse was soaked through at the armpits, dark with sweat. When my knees buckled I sat down hard on the closed toilet lid, breathing deeply. It wasn't enough; I was going to faint. I lowered myself to the floor, staring at the ceiling until my eyes closed and the light in my mind briefly switched off, then on again.

I awoke in a drowning house.

3

The home was unfamiliar to me. The building was abandoned, and its undisturbed filth had not seen a visitor in decades. Every corner had been invaded by black mold which penetrated the rotten carpet and crept up the walls in blurry streaks like smoke stains. Atop the walls was nothing but sky; there was no roof or ceiling, having been torn away long ago. Overhead, a powerful storm was gathering; the maelstrom spun languidly above the house, picking up speed as it rotated in place. When it gained enough strength to touch down, the eye of the storm would swallow me.

Husks of nondescript wooden furniture, warped with water damage and rot, were piled in the corners. Algae and fungus sprung from every nook and crook it could take hold in. As the funnel cloud over the tops of the walls elongated and reached toward me like an octopus arm, wind tore through the rooms, trembling clumps of dessicated weeds growing up through the flooring. Somewhere nearby a door crashed again and again.

I walked into the center hallway, from which I could see rooms in every direction. The house stood high on a hill; through broken windows in a room to my right I could see the earth drop away for a mile. In the distance I spied a town as desolate as the house I stood in; bleached from relentless downpours, abandoned, grey.

A great gust of wind slammed into the house, rocking it, and a moment later the sky exhaled a torrent of cold raindrops which washed over the open walls, the cracking furniture, and my shivering body. Streams of water coursed down my skin, making my clothes cling and sag. There was so much rain I thought it must fill the house up like a washtub. I would be drowned.

Harder and faster the rain came down until my visibility was reduced to inches. I raised my hands to my face, watching small rivers race down my palms. The weight of the rain became like standing under a waterfall, yanking at my hair, bruising my flesh. The tears from my eyes were as insignificant to the downpour as grains of sand in the galaxy, and I could not hear my own cries over the sound of the crashing water.

"Maman."

It was Bird's voice; her pet name for me. She was calling to me.

"Maman, wake. Please wake up."

I realized my eyes were closed; I could not open them. Yet, in the storm-smashed house, I could see. I stumbled forward to lean on a spongy wall the texture of a mushroom cap. I found a firmer grip on a door frame and moved toward the opening, hoping it would protect me from the torrent.

"*Maman!*"

Bird's voice was becoming more insistent, now. She sounded frightened. I knew I must return to her, to comfort her. As I stepped toward the protection of the door frame, the opening blurred. The air swirled, and my vision lost focus.

I woke up.

Just as she had done in the hospital, Bird hovered over me, her eyelashes nearly touching mine, butterfly kisses damp with tears.

"Hi baby," I said. "I'm okay. I just fell asleep."

Bird scowled at me. She knew I wasn't telling the whole truth.

"Why?" she asked. She was always asking that question.

"I don't know. I just felt tired, suddenly."

"Bathroom?" Bird glared. "Why?" She crossed her

arms. "Doctor."

"Okay, honey. I'll call the doctor tomorrow."

"*Promise,*" Bird said.

"I promise. Pinky promise."

Bird solemnly lifted her little finger in front of my face, and I gripped it with my own.

"Legally binding contract," Bird muttered. The pinky promise was eternal, unbreakable.

"Yes," I agreed.

4

My doctor said all the things I had expected him to. I was working too hard after the concussion, he said. I needed rest. I'd be fine. I should drink more water. The incident on the bathroom floor might have been a tiny seizure, so he'd prescribe some medicine, run some tests. Expensive ones, of course.

Bird was not satisfied. "But, why?" She asked, as she always did.

"The doctor doesn't know. He said I need rest, so I guess I'll take a couple days off. Mrs. Connolly won't like that though. Her pantsuit will be overdue."

The drive home was a slow creep down the highway in evening traffic. Bird gazed out the window. I knew she was pretending to follow an imaginary deer with her eyes, watching it bound over each signpost and distant tree, making impossible leaps from hilltop to hilltop. It was a game she played in the car when she was anxious or did not want to talk to me.

"Mrs. Connolly stinks," she finally said.

"Yeah, a little," I giggled. "She wears that horrible perfume."

Bird relaxed a tiny bit, conceding to glance at me out of the corner of her eye. "Doctor stinks, too."

"He does? I didn't notice that."

"No, just…" she began, then paused to consider. "Bad doctor."

"He's not bad. Neurological problems can be really complicated. Sometimes people have seizures, especially after hitting their head. He didn't seem too concerned, and I have medicine now. I'll be okay, Bird. Try not to worry."

"No," Bird said.

And that was that. She didn't speak to me again until almost bedtime. I tried not to take it personally; she was frightened.

I was frightened, too.

In regards to the car accident, the judge ruled in favor of the other driver. I should have fought harder, probably—but I knew it really was my fault. I had been distracted by my concern with being caught on the highway in the storm, the thought of Bird trembling in her seat, frozen with terror as lightning crashed around us, our car an exposed bump in the open road just begging to be hit by a bolt from the sky. Of course I knew we weren't in real danger, but Bird's fear could be so intense it was hard not to be affected by it. She would have handled it like a champ; no whining, no tantrums. She never wanted to be a burden to me, but I hated seeing her frightened. It hurt my soul.

To pay off the accident, I took a second job for a few months at the shoe rental counter in a bowling alley. Bird was left home alone most of the time, although she was occasionally visited by her cousin. Robby was fifteen, and a good kid. He brought her sweets from the market, and taught her how to play poker using M&Ms for bets. He complained she was too easy to beat, though; whenever she had a good hand, her face beamed with excitement.

For a while Bird did okay on her own, but eventually she became gloomy and withdrawn. Robby was a busy kid—trying out for the football team and doing pretty well, according to my sister, although she had a tendency to boast. He couldn't visit Bird every day, and on the days he didn't come, I often discovered Bird hadn't left her room the entire time I'd been out. Many evenings when I returned home I found her in a trance, drawing pictures on her walls.

I guess I should explain that. Wall Drawing was something I came up with when she was ten years old. There was a feeling of fun irreverence to the activity, covering the walls with sprawling pictures and doodles. Our New Year's Day tradition was to paint over the drawings and start the year fresh, a reminder that nothing lasts forever and change can be good—a lesson particularly useful for young Bird, who had a tendency to cling to strict routine and well-known objects with unhealthy ferocity.

I worried about her loneliness, and the possibility of regressing away from her hard-won acceptance of the chaos of the world and back into obsessive repetition. So one evening on my way home from work I splurged on a gift.

Bird was watching television on the couch when I walked in the front door with a white wire cage holding a red-cheeked cockatiel that fluttered and chirped as it swung from its perch. The cage included ladder catwalks that the bird strutted along with confidence, making happy little whistling sounds from the side of its beak. The whole setup had been expensive, but sometimes you just know when a gift is the right thing for someone. When a gift is given well, it works like medicine.

"A bird for Bird!" she said laughing and jumping up from the couch, nearly upsetting the coffee table.

"It's a new friend for you. I'm sorry I've been away from home so much, honey."

Bird pressed her face to the cage, grinning. "Beautiful," she whispered.

She quickly taught the creature to perch on her shoulder, pretend to talk to her with his little beak nibbling at her ear, and fly to fetch ribbons from her dresser in exchange for seeds. Every time I ran the laundry, clumps of birdseed spilled from her blue-jean pockets into the basket.

Inexplicably, she named him Corduroy.

Our weekly trip to the pet store became Bird's new favorite outing. She would head straight for Aisle 3 to run her finger along the bags of seed and the elaborate cages and the bins of tiny toys with bells attached. The store was something of a local zoo, with a rotating stock of pets for sale in collaboration with pet shops in other cities. For several weeks, a large blue macaw was on sale—"Discount! 30% off!" read the tag—until a tourist purchased it and took it out of town. Bird watched the busy gatherings of parakeets in the cage at the end of the aisle, marveling at their bright Easter-egg colors. Next to the parakeets hung a giant cage with a snow-white cockatoo. It whipped its head to the side and raised its feathery head crest into a curious mohawk in response to Bird's wide-eyed stare.

Behind the counter you could usually find John Hadley. He was one of the few people Bird really trusted, although I could find no special reason why. She would walk around behind him, catch my eye, and wink at me; she thought I should ask John on a date, she told me. I told her I was too old for him—he couldn't be older than 30—but she wouldn't accept that excuse. Every time we visited the shop, she would make her regular run through the aisle, visit the birds for a minute, then end up behind John's counter, squinching her left eye shut at me from behind his shoulder with a giggle and a nod as he tallied our purchases.

I liked John. He had a boyish, crooked smile which

broadened whenever Bird burst through the pet shop door. He spoke to her with respect, and treated her like the mature adult she really was—unlike some people in town.

I didn't have time for dating. If I'm being honest, though, that wasn't the only reason I didn't ask for his number.

To my shame, I admit I was worried about Bird being a burden on any long-term romantic relationship. But who else could love her as much as I did? She was unpredictable, and occasionally unstable. In short, she was a lot of work. I loved her with my whole heart and didn't mind spending every minute of my life with her—but how could I expect anyone else to do the same?

5

August passed, and by mid-September the Halloween decorations were already beginning to appear in the stores. The weather finally cooled—although there was still no prediction of rain in the forecast—and Bird and Corduroy spent all their time indoors, sitting on the couch watching television together.

Bird held out her hand with three sunflowers in her palm. "Three seeds," she offered.

Corduroy chirped. The agreement was struck. He flew from her shoulder and swept around the corner into the kitchen where I was preparing dinner. Before I could stop him he plunged his face into a bowl of trail mix on the counter, swiftly plucked out three raisins, and returned to Bird with his bounty.

Having made the exchange, he munched on the sunflower seeds while Bird chewed the raisins.

"How did you teach him that?" I asked.

"Didn't," Bird said.

I sat on the couch next to the pair and rested my

aching feet on the coffee table. "Dinner's ready in five minutes, Bird. Go wash your hands and put Corduroy in his cage."

Bird groaned and held up her hand as a perch for Corduroy. But just before she stood, she turned her head toward me. I was shocked to see she was staring at me in much the same way she had as an infant; the look in her eyes was distant, searching for information in a vast darkness my own eyes could not sense.

"Don't go," she said.

"What? I'm not leaving, Bird. I'm about to serve dinner."

"Don't go," she said again. "*Don't.*"

"I'm not-" I started.

But my ears were ringing. My vision narrowed, and flashes of light popped like camera snaps at the edges. I was going to have another seizure.

I laid down on the couch and propped my feet up on the back cushions in hope that the extra blood flow to my brain would derail my descent into unconsciousness. But it was in vain; I was fading. The sound of Bird's whimpering faded, and the light in my brain went out for just a moment…

I woke up in a dark house.

6

The great-room was long and narrow. Picture windows spanning the length of the longest wall overlooked a slope which swept down and away from the house for a mile. Velvet curtains hung in swags over each window section, dusty but not derelict. The room was dressed in burgundy and mahogany. A vast dinner table in the center of the room was set for fifteen people. At the end, an elaborate host chair was positioned directly under an enormous moose head attached to a shield-shaped wooden mount. In the silence, I could hear the buzz of a fat fly circling the animal's dry muzzle.

The room was empty, but I was being watched. A mirror, caked with the grime of passing time, showed a partial silhouette of a figure with large horns, just down by the corner of the gilded frame. But the figure was immobile, and I could not find any object in the room with a shape which might cast the reflection; a trick of the light.

I feared leaving, but it did me no good to stay. I had to find a way out. The door at the end of the room was deep red in color, like the rest of the room's appointments. On the other side, I discovered a winding hallway. As I walked, the walls changed color; the mahogany paneled walls had been clumsily painted black, spoiling the fine textures of the wood grain. After a sharp bend in the hall I found a sitting area; a round-backed velvet chair sat alongside a pedestal table adorned with a vase holding a spray of dead flowers. Hung high on the walls were long shelves cluttered with antique junk; long-dry perfume bottles, an ancient rat trap, and a human skull missing its lower jaw.

"Hello?" I called. "Is anyone here?"

To my relief, I received no reply. Resuming my course I soon reached the end of the hall and discovered a small theater. A hundred wooden seats on ramping bleachers offered a clear view of a worn stage framed by blue velvet curtains on pulleys. Dim yellow spot lights cast a sallow glow from each side of the stage. The room was very tall; the ceiling at the back disappeared into darkness. Along the bleacher steps the walls were draped with large ballyhoo banners from long-forgotten sideshow acts; a disembodied head, an angry looking young man with crab-claw fingers, a sullen pair of conjoined toddlers. At the back of the theater before the walls surrendered to the shadows I could make out a decayed yellow banner which screamed *"Ten-In-One Show!"*

I chose seat number 50, in the dead center of the theater, and waited for whoever had turned on the spot lights to return.

Several minutes passed before a breeze from behind the blue velvet curtains caused them to briefly lift and sway, as if someone had opened a back door. I watched them bulge from right to left as someone moved across the stage toward the center, where golden tasseled ropes were visible through the part in the cloth. As the curtains drew back I watched from my seat, curious to see the theater's custodian.

I was disappointed; in the center of the stage stood only a large mirror. I saw my own reflection for a moment—a middle-aged woman frowning from a splintered wooden seat—before dark shadows appeared, obfuscating the mirror. The shadows grew and multiplied, crowding close inside the glass, gradually turning it black like a window looking into the night. When the mirror was filled with darkness and my reflection was gone, it cracked into sharp puzzle pieces, each shard too small to effectively depict its surroundings. They rained down onto the stage, tumbling and tinkling. The mirror fell backwards to the floor with a sharp crack, and from the empty frame rose a hazy figure, flowing and sinuous, like smoke streaming from a stained glass window of a burning church. It coalesced and became human-shaped but it was no reflection; it did not look like me.

The figure was hulking, male in both shape and bearing. The entire entity was massive; five feet across and at least eight feet tall, but with the normal proportions of the upper half of a man—except that the head was much too large. Its torso was draped in the tattered shreds of a ruined butler's uniform, and its hair was neatly slicked. Draped over its bent arm was a folded towel with embroidered initials, MJP. Below its tidy vest the legs faded away, causing the figure to appear to float several feet above the stage boards. Its enormous face assessed me with grey, serious eyes the size of grapefruits.

"So. You have properly arrived," it said. "And so have I. Welcome, Dreamer."

"What are you?" I asked. "And why am I here?"

The entity tilted its head, considering the question. "I am the Simulacrum," it replied.

"Are you a ghost?"

The entity giggled. "Not in the sense your question intends. I am not a dead thing."

It looked down at itself, regarding its appearance with a disapproving frown. The towel disappeared.

"What are you doing here?" I asked.

"What are you doing here?" the Simulacrum replied.

"I was pulled here against my will," I answered.

"As was I," it said.

"Are we both prisoners, then?"

At my question the entity flickered, trembling with something like fear. In its anxiety its projection dimmed and dipped toward the stage floor, revealing some of the backstage area the mirror had blocked from my view. Set decor, makeup vanities, and costume racks were pressed against a back wall festooned with spider webs.

"Why a theater?" I asked.

"Why a tailor?" the Simulacrum snapped.

I stood. "I'm leaving," I announced, sidestepping past the seats toward the door.

"Wait!" the Simulacrum cried. "I am supposed to tell you…"

"What?" I asked. "If you must talk, do it quickly! I need to find my way out of here. I need to return to my daughter."

The Simulacrum whimpered. It drifted forward slowly as if being flown in on battens from backstage.

"The house changes," it said.

"The theater, you mean?"

"This theater, yes. The flooded house, too. It is all one. It changes itself, and then it changes you."

"What flooded house? What are you talking about?" I asked.

"If you don't remember, then don't worry about it. He is just trying to distract you. But look," it said, pointing at one of the sideshow banners. The picture was clear; a man's head with bulging eyes, suspended in a jar filled with green liquid. Over the painting I could see printed words—but I could not read them. The letters were written in English, but the spelling was nonsensical.

"Don't you know? In dreams, you cannot read," said the Simulacrum.

"So, I'm dreaming?" I asked. "How do I wake up? How do I leave?"

"That's simple. You're alive, so he can't really stop you. Just look for the door."

The Simulacrum disappeared in a flash of darkness.

The doorway I had used to enter the theater looked indistinct now, filled with white mist like milk in a bowl. Swirls of purple streaked the white; a pretty but unsettling effect. I knew I had seen it somewhere before, but I could not remember where.

My attention drifted. It was peaceful here, quiet. In the backstage area, I saw the outline of a broad, muscular man. Handsome, he was—even with the big horns.

"*Maman.*"

Bird was calling to me from the mist. She needed me, and nothing would stop me from reaching her. Anyway, the Simulacrum said I could leave. What was I waiting for? I couldn't remember…

The moment I stepped through the doorway, I felt the warmth of Bird's body pressed against my own. We lay together on the couch, and my shirt sleeve was soaked through. Evidently my girl had wept until she had fallen asleep beside me. My arm was numb under the weight of her body.

"Bird," I whispered. "Bird, wake up."

Her eyes flew open. "*Maman!*"

"It's okay, honey." I said. "I'm back. I'm awake."

7

Taos, New Mexico in the late 1960s was ground zero of the counterculture war of the west. Hippies and activists arrived in droves to find enlightenment in Native American teachings on spirituality and connections with nature. They camped and danced on the old Hispanic territories, trampled the local wildlife, smoked cigarettes, and made love under the stars. Some of the micro-communities they formed were strictly sober, while many others were rife with drug and alcohol use. I arrived at one of the latter types in the summer of 1967.

I suppose it could be said that I had run away from home, but I never saw it that way. Dad had left when I was five. My mother and I were disagreeable roommates, and by the time I was eighteen she understood that I would leave the house whenever it pleased me to do so. I spent a year each in Austin, Wichita, New York City, and Tijuana. I was independent and arrogant, thought I didn't need anyone. But that was because I'd never really known what it was like to belong anywhere. When I was twenty-two, I arrived at Big Jack's camp—and in a way I never really left.

The tiny house I share with Bird is only a couple miles from the place, and I still sometimes visit on hot summer nights after Bird falls asleep in her hammock. The campsite has sat empty for decades, except for Big Jack's derelict trailer and Sharon's old broken Chevrolet she spray-painted purple the night before she overdosed in the back seat. Often when I walk through the lot I find mementos from those days; glass beads, old beer bottles, cigarette lighters.

Big Jack was…well, he was something else. He didn't talk much about his past, but I knew some things. His family was from Louisiana. Both of his parents had died in a car accident when he was a boy. The rumor he liked to spread was that he joined the circus and grew up among clowns and contortionists. Over time his tales became ever more elaborate, even to the point of crafting stories about "Ranger," a clown who had supposedly murdered a busload of school children before joining up with the circus to hide from the law. But I knew the truth, because Jack trusted me. He liked to talk to me late at night after the other campers had wandered off to bed. He had spent a couple years at the circus, but that wasn't his main gig; Jack was a con man, and a good one. But he was also a nice guy, so when his conscience eventually won out he saved enough money to retire to a little piece of desert with a trailer on it. That's how he ended up in northern New Mexico.

If Big Jack hadn't been strict about non-spiritualism, his camp could have been mistaken for a cult. Our only subjects of worship were freedom, rebellion, and simple pleasures. We accepted and welcomed the wildness of the high desert, and understood that it would take our lives if and when it pleased it to do so. Under Big Jack's guidance we surrendered ourselves to fate but also worked hard to construct our own ideal world. To outsiders, the camp looked like a childish fantasy, but for us—a group of artists, individualists, and a few harmless criminals—it was the only life we found meaningful. Over time we moved out of our cluster of tents and into simple wooden huts, and finally into interconnected sheds built on cinder block foundations which could be kept warm in the winter and cool in the summer. They were painted pink and orange and blue and yellow, splashed with buckets of rebellious color to express our defiance to the drab outside world and the mindless social structure that watched us with jealousy from beyond the borders of our little paradise.

I am now the sole owner of the sad site of those crumbling memories.

Six months after I arrived in his camp, Big Jack died. He had been out on one of his solo retreats. Somehow, being a million miles from nowhere wasn't always enough distance for Big Jack. Occasionally he felt the "call of the wild," he said, and retreated into the hills, carrying his embroidered satchel that contained granola bars, water, and mescaline. He would reappear a few days later, filthy and sunburnt but light on his feet and filled with a distant, starry-eyed contentment. After returning to camp, he would sleep for a full day until someone woke him out of concern, just to see if he was still breathing. Whoever checked on him would be received with a laugh and a loving bear-hug that squeezed their breath away, made somewhat unpleasant by the smell.

But one time he didn't return. We waited five days, six. Wild-Star finally went searching and found Big Jack leaning in the lee of a boulder. He died with a smile on his face, his water bottle tipped into the sand. Probably a heart attack.

Big Jack left me the camp in his will—a fact I did not know until after he was gone, and to this day only vaguely understand. We had been close, but I wasn't his favorite. I was too responsible. But I think he believed that if anyone could keep the camp running in case of his death, it was me.

He was wrong.

In the winter after Big Jack's death, I fell pregnant with Bird. I had been working hard to keep the camp alive with the help of Ravenbeak and Wild-Star, but none of us really knew what we were doing. When we had first arrived at the camp, the balmy mid-summer season was peaking. We slept during the hot days and partied at night after the temperature dropped. Without Big Jack's help, we were unprepared for the icy climate when the weather turned. We still welcomed newcomers from time to time, and provided shelter where we could, but as the year—and the decade—aged, fewer young people showed up seeking peace and enlightenment from the increasingly inhospitable desert.

Wild-Star disappeared the day after I told him he was going to be a father. Ravenbeak followed him—I now understand he had probably always been in love with him—and I, suddenly alone and pregnant, found the camp impossible to maintain. So, I locked it up, with some guilt. But what else could I do?

I retreated into the city, to safety and adulthood, abandoning the campsite to the rabbits and mountain lions and all the truly wild things of the high desert.

8

A tall woman leaned against the pet shop counter with her ankles demurely crossed, tan and graceful in a yellow summer dress dotted with red flowers. Her long hair was flowing and brown with sun-baked golden highlights, and a clip in the shape of a carnation held a sweep of bangs in place behind her ear. John was grinning at her with his boyish smile as he busied his hands wiping the counter, reorganizing merchandise, opening mail.

I surprised myself with a pang of jealousy. Did John have a girlfriend? I didn't recognize her. And did I have any right to be jealous? Bird was the one who was so fond of him, not me.

As the glass door swung closed behind us and the ring of the entry chime faded away, I followed Bird down the pet food aisle instead of approaching the counter like I usually did. I didn't want to meet this pretty young woman. She reminded me too much of myself; the beautiful and stupid version of me from twenty years ago who danced in the flicker of desert bonfires and made love with strange, handsome young men named after wild animals and natural magics.

I also didn't want to interrupt John's flirting—if that was, in fact, what was happening. I slipped into the aquarium aisle, pretending to watch a school of neon fish circle a tiny green castle.

John found me.

"My favorite customer! Are you looking for a fish to keep Corduroy company?"

"Oh!" I said. "No, it's nothing! I mean, I'm not looking for anything. I think Bird wants a new seed treat for Corduroy. You know, the kind shaped like a little bell?"

"Oh sure, we have those! Come on over this way…"

John headed for the treat bins, beckoning for me to follow. I could hear Bird making squeaking noises at the parakeets. I selected a seed bell and called for Bird; we had what we came for now, and I had no choice but to approach the counter to pay for our purchase. I wished with my entire being I had never suggested an outing to the pet shop that morning.

The pretty young woman dug lipstick and a flip-up mirror out of her purse. She was smiling into the mirror, admiring herself. When I approached the counter she leaned away without glancing up from her mirror, either to make room for my ungainly daughter and I, or perhaps simply out of disdain—I couldn't tell which.

As I paid John, Bird glared at the woman. She didn't run behind the counter like she usually did, but instead froze in place, frowning at the imposter and looking back and forth between the woman and John, assessing the situation. I should have told Bird to say hello or attempted to introduce her, but I found her blatant disapproval of the situation wickedly comforting. She was expressing the disapproval I had no right to, and I loved her for it.

"Here's your change," John said. "Oh! I almost forgot to introduce you! Bird, this is my friend Janice. She's here all the way from Austin, Texas."

Bird's upper lip twitched in a brief snarl. "Hi," she grumbled, before turning to glare at John. I could almost hear the question I knew she wanted to ask: *just what the hell is going on here, John?*

Janice's mouth smiled, but her eyes were dull with scorn and distaste as she looked Bird up and down, noting her oddness. "Nice to meet you," she said, clutching her makeup bag close.

Bird growled.

"Well! It's time we got going!" I said, taking the seed bell and receipt from John. "We have lots of errands to run. See you later, John! It was so wonderful to meet you, Janice!" I blurted in a rush, spinning on my heel to leave the shop. I hoped Bird would follow without coercion, and was relieved when she caught up with me on the sidewalk.

As we walked home, Bird furiously aimed at me the questions she had wanted to ask John.

"*Who was that?* She doesn't like pets! I can tell. John loves *her?* Why her?" For Bird, it was a rare and lengthy diatribe.

"I don't know, Bird! You don't know that he loves her. Maybe they are just friends. And maybe not! But we can't tell John who to spend time with. It's none of our business."

"Is, too!" Bird shouted, but then lapsed back into quietude. "John's sweet. Too sweet for her."

"You don't know that," I said. "She's probably really nice."

Bird scowled. "He's too sweet for you, too."

"Aw, Bird." I sighed.

But John was sweet. Always had been.

And I had a disquieting feeling that I had made a mistake.

9

"Sorry, honey. The weather report didn't say anything about this."

Bird and I were standing under the awning of Mason's Department Store, watching the rain come down. The downpour was incredible; water breached the building's overflowing gutters. Lightning flashed in the distance, still too far away to be loud but close enough for Bird's nose to crinkle with anxiety and her eyes to open wide and dart from side to side. Her muscles twitched like a frightened deer standing in the middle of a road at night. The downpour probably wouldn't last long—certainly not long enough to break the ongoing drought—but it was intense, and inconvenient.

If we tried to wait it out, I'd miss work.

"Thank god we got the car back from the shop. It's really coming down! We'll have to run for it. Ready?"

Bird whimpered, but did not protest. It would have to do.

I held her hand and we ran, leaping over puddles, gripping our shopping bags tight so the water could not soak our purchases. As we ducked under a tree, a shivery-cold stream of water spilled down my spine and for a moment I was transported. Where had I felt that sensation before? It had been recent. But it hadn't rained in months. The drought…

I felt dizzy. Intense déjà vu overwhelmed me as my mind played over and over again the vague memory of pouring water, a spinning storm overhead, shivering in the cold. Where? When? My brain tried to pick apart the memory, to place it in my recent past, but could not find where it fit in.

There was something overhead, a massive shape in the clouds. A figure, human but not quite a man, powerful and horned. Where had I seen him before?

"*Maman!*" Bird cried. I had halted and was standing still in the parking lot, just twenty feet from the car while we both were being drenched in the downpour. Bird pulled on my hand, refusing to leave me behind.

"Sorry!" I said, jogging to the car. "Here, it's open," I called out, wrenching the key in the rusty door lock.

As we tumbled into the car with our wet bags in our laps, the false memory was already fading away. How could I remember something which had not happened? I decided it must be a result of the concussion; my rattled brain was still playing tricks on me. Best to ignore it. I set the thought aside.

And I woke up in a dark house.

10

A miasma of evil; helpless sorrow and inflicted pain. Footfalls so heavy as to defy reason crashed through the earth's crust at each step, punching holes into the molten lava below, their weight pressing the rock into sandpaper sheets of razor-sharp diamonds.

Hatred. The epitome of agony and utter destruction, not just in the present but permeating time and space, the past and the future. Each step foretold the ruin of myself and my family and my sanity; all that I loved and held dear.

The Demon encompassed it all. And it could *smell me.*

It was still several stories below the level I was on, but it would catch up to me soon. It moved faster than I did, roaring as it approached. For a moment I saw through its eyes; the vision was a flicker that showed me a deep tunnel in the dirt, far below where I stood. It ended at a small wooden door, too small for the Demon to fit through. The Demon roared, and the sound was an explosion; the earth was blasted like a crater, obliterating the wooden door. It stepped through the opening and sniffed the stagnant air, its nostrils snorting like a bull's.

It knew I was here. It felt my fear.

Adrenaline buzzed in my body. I wanted to run, but I was confused by my surroundings; a sprawling mansion which was a maze of ornate parlors and gilded powder rooms. In its heyday it must have been the home of an individual of impressive wealth; every surface was papered, plated, or paneled in the finest materials. Murals spanned the walls of nearly every room. The decor was impossibly lavish, but backed off just before crossing the line into gaudiness. Even in my terror of the thing hunting me below I could see the craftsmanship was unlike anything I had ever seen before.

Through hallways and passages I sprinted, but the rooms were endless. I stood frozen in a tea room, breathing hard as my bare feet pressed into the deep pile of a plush Indian rug. A crash shook the house. Overhead, a crystal chandelier rocked and tinkled. Cordial glasses in a display case rattled against each other. The walls creaked and groaned as the Demon forced its way up through the building. Would it use the stairs, or could it tear up directly through the floor? Either way, it was coming for me. I had to move.

As I resumed my run down the hall, the floor shifted beneath my feet like an earthquake, slamming my body into the wall. Something in my hand snapped; a small bone was broken.

I kept running until I burst into a massive kitchen. Everything was stainless steel; giant refrigerators, soup pots, cabinets. The house trembled again as the Demon struck the walls with rage. Hanging utensils swayed overhead with the force of the blows. I could not stay here.

I found stairs, and ran up them. Through a bedroom, a bathroom, a sitting room. Finally, I came to an end; a balcony overlooking a void. And the empty sky was raining; of course it was. Why was it always raining?

The Demon entered the room behind me. I had nowhere left to run. It paused behind me, watching me. What was it waiting for?

I threw my leg over the banister, preparing to jump. I could feel the malevolence of the evil presence behind me. It was a hand on my back, pushing. Death would be better than surrendering to that thing. Anything would be better.

Into the void I jumped, keeping my eyes fixed on my bare toes as I plummeted from the balcony into the swirling purple mist below.

My body tumbled through the mist, piercing a hole through the thick clouds. When they parted, I saw I was over water—a vast ocean from which rose a great wave of water which sloped away for a mile under my feet.

I plunged into the water like a needle into flesh. I

felt relieved, despite the pain; the Demon would not follow me here. Hands reached from the depths, gripping my sides, brushing my hair back from my forehead. How was that possible?

I was being held, then shaken. "Wake up! Are you okay? *Hey!*"

A grocery clerk cradled me in her arms, trying to prop my limp body upright as I slumped back into a shelf of cereal boxes.

"Hey, you just fell down! Do you need me to call an ambulance? How many fingers am I holding up?"

The clerk flashed a peace sign in front of my eyes.

"Two. Two fingers. I'm fine." I struggled to get my feet under myself, to stand. I leaned on the cart I had been using before I fell. The memory of what I had been doing flooded back to me; cereal for breakfast, green salad for dinner. Laundry detergent. Bar of soap.

The bright red detergent bottle in my cart featured a smiling sheep with little curling horns. The image caused my mind to rock and reel—no good. I would fall back into the dream if I didn't look away and clear my mind.

I lifted the bottle of detergent to put it back on the shelf and dropped it again; my hand was hurt. It felt broken. How…? I couldn't remember.

I used my other hand to shelve the detergent and select a different brand—a yellow bottle with a teddy bear on the label. Better. This one didn't make my head ache.

"You looking for something in particular, ma'am?"

Ugh. She called me ma'am. I knew I was getting older, but…

"No, nothing in particular. That red bottle's no good, though. I'll go with the teddy bear."

The clerk shot me a look of concern, but let me continue shopping. I turned away from her and waved her off, concentrating on keeping my balance. I shuffled slowly down the aisle.

"All right, ma'am," the clerk called after me. "Let me know if you start feeling sick or anything."

"Yep. Will do. Thanks."

11

The end of the season passed slowly. Corduroy learned new tricks as the weather cooled and we got our first snow. He could sing on demand, change position from Bird's shoulder to her head and back again, and dance to music as Bird capered around him, giggling and wiggling. On Thanksgiving day, she showed off a tiny cardboard stage she had built for him, complete with a banner at the top which read "Corduroy" in rhinestone letters.

I finished paying off the accident and quit the bowling alley so I could get back to sewing full time. Taos began to fill up with skiers and snowboarders for the winter season. Noisy, alcoholic tourists arrived in caravans of party buses. They crowded into the restaurants, complaining to each other about the machine-manufactured snow which was necessitated by the stubborn drought. I generally avoided the shopping malls and chain stores this time of year; the One-Stop would have to do until the outsiders left in March. The winter months were inconvenient—but they made life simpler, too.

John's girlfriend apparently fucked off to wherever she came from. I never saw her again, and I didn't ask John about it. To my relief, Bird didn't ask him either; she seemed to have forgotten the woman was ever there.

Bird had been hoping for a white Christmas that year, but the ground remained brown and dry. She spent hours raking through leaves and picking out her favorites—she favored most of all the ones with burgundy, orange, and golden hues. She fashioned the prettiest leaves into wreaths which decorated our fence and door. When she found a pine cone she would glue it right in the middle as a centerpiece, where it would sit like a bird on a swing. She gave her biggest, grandest wreath to John, and a smaller one to Robby. She called them "harvest fairy rings."

At the pet store one day, John gave Bird a gift to pass along to Corduroy: a seed treat in the shape of a Christmas tree. I wondered if a nice bottle of wine was too extravagant to give in return to someone I only talked to when shopping for bird seed—then dropped by and gave it to him anyway, along with an invitation to Christmas breakfast. He agreed. Bird was elated.

Christmas morning was a flurry of cooking and cleaning. I was unused to company, and even less used to hosting fancy dinners. Well, it wasn't a dinner, just breakfast, but I wanted it to be nice; a semi-formal occasion, with a white tablecloth and our better dishes. Bird managed the waffle batter while I created a variety of toppings—fruit preserves, lemon custard, whipped cream, walnuts, fresh blueberries—enough to feed a small army. I didn't know what John liked, and I wanted to be prepared for anything. Complicated meals were not my forte, and I almost didn't have everything ready in time. With five minutes to spare, the coffee was ready, tea and hot water was on standby in case he didn't like coffee, and Bird had picked out her favorite skirt to wear for the occasion; the purple one with the little lighthouses all over.

I lit the candles on the table. All set.

"I'll get Corduroy!" Bird said.

"Maybe later, honey. Let's have breakfast first, and then Corduroy can visit with us, okay?"

Bird pouted. She moped into the living room and peered into Corduroy's cage, making the tiny squeaking sounds she used to train him.

Then the squeaking stopped. "*Maman!*" she yelled.

I dropped the pan I was rinsing and it fell into the soapy sink with a splash, dousing my dress. As I rounded the corner into the living room, I saw Bird backing away from the cage.

"Corduroy's dead! He's *dead!*" she screamed, recoiling with her hands in front of her mouth.

Corduroy was a cold lump of feathers on the newspaper floor of his cage, his little claws balled tight.

Bird screamed and ran into the kitchen.

"Wait! Bernadette!" I cried, chasing after her.

I was too late.

She collided with the table, tipping the lit candles onto the cloth. The fire spread quickly, devouring the settings and a beautiful leaf-wreath Bird had carefully set in the middle of the table for decoration. She screamed again and again, whipping her head back and forth, her hair lashing her face as she was trapped between the fire in front of her and the death at her back.

I grabbed her wrist but she pulled away, stumbling dangerously near the flames.

"We have to get out of here, Bird! Come on! *Now!*"

I grabbed for her again but in her panic she was too strong for me. She ran back into the living room and fumbled at the latch on Corduroy's cage.

"Fly away Corduroy!" she screamed. "*Fly away fly away fly away!*"

The fire ate at the carpet, working its way into the living room. The heat was already stirring the air in the house into a fury. Smoke stung my eyes and lungs, but I could not leave Bird and I could not reach her through her terror.

A figure appeared beside me in the swirling ash and flames. It was John.

He grabbed the birdcage and charged with us toward the front door.

We collapsed onto the sidewalk, coughing from deep in our lungs, wiping tears from our eyes. John sat beside us, still gripping the birdcage in one hand and holding the bottle of wine I had given him in the other.

"Oh Bird, I'm so sorry. I think Corduroy…didn't make it," he said, ever so softly.

Tears streamed down Bird's shocked face as she tucked her head into John's chest.

Together, we watched smoke billow from the windows as sirens in the distance gradually became louder until our ears buzzed with the sound. The fire trucks pulled up, bright Christmas-red with merry green wreaths wired to their grilles, and aimed their water hoses at the house. But it was too late.

In less than an hour, at a time in my life when I finally felt safe enough to write a new chapter of our lives after years of solitude, our sanctuary was gone.

12

The mobile homes in John's tract were decorated from top to bottom with twinkling holiday lights. There seemed to be a kind of competition going on; nearly every house was adorned in elves, Santas, reindeer, and giant cardboard boxes wrapped up like gifts. The glow was so bright, the street lights were almost unnecessary.

"Just stay at my place *one* night. Take a shower, get everything figured out. It's okay, I promise," John said.

"Maybe. I guess. I'm going to find a motel tomorrow, though. I don't want to intrude."

I wished I could call my sister, but it was out of the question. Robby liked us well enough—or, at least, he liked Bird. But Susan and I had never gotten along very well. She was younger than I, and hadn't liked mother any more than I did. When I ran away from home I left her alone with mother, and she never forgave me for it. So, we didn't talk. And I didn't have any close friends; I spent all my time with Bird. The motels were all full up for the Christmas holiday. John was my only option.

As John pulled his car into his narrow driveway I saw his home was less elaborately decorated than his neighbors', but still he had put strings of lights around the windows and a row of lawn-stake candy canes across the front of the yard. Hanging on his front door was the large leaf-wreath Bird had gifted to him weeks ago.

"It's practically mandatory. The Christmas decorations, I mean. The homeowner's association doesn't exactly force us to decorate, but I skipped it one year and Mrs. Paulson didn't speak to me for months. It's just easier to comply." John tried a smile, but I was unable to reciprocate.

"Sounds rough," I managed. I was so, *so* tired. I wondered if someone could die of tiredness.

John tried to make us sleep in his bedroom, leaving the couch to him. I wouldn't have it. I gave Bird the couch and made a bed on the floor next to her out of blankets, using a bathroom towel as a pillow. All we had were the clothes on our backs and a big white birdcage. My cash, car keys, driver's license—all lost. So was my career; my sewing machines and materials were gone. But we were alive. We weren't physically hurt. Even through my grief at the loss of our home, I felt a deep gratefulness surge within me when I thought of how much worse it could have been.

John let us bury Corduroy in a small strip of dirt in his back yard. The day after the fire, I went back to the bowling alley and they graciously re-hired me. When I returned to John's house that evening, he had filled Corduroy's old cage with live plants and set it as a grave marker. I sobbed at his display of kindness, and Bird was inconsolable but deeply grateful. She tended to the plants with the same care she used to give her pet.

We stayed at John's the entire week, and the next. The insurance company sent us money to rent a small house, but without my sewing studio a house felt unnecessary. While I tried to decide what to do, we stayed with John, who never tired of our presence in his home—or, at least, he never showed it if he did. I began to worry that Bird was becoming too attached.

The desert called to me.

Instead of renting a house, I bought an RV and drove it out to Big Jack's camp. We pulled into the lot early one morning about two weeks after the fire. John followed after us in his car, ready to help us "settle in." His kindness had been welcome at first, but gradually it had become somewhat nagging. I was used to taking care of myself and Bird, and I loathed to ask for anyone's help. My growing resentment toward John was the effect of stress, and I recognized that, but controlling it was becoming increasingly difficult.

But that would all change, now. We had our own place again! It was eerie being in the camp with the familiar ridge of mountains to the east, the town to the south. I was not assaulted by a rush of specific memories, but rather an aching nostalgia struck me, deep in my gut—the feel and the smell of that magical place, the wild danger and freedom and excitement. The town had crept closer over the years with the addition of some tract housing and a small strip mall. But the camp was far enough out that the wilds were still wild, and it still felt like Big Jack's haven. And in my heart I was still the twenty-two year old girl who had fallen in love with the desert in that unsullied late '60s sunlight which shone so bright in my memory.

"Look at that!" Bird pointed at a car which appeared to be sinking into the desert floor. It was Sharon's old Chevy, with its blotches of purple paint still visible under layers of windblown sand.

I noticed Big Jack's trailer was burned. When had that happened? It had only been a year or so since my last visit to the lot. I hadn't received a notification about any kind of fire, just my regular tax bill for the property. It was just as well, though. Squatters wouldn't be as interested in a burnt-out husk. And Big Jack certainly didn't need it any more.

Bird wandered a few yards into the open desert, fascinated by tiny sparrows which flitted among the dry shrubs. She looked both excited and content now, but how long would it last? An RV in the desert would be nothing like the cozy home she was used to.

The look on John's face told me he was not only skeptical, he was worried. Annoyance with him overwhelmed me. He didn't know my past, didn't know who I was or what I was capable of. I was weary of his company, and of his eternal doubt.

"We'll be fine here, John. Really." I tried to smile.

"You actually own this land? Why? How did that happen?"

I sighed. "Long story. Very long. Look, give us some time to get settled in here and then you can come check on us in a few days. I really do appreciate all your help. But we'll be fine for now. Okay?"

"Okay. If you say so. Just…look out for snakes. And scorpions. And…dammit, wouldn't you rather be in a motel?"

I reached for him, pulling him into a grateful hug. Despite my fatigue and my frustration with his nagging, it was so nice that someone really cared. It gave me hope, a buoyant emotion I had forgotten how to feel. He held me tight for a minute before grasping my shoulders and touching his lips to mine, hesitantly at first but then with more confidence as I responded. Our kiss was long, languid, intense. Perhaps the wildness of the land had affected him as well; we burned together, standing on the desert sand, my reliance on him fading and being replaced by the freedom to act on our desires without the burdens of grief and recovery affecting our relationship.

I pulled away first, but I was finally able to give him a genuine smile.

"Tomorrow," he said.

"No, Friday. We have a lot of work to do here. Give us until Friday, then you can check on us. We'll have a little party, to celebrate."

John nodded and squeezed my hands tight for a moment before walking to his car.

"Maman?"

Bird! I turned around, an apology or excuse already forming in my guilty mouth. Had she seen our kiss?

But it was unnecessary. Bird's eyes were brimming with tears—happy ones. Her mouth was pulled into a ridiculous grin, and her cheeks were pink with joy.

"You did good," she said.

13

The following Friday, I kept my promise.

We finally had our party. Where there had been gourmet Christmas waffles, there were now s'mores cooked over a campfire, and where there had been linens and fine dishware there was now a wobbly card table and paper plates which kept trying to blow away in the breeze. But I think we had more fun that night than we'd ever had on any holiday.

John brought the bottle of wine again and we finally opened it, to christen the camp.

"To Big Jack's Camp!" John said, raising his wine in

a plastic cup.

"No. It's not Jack's any more," I said. "It needs a new name now."

"Bird! What do you think?" John said. "What should your new home be called?"

Bird chewed on a bite of graham cracker, then chased it with a tiny sip of wine—a treat I had allowed her for the special occasion. As she mulled over the question, she picked at a thread on her skirt until she was able to tug it free from the hem and send it riding on the breeze.

"The Birdhouse," she finally said.

John roared. He leaned back at a precarious angle in his folding chair, kicking his leg in the air and nearly upsetting the fire pit as he laughed.

"Perfect!" he shouted, as Bird blushed into her wine.

I tipped a few drops of wine into the fire where they sizzled on the lava rocks lining the pit.

"I formally dub this little plot of land 'The Birdhouse,' in honor of John and Bernadette, who have both been so helpful in making it into a lovely new home," I said.

"And Corduroy," Bird said.

"And in honor of Corduroy, who was a very wonderful friend," I said.

Bird sniffled. I hoped she wouldn't cry. We had both been doing a lot of crying recently, and I wanted—*needed*—tonight to be a happy occasion. Of course I couldn't tell her not to cry; she needed to mourn her little friend, and the loss of our previous life, too. But I desperately wanted a break from the grief, the frustration, the fear. I needed a desert night under the stars, thinking about nothing but the crisp air, the sweet wine, and the man sitting beside me.

Car headlights cut through the darkness, illu-

minating the hard-packed dirt road running alongside
the camp. The vehicle rocked as it drove through potholes, causing the light from the headlights to ballyhoo
in a cloud of dust kicked up by the tires. We watched it
approach in silence—and a little trepidation. Crime in
the camps was rare, but when something did happen, the
police were slow to respond. I checked my pocket for my
knife.

"It's Robby!" Bird cried.

"Robby? Your cousin has a *car?*" Of course, he had
turned sixteen in early January. After the chaos of the fire,
I had lost track—hadn't even thought about him in weeks.

The young man pulled alongside Jack's trailer in a
huge junker of a truck, stalling the engine before yanking
on the emergency brake. He tumbled out of the driver's
seat, briefly airborne before his heels landed in the dirt.
Bird ran to the truck and touched it softly as if to reassure
herself it was really there.

"Great, Robby!" she said.

"Hi, everyone," Robby said, approaching the fire
with his hands in his pockets.

"Congratulations on getting your license," I said,
eyeing Bird's excitement with a sinking feeling. She would
want to ride in the truck with Robby—and I really had no
reason to deny her the experience. Bird was unpredictable, sure, but she was an adult, and must make her own
decisions. I had to prepare her for the day when I wouldn't
be around any more; the loss of our home in the fire had
made that even more clear to me.

"Thanks! My Da' bought me the truck as a birthday
gift. Well, he didn't buy it for me really, I have to pay him
back. But the title has my name on it!" Robby beamed.

"Nice looking truck, son. Stick shift?" John said.

"You noticed, huh? I don't usually stall like that,
but the bumpy road…"

"Maman!" Bird called out. I knew what was coming next. "Can I?"

I breathed deep and exhaled, bracing myself to make the correct decision, the only decision.

"Yes. Go ahead. Don't stay out too long, though, okay? It's really dark out there. No street lights in the camps."

Bird's jaw dropped in amazement; she clearly hadn't expected my swift endorsement. She rushed around the truck and climbed into the passenger seat before I could change my mind. As Robby turned the key and the truck roared to life, I looked away, gazing into the fire and holding myself back from running after and warning them about the dangers of the road, the cold, the snakes, the potholes…

"That must have been tough," said John, watching my downturned face.

"She's not a kid. I have no right to treat her as one."

"No, of course not. But, still, it's Bird. She's a little…" John searched for an apt description which would not offend, and came up short.

"I know. But she'll be okay. I trust Robby. But… yeah, it's tough."

John leaned forward and took my hand in both of his. He kissed my forehead softly, and I could feel his breath in my hair, sending chills across my skin.

We had already christened the camp; for the next half-hour, we christened the RV. I learned then that he had been waiting for me for a long time; as he pulled off my blouse, he whispered, "*finally.*" He said it not to me, but to himself. I'm not even sure he knew he said it out loud. His lovemaking was gentle and careful, but eager. We stopped before he wanted to, but he understood my need to return to the campfire before Bird and Robby came back. He helped me dress and sent me out of the RV with a kiss.

By the time Robby and Bird pulled into the lot, we were sitting together by the fire, drinking the last of the Christmas wine. Bird was flushed and giddy after the bumpy trip in the truck, and Robby was grinning as she bounced and cheered him on from the passenger seat. Robby parked the truck again—without stalling, this time—and they tumbled from the cab, giggling their way through the camp until they collapsed on Bird's blanket by the fire.

"We saw a skunk!" Bird said.

"Almost hit him! Swerved just in time." Robby grinned with pride.

"Good job! Have fun, Bird?" I deadpanned, trying not to show how relieved I was at her return.

"Yah," she breathed, staring into the fire as she calmed.

We sat in silence for a few minutes, watching the fire. I wasn't religious, or even spiritual. I didn't believe in anything supernatural, back then. And yet, there was always something about fire that felt like magic to me. It could incite or calm, build or destroy. But aside from all of that, the sight of a central bonfire tugs at primal urges, creates feelings of deep yearning, and reinforces the importance and safety of belonging to a tribe.

Our tiny group bundled up in blankets and watched the fire dance. Near midnight it burned itself out, shutting off the light on our first night at The Birdhouse.

14

It took a week for me to work up the courage to peek inside Big Jack's burnt out trailer. The fire had started as the result of a lightning strike; I could see the damage to the roof, where the radio antenna now looked like a crumpled spider. The outside of the trailer was badly scorched, but much of the interior was intact. The fire must have occurred during that rare storm a couple months ago—the one which had drenched Bird and I outside the department store—and then been put out by the sudden downpour.

Stepping into the trailer felt like entering a room full of ghosts which turned and stared at me as I walked through the door. I didn't just feel watched—I felt pressed on all sides, touched and crowded by haunting memories.

Most of the electronics had been looted from the trailer, but many of Big Jack's personal items remained. On the wall over the dining table hung his Playboy calendar. The ceiling was still covered in stickers, concert playbills, and chunks of old broken records. His embroidered pouch hung on a hook near his cot, now inhabited by spiders busily spinning white balls of web. The linoleum cracked under my feet.

I slid into the vinyl bench seat at the dining settee. The table before me was covered in layers of filth. Under the deepest sediment rested a paper receipt for nine jugs of water, two cartons of cigarettes, and a Hershey bar.

The logo at the top of the receipt was a familiar one; Kmart. That gigantic "K," followed by "*mart*" in a neat rectangle. The K would have been red if the receipt had been printed in color. As I watched, it glowed like an ember burning away the dirt which coated it. Red K, blue *mart*. The image brought up nostalgia in my throat like bile.

I swooned. The muscles in my neck went weak and my head became too heavy to hold up. I rested it on the back of the seat. Before my mind checked out, the last thing I saw was half of a broken record pasted to the ceiling, which read "Groovy Kind O".

I woke up in an ancient castle.

15

Servants and craftsmen hurried past with their eyes averted. A bearded man with a hammer brushed past me, then tripped and fell to the floor when he noticed me standing there. The hammer clattered on the stone pavers as he stared at my face with terrified recognition. His mouth fell open, and he said "Pardon me, master, have mercy," before rushing away down the hall, tucking his head to his shoulder as it expecting the lash of a whip to follow close behind.

Only half of the goliath structure was intact; massive block-walls stretched toward the sky, dressed in hanging ivy and moss which was dotted with tiny white flowers. But connected to each solid piece was a terrace, tower, or walkway which had collapsed under the weight of time. Workers hoisted blocks of stone on winches and pulleys before drawing on an elaborate system of ropes to swing them into place. In the distance I heard the steady clank of a blacksmith's mallet pounding chunks of blazing hot metal into serviceable shapes. A flustered chambermaid rushed past me with a rag in hand, ready to polish tarnish from a row of bronze statues. Her skirts whipped around a corner before I could see her face.

"Which section shall we address next, master?"

A man stepped up to me, with his head tilted at an inquisitive angle. He appeared to be the foreman; a luxurious ostrich feather was stuck in the velvet band on his hat. His creased fingers were adorned with chunky gold rings.

"What?" I said. "I'm not in charge here. You've made a mistake."

"Which section would you like repaired next, master? The entryway? Or perhaps the bedroom?"

"I'm not who you think I am. I-"

"The kitchen? Bird will be wanting dinner."

"What-"

"The hallway? The pillory? The torture chamber? The wine cellar?"

"*Stop it!* Stop asking me things! I can't make all the decisions! What if I choose the wrong thing? I have no idea what I'm doing!"

"Immediately." The man disappeared in a puff of purple smoke.

"Wait!" I yelled, but the man did not reappear. In making no decision, had I made a decision? I panicked.

I was apparently the owner of this horrendous ruin. I wondered who was responsible for its current state. It seemed like it must be my fault. Everything was always my fault. Because everything was always my responsibility, which seemed extraordinarily unfair. How wonderful it must be to have the freedom to leave the difficult decisions up to someone else, to be able to-

The floor vibrated beneath my feet. What force was strong enough to disturb a structure of solid stone? A deep and threatening rumble—an energy which was felt more than heard—shook the castle. Then, I remembered.

It was the Demon.

The foreman was at my side again. "Master, we cannot keep up."

"Keep up? What do you mean?"

"It all gets torn down again, as soon as we make any progress. The shaking…the stones fall, and my men are crushed. They are so busy dying, they hardly have time to cut more stone."

"Who are you?" I asked. Something about the man was familiar to me.

The foreman giggled, and transformed into a more familiar figure. "Don't you recognize me, Dreamer?"

"The Simulacrum! You're the butler from the theater."

"Well…I'm not *really* a butler, you know. But listen, you have bigger things to worry about right now. Much bigger. Don't you feel it? He's coming."

The floor dropped an inch, sending my stomach into my throat. The castle crashed and vibrated, its stone bones grinding against each other, sending falls of sand tumbling from its joints.

"What can I do about it?" I asked.

"Well, you can't beat him, you know. He's far too powerful."

"Whose side are you on? I need to know! Who are you?"

"I support the reversal. He doesn't."

"Reversal?" I said. "What's that?"

"I don't think you support it either, so I guess that puts me on your side."

"Well, you aren't helping!"

Another massive crash rocked the structure, and the Simulacrum grasped a wobbling bronze statue for support. "He's just trying to scare you, you know."

"*It's working!*" I screamed, stumbling painfully to my knees on the stone. The air grew dense; my skull felt like it was twisting, cracking. A tiny trickle of blood dripped from my nose.

A worker clutching his broken arm to his chest ran up to us, his face contorted into an expression of extreme terror.

"You will die," he whispered, the words wheezing out of him on the tail end of his breath. Blood ran from his nose, ears, and eyes in thin streams.

The ground shook again and again, throbbing like a massive heartbeat. Stones tumbled from the craggy, unfinished tops of the walls, crushing the workers. The faint sounds of their bones breaking was magnified in my ears; I heard cracks and snaps as the bodies were mangled under the weight of the debris a hundred feet below. The worker tumbled into the depths to die with the rest of the craftsmen.

"What do I do?" I cried. The moans of the gravely wounded rang in my ears.

But the Simulacrum had transformed. He was a stone statue, turned to the same material the castle was made from. Every laborer below had turned into a statue, too, and they were all crumbling under the falling blocks. Below the broken floor on which I stood I could see dismembered stone limbs, heads, and torsos, where minutes ago there had stood living men and women.

The Simulacrum's eyes, encased in their petrified sockets, darted toward me as a final breath gasped from his mouth along with a trickle of sandy blood. He said, *"What is your pain level?"*

The castle shook. The floor weakened and pieces fell away, creating a gaping hole behind me as bricks eroded from the raw edges. Purple mist reached up from the opening, wrapping me, soothing. It was all familiar, somehow.

"What do you mean?" I asked.

A nurse hovered over my hospital bed. "On a scale of one to ten, what is your pain level?"

Her lipstick was a lovely shade of carnation red. But she wasn't wearing any eyeliner. Strange. Why bother with lipstick if you aren't going to wear eyeliner?

"Zero," I said, then corrected myself. "Three." I discovered that my head was pounding.

A tiny cup was held up to my lips, parting them. An uncoated pill, sour and powdery, was tipped into my mouth.

"Drink," the nurse said. Kool-Aid in another cup, so sweet it made my eyes water.

"Where am I?" I asked.

"Bishop Glen Hospital. You had a bit of a fall. I'll call your daughter," she said, before whisking away.

"Wait, don't-" I called, but she was gone.

So I retreated again into the purple mist, where it was safe and warm, and

<u>(EDIT: should maybe remove the part with the nurse…It's all true, but maybe it's not important. Ask John what he thinks.)</u>

(NOTE) *My name is Robert Benton. I'm the "Robby" who was mentioned earlier in these memoirs. I was just about sixteen years old when all this weird shit happened, but I'm almost thirty now, so it has been a while.*

Bird was my cousin, and I loved her as much as anyone else did. She was always there for me when I needed her, and she never judged me. She was special, for sure. So when things started to go wrong, I stepped in, even though I was just a kid.

I still don't completely understand what happened, even now. But I found this old book hidden in the debris, and I thought it would be best to just get it out there to the public, considering all the stuff that's been said. There was some press coverage of what that happened during those last few days, and I know there have been a lot of questions. Poor Bird got a lot of phone calls that really messed her up for a while.

So I wanted to set a few things straight. The part that comes next isn't really my fault. It took me a few years to understand that, though. For a long time, I blamed myself for some of what happened. Now I'm not so sure. But I guess you'll be the judge of that when you read on.

I'm not such a good writer, and I won't write too much more, but I just wanted to say that I loved Bird as much as anyone in the world and I was scared for her safety

sometimes, so that's why I did all the stuff I did. I hope you can see that.

Some of what is written next isn't quite true, at least from my point of view. But I wanted to get everything printed in this book just the way I found it, because it's a memoir, and I didn't think I had the right to change it. It's not my memoir. And I'm not the one who was really hurt, in the end. The truth has to come out, even if we can't press charges. So here it is. (END NOTE)

16

I didn't get out of the hospital for days.

John sat by my bed a bit, but I could tell by the starey look in his eyes that some of what I was saying didn't make any sense. I only remember a little. There were fat ticks crawling on the ceiling, and wild dogs running in the hall. The soup tasted like bananas. He nodded and agreed.

Bird didn't visit much. I think John was keeping her away. She was tougher than he thought, though. I missed her desperately.

I couldn't stop thinking about the sparrow bashing against the glass. He was trying to fly through the window, but from my position on the bed I couldn't talk him out of it. Every time I started to fall asleep I would hear him again, smacking against the glass, his beautiful wings crumpling, his tiny beak clicking. He woke me again and again, asking me what month it was, who the president was, what year we were in, how many fingers he was holding up. He was nice, but stupid. The window wouldn't open, and I couldn't get him to go away. He was in danger, but I was so helpless…

John looked in on Bird at the camp for me. He said she was doing pretty well considering my total absence.

She had adopted a small flock of tiny desert birds who inhabited a big shrub like it was tenement housing. Much of her time was spent feeding them bits of seeded bread and singing songs she made up about the desert. John brought pictures of her sitting happily near the bush, grinning as a wild bird cautiously perched on top of her head. She hung little seed bells from the bushes like Christmas ornaments.

Robby visited me once, but he was strange toward me. He didn't say much, and seemed disapproving of my condition. At the time I assumed he was simply uncomfortable being in a hospital, as many people are. The truth was far worse. But more on that later.

They ran a lot of tests; CT scans, MRI, blood panels. Nothing wrong, of course. I felt great, physically. But once or twice a day I would see an object which somehow gripped the full attention of my subconscious—always a random item, like a street sign or a pencil or a stray cat—and that intense déjà vu would flood into my brain, even if I'd never seen the thing before. My mind was fixed on the idea that my life was folding over itself like pleats in a skirt, where time was continuous except sometimes it bent backwards and touched on itself before moving on.

I heard the word "dementia" whispered in the hall outside my room, but the word always lilted into a question mark at the end, so I did not take it seriously. The woman who uttered it was a bitch anyway—Dr. Bannon. She hated me, I could tell. I think she was mostly jealous; her love for John was obvious, and I heard them kissing one time behind the curtain near my bed. I noticed red lipstick on his collar later that day. He said it was just Kool-Aid, but I knew better.

That's okay. He deserved some happiness after our long, stale marriage. God knew.

Eventually my insurance ran out and they sent me home with no specific diagnosis. Returning to our RV after my hospital stay felt like slipping into a favorite pair of jeans. *This* was where I belonged. The old camp! The night after my homecoming we had another bonfire, and I felt my mind clear. The sterile hospital seemed like a bad dream; maybe I had imagined it all. I had a tendency to do things like that, it turns out.

But I didn't get better after going home, even with all the medication they sent me off with. The seizures became more frequent, from once a week to once a day, and eventually I became housebound, unsure when I would next be traveling to the depths of my own mind. The purple feeling of being in the dreams, breathing that mist, being the version of me who traveled, who wandered, has become a sort of addiction. Even when I am not there, I can think about little else.

I have stopped taking the pills. My body belongs in The Birdhouse, but my mind belongs in the dreams.

The Demon is only trying to scare me. Why?

Bird is the only one who knows about my battle. John and Robby think they know, but they also think I'm sick. I'm not. I just live in two places at once; lots of people do. The dreams are just a summer home.

I still don't know who the Demon is. I think Robby knows, but I'm not sure I can trust Robby any more.

Here's why:

One evening in I think it was late February I was building up the fire pit when I bent over to pick up a log, and time folded on me. I had done all this before. Of course I had; I built up the fire most days it wasn't too cold to have dinner outside. But I had also picked up this exact log before, and burned it. Get it? And of course I know I also hadn't; that's impossible. But then my ears rang, and my vision darkened.

I woke up standing in the yard of a broken house.

17

An impressive tree dominated the street view of the building. Reaching branches spread out from the center for forty feet in every direction. Some of the branches grew out from the middle and then went straight down into the dirt, digging for bodies. Ten children couldn't have held hands to hug the girth of the trunk. The shade underneath was so dark nothing could survive but hundreds of criss-crossed footprints tracked in the dust. The tree was ancient, maybe thousands of years old. And it was waiting for me.

Someone had decorated the tree. The job must have taken months. Countless trinkets danced in the canopy; hanging lamps, ornaments, ribbons, and odd items like shoes and silk flowers were attached to limbs and boughs. You could stare for hours and still find new pieces you hadn't noticed; a red wooden apple with a smiley-face carved on it, a glittering spun-glass bunch of mistletoe, a little slot machine with "I ♥ Las Vegas" printed on the back, a raven's skull. When the wind picked up the items rocked and swung, clinking against the branches. Ornaments with bells attached tinkled as they trembled in the breeze.

The house itself seemed an afterthought. It was dark and low, looking out over the long sloping hill on which it stood. When I stepped through the front door, the smell which met me was stale and tired; old moldy bread, dog hair, smoke from a snuffed candle.

The person who lived there welcomed me, but did not set me at ease. She watched me from a wooden rocking chair, and I saw that around her neck she wore more trinkets like the ones in the tree; a bunch of dried flowers, a tiny ceramic goat, a clutch of dull crystals wrapped in leather and wire. The bundle was woven through with dark magic; swirls of purple mist wafted from the talismans.

"Who are you?" I asked.

"Who do you think?" the witch answered.

"Are you him? The Simulacrum?"

She did not answer. With trembling hands she raised a cup of tea, slurped it, and burped before setting it on a table next to her chair.

"Why are you here?" she asked.

"I don't know. I didn't ask to be here," I said.

"Didn't you," she stated; not a question. Perhaps an accusation.

A strong breeze rose up outside. Through the screen door I could hear the tree creak and sway as wind rushed through the leaves with the sound of a waterfall.

"Where's the Demon?" I asked. "Is he here?"

The witch chuckled. "Always," she said.

"Who is he? I have to know."

The witch leaned forward alarmingly, then pushed herself out of the chair with a wet grunt. Her odor wafted ahead of her through the humid air; a layer of strong incense did not quite mask the smell of fungal grit and old sweat.

"You're running out of time," the witch said.

"What do you mean?" I asked.

"You're running out of brain," she said.

Bright flashes like lightning burst inside the oppressive room. Pain exploded near the back of my head, pressed on my eyeballs. My skull creaked under pressure; my ears nearly popped from the force. Blood tears trickled down my cheeks.

"He found a way to get you. Outside your dreams, I mean," the woman said.

The Demon was here. This time, the house only had one story. He was close, just down the hall, and he could smell me.

A back door crashed on its hinges. I heard him call my name. I don't remember ever telling him my name.

How did he know it?

I ran from the witch's room down the hall, and sidestepped into a bedroom. It was all yellow; the sheets and blankets, the curtains, the swooping canopy over the bed. It was dusty, too.

I was enjoying myself. Was that right? The house was a comfort to me, even being pursued by the monster who so relentlessly invaded my mind.

I should not be enjoying this.

The floor vibrated with the force of the Demon's footfalls.

Under the bed I went; no where else to run. I pushed my way through fluffy dust bunnies, spider webs. My foot upset a tattered old shoebox in the corner; keep-sakes and trinkets spilled out onto the floor.

The Demon was in the doorway.

I heard his breath, felt it in my hair. His massive hand closed around my ankle and yanked; I slid from under the bed, scraping my fingernails on the wires under the mattress. He picked me up and held me upside-down. My leg ached and popped, threatening to dislocate as I screamed until my voice gave out. When he threw me on the bed I nearly bounced off of it, but he pinned me before I could crawl away.

The weight of him on my body, crushing me. Pain between my legs, his knee crushing my thigh. His breath was so hot in my ear it burned like fire.

So this was it, then. This was what I was afraid of, all this time. But what was it?

His body was on mine, our breast bones crushed together; he was twice my width, ten times my weight. His heart beat so hard it thumped into my chest; I could feel every beat.

I raised my arms and gripped his horns, one in each hand, and pushed up. With all of my strength, I was able to move his mouth away from my ear. His eyes met mine; and he laughed.

He was mocking me.

"*Don't laugh!*" I screamed, abruptly aware of my prone position under his body. We weren't fighting; the idea that I could defend myself against this powerful crea-ture was preposterous. We weren't mating; he despised my body, and my mind.

Old. Stupid. Weak.

I screamed again, sobbing with frustration and shame.

"*Stop laughing at me!*"

The Demon's bellowing laughter shook the house until it splintered and fell down around us.

18

I woke up on the floor of the RV's tiny bedroom, my fin-gertips and toes twitching, squinting through a thick cloud of pain. Shattered bits of 7-inch records floated over my head; surely that was a hallucination.

Robby's face, contorted into an expression which was a mix of fear and disgust, loomed over me.

"You okay? I called an ambulance," he said.

"I'll be okay," I replied. "Where's Bird?"

"I sent her away with John. She doesn't need to see you like this."

"See me like what? Sometimes I pass out. She knows that."

Robby stood and frowned. "I know what a drug overdose looks like. My mom used, and I know you do too. You can't fool me. I know the signs."

"What? Robby, no! I have a health condition. Ask Bird, she knows…" but my speech slurred, and my eyelids became heavy. I was going to pass out again—but it was not another seizure. I felt a deep, passionate longing for sleep.

"It'll be here soon. The ambulance. Just hang on." Robby's words faded away.

Since Robby ambushed me and sent me back to the hospital, the social workers have been on my tail. They are convinced I am using drugs, and as the primary caregiver for Bird, I am under intense scrutiny. Even after I let them into my house and they turned the entire place—dumping drawers onto the floor, pulling our food from the cupboards, pawing through everything they could find—they will not leave us alone. Robby isn't helping; he's on their side. They visited several times, and always took my pills away for hours when they did, claiming they were checking them for illegal substances. They would call my doctors, verify the stickers on the bottles, and watch me carefully for any sign of desperation.

I can handle the harassment, but Bird has started to shut down. The aggressive invasions have worn her out, strained her bravery. Her unease is growing, like a wild creature which is being forced to migrate over and over again. Her sleep is fitful and irregular, and she spends too much time singing to the birds in the shrubs.

I am furious with Robby. He will not be swayed on his opinion that I am using, no matter what I say. He won't even listen to Bird. I'll get thrown in jail, he says, if he ever finds even a hint of drugs or paraphernalia in the house. What a brat he has turned into. This entire thing is his fault, the little bastard. I should sue my sister for the unnecessary ER bills. I'd ban him from the property, but I can't do that to Bird. He's the only person she'll talk to any more, other than John.

I am running out of money for tests. I still have health insurance, but the copays are getting out of hand. The doctors can't help me anyway, so I have stopped going to my appointments.

Once I surrender myself to the dreams, things will go easier. A couple times a day I check out, that's all. Half of my life is in the motorhome with Bird, and the other half is running from the Demon in whatever place he drags me to next. No biggie.

That *laugh.* I go along with what he wants so he won't make fun of me.

John comes by less often. One time I saw him and Robby talking about me, out by the mailbox. I couldn't hear what they were saying, but Robby was shaking his head, and John had an awful look on his face.

I only saw him a couple more times after that.

(NOTE) *Regarding Case File: Ms. Mary-Jo Pruett*

My name is Dr. Shauna T. Bannon. A family member of the patient has requested my testimony be included in this memoir.

The patient originally presented with a rare form of severe early onset dementia, possibly episodic. My initial diagnosis was vascular dementia as the result of recurring undiagnosed TIAs (strokes) which had generally degraded the brain tissue. I never discovered any indication of illicit drug use, contrary to the repeatedly voiced concerns of the family.

Despite my preference to maintain total patient privacy, the family has established conservatorship and wishes certain matters to be made public. At the request of the patient's family, I have conceded to describe an unusual incident I witnessed in the patient's room with as much detail as our previously agreed upon confidentiality agreement permits.

On the night of March 26, 1989, the patient was admitted to the emergency room via ambulance. She was experiencing intense visual and auditory hallucinations. Administered medications had no effect. All vital measurements were normal, aside from slightly elevated blood pressure.

My final rounds were scheduled for 3:15 am the following morning. As I completed my routine checkup with the patient, she spoke to me in a voice that was entirely unlike her normal speaking tone. Her vocal cords had altered to create a sound like that of a growling animal. Her voice deepened to an extreme, and she spoke to me many words in an unknown language I did not understand. Her family has stated that she knew no secondary languages.

As I bent close over the bed in an attempt to shine a light into the patient's eyes with the purpose of examining her pupils, her left hand gripped my right bicep with incredible strength. Her fingertips pierced through my uniform and into my skin, causing me to bleed copiously from five small wounds. As she gripped me, she spoke again in the language I did not understand, but every sentence ended with one word I did understand; "Demon."

I required the assistance of two security guards to remove her hand from my arm. She had partially torn her nails away from her fingertips with the force of her grip.

Patient was prescribed quetiapine and dismissed the next day into the care of her family. I filed my full report on the incident with Bishop Glen Hospital. As there was cross contamination with the patient's blood, I was required to submit to extensive blood work. All tests came back negative for disease and—I would like to reiterate—no evidence of illicit drugs.

I am reluctant to include this final observation, but it would be remiss of me to exclude it. Before I left the patient's room, the corneas of her eyes appeared purple and in flux, as though they were made of glass in front of a churning mist. She screamed names her family claims are unknown to them; Marie, Joanna. She appeared to be in some level of intense delirium, but her eyes appeared sane and her urgency was genuine. After crying out the names several times, she retreated into a deep sleep from which I did not wake her. (END NOTE)

19

Last night, it finally happened. The flip.

I wasn't asleep yet when the shaking started. It wasn't really a shaking, either, not like an earthquake; more like the air itself was trembling. There was a distant sound that kind of reverberated, like a bell after it has been struck by a hammer. It grew louder and louder, until I felt pressure on my eardrums and my eyes began to tear up.

I saw him in the mirror first. I don't know how I recognized him, because he was always different every time I saw him in a dream. But it was him, no doubt about it.

I had been putting on some foundation under my eyes, trying to cover the dark circles which were the result of traveling instead of sleeping every night, when I saw his reflection over my shoulder. This time, he looked like a sixty year old woman. Like my mother, if she had lived long enough to be that old. But it was him; the Simula-crum. And he was finally out of my dreams.

"The Demon is coming here," the Simulacrum said. "He has broken through into your world, and he will not be denied. He is coming over the hills. Do you hear him?"

In the distance, that twanging sound grew bolder, deeper. It was musical, yet not, like an accident of nature which resembled a creation of man.

"How did he get out of my dream?" I asked. "He can't come here! Bird…she could get hurt."

Twang TWANG *TWANG*

"He is coming for you. You have to stop him. Lead him back to where he came from."

"Back into a dream," I said, understanding. "I have to drag him back in. Away from the camp."

"He's not supposed to be here. He's getting desperate."

In the distance, a sound like an explosion, then another, and another. Rhythmic footsteps like asteroids crushing the hills in time with the twanging sound. The sky darkened with his approach, and I saw his shadow through the window, a lake of black thousands of feet long, casting darkness over the earth. He had grown outside my dream; he was stronger here, like a god. And he was fixated on me. I would have to lead him away from this place, or he would crush the world.

"What do I do?" I cried.

I sat on the floor and my mind spun like a carnival ride. Empty memories crashed in on me—they took away more than they brought, evaporating my thoughts.

"You have sisters. You need to call out to them now, share their strength."

"Susan? I can't call her. She doesn't even-"

"No. Not her. Yours is a shattered soul, which gives you more power than you know. You have sisters who you have never met, but if you can reach through time and space to contact them, you can initiate the reversal. Only you can do this."

"How did that happen? Why is my soul split?"

"Bad luck."

"I don't accept that."

"Good. Because accepting that the universe is total chaos brings hopelessness, and you need all the strength that hope brings. All of time—and therefore all of the universe—is ending. It's happening right now, in every dimension. This destruction looks different on different planes, because the planes are all different—but it is total destruction, nonetheless. And you can stop it, with your sisters' help, because of an incident at birth that was orchestrated by those who approve of the reversal of time."

"Reversal?"

"Time is ending, but can begin again in the opposite direction. The pendulum must swing. The Demon will try to stop it. You must prevent him from doing so."

"How?"

"Wait a little longer. Your sisters are working hard. Keep them in your mind, and don't lose hope."

"I...I'll try," I said.

"You will never see me again." The Simulacrum bowed. "It was an honor to meet you, Dreamer."

He vanished, and with him the hills went silent. As the purple mist receded, I heard him scream in agony before his voice was cut short. He had taken the Demon with him—at a great cost to himself.

(NOTE) *This is Robert again. These next few pages I found crumpled up and thrown under the old burnt out trailer. I think they were hidden intentionally from someone. But why did she write them if she didn't want anyone to read them?*

I know now that she wasn't on drugs. If I had known for sure back then, I still don't know what I would have done differently. Maybe nothing. I was just a kid, after all.

I'm not trying to make money by getting all of this published, by the way. It's an interesting story, mostly, and you never know. Maybe someday the state will let me sue.

Someone ought to pay for what happened. (END NOTE)

20

Bird is mad at me again.

She says I shouldn't be driving my own car, or cooking my own food. What does she know about it? She's just a baby! I'm the parent, she's the child!

I guess it is possible I could black out again while I was on the road. It has happened before. She has a point, I guess.

Still, she's not in charge. Who's going to take care of her? Robby? Don't make me laugh.

I woke up in a rich man's house.

The furniture was minimalist and sleek, space-ship-chic. Blue and white lines of light shined on the walls from hidden floor runners, splashing tasteful illumination throughout the room. The effect made me realize how garish a single point of light was; no lamps were necessary here, the room simply glowed.

A huge aquarium was set into one wall and filled with the most outlandish creatures I had ever seen. Their colors were brilliant, indescribable. One huge fish was cobalt blue with perfect orange geometric shapes; triangle, rectangle, circle. A small silver shark zipped past with gold chains dripping with diamonds fixed onto its body like a harness. A clump of seaweed waved and smiled at me, and it was then that I noticed I was looking at an extremely realistic television screen. It was flush to the wall, almost totally flat. And the fish weren't real; they were animated, and incredibly lifelike. I had never seen anything like it. The effect was enchanting.

In the corner of the room was a pristine grand piano; I wondered if it had ever been played. The lid was propped open, and the underside was painted with an elaborate scene as if it were a harpsichord. The image showed two young lovers, naked but for piles of leaves, embracing under the watchful eye of a horned satyr who hid behind a tree. The entire scene was in grayscale to match the monochromatic aesthetic of the black piano.

Outside, it was night. Through the windows I saw a long path arcing away from the house down a slope. It was flanked by an illuminated pool, glowing pink instead of the usual blue. Clusters of brightly lit trees created interesting sitting areas, just waiting for someone to visit. Whoever sat there would be society's finest, the truly elite; the wine they sipped would go unnoticed unless it was bad. No poor weather would be permitted. No sadness would be allowed. No grief understood.

The house seemed to be holding its breath for the arrival of guests. It was those last quiet moments when all preparations are complete, when the hosts know that the party will be the best of the season—perhaps the best of the year. Everyone will enjoy themselves, will drink to excess, maybe fall in love. Memories will be created which will last for lifetimes.

The house waited.

And for the first time, I did not belong there. It was someone else's dream. But I wanted to stay.

"Welcome," a voice said.

I started, and jumped back a foot, nearly colliding with the faux fish tank. In my previous dreams, I had always found myself to be capable. Confused, perhaps, but able to take care of myself. Now, I was unsure of myself. This dream wasn't mine. And if not mine, then whose?

"Who's there?" I asked. I saw no one.

"Knock knock," the voice said.

"Who's there?" I asked again, trapped by the joke.

"It's you," the voice said.

"Me, who?"

"No, you," the voice said.

(NOTE) *These next few chapters I have personally recreated from notes I found in the motorhome. Most of it is from paragraphs scribbled on napkins, paper plates, scraps of junk mail, old receipts. I collected everything I could find, but it is possible there are a couple pieces missing. Bird brought me a few more that she found in the burned trailer. Some of it is written out by me, based on what she told us during one of her delusions. I tried to copy her style a bit, but I'm no writer.*

An editor and a lawyer helped me piece it all together into a story that makes some kind of sense. I paid them pretty good money, too. Like I said, I'm not trying to make bank off of all this. I'm just trying to get the information out there for anyone who needs it, who is still wondering what happened.

She came out of the coma on Christmas Day, 1999. Bird thinks it's the storm that woke her up; there was rain that day, more than any I'd ever seen in my life, and lightning too. Making up for past years, I suppose.

She never really woke all the way up, though. It's like she woke up just long enough to write the rest of this stuff out before she checked out for good.

I do have my suspicions about who the "Demon" was; she was right about that, at least.

She screams two names over and over when I visit her. "Marie! Joanna! Marie! Joanna!" But I think it's just her trying to remember her own name. So sad.

One time when I went to visit her in the hospital she wasn't wearing any clothes, and an orderly (who the lawyer says I can't name here) was walking out of her room. He was a really big guy, kind of scary, so I didn't say anything at the time.

Please believe me when I say that I wish I had.

So here you go.

–Robby
P.S. - I did the best I could. I really did. (END NOTE)

21

The Simulacrum was gone for good. For the first time, I missed that being; he had been something of a guide, even if he had often been mostly unhelpful.

I knew the Demon had done something to me. He had hurt me. He was so *powerful*.

It had to end.

"You're right, you know. It has to end. But do you know what that means?"

A woman appeared in the room, right in front of the aquarium. She wearing a professional pantsuit, but it was torn and caked with mud. One of her boots was missing. She was semi-transparent like dirty glass; through her body, I could see the fake fish swimming in their tank.

"How do I end it? What do I do?"

"It's going to hurt, you know. It will probably leave a scar inside you. It might kill you. But you have a job to do that isn't here. It isn't in this life at all."

"I don't care. It has to end. I have to leave the house behind, whatever it takes."

"You're not listening to me. The dreams are a byproduct of a greater purpose. Do you know the name Marie? Do you remember hearing it whispered to you? Do you remember Joanna?"

"What are you talking about? I don't-"

But I did. The names reverberated inside of me, like a plucked string. Where had I heard those names before?

"I don't know who those people are, and I don't care. Bird is the only one who matters to me, and I'll do whatever it takes to protect her—even from myself."

"Fine. The next time the mist comes to take you away, you have to fight it."

"How?"

"Don't breathe it in. Hold your breath as long as you can. Keep your mouth shut, close your eyes, and don't let it in."

I nodded, feigning understanding. How do you fight air?

"He's here."

From the doorway, from a vent in the ceiling, from a cracked window—from every side—came the purple mist. It smelled like grape syrup, like an Otter Pop, like liquid candy. It was sticky-sweet and comforting, and promised rest and the gentle peace of amnesia.

Before the mist could caress my face, I inhaled deep, clean air, and held it.

The mist touched my skin, causing goosebumps to pop on my arms. Tingles ran up my back as the purple air touched me like soft fingertips. My lungs ached and screamed for oxygen, but I did not open my mouth. Instead, I shut down.

"Good luck, sister," the woman whispered.

I felt faint. But if I passed out, the mist would get in. I struck the side of my face with my hand, shocking myself to full consciousness. At my actions, the mist retreated, as if in surprise.

I struck myself again, but the pain I was causing myself was soon drowned out by the agony in my lungs. It felt like they were beginning to collapse in on themselves. My eyeballs throbbed in my skull, and my chest howled for oxygen, but I would not breathe.

A third time I struck myself, stinging my skin.

And then I woke up in a hospital bed. And this time it was real.

"She refused her medicine," a voice said.

"That's impossible," a different voice said.

Faces appeared in my line of sight.

"She's coming out," one of them said. "I've never seen anyone come out of a coma after being in one for so long."

A woman with a pinched nose and clear spectacles frowned down at me. Next to her-

The Demon.

He was wearing a pinkish flesh-suit like a man, but it was the Demon. I knew him immediately for what he was. I knew his smell, his voice. He held in his hand a tiny plastic cup filled with purple mist; it looked like liquid, but I knew what it really was. The Demon had come to send me away so he could hurt me again. And again. And again.

I screamed.

"Oh my god, she's really awake!" the nurse cried. "Get Dr. Bishop!"

The Demon disappeared, presumably running for the doctor. But I knew he would be back. And I knew he would have the purple mist with him when he returned.

In that little cup.

I screamed again, this time vocalizing my only desire; my daughter. "*Bird!*"

"I'll call your daughter right away, ma'am, don't worry. I'll call Bernadette."

(NOTE) *Me again. Sorry, I forgot to say this part before.*

The orderly I mentioned in this memoir was dismissed from the hospital, and he skipped town soon after that.

That's most of what we know.

Bird and I visited her so many times in the hospital, but we never knew that anything weird was going on. It's understandable that Bird wouldn't notice something was wrong—she doesn't really pick up on things like that, she's just not that smart—but I feel responsible. I should have known better.

Bird grieved for a while, but she'd really already lost her mother years ago, just about six months after the car crash.

I mean, the woman was in a coma for over ten years.

But I wonder.

The coma was always light. She always seemed just on the verge of waking up, coming back to us. Her eyes would open, and her mouth would even move. I could swear she looked right at me once, and her hand twitched. But then it would deepen again, she would slide away.

Her lips were often purple. From the medicine, the orderly said.

So, here's the very last of it. I didn't have to hunt down this next part on my own; she actually sat me down one day and asked me to help her type it out. So I knew this part before we even found the rest of the pages, but it all just sounded like crazy jibberish to me until I understood where it went in the story. This is the last bit of writing I have found, and to me it's the scariest because this part happened AFTER the coma; not when things were weird, not when she was in the hospital.

This part happened one night at The Birdhouse.
(END NOTE)

22

I was free of the mist.

The house I woke up in was our old motorhome at The Birdhouse. The grounds had deteriorated quite a bit during my years in the hospital, but Bird had maintained them as best she could.

How much of what I remembered was true?

I know my memory started to fragment after the car accident, so long ago. But the part about the Christmas fire, and moving back to Big Jack's Camp must have been true, because here I am.

In the end, the only thing that matters is that Bird is real, and she is here with me.

She's twenty-five or thirty years old now. I can't remember exactly. One day while she was cooking a pot of macaroni on the kitchen stove I noticed she had a single long silver hair. It started just at the bald line of skin on top of her scalp and wove itself all the way down through her brown waves like an icy stream running down the side of a mountain. I didn't tell her; I didn't want her to tear it out. It was beautiful.

We haven't talked much about what happened to her while I was in my coma. This is my fault. I am afraid to ask. I don't want to lose a lovely memory I thought was true, or be told about anything which might hurt or frighten me. Cowardly, I know. My episodes of terror in the hospital had left me with deep fatigue and an aversion to introspection. I wanted to deal with tangible, real-world problems for a while. My broken brain would have to mind itself.

Of course, that's not how the brain works.

I haven't told her what happened to me during my coma, either. So many years, so close to the Demon. I'm still not sure how I escaped; I think someone helped me, there at the end.

Late at night when I was lying in bed in the motorhome, I tugged at the loose strings, pored over each memory looking for holes. I remember visiting each house, each encounter with the Demon. During the confusion everything had been a bad dream, just floating along, trying not to either collide with reality or slip all the way into oblivion. Then once I entered the coma, everything was worse—but simpler. Like winter.

I worried and gnawed at the fabric of my life, tested each stitch, examined each episode whenever I forgot not to think about it. And despite my fears, I became complacent. I was comfortable living under Bird's roof, other than the nagging feeling I was forgetting something.

What was real? I wondered sometimes if I was forgetting to call someone. Two people, actually. Sisters… Sometimes I lay and thought about them, wondered what they looked like. One of them was probably some kind of professional; a realtor?

I should have left it alone.

I picked and pried a door wide open in my mind, and the Demon walked right through.

23

"I'm tired from work, Maman," Bird said. "I'm just going to order pizza."

"Sounds wonderful, honey. Get one with mushrooms for me, please."

Bird sent in the order on her computer. I wondered where she'd gotten it, but I didn't ask. Apparently she had subscribed to some kind of on-line service for The Birdhouse, which I couldn't quite understand. It had something to do with sending messages electronically. There were a lot of services available, too; Bird signed up for some veterinary classes she didn't even have to show up for. My heart surged with pride when she told me, but it sounded too good to be true and I was unable to feel as excited as I suppose I should have. It all seemed like another fever-dream.

We watched the news. That was another thing Bird

was into now; world news. She drank it in as if she'd never heard about other places, other countries. But she'd always had her books and her television. So much had changed—for me, it had happened abruptly—and I never knew what to feel about her any more. She was still my baby Bird, but wounded now, and tired.

The weatherman predicted a storm for that night; lightning, thunder, pouring rain. For a moment I worried about Bird, before remembering who she was now; a grown up woman taking care of her demented old mother.

By the time the pizza arrived, big drops of water were falling from the sky. They spattered the top of the pizza box with sharp popping sounds. I tipped the driver and watched him run, hunched under a black raincoat, to his car. As soon as he got in, an enormous *bang!* erupted directly overhead. The storm had started.

The lights flickered and quit, draping the RV in darkness. Bird gasped in fear; not so grown up after all, then.

"Bird? Do you have any candles?"

"N…no. I don't keep candles in the house."

"Whyever not?"

"They make me nervous. I'm not sure why."

Her voice quavered in the dark. She was frightened…of what? The fire on Christmas morning, so many years ago? I had assumed that night had never happened, that it was part of my dreams. I longed to know the truth, but could not ask Bird to recall that event. If it had actually happened, the memory would be painful for her. I let it go.

"What about a flashlight?"

"Let me see…" I heard Bird rummage through kitchen drawers, then suck in a quick breath as something sharp poked her hand.

"You okay, hon?" I asked.

"Yeah. Got it," she said. There was a click, and the

kitchen was awash in blue-white light. The shadows cast by her full lips and wide nose created a ghost mask of her face.

"Let's eat the pizza before it gets cold," I said. "Get some paper plates."

I sat the flashlight on its butt, and we ate as we listened to the storm pummel the RV. The drought had been over for years, but I still marveled at the sheer amount of rain that could hit the desert. I knew the water would be carving deep channels into the slope outside, creating smooth grooves in the mud that would dry into beautiful miniature canyons until someone finally crunched them out of existence with their boot heel.

"Really coming down," I said, wiping the grease from my chin with a paper towel.

"Mmm," Bird agreed.

I set down my pizza crust. Bird eyed it critically; she didn't want to eat the crust either, but neither did she want me to waste food on our low income. I hoped she wouldn't say anything about it. I didn't like crust. When did she become the parent, and I the child?

My hair raised on end, and tiny jolts of static tingled my ears. "Get down!" I screamed, knowing what was to happen next.

We dropped to the floor the moment before a lightning bolt struck the roof. Even through my shut eyelids I could see the outline of my dining chair and the cabinets behind it. Bird screamed, a child again; her high thin wail sounded like madness. Then all sound faded away; I was deaf and blind, and filled with a particular dread.

That fear was familiar to me, and had no place in this world. It was the unique terror I felt when the Demon was near. But he was not here.

Was he?

"Bird," I called, unable to hear my own voice in my

ringing ears. "Bernadette, come close to me now!"

She didn't respond; she was as deaf as I was after the bolt. I reached for her, and hooked my fingers into her shirt sleeve, pulling her close. The warmth of her body pressed into mine. I could smell her hair, her skin; my beautiful daughter, grown up now but still under my wing.

I knew this fear.

"He's close," I cried out. Rain ran through a black-seared hole the lightning had blasted in the roof. It coursed in cold rivers down our bodies; where had I felt this sensation before?

"Who? What are you talking about?" Bird yelled.

I blinked my eyes, trying to restore my vision. The chair which I had seen in relief during the blast had disappeared immediately after the flash, but was now coming back into view in grayscale. The cabinets manifested beyond; nothing so detailed as shadows, but shapes were forming, pieces coalescing.

The dark doorway to the bedroom was not as dark as it should have been—and it was not my eyes which were in error. It was reality which was in error, for there stood the Demon.

He was the most solid, the most *real* I had ever seen him. He had found his way into reality again. His body was thickly muscled and naked but for thin patches of coarse hair. His thighs were strong and human but at the knee his legs bent back like a bow, where they conjoined with great hooves topped with black tufted hair. A tail wrapped around from the back; it was tipped with a barb like a fish hook. His hands, massive and tipped with claw-shaped fingernails, gripped the door frame on either side, splintering the wood. His head was bowed to allow his horns, as thick as his arms, to fit under the motorhome's low ceiling.

"No," I whispered in horror. "You cannot be here.

The Simulacrum spirited you away, long ago. You are not real," I hissed. My mind recoiled in disgust and fear, but my body had a different reaction.

I was filled with a powerful lust for this vile creature. The sensation was stronger than any I had ever felt before; more urgent than love, more undeniable than a craving for natural procreation. I needed this animal to take me and to keep me, no matter the cost.

"Maman," Bird started. "Who are you-"

"*Come, bitch,*" the Demon rumbled. His mouth did not move; it was not crafted to speak human words, anyway. I heard his voice only in my mind. He rushed at me and caught my wrists in his clawed hands and pushed me against the wall, pressing his body against mine. His breath was hot on my neck, hot enough to burn my flesh and melt it away like candle wax. My flesh boiled, and blood ran down my neck. In the distance, the sound began again; twang, twang, twang.

Bird saw him, and gasped. He was finally fully manifested in our own world, free of his prison in the void.

"You are the one who threatens my mother!" She screamed. "It was *you!*"

"Bird! No!" I screamed, my voice muffled by the Demon's bulk. He threw me away, and in the moment before I struck the wall I saw a young woman, thin and worried. She was grimacing, and every tooth was a fang. I put my hands up to cushion my collision with her but she flickered and disappeared before my body met hers. I collided with the motorhome wall.

Behind me, screams, in Bird's voice.

She had thrown herself at the Demon, scratching with her nails, totally without fear. He smiled and looked down at her before grasping one of her arms and lifting her off the floor. I stood and leaped toward them, but I was too late.

The Demon tore Bird in half with a single effortless motion from her shoulder to her pelvis, ripping her spine from her head and collarbone. He threw the pieces to opposite corners of the room, casting them away as if they were plucked butterfly wings on the breeze. Thick trails of blood streaked the floor where they landed.

All my hope drained from me. Bernadette, my daughter and greatest love, was the entirety of my strength and my purpose. And she was no more.

I screamed, over and over. In my delirium, I remembered I had sisters, and I cried out their names in desperation; "Marie! Joanna!"

Purple mist swirled.

(NOTE) *That's it. That's all we have.*
    –Robby (END NOTE)

-5

Marie looked around the crumbling casino—the last one standing on the block. It was filled with people she had grown to love over the last ten years; good old Pete, of course. Carlos. Katy. Bryce, who was grown-up now, and had a boy of his own. The small group consisted of individuals who had wandered in from the desert over the years and the few survivors of her father's murderous rampage. A small, sad community, with little hope for the future. But she had managed to keep them alive.

What would happen to them after she was gone?

For a moment, she felt deep resentment that she would be the vector of change. The odds against being the lynchpin which must be pulled were not just astronomical; they were unreal. In the end, her little army had been useless against forces of nature she only loosely understood; they had fought together to survive, but the greater issues were beyond their power to solve. The universe must reset, and someone must be there to *push*. And that person was Marie.

So, was it all for nothing? Their long journey, their survival against all odds?

Low conversation rumbled around her. In recent days, the group had become more distant toward her, as if they sensed the magnitude of the forces at work. They didn't see all that she saw—the mist, the visions of the Demon—but they saw the glow in her eyes, the purple around the edges.

Everything had already changed, and it was impossible to put the end off any longer.

"Pete," she whispered. The man had hardly left her side for the last three weeks as the choking mist had rolled in over the hills and the airquakes grew ever stronger. He held her tight during each quake, as though he was afraid she would shake apart.

"Pete, it's time for me to go," Marie said.

"Oh, God. I know. I hate it, but I feel it too. It's now or never. But I'm going to miss you like hell, Marie. If I still exist after you go, of course," Pete said.

"I don't know what's going to happen. But it's for the best. It's the only way."

"I know," Pete said. "That doesn't make it any easier."

Marie hugged him, resting her forehead on his shoulder as she had done a thousand times before. "I couldn't have come this far, lived this long, without you. And if I hadn't made it, the whole universe would have collapsed. That means you're the savior of the universe, Pete."

"I'm a short-order cook, and that's all I want to be,"

Pete said, grinning. "You're the savior, hon."

"I'm just a little girl with bad teeth, from the edge of nowhere," Marie said. Her tears soaked through Pete's shirt.

"You're magic, hon. And most of all, you're loved. And that's all anyone really needs to be special."

"You're talking like a Hallmark card again," sniffled Marie.

"I guess you just make me wax poetic," Pete said, his voice rough with emotion. "It's 'cause you're so gorgeous."

"Shut up," Marie whispered. "Are you…are all of you going to be okay?"

Pete fell silent. "That's not a good question to ask, Marie. You know that. So don't ask it."

Tears streamed from Marie's face. "I can't…I can't leave."

"Whether you stay or go, we're dying, Marie. No sense in you dying here with us. You have a chance to stop all this, somehow. I'm not sure what that means, but you need to figure it out for yourself and that's not something that can happen here."

"I know." Marie sniffled. "I guess…I'll go. I better do it right now."

"How does it work?" Pete asked. "Do you know what to do?"

"Yeah. Someone called Simulacrum told me what to do during the airquake last night. He's kind of a jerk… but I think he's telling the truth. I just have to close my eyes and concentrate like I do during the quakes, and he'll take me where I need to go."

Pete pressed Marie's hand for a moment, then backed away.

Marie took a deep breath, and closed her eyes.

"I love you, Marie," Pete said.

Marie smiled.

An air quake began, and for the first time ever it was out of schedule. The small community gasped in shock and ran to close the windows and doors. From every opening rolled in a cold purple mist, which flowed into a maelstrom around Marie.

And when it had consumed her, she disappeared.

-4

Joanna had returned to Samuel's old camp after her conversation with the Demon in the cave, and helped Christian build a home for the children. For ten years they had worked hard to prove to social services that the community was safe and healthy; Joanna set up home schooling for the younger ones, and Christian taught the older ones to farm. It was a difficult life, but it was free.

But now, the earth was wounded, and the cut was lethal.

It had happened on a calm spring morning, weeks before the weather was due to turn hot, and the disaster had come swiftly and silently. Simply, one minute the camp had been centered on a meeting area with straw pillows circling a boulder that served as a podium; the next, the earth had been disemboweled, as the dirt beneath the heart of the camp fell away into a massive empty hollow. Many campers had fallen, screaming, into the pit. Without warning, the center of the grounds turned into a crevasse a thousand miles deep.

The remaining ones began screaming Samuel's name, for he still haunted their nightmares, but the damage was beyond human capability. Samuel hadn't caused this in some long-planned plot. He had been a small, petty man, a desert mouse whose family had been caught up in the cosmic plan of a being much greater than him. His mind had been twisted by the efforts of the Demon.

The abyss grew as the cliff sides crumbled into the darkness. Soon, it would encompass the hillside, then begin eating into the desert. Joanna sat at the edge, watching mist whirl in the darkness.

"Monster," Chris said. He sat next to her and peered into the depths. Ever at her side, he was. An eternal and unwavering friend.

"I love you so much, Chris," Joanna said, wrapping her arms around his twisted torso, as she had done a thousand times over the years. "I have to fix this—and I can, but only if I leave. I've already waited too long."

Chris grunted. "When will you go?" he asked.

"Now. This disaster is just a symptom. I have to help stop the cause."

Chris shuffled around in his cloak, then pulled something out, hidden in his sleeve. "For you," he said.

Into Joanna's hand he dropped a shiny red apple with a strange face carved into the skin. The mouth was smiling.

Joanna grinned. She reached out and took the apple, then planted a kiss on Chris's cheek.

"Thank you, Chris," she said. "For everything."

She braced herself against the cliff edge and jumped into the gaping wound. The mist swirled around her, then carried her away.

-3

Mary-Jo was suspended in an empty sky.

Everything was gone—Bird, their home, and the Demon. There was no ground beneath her feet, just the mist. And in the distance, someone was calling her name.

Mary-Jo.

How did they know her name? She hardly remembered it herself.

Mary-Jo, it's time.

Two women drifted with her in the mist. One appeared to be in her mid-twenties—far too young for the fall of long, white hair on her back—and deeply sunburnt. She looked tired and dirty, but her eyes were filled with a complicated expression of love and determination. The other woman Mary-Jo recognized, as she had appeared to her before. She was younger last time; now, she was in her forties, and dressed in tattered work clothes like a farmer. Her jaw and fists were clenched tight with powerful resolve. The women looked toward Mary-Jo with an attitude of expectation.

"It's time," the younger one said.

"Time for what?" Mary-Jo asked.

"Time to reset the universe," the older one said, smiling.

They held out their hands.

-2

In the void, the Demon stood in the path of time and waited.

Nearby, three women appeared. They watched the Demon, but hesitated to approach him. Instead they drifted, spinning, holding hands in the mist.

The pendulum was slowing as it approached its zenith, where it would peak, pause, and reverse direction to restart the flow of time.

In that moment, when time was unprotected by its speed and energy, the Demon knew the fabric of the universe would be at its weakest. It would be vulnerable to being caught and held forever, ending the eternal cycle.

"How many times have you tried this?" one of the women asked.

"The number is greater than your mind is capable of understanding," the Demon replied.

"And how many times have you succeeded?"

The Demon laughed.

The three women drifted in void, waiting for the pendulum. As it approached it whirred and whined, impossibly fast. The Demon readied himself in its path.

Two more figures appeared; the Simulacrum, doubled. The third was missing, having sacrificed himself years ago to keep the Demon in the void.

"Five against one?" Marie said. "What are we supposed to do?"

"You can't affect the pendulum prematurely. You must disrupt the Demon instead," said one of the Simulacrums.

"How? He's too powerful."

"The same way he tried to disrupt you. You must affect his mind."

The Demon overheard and snorted, flaring his nostrils.

"I can do it," Marie said, her eyes widening with revelation. "The airquakes-"

"The what?"

"Nothing. I have been…training. To withstand the power of the Demon. I can survive his mind, but you must disrupt his body."

"I can do it," Joanna said, and smirked. "I'm actually starting to think I can't be killed. Let me take him on."

"One of you must also protect the pendulum. It is fragile and infinitely important. It needs care, and will need redirection at its climax," said one of the Simulacrums.

"I can do it," Mary-Jo said. "I can take care of it. I always do."

"It's time. Go now, and restart all of existence

before it's too late."

The three women pierced through the void like tines of a fork.

Marie closed her eyes as she always did during the airquakes, and felt for the Demon's consciousness; it was nebulous matter in a void, like the purple mist, yet thick with hatred and suicidal desires. She reached for him like a wind, disrupting and confusing him. He thrashed and growled, but kept his claws raised. He tilted his head back and roared.

Joanna leaped. She gripped the top of his head in one hand and his jaw in the other and pulled, stretching and tearing the skin at the corners of his mouth. She felt something pop; his bones were cracking. It took all her strength to keep his mouth prised open; if she weakened, he would sever her hands before she could leap away.

The pendulum approached. Mary-Jo rushed alongside it in the void, pacing its progress, until it decelerated at its ultimate point. The Demon thrashed in the void, whipping his attackers as they held him. Joanna felt her arms snap at the elbows, and the Demon's mouth began to close. Marie was being pushed from his thoughts; he was too strong for her. She felt madness approach in her mind as he fought back; her nose bled as aneurysms burst in her brain.

"Hurry!" Joanna and Marie screamed in unison.

"Hold on!" Mary-Jo cried. "It's almost here! Just *hold on!*"

She glided into the pendulum's path and caressed it. Her fingers tingled on its massive surface; it was the embodiment of all time, and therefore all existence. It thrummed with life and energy. It slowed, and slowed further. Mary-Jo closed her eyes and concentrated; she must not apply pressure until the last possible moment, the moment at which all energy had been expended and it was ready to begin its return journey.

The air vibrated and stretched. Enormous forces of gravity pulled space and time like a rubber band. She sensed the entirety of reality strain, ache, and slow to a perfect stop. For the smallest fraction of the smallest moment, everything was utterly, totally still. No atom in the universe moved, no cells split, no time passed.

The pendulum stopped.

"Now!" the Simulacrums cried in tandem.

Mary-Jo pushed. Screaming, she bent her entire body and mind into galvanizing the pendulum's new trajectory. It trembled with power and anticipation, then followed its ancient path with new energy, reborn.

The Demon thrashed with rage, screaming from his broken skull, a noise that shook the heavens. Marie and Joanna freed him. The second he escaped their hold on him, he turned and once again started his pursuit of the pendulum, pacing it, following it to its distant threshold in his eternal race through the void.

"You only have a moment," one of the Simulacrums said. "Talk if you like. Soon you will be swept up into the time reversal."

The other Simulacrum smiled as they both disappeared like mist in the wind, whispering; "*You did it.*"

-1

Mary-Jo watched the younger woman drift toward the older one, and they clasped hands. They held their hands out to her, beckoning her to close the ring.

"Who are you, really?" she asked.

"You already know," the younger one said. "I'm Marie, and this is Joanna. We are your dimensional sisters. In a way, we are you."

"I know," she said. She took their hands, and they

spun slowly together in the ether. "But I also don't know. What is actually going to happen?"

Marie smiled. "Everything, all over again. The Simulacrum told me everything that has ever happened will unhappen, so it can all happen again. This cycle has only minutes remaining, and we three are always at the center of the universe when it ends."

"But…the Demon?" Mary-Jo asked.

"The Demon has a different perspective. He thinks we're all trapped in a sort of hell, where everything repeats into infinity, and the cycle should be ended. The Simulacrums disagree. As do I," Marie said.

"We aren't exactly special, you know. It's coincidence, really. Even though many stories have been written about us," Joanna said.

"What stories?" Mary-Jo asked. "Who wrote them?"

"We are spoken of throughout the history of man as the three aspects of Fate," Joanna said. "We are also the three forms of The Morrigan, and the three Witches of ancient folklore. We have been spoken of and prophesied over and over again by people of many cultures, who all sensed the importance of the three women at the end of the universe. That's us."

"We're just people," Marie said. "In the right place, at the right time."

"What happens now?" Mary-Jo asked.

"We say goodbye, and usher in the new age," Joanna said.

"I'll see you again," Marie said. She started to fade, slipping from the void into her own time and space. "*Next time.*"

Mary-Jo woke up in the motorhome.

Bird was handing money to a pizza delivery man at the door. The box he handed her smelled of mushrooms and mozzarella cheese.

As she watched Bird close the door, her memory of the void faded away. Her life began its race back along its own well-worn track for the millionth or billionth time—but was it moving forwards, or backwards?

In the end, did it matter?

Finally, Mary-Jo allowed herself to forget. She surrendered herself to the perpetual rhythm of nature with the satisfaction that everyone and everything is immortal, even though it dies. Lives and events repeat in an unending dance in a universal ballroom, forwards and backwards and forwards again, for all of eternity. There was a certain undeniable comfort in the assurance that nothing, and no one, is ever truly lost or forgotten.

She could live with that.

0

If you enjoyed this book, please leave a review!

Independent authors can not keep writing awesome books unless readers leave reviews. If you want to support writers, leave your opinion or rating wherever you found this book so others can learn from your experience.

You can also sign up for my newsletter at www.ccluckey. com and get early access to FREE short stories, information on becoming part of my limited advance reader team, and updates on my upcoming new releases.

Thank you for reading!

– C.C.

C.C. Luckey writes uniquely imaginative and eerie stories influenced by her studies for degree in Philosophy. Prior to beginning her writing career, she spent many years working as a costumer for a variety of productions ranging from volunteer theater troupes to Hollywood feature films. As a multi-talented actor and musician, she has had many unique experiences including performing on stage to sold-out Los Angeles amphitheaters, extensive cross-country travel, and playing live music to an audience of millions on national television. She lives in Long Beach, California in a 100-year-old house with her husband and two corgi dogs. Follow C.C. Luckey at **www.ccluckey.com** for free content, information on how to become part of a limited advance reader team, and updates on new releases. She can also be found on Facebook at **@ccluckey** and Twitter **@ccluckey_author**.